I0822782

The Summer of Ice and Honey

By: Gail McDonald

Table of Contents

Chapter One

Charlotte rolled a mint leaf between her fingertips, inhaling its delightful fragrance. Its pungency reminded her of the many lazy summer days before the Civil War when she had sipped refreshing cool drinks beneath the shade of the magnolia in the front yard of Oak Haven plantation, her Virginia home. Often with a good book, frequently in the company of a close friend or two, Charllie had once spent untold hours daydreaming about future balls, potential beaus, and romance. A young servant often brought her a plate of freshly baked cookies, a cold drink, and her hand-painted fan.

Charllie had often luxuriated in the cool shade until it was time for lunch, and here in her outdoor bower, she would greet visitors, pore over the invitations and calling cards, write notes and letters to friends to be sent out by courier, and occasionally jot down dining suggestions of her favorite foods for the cook for future menus. Her life in those days had been full, though also more than a little self-indulgent, and she had always anticipated a joyful, smooth entry into womanhood. She had dreamed about the many future social engagements where she would wear gowns of increasing color and allure, for events that would anticipate the eventual debutante ball. This ball would signal her introduction to the world at large, where she would take her rightful place as an alluring young woman on the verge of adulthood, romance, and the proposition of marriage.

Those days were long gone, however. The Civil War had made that determination. The world that Charlotte had once known and accepted without question no longer existed. It had been replaced by a fledgling Southern society still reeling from a spectacular defeat that had riddled every state with the loss of lives, livelihoods, and property. The South, out of necessity, now dealt with new philosophical and economic mandates for these fractured states, which were struggling to reunite with the North as they resolved their differences peacefully. It was, frankly, a very tall order.

Charlotte knew that she was more than ready for the world to change. She had become disillusioned with life and no longer knew where she fit in. When Charlotte was just a child, her closest friends and then her family had begun to call her "Charllie" because of her independent streak and tomboyish ways, rightfully perceiving *Charlotte* as a name far too proper and staid for her true personality. For a girl, she had been tall and lanky in build. Her luxurious golden-streaked hair had more often than not been casually subdued in an upswept topknot; for she had seldom been overly attentive to her own presentation. So, Charllie had become her favored nickname, and by this time, only the very closest members of her family and friends remembered that she had ever gone by the more formal name of Charlotte.

Charllie, most assuredly, seemed to be a more appropriate name for someone who was no longer ruled by the indolence and narrow rules that once applied to a young, yet-to-be-married female in the rather rigid society of the old South. With the changing circumstances on the plantation, Charlotte no longer had the luxury of wiling away her hours in the shade. Her name was a more accurate description of an active, vibrant person who could think for herself, make her own decisions, and flourish in this new society where she was now forced to aspire to real change if she did indeed wish to find true happiness. Though Charllie had long ago developed into a beautiful woman with soft curves, a seductive smile, and sparkling blue eyes, her long golden hair was now tamed and sedately tucked into a stylish bun—for practical reasons. Her dream of a debutante ball had been erased in this new world of changes, and her lot in life now left little room for romance.

Charllie's plantation home was no longer able to rely solely on the intensive labor of the many servants whose lives had once been irrevocably intertwined with the fortunes of her family. Servants no longer answered to the orders of an overseer under the direction of her father, the owner of the plantation. They were no longer tied to a family that condescended to think they owned them. Slaves had been given their freedom and had immediately become responsible for choosing their own destinies. Some had chosen to remain with the Wrights, confident in the familiar, while many others had chosen to strike out for new lives elsewhere. The future of Oak Haven now relied on setting priorities for success based on ingenuity and hard work from all who remained, and the continued support of a new, tight-knit society of family, employees, friends, and neighbors who were committed to seeing a new world arise from the ashes of what had once been.

The Wright family had experienced numerous personal tragedies during the war as well as material losses, and the world in which they now lived was filled with the many changes that required them to move forward, changes that the family was still adapting to on a day-by-day basis. Thankfully, they were still able to rely on Oak Haven, their plantation home, which offered them a certain amount of comfort and security in these tumultuous times of accommodations and sacrifice: political, economic, and personal.

Charllie filled the wicker basket that was tucked securely under her arm with the pungent sprigs of mint to be steeped for later use in an aromatic and refreshing tea. She planned to hang small bundles of mint in the attic to dry for use over the winter months. The carefree days of ease and indolence had faded into the mists of yesterday, along with most of her dreams. All servants, excepting Mr. George and Hattie Mae, had either left Oak Haven in pursuit of their personal dreams or had accepted sharecropping employment on the Wright plantation where they were also provided housing in the estate's dependencies, which were small but solidly built shacks that came with enough yardage for vegetables, fruit trees, and herbs as well as a few chickens and pigs.

The decisions about the future had been weighty for those slaves who had left, as well as for those who remained, and the family itself. The Wrights and the former slaves had once been totally dependent upon one another for survival, but the old system had required total servitude to make it work, and all men thirsted for freedom. With the laws of the land in flux, the Wright plantation was no exception to the new changes that were sweeping through the South. Mr. George and Hattie Mae had lived on the plantation forever, it seemed, and they were too loyal to the family and set in their own ways to wish to continue their lives elsewhere. They and their families had opted for the security of the "familiar," comfortable with the relationships forged with the Wrights, expanded opportunities for personal financial growth, and the security of freedom from want. They had felt mixed emotions about their new status: exaltation for the new freedom now bestowed upon them and their colored brethren, but also sadness at the many changes that they now saw here on the plantation, especially the sadness felt by the departures of so many of their family members and friends. A gaping hole in their hearts would always remain due to the loss.

Though the previous slaves had been fortunate that their owners had always been kind, considerate, and humane, they certainly knew without a doubt that that was not the way it was on many of the plantations. A few of their children, who weren't willing to risk the possibility of ending up worse off than they already were, remained to farm plots of land at Oak Haven on shares; but many had gone further afield for better job opportunities, many were now seeking out their fortunes in the North where employment was far easier to come by than here in the South. Virginia had been especially hard-hit by the ravages of the war, and its recovery would take patience, diligence, and precious time.

Hattie Mae now lived in the house proper in her own apartment, and Mr. George had his own comfortable living space above the stable. The Wrights relied on Aunt Bethany, a distant cousin of the family, for coordinating the housekeeping; Hattie for overseeing the kitchen; and Mr. George for managing the stables and livestock. All were now compensated with food, lodging, and meager wages for their labors, with a promise for increased wealth as the estate's fortunes reversed in time. All were perceived as a part of the family.

The ranks of workers for the plantation had drastically shrunk with the many changes, so Charllie now worked rather closely with those who had decided to stay. For the first time in her life, manual labor was part of her life. She had gone from needlework to gardening, piano lessons to assisting in the kitchen, and personal letters to assisting with family correspondence. This new world demanded an uneasy transition of changing philosophies, morals, work ethics, and management that was unfamiliar with anything found in the past. The owners and those who had decided to continue working at Oak Haven were bound by the necessities of life, the love of the land, and the familiarity and respect of all the plantation's people. For the happiness of those who remained, it was essential that all make their best attempts to work together in guaranteeing the success of the plantation, as it was only through this that they could survive and prosper.

Charllie steeped some of the refreshing mint tea for both family and staff, especially for her mother, who was feeling a bit under the weather this morning. The heat and humidity were taking their toll on everyone. There was no ice left in the icehouse, for little had been stored during the past winter months due to the lack of help. And now, as they continued to adjust to a post-war way of life, the family was continuing to learn how to do without and making many necessary adjustments to get on with their lives. Charllie mixed the mint infusion with cool spring water and honey and then left it in stoneware crocks in the deep, ferny shade to the north of the house. This liquid refreshment wouldn't be ice cold, but it would be cool and refreshing enough to quench the thirst.

Charlotte brushed a wayward, damp tendril away from her cheek. Her blonde hair was disheveled, and a trickle of perspiration followed her cleavage down into her cheap, simply-made gingham dress. Standing over five feet nine inches in her stocking feet, Charlotte was considered rather tall for a Southern woman, but she also had the advantage of being both slender as well as buxom: tiny waist, slender though rounded hips, and full breasts. She had intelligent blue eyes, a creamy complexion which had become slightly ruddy by her increased exposure to the sun, and a pert nose that gave signs of a rather independent nature.

Now she looked down at her wrinkled, soiled gown with scorn and thought how nice a cool-water bath sprinkled with lavender would feel on her hot and aching body. She would love to change into a simple, colorful day gown following her imagined bath. Perhaps she would choose to sit in the shade with her needlework or write a letter to her cousin in Louisiana. However, her gingham dress would have to see her through the morning. She still had numerous chores to attend to, and she couldn't squander good lavender on her bath when the linen chests needed to be refreshed with its fragrance. She quickly wiped her hands on her apron as she finished preparing the tea. She would freshen up later after she completed her chores. The War of Northern Aggression, as many in the South had once referred to the war, the War between the States as many scholars chose to describe it, or the Civil War, which many in the North preferred—though there were those in the South who could never appreciate how bloody devastation could be described as "civil," had changed so many things in the Wright household. It had left Charllie's father helplessly crippled and confined to a wheelchair. Charles Wright had enlisted in the war out of duty to Virginia and the South more than for any abiding support of slavery. He had become a lieutenant in the war and was fortunate enough to survive the four grueling years in some very bloody battles.

Unfortunately, one of his last forays in the fourth year had left him with a shattered hip caused by a cannonball. His life had been saved, though he had lost the use of his legs. Being confined to a wheelchair, where he would stay for the rest of his life, took him away from the fields he had so dearly loved. Now he was forced to supervise his workers through the direction of others, but he knew he was blessed in that he had been able to return to his beloved Oak Haven, knowing full well that many others had not been so fortunate.

The Wrights' younger son, Jeffrey, who had enlisted during the second year of the war, had not been so lucky. He had survived just one year of the war when the unit he was in was completely wiped out by Union forces. His untimely death at nineteen had greatly aged both parents and sent Charllie into deep mourning. Jeffrey had not just been a brother, but a favorite friend and companion. She would miss him greatly for the rest of her life.

Sophia Wright, Charllie's mother, who had dealt with the loss of a son on the battlefield as well as having to come to grips with the return of a forever-crippled husband, had always been a strong and rather feisty woman; but the ravages of this war, which had personally cut so deep, had been devastating. She tended to sometimes distance herself from the reality of her day-to-day life in this rearranged new world and was only now beginning to recover from the many changes wrought by the war. Both parents were recuperating and gradually learning to accept and adapt to their post-war lifestyle, but it had been an ongoing struggle and would continue for many years.

The Wright family home, once a thriving and bustling plantation of tobacco, livestock, and fodder crops, along with vegetable gardens, groves of fruit trees, and acres of wheat for both the family's use as well as commerce, was no longer providing the substantial means it had in the past; prosperity was now but a fading memory. Many of the fields were overgrown, sprouting armies of weeds and wild saplings. Most fields lay fallow, the soils depleted from the overproduction of tobacco, the lack of fertilizer, especially manure, and neglect because of a severely depleted workforce. Rabbits now burrowed beneath numerous wild blackberry patches that had sprung up where tobacco once grew; here they raised their young and hid from the talons of the red-tailed hawk; and squirrels raided the untended peach trees in the overgrown orchard, eating most of the fruit while still green. Hardy vines of woodbine, wild clematis, grapevines, and once-tame wisteria had taken over fences, wind rows, dilapidated buildings, and even some towering trees. The fields currently under cultivation barely provided a living for those who remained at Oak Haven. Its inhabitants, once used to the tremendous bounty which had provided for everyone for decades, had been forced to make-do with what was left. of "needs."

Much of the time, Charllie didn't mind the many new changes in her life. She had always been far more independent and headstrong than the average Southern miss. She had never found choosing patterns, fabrics, and ribbons to be an exciting pastime for someone who craved action and adventure. She welcomed the additional activity and quickened pace of life, for she had an active mind and enjoyed learning new things and challenging her body with physical tasks. Being sequestered inside the house with an occasional visit to the backyard had always seemed far too confining, and she had always delighted in her visits to the stable, the walks in the woods, and learning to ride the horses. She also found that she had an ambitious streak. Problem solving, accomplishing positive change where needed, and instructing others as to how tasks might be approached in a more productive manner provided a welcomed challenge for her new life, a challenge both invigorating and heady. Charllie enjoyed working in the house as well as outside in and around the stables and outbuildings. She quite enjoyed the new tempo that she found blossoming on the Wright estate.

In the early dawn hours, before Charlotte had to begin her chores and duties, she often enjoyed dressing in her brother Jeffrey's old clothes before most of the plantation's inhabitants had begun to stir. She would hurry to the stable where Mr. George saddled up her beautiful roan filly, Merilee. Charllie would then canter across the fields, through the wooded copses, and along the boundary separating Oak Haven from the neighboring plantation of Danbury Dell. The stillness of the morning, when the air was yet untainted by heat and humidity, the fragrance of grasses and flowers, and the awe of the workings of farm life always filled her with joy. She refused to ride sidesaddle but rode astride instead, and she never hesitated once when deciding to jump those split rail fences that she was confident of jumping. At the end of each ride, she would give Merilee her head, and the roan would fly across numerous open fields on her way to the meandering stream nestled in a wooded glen where she would take a cool morning drink.

With the changing circumstances on the plantation, Charllie now felt free to assist Mr. George with the chores in and around the stable. The livestock had dwindled to a mare, a stallion, a matched pair of carriage geldings, a cart pony, an ox, a milk cow and three goats (a Billy goat and two nannies). A few chickens and a dashing black rooster with a bright red comb were fenced within a chicken yard, complete with their own hen house; a few guinea hens roamed the grounds and roosted in the trees; and a sow with her eight newborn piglets had been installed in their own pen.

Charllie was a true horsewoman who also enjoyed helping with the grooming responsibilities of the horses. She frequently curried them until their coats shone, sometimes plaiting their manes and tails, and she often brought them treats of apples or carrots. Charllie also fed the chickens and guinea hens, gathered the eggs, tossed kitchen scraps to the pigs, and made sure that the milk was brought to the spring house, where it was kept cool until used in the kitchen, churned into butter, or aged as cheese. She enjoyed her visits to the stable and barnyards, where she always felt useful as she met the needs of the animals and the fowl.

Charllie hurried through the back door and went into the large kitchen, where she hoped to grab a piece of bread and a cup of milk for refreshment. Her day usually began in earnest at this time, though today she would have some respite as the family would be celebrating her father's birthday.

Normally, Charllie provided oversight for the sleeping quarters, parlor, and dining room; pitching in to help Aunt Bethany where needed; working in the kitchen with Hattie Mae: baking breads and pastries, preserving jars of jams and pickles, and preparing the meals for the day. Working alongside Hattie, Charllie was becoming a proficient cook in her own right. She had quickly learned how to baste and season meats; bake breads, cakes, and fruit and custard pies; cook stews and soups; and churn butter and make cheese.

Charllie had also become an exceptional gardener, and under her hands, vegetable, herb, and flower beds all flourished. Thomas, Hattie's grandson and Charllie's mainstay helper, had been eight when the war started, and he was now a responsible fourteen-year-old who worked closely by her side in all things related to the grounds. He was mastering valuable gardening skills that would one day lead him to becoming head gardener at Oak Haven, but, for now, he watched and assisted Charllie in bundling fragrant bunches of herbs and flowers in preparation for hanging them in the attic to provide seasonings, medicines, potpourri, and dried flower arrangements. Thomas sorted, snipped, and organized foliage at her direction—flashing her a wide smile whenever she gave him special approval for his work.

Charllie's desire to make family members comfortable in their daily lives, providing them with items for health and beauty, all came together in her fresh and dried flower arrangements and bunched herbs as ways for her to make the plantation ever more prosperous, pleasant, and productive following the war. She did not feel oppressed but felt that her contributions really did make a difference. It fueled her desire for independence and strength against all adversity, and she took joy from the support and love of her family, which included the entire Oak Haven staff.

Charllie looked forward to arranging flowers, fresh or dried, for the bedrooms and parlor, and she took much joy in tending a flower garden in addition to the vegetable garden, a flower bed that flourished beneath her direction and the toil of her hands. Delphinium, yarrow, iris, mountain laurel, roses, lavender, spirea, honeysuckle, and butterfly plants grew on either side of the garden path as it meandered to the fenced-in vegetable garden. The flowers' vivid colors and arresting fragrances permeated the air for those with the spare time to relax on the verandah. Honeybees wallowed in their luscious scent, and hummingbirds dove headlong into their nectar. Delicate, fragrant blossoms were such a gift, and when they graced a bedroom or a drawing room, fresh or dried, they contributed to making the house a home. Charllie knew that if these blooms, at once both so fragile and resilient, could endure and provide beauty following a devastating war, then she too would be able to survive the desolation she had endured.

The herb garden was carefully planted with foxglove, witch hazel, peppermint, spearmint, onion, sage, thyme, parsley, dill, chives, and basil. Charllie had transplanted a large butterfly bush into the herb garden for color and to attract the butterflies. A row of beehives was stationed in the back of the garden near the fruit orchards for pollinating the crops and providing honey, and George's son Buster, an Oak Haven sharecropper who managed one of the estate's largest holdings, was now the plantation's chief beekeeper. With his sturdy coveralls and smoker, he kept the bees from swarming and harvested most of the honey for the plantation's use, leaving just enough combs to support the bee colony through the scarcities of winter. With sugar expensive and hard to come by, the plantation was indebted to Buster for the stores of golden sweet honey set aside for drinks, baked goods, and medicinal syrups.

Charllie studied her hands and thought what a difference a few years could make. Six years ago, these very same hands had been soft, white, and carefully manicured. They had been graceful, adorned with delicate bracelets, often displaying cherished heirloom rings. Now they were callused, brown as a berry, with nails clipped short for daily work; the bracelets and rings no longer adorned her fingers and arms. An engagement ring was one exception; it was affixed to her left ring finger, upon which it had once been bestowed, and it was still an important part of Charllie's identity. She looked at this ring now, marveling at the beauty of the diffused sunlight that flashed from this delicate prism of opal and gold. She felt a sharp pang of remorse and sadness, knowing without a doubt that this ring was no longer a truthful representation of a bright, hopeful future.

Charllie was proud of her hands' strength and durability, but she often felt that they belonged more to a field hand than a young lady. Was she still a "lady"? What did that title now mean in a South where all the rules and morés had changed—where everyone had been forced to start anew? Emotions still ran high in Virginia, where loss, destruction, poverty, and grief still settled as heavy as a broody hen upon the land.

The war continued to rule their lives. There had been such a tremendous loss of life. Though the soldiers had taken the brunt of these losses, death had not been partial to them alone. Due to many of the harsh circumstances of war, many women, children, slaves, livestock, pets, and wildlife had also perished during the four years that the war raged. It is true that bullets, cannonballs, sabers, and bayonets had taken many soldiers' lives on distant battlefields, but Union prisons were no less brutal and often dealt out disease, starvation, and neglect as alternatives that were equally fatal.

Other tragic deaths increased during the war as well, caused by disease, famine, childbirth, grief, fires, excessive heat and cold, and drownings. Most doctors had been called to service on the battlefields, and only a few midwives and women schooled in herbal medicines remained by the hearth fires to combat the many other maladies. All deaths had contributed to the many additional headstones found in numerous family burial plots throughout the area, if the occupants had been fortunate enough to die at home. The four years of devastation by the war, followed by two years of a difficult reconstruction, had taken a terrible toll on the people, their livelihoods, and their land.

Thankfully, most Virginians were resilient, and they welcomed a great sense of relief when the war finally ended. It was comparable to having just witnessed the last vestiges of a terrifyingly severe thunderstorm roll through a landscape. A sky roiling with blackened clouds against a backdrop of yellow sky intermittently slashed with vivid lightning and the ear-rending crashes of thunder evoked the emotional turmoil of a bloody war with cannon fire and massive destruction, a war which had pitted northern states against southern, brother against brother and father against son, sweeping through until its conclusion where victory often felt lost in the grief and destruction that remained to the vanquished. When the ferocious storms of war had finally come to an end, there had been an unnatural silence for a time, an uneasy peace, and finally—a cessation of fear with a tremor of hope.

People began to pray that their lives would find a peaceful channel forward, and then they counted their blessings. They began to realize what mattered most in life and set priorities that dealt more with love, honor, and faith than money, prestige, and material accumulation. Once again, people began to think about their futures—beyond just their daily survival. And that was a precious commodity.

Though the war had robbed Southern families of much of their inheritance, it had also robbed young men and women of more: their hopes and dreams for a brighter tomorrow. Now they seldom, if ever, experienced the important social engagements, balls, and holiday parties that those living in wealth and privilege had once come to depend on for their rite of passage. The constant and pervasive upheaval, poverty, and uncertainties brought about by the war had destroyed many hopes of social interactions where young women in long, sweeping gowns would be waited upon by potential beaus who sought their favors as they searched for a life partner. The balls that had once signaled the readiness of beautiful young women of wealth to accept the well-chaperoned pursuits of young men anxious to make advantageous matches with them were very rarely held.

Chapter Two

Charllie had been extremely fortunate in that she had never needed the matchmaking services of any ball to chart her course for marriage. Seven years ago, her next-door neighbor and friend, Thomas Danbury, had come forward to offer her friendship, love, and matrimony. Charllie, still no more than a young girl of fourteen at the time, had been a bit infatuated with this elder Danbury brother. Thomas portrayed the quintessential Southern gentleman who was handsome, poised, well-mannered, and highly educated. He was a true gentleman in every sense of the word, including how he wore his well-tailored clothes, sat his horse, bowed as he acknowledged each beautiful young lady, and masterfully guided a partner in dance upon a ballroom floor. Even when she was very young, Charllie had often viewed him as a rather romantic prince, though this infatuation had always been maintained in secrecy, for she was still a very young lady while Thomas was already a man about town.

Amazingly, to Charllie's total shock and amazement, Thomas had one day decisively stepped forward and designated her as his chosen future wife. His marriage proposal had been made on a balmy April morning when trees were brilliantly garbed in pastel green, and blooms filled the air with a profusion of perfume. Charllie, at that time, was no more than a young girl barely budding into womanhood. She had only just begun to dream of what her future might hold. However, Thomas had already taken it upon himself to make detailed plans for her. He had begun his aggressive pursuit by immediately seeking and receiving her father's permission to court her, and then he had quickly taken up the mantle of a most devoted suitor. He had begun calling on her with brief, informal visits—frequent in nature.

Thomas had not taken advantage of her youth, for he gently pursued her by giving her the time and space she needed to get to know him better and to learn how to handle this mantle of betrothal that she had taken upon herself at such an early age. Charllie had gleefully accepted his gifts of flowers, candy, ribbons, and even a kitten. He squired her to various dances and social events, accompanied her on morning rides, shared church picnics with her, and took numerous teas in the Wright parlor with her and her family. Thomas treated her with deference, patience, and kindness—a young lady who was more than worthy of his attentions. He sought to learn of her preferences in all things and gradually introduced her into the very realm of adulthood with many of its benefits and pleasant distractions.

The Danbury and Wright estates adjoined one another, so the future marriage of the Danbury heir and the Wright's only daughter seemed to be heaven-sent. The marriage would take place after a couple of years of planning, which would allow Charllie the time to mature and the family time to prepare for this most auspicious of occasions. The wedding attendants had to be carefully chosen, and the bride's mother had to arrange for the tailoring of the wedding ensembles for the bride as well as for all those in her circle of attendants. Fabrics and colors would be carefully perused and then chosen, and tedious days would follow with fittings and alterations.

The repasts for the wedding breakfast, as well as the wedding dinner and the evening ball, would be meticulously chosen from recipes handed down by ancestors over the years, friends, and neighbors. Additional linens for those guests staying at the Wright plantation had to be purchased, carriages refurbished, the plantation house cleaned and painted, landscaping updates begun, and coordination of the servants for both the farm chores as well as the wedding organized. Important incidentals such as flowers, decorations, musicians, a spectacular wedding cake, and a vintage wine would also require much thought and attention. The wedding would be the highlight of the year 1860 for Oak Haven and the surrounding countryside. The wedding would emphasize the continuing good fortune of the successful and prosperous families—the Wrights and the Danburys. Therefore, all the arrangements must be perfect.

However, as the time approached for commencing wedding arrangements in earnest, the political climate in the country grew more and more dire. What had begun years ago as points of contention and disagreement among the states began to maliciously bloom into a total separation between the Northern states and the Southern states regarding a national philosophy and will to go forward as one nation. The ways of the South, which had relied on the engine of slavery to amass its wealth and good fortune, now came up against the ways of the North, which valued a more diverse system of economics where personal freedom and dignity happened to be the unalienable rights for all. The arguments and dissension went from the back rooms to the main streets, from the communities to the cities, from the North to the South. There would be no easy solution and no peaceful compromise for the continuation of commerce in the South, which allowed for the existence of slavery. The willfulness of both sides would, unfortunately, be resolved by man's most violent arbiter—war.

Many citizens continued to turn a blind eye to the storm on the horizon, but eventually the eyes of the nation were trained on the attack of Fort Sumter, and every man and woman now knew that there would be no turning back. President Abraham Lincoln was determined that the country would be of one accord, but it would take the South's cooperation, and that was most definitely not a possibility. As soon as war had been declared, many Southern men from all walks of life joined to take up the cause against the North, which they believed was set on destroying the very foundations of their economic system. The Southern states could not allow the Northern states the ability to direct their lives, their fortunes, and their destinies. These decisions were sacrosanct to their independence.

The homes that they had built, and, most importantly, the plantations that they had carved from the land, depended upon slave labor. They would not, could not, allow others to force their will upon them with these new prescriptions for commerce, and they, after all, were the ones who would have to live by these drastic changes that were being foisted upon them.

Thomas Danbury, Charllie's betrothed, had been no exception to those who had become outraged, and he too had caught the frenzied fever that especially raged through the aristocratic circles of Southern society. At the age of twenty-five, he donned the gray uniform and prepared to leave for distant battlefields with his regiment of fellow soldiers.

The wedding of Mr. Thomas Danbury and Miss Charlotte Wright, out of necessity, was immediately postponed. The war had taken precedence, and no one's life would be the same until it was resolved. Charllie was distraught, of course, because it waylaid all her matrimonial plans with Thomas;

however, at the very beginning, the reality of what this war would come to mean had not been truly understood. Thomas' life now took place on the battlefield, and she could only pray for his safe return. With the world embroiled in war, there was no longer any time for love.

At first, the war felt as if it had been born out of an exciting, patriotic fervor. Everyone anticipated a contest of short duration where the losses would be minimal; the war itself nothing more than a learning experience, a flexing of wills; and the winning of it, just a way of fostering pride for the Southern way of life. The war, in all actuality, became little more than a time of loss.

Charllie's yearning to become a cherished wife, to preside over a loving family, and to begin her own life had been abruptly destroyed one rainy day on a distant battlefield in March, two years into the war. Thomas Danbury, the beloved man to whom she had become betrothed, had been wounded and captured. After languishing in a Yankee prison for two months, Captain Danbury had finally succumbed to the infection of his wounds and a raging fever. He had paid the ultimate price for his beliefs. He had left Charllie with an engagement ring and a gold locket brooch containing locks of their hair delicately entwined in a love knot. Thomas had been killed prematurely at the age of twenty-seven, and Charlotte, only eighteen at the time, had no option available to her but to learn to survive her loss. Charllie had felt that a precious part of herself had died with him. Never again would she feel the deep sense of love, joy, and hope that had once coursed through her body when she had promised herself to him for a lifetime. Her dreams, and most importantly, his dreams, had been lost forever.

Charllie could no longer even begin to imagine the thrill of romance she had once felt, for only the deep, cold sorrow of loss remained with her. Keeping active and busy had become a tonic she prescribed for herself, and for the most part and most of the time it worked, except on those fragrantly, still summer evenings when the gentle breezes beckoned her to walk the garden paths to catch a glimpse of the silver moon reflected in the lily pond. Then, in agony, she would remember breathless promises, the pressure of warm lips, and the comfort of an embrace.

Shrugging the negative daydreaming aside, Charlotte walked up the path to the house.

This house had been in the Wright family for three generations, but its glory days were now gone. It had gradually fallen into disrepair during and following the war. Neglected due to lack of money and lack of help, the once pristinely white mansion with stately pillars and graceful porches now sported a shabby, gray appearance. Its paint was peeling, its porches were sagging, and its shutters were hanging unevenly around its perimeter. The house's down-at-the-heels look was compensated in some part by the English ivy that trailed up and down its walls, the stately oaks that shaded its porches, and the quaint raised beds that held orderly plantings of flowers and herbs along the walkway. That it had survived the war at all was indeed a blessing. Many ancestral homes had been destroyed by insolent soldiers and voracious flames. Oak Haven had seen more prosperous days, but at least its graceful presence had not been destroyed.

"Charlotte dear, for pity's sake, can't you do something with that hair? And that dress! It is just plain hopeless.

Today is your father's birthday, and we never know when our guests may begin arriving."

Mrs. Charles Wright, a rather florid-faced woman nearer fifty than forty, and who looked even a decade older, berated her youngest daughter with much-veiled fondness. Sophia had endured much fear and sorrow over the past years, but, remarkably, her recovery was taking place in fits and starts. She was a strong woman who felt blessed that, though she had lost one son and a potential son-in-law, she had retained a loving husband, a daughter, and her eldest son. Life went on. She was extremely fond of Charlotte, for her birth had taken place when she had almost given up any hope of ever having a girl child. Neither Charllie nor her mother would ever admit, to themselves or each other, that they both shared many personality traits, such as willfulness, sharp intelligence, and independence. But, despite the mother and daughter's playful bickering, they were very close.

Mrs. Wright had first presented Mr. Wright with three healthy male children, though, unfortunately, only one had survived to the present day. The youngest son, Martin, had died shortly after his third birthday of diphtheria, and the middle son, Jeffrey, had died on the battlefield just two weeks short of his nineteenth birthday. Only the eldest son, Frank, and the youngest child, daughter Charlotte, had survived. Frank was now twenty-eight, wed, and the father of an eight-year-old son and a five-year-old daughter. Only Charllie still remained at home, the "old maid" of the family.

In exasperation, Charllie hastened to her mother's side. "I had planned on changing as soon as I made you a cool glass of mint tea, Mother. It is so warm already, and I didn't want to ruin my only good day gown with the grass and dew."

She gave her mother, who was reclining on the worn gold brocade settee, a quick hug. She noticed that the yellow roses on the tea table were beginning to drop their petals and made a mental note to pick a fresh bouquet as soon as she changed. She knew that the delphiniums were just beginning to bloom, and mixed with a few graceful fronds of fern, they would make a striking centerpiece: cool yet summery. The garden roses were withering in the heat, but until she could find the time to water them sufficiently, she would have to pick alternative blooms.

Less than half an hour passed before Charllie once again entered the parlor where her mother reclined. She had changed into a faded blue summer gown that highlighted the brilliance of her blue eyes. Her blonde hair was twisted into a loose knot at the base of her elegantly slender neck, but it was not totally subdued, for curling tendrils had escaped around her forehead and at the nape of her neck. The engagement ring and gold locket brooch, mementoes from her lost love, were the only ornamentation worn to complement her simple attire.

"Charlotte, dear, I do wish you would leave off wearing those trinkets of Thomas's. They are so morbid! A young girl like you should be wearing all her finery. Thomas has been dead and gone these four years now and more. You're young and beautiful and need to get out and embrace life again."

Sophia Memsey Wright had, herself, once been the belle of every Fredericksburg ball, and she could not fathom how a young, single child of hers could go out of her way to avoid all the gaiety and frivolity of being young, beautiful, and single. The South was beginning to heal, and she felt that Charllie's heart was long overdue for its own healing. Long before this time, Charlotte should have been married with children and managing her own household, but no suitor had yet appeared on the horizon to entice her away from her doldrums. Sophia was beginning to lose patience with this headstrong daughter of hers.

"Mother, I'm no longer what you would call a 'young girl.' And forgetting someone you've been betrothed to for many years is just not that easy. Besides, true love never dies. Even death is not as final as some people may believe. Thomas still exists, at least in my heart, and I just can't betray him with another love after all the promises we made to each other. Our pledge was sacred. This jewelry is all that remains, but it does remain, and it will always be a remembrance of him."

Sophia left off preening and gave her favored daughter a withering and exasperated look. "Pooh, Charlotte. What balderdash! You always were a stubborn girl. But I suppose you will just have to get over him in your own sweet time. Just remember, the bloom stays on the rose but a little while. You don't want to become a spinster while mourning a lost love who will never return. You were but a child when you and Thomas became engaged. Hardly old enough to know what true love is really meant to be."

Mrs. Wright reached for her fan on the curio table and began to slowly wave it as she continued, "Charlotte, live life now. It won't wait for you. Regret is a waste of emotions, and many of us spend far too much time living with it."

Charlotte, hurt and frustrated by what she perceived as an attack by her own mother, replied, "Spinsterhood rather appeals to me, Mother. I need no strange men posing with false love to attract my attention when the one who could have given me all the happiness in the world has so recently departed. Sometimes memories are quite enough to last a lifetime if they must. As for regrets, the only thing that I regret is that Thomas was taken from me before we could become husband and wife."

Sophia scowled, rearranging her gray-streaked chignon and smoothing the front of her green day gown. "Darling, please don't be so negative and stubborn. I only want what's best for you. All the mourning in the world will not bring Thomas back. To remain cooped up with us old folks is not what I had envisioned for my daughter. I want you to live as I have lived: parties, romance, eventually a marriage and children. I can't imagine that you would wish to continue wallowing in your own unhappiness, and as your mother, I wish for you to move on with your life. What's wrong with that?"

Charllie did not respond at first, but her eyes began to tear up. She bent over to remove the vase of wilting flowers, and then quickly focused on her mother with anger and sadness. "Your betrothed did not perish in a cruel and bloody war that turned everyone's life upside down. That's what's wrong with that!" Charlotte stalked out of the room with the vase of wilted roses and, though her jaw was set in anger, tears threatened to spill from her over-bright blue eyes.

In the sultry summer kitchen, rotund Hattie was busy basting a scrawny stuffed chicken. Rivulets of perspiration traced paths down her glistening, round cheeks. Still, she had a merry smile, and her round black eyes flashed with goodwill and humor. "Some hot day to be cooking up a storm, Miss Charlotte. I sure do hope Mr. Wright appreciates all we do just to keep him gay on his birthday. Cake's cooling on the windowsill. Chocolate's all spent, but with this heat, maybe a taste of blackberry frosting will be even more tempting. Is your mother feeling any stronger this morning, love?"

"Oh, Mother is feeling just absolutely fine this morning, Hattie. Enough so that she continues to boss my every thought and deed, attempting to run my life for me! She can always bring out the worst in me, and I swear I never am as sassy with anyone else like I am with my own mother. I wish she would just let me live my own life as I see fit." Charlotte tugged on an apron and began to knead the dough that was sitting on the pastry board. She needed activity and often found that hard work was the most effective therapy for a bruised heart.

"Now, Miss Charllie. Don't mess up that pretty blue dress. I can take care of these rolls as soon as I frost this here cake. Don't you know that when girl children reach an age, they always clash with their mommas? The mommas want what they consider is best for their children, and the children, who have just come of age, want what they think is best for themselves. It's as natural as getting a rash from poison ivy." Hattie began to slather blackberry frosting on the cake. Though she tried to maintain a serious demeanor, mirth was flickering around her lips.

"Poison ivy. How apt. That's exactly how I feel about my mother's bossiness. I just can't abide it. She has led her own life, and there have been times that she also led my father's life, as well, if I am not mistaken. But I'm an adult now, Hattie, and I need to lead my own life—without her interference. Would you know of any soothing lotion that will cure me of my mother?" Charllie thumped and pummeled the dough unmercifully, and the flour billowed from the board into the air in white clouds. Her face became streaked with flour and tears, but when she wiped it with the back of her hand, it only left more streaks.

Hattie's mirth erupted, and she chuckled and then laughed until her sides ached. "Mercy me, Miss Charlotte. We want rolls for our dinner, not pannycakes. You don't need to beat that dough to within an inch of itself, or it'll be harder than Mr. Wright's brick sidewalks, and that's a fact. Your poor face. What a sight! Here, you give me that dough. I'll make us some nice rolls and let them rise near the oven. You go wash up and cool down. Just remember this, child. Your momma loves you, and she only wants what's best for you."

"Like poison ivy," Charlotte muttered as she left the kitchen, wiping her hands on a dish rag.

Hattie continued chuckling as she twisted the rolls into shape. "I dearly love that Miss Charlotte, but sometimes she can be so headstrong! She is often her very own worst enemy. But there is no one around who can ever convince her of the difference. She is one female who will just have to learn her lessons all by herself. And sometimes that's a real pity."

Chapter Three

In the garden, Charllie washed her hands and face at the well. The water was deliciously cool, and she soon regained her good nature. A fresh kitchen towel hung nearby on a tree limb, and she industriously dried her hands. She took out a pair of scissors from her apron pocket and wandered further down the path to the patch where the delphiniums were in bloom.

As she bent to snip a stalk, a deeply masculine voice greeted her, "Charllie, I didn't expect to see you so soon on this beautiful morning. I thought you would be fussing and primping for your father's party, though God knows your beauty needs little assistance."

Charllie quickly turned around, and her cheeks reddened with anger and exasperation.

She had quickly recognized the voice—Thomas Danbury's younger brother, Sage, and it was clear that she was most definitely not pleased to see him.

"Oh, it's you, Mr. Danbury. What brings you to our home this morning? I hope no one at your home is ailing. As you can see, I'm quite busy and really have no time to spend in idle chitchat with a neighbor." She quickly turned her back on her unexpected guest and continued to busy herself with gathering the delphinium.

"We are far more than neighbors, Charllie, and you know it. *Mr. Danbury* is my father, and I have been Sage to you since you wore pigtails and ran wild through these gardens. Your mother kindly invited me to take part in your family's festivities today. My folks were also invited, but my father was called to Philadelphia on business, and my mother decided to accompany him, hoping to find some respite from this Virginia heat. So, I'm here representing the Danburys. Friends' birthdays are always something to celebrate, and I've been looking forward to this day." His smile was engaging, and his green eyes sparkled with amusement.

Charllie shot him a withering scowl. "Just because I was once betrothed to your brother does not give you the right to seek familiarity with me. We might have become brother and sister once, Sage, but, unfortunately, fate stepped in and now that will never be. We are still neighbors, however, but that is all, and we must leave it at that. I'm glad my mother extended her hospitality to you, but I took no part in the invitation. Had I been consulted, I would have opted for a far more private family celebration—without outside guests." Charllie's inhospitality belied the effect Sage had on her. His dark good looks and charisma could not go unnoticed, even by Charllie, who falsely claimed indifference—even dislike.

"We've lived side by side our entire lives, *Miss Charlotte,* and we have the right to at least acknowledge friendship. You need to let my poor, dead brother go. He doesn't deserve such fine feelings of loyalty. They're entirely a waste. He has passed on and become a fond memory. You need to get on with your life. You know that I have had my own hopes in that regard, though it seems that you never take my suit for your affections seriously. I often wonder why there is so much reluctance on your part."

Sage Danbury picked up a spray of delphinium that had fallen unnoticed to the ground and tucked it back within her bouquet. He towered above her with his dark, unruly locks and ruggedly chiseled features. His light gray summer-weight jacket molded broad, muscular shoulders before tapering to his slender waist. A broad-brimmed black hat shaded his tanned face, adding to his rather swarthy appearance.

"Your impertinence is outrageous, Mister Danbury." Scowling, Charllie prepared to dress him down with her sharp tongue, "Your conduct does not give credence to your being called a gentleman, and certainly does not offer encouragement for me to call you by your given name. Perhaps you need to consider moving on yourself, for it seems to me that you could be beating a dead horse on my account."

Charlotte straightened up, haphazardly brushed herself off, and quickly gathered her flowers and scissors as she attempted to vacate the space both shared with overmuch familiarity. There was something about his very presence that always made her feel extremely uncomfortable. She felt as if her very innermost emotions were exposed and under attack, her heart raced, and her palms began to sweat. How one man could produce so much turmoil within her, though they were nothing more than neighbors and acquaintances, was unfathomable. She slowly backed away from her visitor to create more distance so that she could scrutinize him from a safer perspective.

Sage Danbury glowered at her. "You, Miss Wright, are nothing more than a selfish prig. Your rudeness is uncalled for, and you should be thoroughly ashamed of your lack of hospitality. As an invited guest who tenders nothing more than the highest of all regards for you, I can only hope that your black mood has more to do with the heat and humidity than with our relationship. I bid you good day and hope that your family's greetings prove far more pleasant than yours."

Charllie watched Sage's retreating back as he sauntered down the path to the portico where her family was starting to gather to greet their guests. Charllie stomped her feet in exasperation. "He is absolutely insufferable! I should have known Mother would invite that scoundrel to Father's party. She has always held him in high esteem, though I, for the life of me, cannot imagine why. If he thinks I could ever possess feelings of affection for him with his boorish behavior, he is greatly mistaken. I'd rather be courted by a water moccasin or a porcupine. Father's birthday party will greatly test my sense of humor. I'll be desperately happy to see this day come to an end." She gathered up her flowers, in a less than gentle manner, and retraced her steps back to the house.

Charllie took her time arranging the flowers and freshening up. By the time she ventured out onto the verandah to join the birthday festivities, she was met by a lively family portrait that she found extraordinarily nauseating. Sage had ingratiated himself with the entire family and was seen lounging with his legs propped upon a stool, mint julep in hand, surrounded by her loved ones. Charles Wright had been wheeled out onto the porch in his wooden wheelchair and sat beaming as he listened to some of Sage's latest escapades. Sophia preened and flirted with what remained of her Southern coquetry. Brother Frank and family had also just arrived, and while Frank sat on a settee with his wife Emily, son Gerald, and daughter Sarah had pulled up chairs next to Sage and appeared absolutely enthralled by his storytelling.

Charllie breezed through the lively group, making light-hearted acknowledgements, though she pointedly ignored their impertinent guest. Finding Hattie Mae hovering near the front doorway, having just delivered celebratory libations for all, Charllie requested a mint julep for herself, "If you please, Hattie Mae. Would you please make it tall and strong?"

"You know, Miss Charllie, this here hard stuff can lead to loose-living and early wrinkles for young women who have so recently just left the classroom. And I know that it can pack a punch!"

Charllie wrinkled her nose, totally ignoring Hattie's dire warnings—knowing full well that she would soon return with her drink as she had requested, though it was clear that she hadn't welcomed the request. Hattie Mae was a sweetheart, and she was always game for pleasing anyone, especially the members of the Wright family.

"I know that I am most definitely in a mood, but I cannot excuse Sage for having riled me up in the first place. He has no right to ingratiate himself with me, especially when he knows that I do not welcome his advances. I no longer view him as a trusted playmate from my past, and I fail to understand why he has become adamant in trying to unite the two of us in some kind of romantic liaison. It is more than I can take. Plying me with cordial friendship would be much more my cup of tea, but his attempts at encouraging a budding romance—never!"

Once her mint julep was delivered, Charllie rejoined her family—kissing her father fondly and wishing him well on his birthday. Then she found an empty chair in a shady nook on the verandah, far removed from the arrogant Sage Danbury, and brooded over her drink. If she could have cast a spell, she would have made their obnoxious guest disappear.

She was lost in thought until a familiar voice jarred her out of her reverie. "One should never drink alone, my dear. I've been told that on good authority. Or is that mint tea that you are sipping with such relish?" Sage had quietly approached Charllie's corner and now stood just behind her chair. He casually fingered an errant curl that had recently tumbled from its loose knot, and she could feel his warm breath stirring the tendrils that rested upon her neck. Red crept from her neck to her face, and the emotions of embarrassment and anger vied for her attention. She suddenly sat up straight, ignoring the few drops of drink that had spilled onto her lap with her hasty movement. She felt both vulnerable and defensive, and these warring emotions continued to do battle as she strove for composure. Charllie delicately lifted her glass to her lips, and she drank deep and long. Then she pierced Sage with a haughty glare.

"Mr. Danbury, your attentions are ill-advised and unsolicited. What I am drinking is really none of your business, though, as an adult, I may rightfully partake of somewhat stronger libations, especially in times of celebration. Furthermore, I wish that you would keep your hands to yourself. Perhaps you should find some James River doxy who would appreciate your advances, as I do not!"

In their quiet corner, their conversation went unheard and unnoticed by the family and their newly arrived friends, who were caught up in their own conversations. And though Charllie attempted to get up to join her family, Sage successfully blocked her way.

"Sage to you, my dear. Still using that caustic tongue, I see. It is bound to get you into some very serious trouble one of these days, Miss Charllie, mark my words. I have never treated you with anything but respect and devotion, yet, like a harpy, you chastise and berate me with that razor-sharp tongue. Could it be that these very same emotions do no more than mask your true feelings? Can it be that you also hold a flame for me?"

He narrowed his eyes and gently held her two hands between his own. Mesmerized, Charllie could do little more than stare into his smoky green orbs. His long, dark lashes gave him an almost feminine look, but the emotion that smoldered in the depths of his eyes was excitingly masculine and gave her pause. She quickly blinked, attempting to regain her composure and hesitated briefly before responding.

"I see that being perfectly blunt with you about my feelings continues to be ignored, Mr. Danbury. With your inflated ego, you seem unable to appreciate the fact that you will never measure up to your brother Thomas, whom I will always love with all my heart. If you choose to waste your time courting someone who ranks you just slightly lower than the vermin on this plantation, please feel free to continue paying your devotions. I, however, will never take your suit seriously. And never, *Sage*, is a very long time."

Charllie drained her julep, smoothed her skirt, and attempted once again to depart. Before she could walk away, however, Sage gently, though forcefully, restrained her.

"Today, you may seem to have all the answers, Miss Charlotte. But as you say, never is a very long time. And let me make it very clear to you that there will come a day when you will become mine, and you will do it with gladness and with joy. If you choose to interpret this as a threat, feel free. I, however, view it as a very solemn promise. A promise made by a living Danbury son, not a dead one, to a most-assuredly-alive Wright daughter. All that is needed, my sweet Charlotte, is the convincing."

Before Charllie could set her glass down on the tea table, Sage had disappeared around the corner of the house. Soon she could hear his laughter mingling with that of her brother's, and she could smell their pungent cigars. For some reason, tears threatened again, but she kept them at bay. She gently shook her head, at a loss to understand her current feeling of vulnerability. How was Sage able to trigger such a deep-seated emotional response when she totally detested him for trying to supplant Thomas's continued role in her life? For the life of her, she was totally unable to understand her errant emotions.

Charllie wanted to pace and scream, but, instead, when she saw Hattie Mae gathering up the empty glasses, she snapped, "Hattie, please, another— strong and tall!"

Hattie, not taking kindly to Charllie's abrupt and nasty mood, put her hands on her hips and scowled at this girlchild who, most times, was as loving as could be. She chose to ignore her ill manners and hurried on into the house to refill her glass with a mint julep, though it was not as strong nor as tall as she had been bid. She would pick her battles with this headstrong woman-child another day.

***

Charllie sat under a large white oak, its verdant shade a respite from the heat of the day. A discarded book lay by her side, and she found herself traveling back to a day when life had been sweet and filled with promise. It was the day after her lavish engagement party.

Many young women would have most likely treasured all the pomp and circumstance of the engagement party itself, where the lucky couple was toasted and acclaimed by friends and family. For them, the memories of this social engagement would have been held dear, and here they would have lingered. And though Charllie had enjoyed the party, and it had certainly formalized the many hopes and dreams that she shared with Thomas Danbury, the memories she treasured most were of a simpler, more poignant nature.

Charllie remembered the day following the party, when Thomas was preparing to join his regiment. They had strolled through the park at Danbury Dell and loitered by the pond. Both had been caught up in the bittersweet emotions that were evoked by Thomas's upcoming leave-taking. As their images were mirrored in the pond, Charllie found herself fighting off a deep sense of foreboding, but she realized that this foreboding was probably shared by most women who were bidding farewell to their husbands, lovers, and family members who were also departing for the battlefields.

Many women had been forced to play a flagrantly false, cheery role as far as good-byes and well-wishes were concerned, neither party knowing when or even if a reunion would ever take place. Most had probably experienced painful qualms as they parted from their loved ones. The dangers inherent in war were great and very real; no outcome could be predicted with certainty. However, often the internal sorrow and fear that all felt were to be kept at bay, shrouded in forced gaiety; they needed to bid their lovers farewell as if everything was right with the world, even if that world was beginning to crumble and disintegrate before their very eyes.

Charllie knew that she had to continue to be brave and cheerful for Thomas's sake. It would most certainly not be fair to send him off to war with the baggage of her emotions, for she knew that he probably had enough misgivings of his own with which to contend. She needed to make sure that their parting was sweetly memorable so that once in battle, he could look back on this day with fond remembrance and have something to look forward to when he returned.

The day, however, was tinged with the sadness of their parting, and Charllie had all she could do to keep her tears at bay. She felt that her smile had been pasted on her face, and that her cheeks might crack from the effort, but she was determined that Thomas would never know the misgivings and fears that constantly preyed upon her every thought and gesture. Her love and support on this day of farewells were the last gifts she would be allowed to give him before he was sent on to his army unit, though she could not help but wistfully explain that she wished life for them could be different.

"Thomas, you don't know how much I hate saying good-bye. It seems now that we have become engaged and committed to each other, that we are immediately being forced apart, not knowing when we shall be reunited again. I suppose I am human enough to question the fairness of all this, and it makes my heart ache to think how different everything should be without this outrageous war that waits upon our doorstep." Angry and a bit fearful of their circumstances as well, she felt a solitary tear slide down her cheek and quickly brushed it away to quickly regain her composure. Imagining the possibility of Thomas not returning struck her with terror, and she quickly tucked her arm even more securely within his, as if the act of keeping him close could protect him from the possible danger that might be lurking in his future. Thomas attempted to comfort her, "My love, you should not fear or anticipate what life has in store for us. Instead, you must immediately begin preparations for my return. Our wedding day will be here before you know it, so you must not waste time thinking of what might be when we are so convinced of what will be. We will have our time together, and we must remain vigilant and confident that all will be as we planned." Thomas' soft, wistful smile and gentle embrace had comforted her tremendously, and she had rested her head upon his chest. Then he had led her over to a bench where they could sit and resume their conversation.

"You must know, Charllie, that I am most anxious for us to be together to start our new life. With you as my future wife, I look forward to the day when our children will fill our home and become the rightful inheritors of the Danbury trust. I am confident that you and I will soon be together, and our home will always be open to both family and friends. As my revered wife, you will be waiting at the door with a beautiful smile and your golden hair—so lovely, gracious, and welcoming." Thomas had gently taken her hand, lifting it to his lips where he gently imparted a kiss.

His warm gray eyes had shared deep intimacies with her that day, and Charllie had reveled in how safe and cared for she had felt at that very moment. She wished that time could stand still and prayed that their separation would be brief and that their marriage would eventually erase any sadness that they were being forced to endure.

"Charllie, you know I have deep affection for you. You are my future wife and mother of our children, so you are precious in every way. Every man needs a loving partner who can assist him with life's duties and challenges. When one finds a woman with such beauty and grace, and he knows that she stands ready to complement him as they make their home, he is fortunate beyond measure. Never fear that I will make my return, for I vow to you that it will most certainly take place."

Realistically, Charllie knew that Thomas' vow could not be taken seriously. She was not sheltered to the point where she did not understand the seriousness of the war in which he was soon to become engaged, and Thomas was human, like everyone else. But he did make her feel more confident about their future together. Thomas was not one to wear his heart on his sleeve, and he did not waste precious time declaring his undying love and passion for Charllie. However, he had held her close and trailed a lazy finger over the fullness of her cheek.

"You and I will lead a full life at Danbury Dell. I will be so proud of you—my gracious hostess. You will conduct the affairs of our home with competence and youthful energy while I manage the estate and its retainers. Everyone will marvel at this much-envied couple who suit each other so well. I look forward to enjoying the many years ahead and, when we are an old married couple, we will look back on these days and wonder why we lacked the confidence to embrace our future without fear and apprehension."

Charllie had been but little more than a child on the day of his departure; yet Thomas had made her feel like a fully-grown woman—one who would soon come into her own as mistress of one of the largest plantations in Virginia. Thomas often talked about their marriage in an almost impersonal manner, but Charllie was not deceived and knew that it was just his way. Though his actions were often rather cool and reserved, she knew it was out of respect, and she fully appreciated his showing her his deference and caring concern.

Occasionally, Charllie felt brief stirrings of passion when Thomas gently kissed her, but he was always the gentleman and never sought more than was proper for their status as an engaged couple. Charllie respected him for this because she felt that he was her protector, her knight, and her guardian in matters of the heart. Chaste caresses and kisses were sweet preludes to the promised rewards of the passion evoked by a future marriage. And this war that the South felt compelled to wage would surely be of short duration, she had to believe that. She could afford to be patient and bide her time.

Thomas had set the standards high for their conduct, and Charllie could only congratulate him on his good manners and restraint. Thomas took Charllie's hands within his own, and his gray eyes became rather somber and serious for a time. "Charlotte, I know that I have already presented you with an engagement ring, an heirloom that represents much history for the Danburys. The gold ring set with opals was a gift to my grandmother from her betrothed, my grandfather, Philip Caldwell Danbury, many years ago, and my presenting you with this ring was based on much family tradition. Now I would also like to present you with something far more personal, something that will be a constant reminder of our own love and promises to one another."

Thomas took an ornate red box out of an inner pocket of his vest. He formally presented it to Charllie, who opened it with joy and delight. A stunning gold locket was nestled in the depths of the little box, and it was attached to an equally stunning gold brooch. As he lifted the beautiful piece of jewelry from the box, it glimmered in the gentle rays of the summer sun. He bestowed it upon her and then softly pressed his lips to her forehead.

Thomas carefully attached the brooch to her dress, and it hung in all its golden splendor. Charllie's eyes took on a softness, and tears glistened within them, emphasizing their brilliant blue. Her smile was tremulous and warm. "Thomas, it's beautiful," she breathed. "I will treasure this for as long as I live and will wear it every day, remembering just how much you love me, and how much we mean to one another."

Charllie was touched by the thoughtfulness of her fiancé. He was such an enigma! One moment, he was pragmatic and all business, and the next, he exhibited glimmers of the romantic.

Thomas opened the locket to show Charllie the intricately-woven love knot within. "I took the liberty of making a request of your Aunt Bethany to provide me with a lock of your hair, so that I could have your tresses and mine entwined within this keepsake. I hope that when we are apart, you will be able to look within this locket and be reminded of all we share as well as all we will share in the years to come."

Charllie had peered within the locket that hung from the brooch now pinned just above her heart, and Thomas had gingerly touched the brooch one last time as if to impart his blessing upon this gift of love. His touch had sent delicious shivers down her spine. The soft glow of love on Charllie's face spoke of vulnerability, delight, and passion. Thomas's cool lips had taken their final kiss, and with it had been given his pledge to return and resume their relationship, the next time as man and wife. The brooch was a cherished memento of the promises they had every intention of fulfilling following their engagement apart.

Charllie, breaking free from her reverie, now touched this keepsake with her fingertips. She looked inside the locket at the love knot made by their hair, hers and Thomas's. As she sat beneath the shade tree, reminiscing about what once was and what might have been, it hit her with violent and emotional force that Thomas was gone. His home was now the grave, his future forever destroyed. And what of Charllie's future? Without Thomas by her side, her future was forever blighted; no one could ever replace what the two of them had once possessed or the dreams they had shared. She knew this with certainty. Mortals, if lucky, get one chance at true happiness, but if that doesn't work out, whatever comes along can only be construed as second best. And Charllie was not about to entertain the idea of ever settling for second best!

Chapter Four

Mauve upon mauve, the twilight crept upon the land, sending misty tentacles of fog through the trees and around the plantation house. Heavy and humid was the night. A star or two shone through the haze, but the atmosphere was charged with environmental emotion. Heat lightning shimmered on the horizon, and Charllie mopped her damp brow with an embroidered handkerchief. Occasional light breezes sifted through the trees, but they were scarce and of short duration. The night was becoming oppressively cloying, and she awaited the approaching storm with heightened expectancy.

The once innocuous lightning, which had been vividly displayed in the distance for most of the evening, was now edging closer, and soon it was followed by the ominous rumble of thunder. The lightning was now much more than a display, its power and savagery more real than imagined. With the first violent clap of thunder, Charllie sought shelter on the verandah. She was tense from the charged night air and prepared herself for the atmospheric show threatening to display all its ferocious grandeur. Brilliant forked lightning lit the sky, and the following crash made by the accompanying thunder sent shivers down Charllie's spine. Cannon fire—that's all she could think of. Maimed bodies, disintegrating limbs, charred remains, and shattered dreams lying forever frozen on a cold and cruel battlefield made too real by the imaginings of her mind. War took casualties beyond the battlefield, sending loss and desolation to those who had waited in vain for their loved ones to return.

Every time a lightning bolt struck the ground, quickly followed by a crash of thunder, Charllie recoiled, and the sights and sounds of destruction went straight to her heart. She could not seek the shelter of the house, for she was mesmerized by this violent performance that both repelled and fascinated her. It reflected her tormented soul and held her in its power. She sat rigidly in her chair, hands clenched and white with fright. The metamorphosis that had taken place from the bright, glimmering day to the dark, forbidding night tugged at her soul and was a constant reminder that the goodness in life was often nothing more than an illusion. It was always subject to change.

The sweep of rain that had begun as a gentle patter now blotted out the stars and hammered the landscape. Huge drops echoed from the roof and ran in rivulets down the gutters. It seemed the world was bent on shedding its tears as well for all the devastation that had been incurred by a bloody war from which so many had not returned, and for whom many were still grieving. Tears slowly glided down Charllie's cheeks. People told her time would heal all, but for now, her loss was still razor-sharp. The edge of grief had become less distinct, but it was still present.

Charllie was now no longer sure about her purpose in this life. She had always dreamed about the love and security that came with marriage and children, but she had never envisioned the possibility that these could be easily snatched away from her by fate. She hated the idea that her life had been kidnapped by external forces. Wanting something and needing something did not always mean that they were easily acquired. Wishes, she had sadly learned, were really relegated to children who could still believe in forces of good that rewarded those pure of thought and deed. Ironically, as each clap of thunder shook the landscape, Charllie could not help but wonder why her punishment in this life had been so severe. Why had she been left alone? Why was her life to be forever blighted?

And then, in guilt, she would soon realize that she still possessed the preciousness of life. Not so for Thomas. His only shot at this life had been abruptly snatched from him, his dreams ruthlessly torn to shreds. For Thomas, there would be no second chance, and he was not alone. Thousands and thousands of soldiers from both sides had also been maimed or had perished. The sky should be shedding violent tears for all these losses.

The savage lightning diminished, and with a last gust of damp night air, the thunder itself rumbled off to the west and then finally ceased. As the thirsty landscape puddled, soft night fragrances permeated the still, humid air, and night sounds swelled, filling the night air with a savage symphony. With the cessation of the heavy downpour, the gentle patter of the storm's finale had unleashed a chorus of frogs and breathed fragrant sighs of damp earth and grass. The tumult of the night began to wane and recede. A brave lone star peeked through a dissipating cloud, then another, and another, until finally a twinkling array of stars was joined by a crescent moon.

Exhausted by spent emotions, Charllie decided it was time to retreat to the confines of her bedroom. Here she would seek solace from her sorrows, and though she had never truly found respite anywhere, her bedroom had become the closest thing to a sanctuary where she could go to seek healing. Memories were hard to elude, especially when they brought those who had been so dear and close to her heart—alive and begging to be remembered by the living.

Charllie hoped that her "mind" could erase all the pain and anguish that continued to haunt her. She could only pray that tonight her dreams would be sweet, for her daydreams were never such.

***

The Danbury family cemetery was situated south of the family home, down a dusty lane that passed between a hayfield and a field of wheat. A stately, ancient beech sheltered the center sweep of the graveyard with its graceful branches, and as the marble headstones spread out in a semi-circle from that spot, they became intermingled with lily-of-the-valley, roses, and ferns. Mossy pathways meandered amongst the headstones, and stone benches offered quiet places of rest and contemplation for the few who visited this area of sorrow and loss. A graceful marble angel, green with time and wear, guarded the gravestone of a young woman who had died of consumption over a hundred years ago. An achingly small, lichen-covered stone was all that remained to memorialize a two-year-old boy who had been bitten by a deadly copperhead snake. A crudely chiseled double heart seemed to pulse with the memories of the untimely deaths of twin girls who had given up the battle for their lives at birth. Death and sadness were everywhere.

Charllie quickly located the stone, which was her destination. Still spotlessly white and free of any weathering, Thomas Danbury's gravestone was nestled on the knoll overlooking his family estate, Danbury Dell, the home where he had once dreamed of becoming its master. As Charllie gazed from that spot and surveyed the Danbury estate in the distance, she saw the sunlight trace a glow across the mansion's sun-bronzed brick edifice. Magnolia trees, oaks, tulip trees, and holly surrounded the clearing while English ivy, climbing its walls, softened the rather stark look of the hundred-year-old mansion. A circular garden in front of the home displayed English boxwood, topiary, and urns of geraniums. White ducks swam on the pond to the right of the house, and in the distance, a pale gray stable was the site of much activity.

The plantation's involvement in the workaday world seemed far removed from the spot where Charllie stood. The stir of life at Danbury Dell was going on without Thomas. The cemetery's somber presence, far removed from this life, held the precious remains of a Confederate soldier who had once made plans for marriage, fatherhood, and a prosperous position in society. Death took center stage here. The older gravestones spoke of infants snatched from cradles before their first teeth broke through; men gored by angry bulls; women losing their battle in childbirth; and children dying of smallpox, whooping cough, and diphtheria. The somber landscape spoke of so many who had given up the good fight, unwillingly and often without warning. Charllie hoped they had all found peace. Perhaps their realities were far more pleasant than the realities left behind for their friends and families. This life and death struggle, often forgotten in the daily routine of living, was only fully understood and appreciated when one was either directly facing it oneself or was forced to face it upon the loss of a loved one.

Charlotte sighed and returned to the purpose at hand. She took out her trowel and jug of water. The hard, dry soil was quickly loosened around the geraniums, stray weeds were pulled, and the withered blooms discarded. Charllie removed the last dead blossom and then gently poured water upon the parched earth. Her pathetic attempts to provide beauty in this spot were in direct opposition to the stark reality of what it represented. In her attempt to bring life to this shrine of death, she hoped in some way to keep Thomas with her, though she knew this was a futile attempt. Thomas was no more a part of this landscape than she was.

Thomas' spirit had departed this place long ago; he had gone home to a place where he was at least at peace—something Charllie had been unable to find for herself in this world. Dealing with devastation was never an easy task, but when one made it an integral part of daily life, it became debilitating. It sapped her strength to the point where there were some mornings she had to unwillingly drag herself from her bed, force herself to eat, and chastise herself for overlooking all the blessings that remained within her grasp.

Her blessings were mixed at best, but Thomas's were no more. When Charllie found herself mourning his passing, she often wondered what his last hours had been like. Had he been in terrible pain? Lonely? Had anyone given him any final comforting words or a friendly touch? Had he been thinking about her and their future together when he had breathed his last? The not knowing was incredibly difficult, and the imagined scenarios were probably more horrific than the reality. She would never know, and now it really didn't matter. So often she just felt guilty that she was still alive when Thomas's very lifeblood had been taken from him so suddenly and so long ago.

Often, it was just easier for Charlotte to lose herself in a fantasy world. As the water continued to seep into the ground surrounding the plants, her mind wandered, and she dreamed of what might have been. She saw herself strolling by the duck pond with Thomas and an elfin child by their side. Thomas, who stood only about three inches taller than Charlotte, had favored his father. His fine, sandy hair and intelligent gray eyes accompanied high cheekbones, a meticulously groomed moustache, and a rather gentle smile.

He looked dashing in his gray officer's uniform, and the gentle pressure she felt at her elbow as he guided her around the estate spoke volumes of the love and concern he felt for her.

Thomas took her hand between his two gloved hands and raised it to his soft, pliable lips. A gentle kiss. He patted their child on the head. A daughter. A son. The image was too indistinct, too dreamy. Thomas tucked a rose behind her ear and promised that they would be together forever. Charlotte closed her eyes and once again smelled roses and Thomas's favorite cologne, a spicy lime mixture. A tiny shudder shook her frame. A smile flickered across her face as she clutched the spent geranium blossoms to her breast. Her quiet reverie was sweet, but brief. It was soon shattered by an interruption.

"Miss Charllie. Here again? I swear, you spend more time on our plantation than we do ourselves. Still visiting brother Thomas?" Sage had intruded upon her reveries—again!

"What morbid fancies has Thomas led you to conjure up this beautiful June morning?"

Sage Danbury had silently ambled up to the cemetery gate on horseback, and Charllie, in her daydream state, had never heard his approach. He narrowed his eyes when he noticed the tenderness and reverence that Charllie gave to the flowers surrounding his brother's gravestone. His lips became a grave, ominous line. His hands tensed on his horse's reins.

Try as he might, Sage could never understand Charllie's devotion to Thomas. It was an unholy relationship that she constantly rekindled. Thomas had always treated her like his kid sister. Their relationship had lacked the passion he felt necessary for a successful marriage, the passion he himself felt for Charllie and was not allowed to express. But, then again, he knew he was biased against Thomas because of his own deep love for her. Had he been betrothed to Charllie, not a day would have gone by without his arms around her pleasing body, his lips pressed persuasively against hers, his body seeking hers for a grand completion of desire. He would have shared his passion and love for her in every sigh, in every gesture, in every caress. But then, he had never been betrothed to her.

"Mr. Danbury, I swear you should have been a spy for the Confederacy. The outcome might have been far more favorable for our side. I'm sure your parents taught you some very fine manners once upon a time, but it seems you have allowed them to lapse. Since Thomas and I were betrothed and should have become husband and wife, I am giving his memory the respect and consideration due what would have been shown by any loving widow—had God allowed me to become his wife. But, since that was not to be, I feel bound to at least perform those loving duties which honor his memory; and for as long as I live, his memory will not be forgotten."

Charlotte stood up in her pearl gray gown, which deepened her blue eyes and cast stormy lights within them. She wore the brooch and the ring, and her hair was pulled back into a severe bun. She lacked but a widow's veil to make the picture complete.

Sage dismounted his black stallion, Ebony and purposefully approached Charlotte by entering through the rickety wooden gate that was held tenaciously in place by the carved stone cemetery wall. He banged the gate shut as he entered. His face was ominous, his demeanor less than cordial.

"When does this period of mourning end, Miss Charlotte? You have become a tragic, blighted rose. You are paying homage to a god who never existed on this earth. Thomas was a man, not a god, not an angel. He died before his time, his friends and family mourned his passing, and now it's time for those he left behind to get on with their lives." In his agitation, Sage crushed his hat within his powerful hands, and he then stabbed Charllie with his emotionally charged green eyes. His face was solemn, and he held his body as taught as the bowstring that prepares to release its arrow to its target.

As he approached, Charllie instinctively backed away until she was prevented from further movement by the presence of a nearby gravestone. With her own eyes flashing anger, yet also damp with tears, she stood her ground. She was troubled by her inability to deal with Thomas's brother without animosity, but he provoked such strong feelings within her whenever he was near that she found herself floundering with mixed emotions. Perhaps in the future she might possibly be able to accept him as a good friend and confidante again, but she could never envision him as a suitor—only Thomas had been adequate for that role. Sage was pushing the boundaries beyond propriety. He was trespassing on her heart, which was no longer hers to give. His tenaciousness was hard to understand and impossible to accept.

"Sage, your brother was more than just a man. He was the finest Southern gentleman one could ever hope to meet in the entire state of Virginia. He was loving and kind, and I, at one time, had had the wonderful promise of becoming his wife. You, as his sibling, may have never appreciated his finer qualities, but as his fiancée, I had the privilege of knowing him like no one else." Charllie's eyes were a bit downcast as she spoke. She felt her statements were a bit stilted and artificial, as if her speech had been spoken from memorization rather than from her heart. Still, her pleas were becoming less than original and heartfelt, and she knew it.

"Charllie, sometimes knowing someone, even those closest to us, may not always be enough. What lies within each person's heart is often secret. And, if we look too closely, we may not always discover what we hope to find."

Sage's tone had become gentle and tender, but his eyes belied this tenderness with the deep sparks of anger that continued to smolder. He slid his hands within his pockets and sought composure. He paced the narrow confines to the side of Thomas' grave, never once looking up. Charllie was puzzled by Sage's speech, for the meaning remained elusive and cryptic. However, his serious demeanor bought her silence.

Sage had trouble containing the volatile emotions he was experiencing and visibly blanched when Charllie gently traced Thomas's epitaph. He quickly turned his back on her and walked back through the graveyard gate. He led Ebony to an especially grassy corner where he tethered his horse so that he could graze. He viewed the serenity of his ancestral home, yet this perceived serenity could not assuage the anger that simmered and curled like a snake in the pit of his belly. "Southern gentleman!" A curse threatened to leave his lips, but he pressed them shut and allowed the profanity to die in a slow, painful hiss.

Chapter Five

Sage narrowed his eyes as he watched the woman he loved caress his brother's gravestone. He finally turned his back on her and sadly shook his head in disgust. Charllie knew little of the true Thomas Danbury. Yes, he had been a great captain in the War between the States. He had been a wonderful son and brother. But he had never been marriage material for someone like Charlotte Wright. Charllie had innocently gone on with her day-to-day existence, never realizing how close she had come to having her precious life forever blighted. The love she cherished, a love commemorated with token jewelry, occasional nosegays, and whispered promises, had been nothing more than a sham. Yet it stood today as shiny and as untarnished as a newly minted coin.

Tragically, Charlotte had the two brothers confused. She had mistaken worthless dross and fool's gold on Thomas's behalf as the true treasure of her world, but she had been misled. Sage, the brother she chose to detest and malign, was the one who had truly cherished her over the past years, not the dearly departed Thomas. Sage's coin was preciously minted, his gold of the highest karat. Unfortunately, Sage did not feel that he would ever be at liberty to divulge this truth to her without destroying her and the memory of his brother. And therein lay his dilemma.

Sage remembered too well the day he had impetuously ridden into Thomas's camp during the early days of the Civil War, a camp which had been set up in a clearing in Maryland in preparation for the next battle. The officer's tent had been pitched in relative seclusion, totally apart from the other soldiers' tents. Sage had recently decided to enlist in the war, and he was excited about sharing this information with his older brother, as he had promised to assist him with the South's struggles. He had hoped to surprise Thomas with a visitor from home, a visitor who might be useful in building his morale and offering some support and news from home. But Sage had been the one who had been surprised.

As Sage had entered his brother's tent unannounced, he was startled to see that Thomas had company, of a most intimate nature—his first lieutenant, Michael O'Rourke. The two men were blatantly naked and wrapped up in each other's arms with little more than an army blanket to cover their lower extremities. The air hung heavy with sex and desire. Sage had stood speechless, reeling in shock because of this most awkward of situations. He surveyed the surreal tableau of intimacy before him and shook his head in disbelief. He could not imagine his brother Thomas, the hero of the family, the leader, the upstanding citizen and army captain, cavorting with another man when he was engaged to marry the sweetest, most beautiful woman in all the world. Sage could not have felt any worse than if someone had plunged a dagger in his heart.

There had been no mistaking the intent of this rather private liaison, and Sage could easily tell that this was no uncommon occurrence. The privacy given to them by the rest of the camp owed two respected officers whose need for planning war strategy meant that they must spend much time in conference without being interrupted. Sage knew better. Army camps were communities of men who had each other's backs, who planned together, trained together, and went into battle together. He knew immediately that Thomas and Michael were a pair: their planned strategies often had very little to do with the war for which they had enlisted. The times when they were alone were important for their frequent dalliances.

Thomas had immediately acknowledged Sage's presence. He casually rid himself of the army blanket and began to don his uniform as if nothing untoward had happened. Sage, however, could tell that Thomas was flustered and furious due to his unannounced entry into the tent, for his face was flushed by embarrassment and irritation. The elder brother narrowed his eyes as he gauged Sage's reaction to the inexplicable tableau laid before him, and then he quickly pasted on a disingenuous smile and faked a pleasant greeting for his brother, whose entry was as awkward as it was ill-timed. However, he smoothly recovered his composure, casually buttoning his breeches and shrugging into his jacket. He attempted to straighten his uniform, soon realizing that the buttons did not align. He meticulously corrected their alignment and then tied a scarf around his neck. Lieutenant O'Rourke, taking only enough time to yank on his breeches and pull on his boots, gathered his remaining scattered clothing and vacated the tent with great speed, making it quite clear that caution was necessary in maintaining the obligatory secrecy of the discovered liaison. He hurriedly left the two brothers alone to sort out their turbulent emotions, something which he most certainly had no wish to share in concert with them.

Sage, masking his feelings, was the first brother to open the conversation. "Not a pretty sight, brother, especially for someone who is engaged to one of the most beautiful women this side of the James River. This intimate little scene was something I would never have anticipated—not in a million years!"

Thomas, slightly on the defensive, attempted nonchalance. Though he was unable to look Sage straight in the eye, he casually replied, "I am quite happy to see you well, brother, though your arrival most certainly came at a rather awkward moment. Perhaps next time you might wish to send me a timely missive so that I might prepare for your arrival."

Thomas soon picked up on Sage's expression of discomfort and censorship. "Don't be such a prude, brother dear. Men have their public lives, it is true, and they must give all due respect and honor to those positions. But they also have their private lives as well, which for some may require discretion, as in my case. It is a matter of record and history that occasional liaisons similar to what you just interrupted have been common in society for centuries—instances like these have even been passed down in ancient literature. It was commonplace for Greek warriors to take male lovers from within the ranks of their comrades in arms. These love matches were often expedient, quelled desires that must be stemmed, and fulfilled a passion that some men happened to share. I have done no more and no less than many others in my situation."

Still feeling as if he had wandered into a bad dream, one from which he could only pray that he might soon awaken, Sage approached his brother with all-important questions on his mind. "I think that this was something more than expediency, Thomas, and certainly not just an overriding attempt to assuage your sexual needs during wartime. In fact, it's quite clear to me that this was more than just a casual coupling. But I'm not here to censor your love life, Thomas, for that is none of my business. What does concern me, however, is how all this fits in with your ongoing engagement. What about Charllie? What of your plans for her future as your wife?"

Sage's face had become white and pinched, and, though in shock, he was giving his brother deference, hoping that much could be explained. Perhaps war had distorted his judgment. Perhaps he was experimenting out of sexual need and frustration. Perhaps he was extremely lonely, and a sexual romp, even with a member of the same gender, provided release. All the rationale that he attempted to conjure up failed to satisfy his sense that Charllie was being seriously wronged by the one whom she held most dear. He turned and waited expectantly for Thomas to explain himself, to validate his position.

Thomas was in no mood to hastily come forward with his reply. He casually folded two of the camp blankets and then lit a cigar, pensively watching its tip glow red as he inhaled his first lungful of smoke. He felt put out that he was being called to task by this younger brother, who was still green in battle and in life. Though he felt no real compulsion to make himself understood, he casually shrugged his shoulders and faced him. There was little of the penitent in his stance.

"This has absolutely nothing to do with my engagement to Charlotte. She is a part of my life that is totally separate from what you rudely interrupted this day. As the elder son, I must do my duty regarding my family, which means partaking of marriage, fathering children—most especially a male heir, and maintaining an honorable presence in society. However, as a man with certain predispositions, I also have those physical longings and attachments that cannot be denied. I see nothing wrong with living my life as I see fit."

Thomas walked over to a mirror and, comb in hand, began preening in front of it, attempting to repair his disheveled appearance. His apparent selfishness in both thought and deed fueled dormant fires within the younger brother.

In disgust, Sage leapt forward and roughly grabbed Thomas by the forearm. "What of love?" he hissed. "Charllie thinks you are marrying her out of love, not duty. She deserves a man who truly loves her in every sense of the word, not someone who is acting out of pretense. The day you walk down the aisle with her, you will be forever sullying the true nature of what marriage is meant to be between a man and a woman. It will all be a lie. You will be destroying the trust and goodness of our dearest neighbor and friend, who has dreamed for years about becoming your wife. I cannot believe you would do that to her!"

Thomas knew he would have to immediately talk to those guarding the perimeters of the camp. No visitors, even those who appeared to be the closest of friends and relatives, should be allowed on the grounds without the expressed permission of the commanding officer. This interview was most distasteful and, had he been able to relive this incident in his life over again, he most certainly would have. It was a most embarrassing predicament to be called upon the carpet by a younger sibling and was distasteful to the extreme. He should never have to answer to anyone regarding his personal life!

"My dear brother, be realistic. Charlotte will never know. She will be totally oblivious to my most discreet private life apart from our times together. I will marry her and do my sacred husbandly duties. She will be with child soon after our marriage, and to all outward appearances, we will be a picture of domestic bliss. I will be a true master of discretion, and nobody but you and I, and some of my closest friends, will ever know that something more exists beneath the surface of this model marriage. Relax, Sage. Don't be so sanctimonious. Not one marriage in ten involves absolute fidelity. Ours will be no different than many that go on for decades, even unto death, with no one being the wiser. Business trips will come up from time to time: Charlotte will accompany me on some, some she will not. Nothing will ever interfere with the marital bond between us, and discretion will ensure that."

Thomas sat down and pulled on his regimental boots, which had been polished to a magnificent shine. He acted as if having one's brother barge in on a very private sexual activity was but a minor distraction. It was evident that he had been caught off guard, but it was also very clear that the gravity of the situation totally escaped him.

Sage, who could hardly contain his anger, savagely removed his hat and began to pace. He was his brother's junior by almost three years, yet at this moment, he felt that he was much the older and wiser; but he also felt the frustration of lacking the power to make any of the major changes that could rectify the unsavory knowledge of his brother's dual life. He felt like a cornered animal that could growl and gnash its teeth, but without effect, for it would continue to remain trapped and besieged. He sought some sense of justice, for some way to right this wrong he had unwittingly discovered. In the end, he dealt with an overwhelming sense of helplessness—and hopelessness.

"You have yet to discuss the issue of love, Thomas. You talk of duty, and outward appearances, and deception. Charlotte is mentioned as one might mention his favorite brood mare, not the woman he loves, not the woman he hopes to make his wife. Have you no common decency? You know the feelings I have tendered toward Charllie. You know I have respected the fact that she chose you over me, even though I myself had deferred to you from the onset and never formally petitioned for her hand myself. But this! To think that I have lost her to a shabby farce, a cruel joke! You cannot mean to go through with this marriage based on deceit, brother. It is unconscionable!"

Thomas Danbury finally had the nerve to look Sage in the eye. He leveled his gaze in a rather cruel and cold manner. "In everything but dowry, this marriage was arranged, my dear brother; and, due to the wealth of both families, a dowry would have been crass, so it never became an issue. The marriage of the elder Danbury male child to the Wright's only girl child has been a cherished dream for both families for many years. I would never compare my sweet Charlotte to a brood mare, at least not directly, but bloodlines do matter—you must see that. Love might have been the icing on the cake, but sometimes one must settle for affection and best regards. The benefits of our marriage will far outweigh any of the obstacles that you may find so offensive. Two powerful families will be able to maintain their wealth and standing in society. Their superior bloodlines will be allowed to mingle so that both of their legacies will live on for the foreseeable future. I, for one, am more than content with this outcome."

Thomas stubbed out his cigar and coldly continued, "I find the arrangement quite to my liking, dear brother. I will be able to savor the best of both worlds, and none will be the wiser. My standing in society will be respectable and secure; my little escapades will add a certain relish to the humdrum nature of my existence; and the Danbury name, yours and mine, will flourish with me at its head. All's well that ends well, as they say." He tucked his shirttails into his breeches and brushed imaginary dirt from his sleeves.

Sage stared at his brother in disbelief, the wretchedness of his cold statements and the mockery with which he had colored his upcoming marriage with Charllie surged within him, cutting and sharp. "Your life is a lie, Thomas, and Charllie should not be dragged into the mud because of your choice of lifestyles. Bachelors are respected and constantly in demand. Break off this travesty of an engagement and allow her to find happiness with someone who desires her as a woman, if not with me, at least with someone who will treat her as a desirable partner in life, not a brood mare. Please don't ruin her life. She is the true innocent in all of this and does not deserve the kind of treatment you have so boldly predicted."

Sage, shaken by the last hour's events, walked over to the doorway of the tent to get a breath of fresh air. The tent's atmosphere had become filled with the contagion of deceit, egotism, and callousness. He was dealing with the sorrow of true recognition. The brother he thought he knew so well was but a lie. The attributes of honor, bravery, and compassion, which he had once easily bestowed upon him, were no longer relevant. He had lost not only the childhood beliefs he once held pertaining to his brother, but he had also lost the very brother himself: the one who could do no wrong, the one who was steadfast, the one who always chose the path of goodness and what was right. He wondered if his brother had always been such a fraud or if the change was recent in nature. He was at a loss as to how to react to the developments that had so recently transpired. Conflicting emotions boiled within Sage, and he could not look at his brother without contempt.

Thomas approached Sage and gently laid his hand on his shoulder. “This will all remain a secret between brothers, Sage. I will make Charlotte Wright immensely happy, I can assure you. She will never be the wiser. Further, I promise that she will be given free rein at Danbury Dell as my wife and hostess. Shortly after our marriage, she will become a doting mother, and she and I will be the greatest of friends until death do us part—mark my words.”

“Friends!” Sage spat the words in disgust. “A husband and wife need to be more than friends. What of love? Passion? Desire? Your word means nothing to me, Thomas. You have broken all pledges of goodness by being adamant in taking this callous route, sullying all that should be sweet and good within a relationship. You don’t deserve Charllie, and she most certainly doesn’t deserve you. And because of that, Thomas, I will never forgive you.”

Spying the flicker of a grin crossing Thomas’s face, Sage clenched his fist and then smashed Thomas’s face with all the pent-up rage and exasperation that had been building up within him during their confrontation. Without a backward glance, he stormed through the open flaps of Thomas’ quarters, leapt upon his horse, and galloped away from the site of moral contagion. He rode as if the very demons of hell had come to light in the officer’s tent, and they now chased him in hot pursuit back to Danbury Dell.

Thomas gingerly rubbed his cheekbone, which was already beginning to swell and turn color. But his smile had not been erased. “My secret is safe with my brother. Sage has always been the more honorable of the Danbury brothers. He will never compromise the happiness of his sweet Charlotte, on that I’ll stake my life.” Captain Danbury slowly shook his head as if to dispel the ugliness of the past hour, and then he went back into his tent to apply cool compresses to his cheek and to imbibe in a rather strong glass of bourbon.

Thomas had died in a Yankee prison six months later, and so many mixed emotions had raged within Sage at that time. He had been devastated by the death of his brother, relieved that Charllie would not have to enter into a marriage that was not as it seemed, and guilty that the loss of Thomas must be sadly tempered by a sense of relief. He had forgiven his brother for his transgressions long ago, but he could never forget the devastating legacy that he had left behind.

Following Thomas's death, Charllie remained infatuated with a lie. A fiancé who had knowingly maligned her in a less-than-sensitive manner was seen by her as a sainted officer of the war who had perished in duty to his country. She continued to deify Thomas when, instead, she should have finally brought her period of mourning to an end so that she could get on with her own life. It was more than overdue. Sage knew that, even in anger, he could never betray his brother's secret; he would never sully his brother's good name in deference to the love he still felt for him and to the loved ones that Thomas had left behind. Most of all, he refused to destroy Charllie's innocent dreams of a man of whom she had known so little. He refused to ever take part in anything that might bring her further unhappiness.

But these very same secrets emasculated him and made him vulnerable. He felt trapped in a nightmare that had been brought about by his only brother, a brother who had never taken the responsibility to do the right thing. This dilemma had become all the keener because Sage was unable to successfully press his own suit with the person he had chosen to love and cherish for a lifetime. Sage knew without a doubt that if his brother's memory had not constantly interfered,

Charllie would have been able to eventually recognize the budding love that existed between them. But until that day, Sage must continue to live with the hopelessness of their relationship, realizing that she might never become *the love of his life.*

***

A deep sadness fell across the topography of Sage's face, but he quickly erased it away with a scowl of anger. An outward display of tender emotion for his brother, Charllie, or even for himself would do more harm than good. It only proved that he had finally given in to weakness. He turned back to Charlotte and, unfortunately, some of his anger and frustration were given vent as he spoke to her.

"Widow's weeds do not become you, Charllie, especially since you have yet to marry. I am certain that you could find more savory pastimes than visiting graves and talking to the dead, even your most dearly departed! He'll never answer back, not even for you."

Charllie turned away from him, trying hard to ignore his very presence. She felt tears pressing behind her eyelids, but she willed them to cease while she struggled with her pain. Her silence did not prevent Sage from continuing with his pleas that up to this point had been ignored.

"Charllie, can't you see what you're doing to yourself? Your cheeks have lost their bloom, and you'll soon take to your bed if you don't shake off this obsession. Must you go on like this when there are those waiting to escort you back into this world? You are young and beautiful, and you know my feelings for you are honorable and true. Don't bury yourself here on this knoll with Thomas."

He handed her a bonnet that had been casually placed upon Thomas's headstone, and Sage cringed at the familiarity she still felt for his brother. Charllie reached over and snatched the bonnet from his outstretched hand, and it fell loosely to her side. Her face was flushed red, and her hair had begun to escape its confines, framing her face in loose ringlets. Sage ached with longing and desire.

Charllie maintained her composure, but inside she was seething with hurt and resentment. Did Sage really expect her to casually discard all precious memories of Thomas? She had barely gotten used to being promised to him as his bride when she had to accommodate his death. Didn't he understand that loving someone was not a disease that was so easily cured? Surely, he should feel some sympathy for his own brother and empathy for the woman who had been promised to him as his bride. There were times when Charllie truly felt that friendship with Sage should be possible, and she knew that she could surely use a friend at this time. But too often the strong responses that accompanied their meetings forced her to keep him at a cool distance. His arrogance and insensitivity always tended to erect barriers over which she refused to climb.

"Mr. Danbury, you wouldn't know what a real gentleman was even if you tripped over one. I've told you time and time again, I am repulsed by your attentions and had hoped to deter your gestures of familiarity a long time ago. You have never given your brother the respect due him. He was a hero of the war in every sense of the word. You can never compare." Charlotte knew that much of what she said was said in anger, but there was much about Sage Danbury that evoked strong emotions within her, some of which she could not even begin to understand.

Restraining his temper, Sage quickly reached Charllie's side. With strong fingers, he lifted her chin, forcing her to look straight and deeply into his blazing green eyes. "You, my dear, may know what a gentleman is. But I will gamble everything I own that you have no knowledge of what a true man is, not one who wishes you nothing more than your own happiness. There will come a day when you will meet one, and I venture to predict that he will look very much like me!"

Totally ignoring the fact that Charllie would not welcome any intimacy with him, Sage roughly pulled her to him in a close embrace. For the briefest of moments, he just held her to his breast as he reeled with the softness of her silky hair, the fragrance of her sun-drenched skin, and the sweetness of her pouting, ripe lips. He quickly bent down, and before she could react to the liberties he had already taken, he covered her lips with his own and kissed her deeply with all the pent-up emotion and strong feelings that had lain dormant for far too long. An aching hunger swept through him, and he soon sought a deeper kiss from her plump lips. Reluctantly, Charllie shared in the embrace. She was not immune to his closeness or his passion, but she was yet unable to realize his worth as a lover. Sage, however, felt totally overwhelmed by her nearness, and a flame gently kindled and threatened to burst into flame. He knew that if he didn't stop soon, he would lose control of the passion that threatened to eat him alive.

Still, he could not immediately pull away. Not yet. He had thirsted for her so long and so deeply that his parched soul demanded at least some dregs from this botched love affair. He softly kissed her eyelids, gently traced her neck with his fingertips, and seductively palmed the rounded swell of her breasts until her nipples hardened into pebbles. Charllie moaned low in alarm and surprise as her cold soul began to melt with the heat of desire. An awakening of passion throbbed through her body, passion that she had never once felt with Thomas. Tiny tremors swept throughout her body, and she trembled at these new feelings that held her spellbound.

Though Sage's caresses had been but a preliminary to love, and he remained reverent and alert to Charllie's reactions, he could not come this close to his own heart's desire without being emboldened to take one final, earth-shattering kiss. His body was clamoring for far more than he had already taken, and his heart and soul strained for further resolution; but, knowing that their time had not yet come, he reluctantly dropped his hands to his sides and slowly backed away.

Sage knew that Charllie might very well be bewildered by the temptations of his lovemaking, even as she battled the passion that he had stirred within her. But she would quickly recover by accepting the guilt for her responses, which would only strengthen her resolve to protect herself from betraying Thomas any further. He knew with a certainty that Thomas was still too much on her mind. Until her grieving for his brother ended, and they were of one accord, he could not jeopardize their current relationship any further. He knew that if he were to begin pressuring Charllie with his own suit, she would view this as trespassing on his dead brother's territory. At this juncture, however, he could not distance himself from her any more than he already had. He would have to continue to temper his passion for her, ceasing to entice her with his lovemaking while he still could.

Charllie had been totally caught off guard by Sage's embrace, and she was also unprepared for this major assault on her senses. Thankfully, she had failed to overreact to his deepening kiss, but her mind and body were spinning with the passion they had shared. He had created rippling waves of desire that still lapped throughout her body, and she was enthralled with these new, unsought lessons in love and passion. Unconsciously, she remembered how she had begun to lean slightly into his final kiss as his gentle tongue sought hers once more, seeking a sweet sharing of intimacy; and she began to question her response to this most mysterious of occurrences—with Sage no less.

Charllie knew that Sage had no right to boldly plunder her mouth as he had done, but she had to battle with her own clamoring senses to stop them from forcing her to quickly enter the fray and fiercely respond by begging him to stay. She had been so tempted to return each one of his kisses with the same amount of fervor as his own, even while she recoiled at the thought of betraying her loyalty to his brother. When he abruptly released her and backed away, she felt totally bereft. Had he realized his judgment was in error? Did she truly mean so little to him?

Sage knew that he had taken far too many liberties this day. He must not continue upon this path of seduction where Charllie was concerned, for she was yet an innocent. Though it would be a seduction born of true love and desire, it was not the kind of relationship he had dreamed of giving her. His deep love for Charllie battled with his desire to claim her for his own. Begrudgingly, he backed down, accepting that the strength of his love far outweighed his physical need.

"Charllie, I must apologize for my lapse in manners. I never meant to take liberties with you, who has been a dear friend and neighbor. You are right that I should honor my brother's memory, for it is clear you are still very much in love with him. Please forgive me."

Sage was overcome with emotion. His words did not echo the agony he felt in backing away from the love of his life. He knew, however, that he could not force his will upon her.

Charllie now felt ice running through her veins. She had been amazed and enamored with this man who had so recently shared so much of himself with her. She had felt herself coming alive, and now he was backing away from her as if he realized that loving her was a huge mistake! Bewilderment turned to hurt, and finally to anger.

"I'm sorry if you found my kisses beneath your expectations. I am not sure that I accept the possibility that your caresses were purely a lapse in manners, Sage. I sometimes wonder if your jealousy in regards to Thomas might just fuel your need for vengeance. Perhaps you feel justified in trying to get back at me, for whatever reason. I will forgive you, but please see that it doesn't happen again."

Even though Charllie was dying inside, she chose to put up a front of nonchalance. She would never let Sage know just how close he had come to invading her heart. He would never know that he had begun to plunder the boundaries of love that had once been established by Thomas, boundaries which were beginning to crumble due to the passage of time, absence of passion, and the lack of substance. How could this have happened? Charllie could not understand it herself.

Sage caught a glimpse of the hurt in Charllie's shadowed eyes. However, determined though he was in fostering this fragile connection, a connection sweet beyond words, he knew that it must be deferred until the time when he determined that there might be a future for them. The break was painful but necessary, and he was now forced to return to his solitary ways without her. He knew that Charllie immediately felt the chill of his rejection, for she immediately turned her back on him—already regretting ever allowing herself to be caught up in emotions for another Danbury.

Feeling Charllie's cold dismissal, Sage turned on his heel, and in rapid, angry strides, he reached his horse, mounted him, and steadfastly galloped back toward the Danbury stables. No kind words of parting passed between them. What their bodies had so recently striven to unite, their hearts had boldly chosen to reject.

Charllie stared after him in puzzlement and amazement. His abrupt departure had created an emptiness, and she could only stare after him, feeling somewhat bereft. She knew that they had left much business still unresolved. She tried to convince herself that she should be overcome by outrage, for she had most definitely not solicited his advances, but she did not. Charllie was totally confused, and her brows knit in consternation. Sometimes it was harder to understand her own feelings than the feelings of others. And she had prided herself on thinking that she knew herself so well. Yet, where Sage was concerned, she always felt a bit out of control and somewhat disoriented. Why was her life so difficult? It seemed that she was constantly attempting to navigate through uncharted waters, and that she was seldom able to fully comprehend her own destination.

The morning dew had evaporated, and the noonday heat felt heavy and oppressive. Her mood mimicked the day. Charllie hoped that the jug of cool tea had been replenished, for she longed for any refreshment that might ease the discomfort of this long, emotional morning. She could not dismiss the uncomfortable feeling that played upon her mind, a feeling that there was more to Thomas' brother than met the eye. Damned Sage Danbury anyway! Who was he to interfere with her life?

Charllie gathered her gardening tools and the empty water jug. She gave one more backward glance at Thomas's gravestone and then climbed up into her trap. With a gentle flick of her wrist, she snapped the reins, and the pony gradually pulled the vehicle away from the Danbury graveyard. She felt some remorse for her treatment of Sage, but not enough to change her attitude toward him. How dare he malign his own brother and continue attempting to change her loyalties! Her grief was sincere, and he had no right to chastise her for it. Then Charllie began to recall with wonder the sense of vulnerability that she had briefly glimpsed when Sage had confronted her, as if she had inadvertently touched an extremely tender wound. Though she still felt simmering anger, nagging doubt accompanied these feelings, and she could still feel the heat that had been brought about by his fervent kisses and gentle caresses. Her ride home proved far more somber and disquieting than even her earlier arrival had been.

Chapter Six

Days stretched into weeks, and Charllie neither heard from nor saw Sage Danbury. Though his very presence was always exasperating and irked her no end, with his absence there now seemed to be something vital missing from her life. She wondered if perhaps he had become a small compensation for the loss of his brother, but quickly refuted that with an angry shake of her head. This new relationship that seemed to be developing with Sage was a total mystery. She couldn't help but be enthralled by the tentacles of passion that had insidiously begun to wrap themselves around her heart when she had been embraced by him in the cemetery. Never before had she experienced the ache of desire that had been sparked by his kiss, her body immediately infused with a warmth that went from head to toe. Not even with Thomas! And her mixed emotions had stirred her senses with anger, pleasure, curiosity, arousal, and fear.

Charllie knew she should be thankful for the reprieve. Without Sage's unwanted advances, she could get on with the sameness of her life, each day predictable in its own way. Now the rhythm of the seasons had more to do with the daily chores of subsistence rather than the appreciation of their beauty and grandeur. But all this activity was rather comforting in its own way because she could attempt to sleepwalk through life without being caught up in any of its emotional turbulence—turbulence which could be so heartrendingly painful! She sought to anesthetize herself from life, especially when it struck so close to her heart. Never again did she wish to feel the sharp pain that had consumed her when she had learned of Thomas's death.

Though Charllie spent hours in the kitchen with Hattie—baking, preserving, and cooking- it was never enough to totally douse what remained of her enthusiasm for life. Mundane chores and monotonous housework could leave the body drained and ready for the release of slumber, but the emotions and the instinct to live life to its fullest vied with the physical exhaustion and usually won. Late at night, Charllie would lie awake and think of a future that was nothing more than a long, dark tunnel, a future devoid of love, passion, and excitement. Her soul constantly strove to rebel. Her youth and normally joyful spirit cried out for more experiences, joy, and love. They begged her to put by her trappings of mourning, to embrace whatever life had left to offer with gusto and passion, but she was never quite able to totally walk away from her loyalty to a cherished fiancé who would never be coming home.

***

Charlotte awoke to a blazing sun. It was still morning, but the dew had long ago evaporated, heat waves shimmered, and the slight breeze that had once tenderly lifted the oak leaves had disappeared without a trace. She stretched and smiled. Today was a holiday of sorts, and she felt that one was long overdue. The local church was hosting a peach festival and bazaar. She had volunteered to spell one of the ladies at the crochet booth from 1:00 to 2:00 in the afternoon. After that, the day was hers. No housekeeping, no weeding, no preserving. She would take a long, cool bath and then dress in the new rose-sprigged gown she had sewn with Aunt Bethany's help. The shimmering moss green material was soft and light; it would be a pleasant change from the heavier gowns she normally wore.

As she prepared her bath, she caught herself humming a merry little tune she had once heard her niece Sarah singing during one of her recent visits. It was a lilting, rather playful melody. She smiled. Lately, she had not been one to give in to her lighter side. The fragrance of the rose petals sprinkled in her bath was delightful, and she luxuriated in the tub's soapy depths. Somehow, somber reflections of the past were unable to subdue the beauty of the glorious summer morning. She felt alive, anxious to greet the day. And she was starved!

Charllie quickly toweled off, dressed, and piled her long tresses on top of her head and fastened them with a blue ribbon that matched her dress. She pinned on her brooch, but the engagement ring—at least for this day—she would leave behind. She glanced in the mirror and was almost shocked to see a beautiful young woman who seemed not to have a care in the world. She had begun to think of herself as someone whom life had totally passed by, someone forever in mourning, a self-made spinster. The woman staring back was adventurous, eager to get on with life, and willing to take on any challenge. Stimulated, but also a bit chagrined, Charlotte hurried down to the kitchen to see what remained from the breakfast menu.

Hattie Mae was just finishing tidying up the kitchen. She, too, had the day off, and she was already garbed in her Sunday-go-to-meeting dress. She removed her apron, dusted off the front of her dress, and then threw a hand-crocheted shawl casually around her shoulders. She knew that she would be encountering wind-blown dust and debris on the carriage ride to the festival, and the shawl would also come in handy when they returned in the cool of the night. A wicker basket covered with a towel was suspended from her arm. Already her brow was beaded with perspiration, but her lips were puckered in merriment.

Charlotte rushed over to her, gave her a huge hug, and then began to scour the kitchen for a quick repast. “What are you doing, Hattie, robbing the kitchen of all the leftovers? And you know I haven’t eaten yet and am feeling mighty poorly from starvation. Surely you can take pity on me this beautiful morning and feed your most favored cooking assistant.”

Charllie knew how to play Hattie Mae like a familiar fiddle, yet today Hattie was having none of it.

“Miss Charlotte, you scamp, you deserve just what you get. You slept till all hours of the morning like a slugabed. There is no stealing taking place this morning. This basket is filled with peach preserves and slab pickle for the church bazaar, and my ride is waiting at the back door. You’d better pour yourself the rest of that coffee sitting on the back of the stove and eat one of the leftover honeybuns that were freshly baked early this morning. It’s the very best I can do with a last-minute notice. Next time, you might want to come to breakfast at a decent hour like most folks—before it’s time for the noonday meal!”

“Oh, Hat, I’m only teasing. You go on and have a wonderful day. I am sure that I will catch up with you soon enough. I’m scheduled to watch over the crochet booth part of the afternoon, but after that— I’m free as a bird!” She gave Hattie a large grin, and for once her laughter was sweet and warm.

“What has come over you this morning, Charllie? You are as pretty as a picture in that green dress of yours, but there’s something about you that seems different today. I just cannot put my finger on it! I haven’t seen you this gay since. .

." Hattie Mae wisely omitted that Charlotte's engagement party had been the last festive occasion when the sparkle exhibited by Charllie had been this evident.

"You haven't been sneaking any of those juleps so early this morning, have you?" She put her hands on her hips and tried her best to look stern and foreboding.

Charllie burst out laughing and gave her one last hug before attempting to shoo her out of the kitchen and on her way to her ride waiting in the drive. "Go on with you, Hattie. There's absolutely nothing wrong with me. I'm just looking forward to a little holiday. Now hurry up and mosey along. Your ride has been waiting quite some time. I will see you at the festival!"

Once Hattie was gone, Charllie poured herself a cup of coffee and fixed herself a plate of buns. The house was blissfully quiet. Everyone had allowed her some extra time for undisturbed sleep, and then they had gone ahead of her to the church to prepare for the festivities. Since she was not responsible for any of the activities herself until close to noontime, she had decided to follow along in her small pony trap later in the morning. Charllie settled in the old rocker located in a shady section of the verandah, after first shooing a disgruntled gray tabby from its cushion. She claimed the chair for herself and quickly took a bite of one of the soft rolls that was laced with honey and black walnuts. She smiled with pleasure and delight.

The air was still, but the shade on the verandah still held morning's freshness. She looked out upon the land that rolled down to the James and thought about the many changes her family had faced in the days during and following the war. The years, though tragic in many ways, often laced with pain, duty, and sacrifice, had also been filled with love and many blessings.

During the war, the Wright plantation had been commandeered by Confederate soldiers for their headquarters. As the Wright family had been Confederate sympathizers, the house and its grounds had been treated with at least a show of respect. A few of the minor chandeliers had turned up missing, deep gouges in the hardwood floors remained from exposed boot nails, and stains and rips were still evident on some of the wallpaper in a few of the rooms. Most of the linens, blankets, and dishes had been confiscated for the army's use, and all the curtains and drapes had been appropriated for extra bedding.

The Oak Haven home had been fortunate, for it had withstood so much in such a short period of time—yet it still remained intact; however, its grounds had been less fortunate. The flower and vegetable beds had been trampled into oblivion once they had been stripped of anything edible for the men and their horses. Many of the beautiful trees on the estate, even those shading the gracious sweep of the main drive, had been brutally axed for the many campfires that had provided flames for cooking and meager warmth for those who had crouched around them night after night as they planned new battles or recovered from old. Now, many ugly stumps dotted the landscape, giving testimony to but a few of the signs of the ravages of war.

When the troops had finally withdrawn from their temporary quarters at the Wrights, moving on to partake of more distant battles, the simple integrity and character of the Oak Haven plantation had miraculously remained. The plantation had passed the test of time and the indignities of a war that had indiscriminately destroyed many lives, homes, and property. Remarkably, a two-hundred-year-old red oak remained as witness to the history of the site, its presence on the knoll behind the barn a testament to the durability and determination of its people in moving forward to a better day.

During the army's stay at the plantation, many of the soldiers had sheltered in the barns with the livestock, some on the grounds in the many tattered canvas tents that were pitched randomly across the grounds, while the officers and their staff had taken up residence in the house. The family, which then consisted of Charlotte, her mother, and a few aunts and female cousins, had lived in the mansion's garret during the weeks when the army was in residence.

The women had used the soap-making kettle behind the house to cook massive quantities of soup and stews with the fruits, vegetables, and herbs that could be gleaned from the gardens, orchards, farmyard, and the woods for themselves and the hungry troops. They had quickly rinsed out a few of their own soiled clothes in the horses' watering trough and then hung them out their windows to dry. Their own personal needs were confined to chamber pots, which they discreetly emptied every night, and buckets of cold, soapy water, which provided minimal sponge baths. Their rather solitary existence on the third floor was voluntary and most definitely precautionary.

Charlotte, her mother, and the other female relatives had chosen to avoid the soldiers whenever possible and to play down their good looks. This necessary form of protection was provided by Sophia's wise counsel, and it had served them well during the army's occupation. Even though these soldiers shared the same cause as the family, they were still men; men who had been without the company of women for weeks on end. And with Mr. Wright and his sons away on some distant battlefields, they could not afford to risk the temptation that female company could offer lonely men hungry for a woman's attention—even if forced. They had spent their days reading and darning by the faint light that filtered through the dusty windows upstairs in the garret, knitting warm socks and mittens for the coming winter, writing lengthy letters to their loved ones far away from home, and quietly sharing plans for the future when they prayed that their menfolk would finally return from battle.

Most of the crops, both in the barns and in the fields, had eventually been eaten, trampled, stolen, or destroyed by soldiers from both sides on foraging missions, so the winter that followed had been a lean one. But they had made do, for it was clearly a matter of life and death. Wisely, prior to the commandeering of their plantation by Confederate forces, the Wright family had squirreled away provisions for just such dire circumstances: hiding foodstuffs under floorboards and buried deeply beneath the hay, hidden in attic trunks in the garret, or sunken in the bottom of the creek. They had also buried some of their best china and silverware in their backyard, and some jewelry and coins were hidden in the knotholes of trees. The canned fruits, vegetables, and jellies, which had been hidden from the visiting soldiers, as well as dried beans and herbs, smoked meats, honey and molasses, and chicory and tea, had been a provident foresight that saved those at Oak Haven that following winter from starvation, keeping them from total want during the following lean months. Once the Confederate army had pulled up stakes and other marauding troops had assessed the Wright plantation as lacking in any useful provender for their soldiers, an uneasy sense of peace had reigned. The hidden provisions had been gradually brought to light and stingily doled out to those remaining on the plantation over the many long months that followed. Survival during the war for those left behind was often as much of a struggle for them as it was for the men in the military.

Only prayers and hard work had helped guarantee the women a replenishment of foodstuffs the next year. They had successfully gleaned numerous foodstuffs: wild mushrooms for drying in the attic, fiddlehead ferns for pickling, apples for cider and vinegar, acorns for pig fodder, and dandelion leaves for fresh greens. The women had hand-tilled enough land to plant the precious seeds that had been stored in waterproof crocks. They had manured the land, seeded it, and cultivated it—all by hand, using the few implements available. But their efforts had eventually been rewarded the following fall with a meager crop of grains and vegetables that helped to replenish the root cellar, garret, and pantry; mainstays that would keep starvation at bay, and when supplemented with wild game, dried wild fruit, and precious corn meal, could be stretched through another season.

Disease and starvation had, unfortunately, ravaged much of the Southern army. A day came when Charles Wright returned from the war in a wheelchair, a very broken man. He was no longer of any use to the Southern cause, so he returned home without delay—hoping to do what he could for the loved ones he had left behind. His homecoming had been bittersweet, but he had been largely responsible for boosting the morale of those who had fought for the survival of Oak Haven and themselves while he was gone. Though Charllie's father seldom spoke of the misfortunes he had faced while serving in the Confederate army away from his family, all knew without being told that his hardships had been numerous and severe. He made a brief reference to his having been gravely wounded in one of the minor battles of the war was all that he would discuss, at least with his children. And they knew without being told that he tended to downplay the hardships he had faced during this episode of the war, turning it into a heavily edited adventure story for the grandchildren to dull the harsh reality of the circumstances that surrounded it. If he was more forthcoming about his experiences in his army unit with his wife, Sophia, it stayed between the couple; for Sophia never divulged anything further with Frank or Charllie.

Soon after Charles Wright returned home, the family was informed by a Confederate runner that their son and brother, Jeffrey, would not be returning home. He had recently been killed in a minor skirmish near Richmond. But it had been enough. Numerous young men from both sides had been felled that day, including Jeffrey and ten others from his regiment. Jeffrey had died a hero as he faced active duty in a war that so many believed in. But his family, who were overcome in their mourning for him, were unable to feel any celebration for the so-called heroism that took place that day.

Charllie knew that brother Jeffrey's death would forever be a solemn remembrance of the fickleness of war. Though it had been a shock to learn that her father had been forever crippled during battle, still, he had remained relatively whole of mind and body. How great would have been the family's joy had the house been blessed with two wheelchairs, for at least both loved ones would have returned to their homes. But the enemy rifle fire that had taken the lives of many men in Jeffrey's troop also took him. The Yankees had been bent on total annihilation of the band of rebels, and survival had never been an option for most of them. What was found of their remains had been buried by a neighboring squadron in a mass grave; the rest had fed the buzzards and ravens, the coal-black scavengers that circled the dying and lay waste to the bodies of the dead.

Jeffrey's bedroom would be forever empty. His voice, his laughter, his very presence might continue to echo resolutely through the hallways in ghostly whispers and haunted breezes, but he was gone. Though he would not soon be forgotten, the emptiness that he had left behind was a stark reminder of the finality of death. The Wrights now mourned the deaths of two of their children: one had succumbed to death as a mere child from diphtheria, and the other had been killed as a soldier in the war. They would continue to grieve these losses for the rest of their lives, but they would always maintain places in their hearts for these two lost sons.

The family had much to grieve, but also much to be thankful for. Today, Charllie somehow felt that the blessings far outweighed any sorrows. The colorful richness of the tapestry of life was forever changing, for its pattern was intricate and bold. Life was indeed for the living. Unbidden, a familiar face came to mind: raven hair with rakish curls, sparkling green eyes, a strong, determined profile, rippling muscles that gave way to slender hips and thighs. Sage Danbury.

With a start, Charllie quickly sat up straight in her chair, in shock and disbelief. Him! Why, she would never lower herself to even give him the time of day! Just what was he doing in her daydreams when she should be preparing to attend a peach festival? It was more than a mystery; it was a travesty! She would see that it didn't happen again. In the kitchen, she rinsed out her cup and then found a light shawl to protect her dress from the road's dust during her ride in the trap. As Charlotte left the house, she slammed the door behind her. For some reason, this gave her great satisfaction!

***

By the time Charllie arrived at the peach festival, everything was all hustle and bustle.

Tables were set up under colorful awnings, and they groaned under the weight of some of the finest peach cuisine in the county: pies, preserves, tarts, pickles, and shortcake. The children were running and shouting, even in the heat, while the adults milled around, conversing with neighbors whom they saw too infrequently, examining the wares for sale in the craft booths, purchasing peach delicacies, and lounging and chatting under the shade trees with their fans constantly in motion.

Georgia Merriweather and Abigail Cory, two of Charllie's childhood friends, were there, and soon the three of them were catching up on much of the neighborhood gossip. Georgia, five years married, had a three-year-old son in tow, and Abigail, married a year ago last September, was already sporting a coming event. Charllie, though pleased to be reunited with her friends, was more than a little bit envious. She felt like an outsider looking in upon a coveted tableau of life, one in which she was not yet welcomed. Without a helpmate, she was unable to share in the experiences of her friends, both happily married.

As Georgia and Abigail chattered on about their husbands and motherhood, Charllie had little to offer in the way of conversation. Her life was composed mostly of work and industry; it certainly seemed very bland in comparison to theirs. Georgia and Abigail continued to go on and on about the comings and goings of close relatives and friends, the recent births and deaths in the area, the love affairs and separations of some of the couples they knew, and even the weather. For the most part, Charlotte was only slightly interested and mildly amused; she didn't pay close attention to the gossip and commentary until Georgia, in confidence, let them in on a little secret.

"I'm sure this will be news to you all. Did you know that Phoebe Somerset, *the* Phoebe Somerset whose father owns that new textile mill in Richmond, might be formally announcing her engagement any day now? Good authority has it that she may have finally captured that elusive neighbor of yours, Charllie, none other than our own Mr. Sage Danbury. Doesn't that beat all? Somehow, I never thought I would see the day. I always thought Sage tended to wear his heart on his sleeve for you, Charllie, though he has protected his single status for quite some time now. But I suppose that when you are filthy rich and beauty-queen gorgeous like Phoebe, you are able to wear down even the most resolute of bachelors after a time."

Charllie felt like the floor had dropped out from under her. She had not been privy to this particular bit of gossip, and she found that tears had immediately sprung to her eyes—her stomach now clenched in a hard, painful knot; but she bravely smiled and acted surprised. She was soon grateful for the diversion created by Georgia's son, Evan. He had wandered away from his mother's side and was to be seen edging closer and closer to the dessert table, where he knew it was quite likely that some kindly bystander would take pity and offer him a sweet. And if not, he might easily snitch a peach tart without anyone being the wiser. His pudgy little hand was gradually creeping up towards its target when his mother spied his attempt.

"Evan Junior! You come back to your momma right this minute! I told you to stay away from those sweets until you had your dinner. Now you mind your momma. Sorry, Charllie. I'll catch up with you later." Georgia, with Abigail awkwardly waddling in her wake, hurried away to catch up with her delinquent son before he turned into a dessert outlaw and spoiled his appetite.

"Sage engaged?" Charllie was stunned. She felt as if the radiant sun had been eclipsed by a wandering storm cloud. Her emotions felt raw and tumultuous, and for the life of her, she failed to understand why. She knew that she often took Sage's attentions for granted, and that she had just assumed that he would always be there for her—even when she constantly treated him with cold disdain. For some unknown reason, though Charllie had unknowingly used him as her whipping boy, she had often relied on his presence for a semblance of normalcy and socialization in her life. When fate had handed her tragedy, she had begun blaming Sage for his misguided attentions toward her. She now realized that she had been in error.

Charllie valiantly tried to shake off the melancholy that threatened to spoil her day. She knew that much of what she was feeling was probably due in part to being reunited with her friends and having to acknowledge how their lives had recently changed for the better. They had taken on the roles of wife and mother, and Charllie had been left behind—feeling as inadequate as an untutored schoolgirl. She began to question how much she, herself, was to blame for having to live a life that was hopelessly stalled.

Against all logic, she had to admit that she had become extremely agitated by the rumors of Sage's impending engagement, and in attempting to understand why this tidbit of gossip should be so disturbing, she realized that he was Thomas's brother after all; and it was only natural that occasionally that link would make the departed fiancé's memory all the more poignant. It certainly couldn't be that she was upset by Sage's becoming engaged. In fact, that would be a pleasant enough occurrence when it took place, for it would relieve her of his odious attentions whenever they happened to cross paths. She smiled at an approaching neighbor who greeted her warmly, yet somehow Charllie felt that her own smile was more for the neighbor's benefit than out of any sense of true joy of her own.

Charllie spent most of the late morning casually mingling with friends and neighbors. She knew that all went out of their way, not to mention Thomas, and for some reason, that angered her. They acted as if he had never existed, and that emphasized her status as a maiden who had yet to experience the joys and sorrows of true love. She couldn't help but feel they were being condescending in their approach to her—well-meaning, perhaps, but a bit heartless in their attitude towards her nonetheless. As she looked around at those who had assembled at the festival, she realized that she seemed to be living in a world of couples. Yes, she recognized a few who had been widowed or who had lost their lovers, but many of them had already paired up again, and Charllie felt a bit of revulsion at how easily the broken bonds of love had been so easily forgotten and then reforged with others.

As she watched the numerous couples laugh and casually touch, she felt truly alone for the very first time. She felt that she was distantly viewing life rather than living it, looking dispassionately at the occurrences that revolved around her rather than taking part in them herself, in true flesh and blood circumstances. It seemed that she could only come so close to the life that flowed around her without finding it almost impossible to connect. This emotional distancing made her feel a total outcast, and she wandered the festival grounds alone and miserable.

Later that afternoon, Charllie was grateful that she was responsible for a stint in the crochet booth. It gave her the opportunity to be productively busy and have a sense of purpose as well. She also found that those who stopped by to examine the crafts and foodstuffs were both friendly and interesting. It made the time go by, and it prevented her from partaking of the morbid introspection that had besieged her earlier in the day. The gaily colored scarves, doilies, and bed throws draped on the tables were wonderful conversation pieces, and Charllie found herself making plans to begin crocheting lessons herself the following week with an elderly neighbor. Together they chatted about her first lessons and which project might be the most reasonable for her to undertake, which yarn would be the most appropriate, and whether or not she might also wish to eventually take up cross stitch, tatting, knitting, or quilting as well. Charllie's time in the booth sped by. She made a few sales, but, more importantly, she found she had begun to reconnect to the life she had temporarily left behind.

Chapter Seven

Later that day, as Charllie was taking off her apron in the crochet booth, she felt someone standing directly behind her. Quickly looking up, she encountered sparkling green eyes and a ready smile fixed above a firm jaw. Sage. Her very first natural reaction was to greet him with an unpleasant scowl, but for some reason, she found herself rather happy to see him, pleased that he had sought her out in the crowd and that he was companionless. All the animosity she normally felt towards him seemed to have evaporated.

She knew that part of this reaction stemmed from the unreasonable feelings of jealousy she had experienced earlier in the day. Learning of his upcoming engagement, and then subsequently feeling relieved at now seeing him alone as he sought her out, had dampened those feelings. For a moment, she felt light-hearted. She knew she could not deny that she was physically attracted to him, always had been. Sage was very charming, especially when he chose to be, and his dark, good looks and vivacious personality had always attracted many female followers, herself included. Charllie, though she would die before revealing these feelings to him, truly felt honored that he had thought enough about her to stop by for a visit. It made her feel very feminine and special, even as she continued to battle the conflicting emotions that she still felt towards both Danbury brothers.

"Miss Charllie, you're the one person I have been looking for. Someone told me that you have been stuck in this booth for the past hour and have not even had time for your noonday meal. I purchased this amazing peach pie, and I was wondering if I could convince you to help me eat it. I beg you to take pity on me. If I'm forced to eat this alone, I might just find myself with an excruciating belly ache." Sage arched his eyebrows in a comical manner, and Charlotte found herself giggling. It was a delicious feeling.

"Why, Mr. Danbury. I've been told that we should never spoil our dinner by eating sweets. You certainly don't want me to live on peach pie alone, do you? Though it certainly does sound tempting." She smiled up at him, and her blue eyes sparkled with mirth.

"Temptation is something we mortals occasionally succumb to, Charllie. I'm game if you are. I've brought along a jug of tea, a blanket, and some utensils. Personally, I think this pie alone will make an excellent picnic. I tend to be in the mood for something very sweet."

Charllie blushed, for she knew that Sage was talking about much more than the pie; however, her vanity was flattered, and she smiled the smile of a coquette. Sage arched his brows a bit in wonderment. This Charllie was a stranger to him. He seldom had the opportunity to experience her carefree side when she was in a happy, flirtatious mood, but he certainly wasn't about to complain.

"Let's go sit under the tall sweet gum tree down by the stream," Sage suggested. He offered his arm to Charlotte, and he was flattered that she gladly linked her arm with his. Charllie wondered how Sage could constantly revert to his own good-natured self, especially after all the provocation she gave him. She had to admit to herself that she seldom treated him in a civil manner, and yet he never seemed to hold a grudge against her. The man must be a saint, she mused, and yet Charllie knew that was most definitely not the case. She dismissed her ponderings as quickly as they had come. A day of pleasure was long overdue, and she, for one, had decided to take advantage of it!

The couple wandered down to the nearby stream, where Sage spread out a blanket in the shade of the towering tree, and they both lounged comfortably with the pie between them. A light breeze played with Charllie's locks, and the humidity loosened golden tendrils that gently framed her face. She sometimes caught Sage looking at her closely and thoughtfully. Though it made her a bit uncomfortable, mysteriously, she felt very flattered. She thought about his alleged fiancée, Phoebe Somerset, but quickly dismissed her from her mind. She did not want to ruin the afternoon, an afternoon that had become wonderfully pleasant and full of surprises. The ice maiden she had become seemed to be gradually thawing in this rarified atmosphere that surrounded the two of them. Instead of trying to understand the change in her emotions, Charllie decided that for once in her life she would just live them—without examining or rationalizing her every thought and deed. And right this moment, she found herself enjoying Sage's company very much.

Sage handed her a server. "Would you please do me the honor, Charllie?" Startled, Charllie quickly looked up. Realizing that he was only asking her to serve the peach pie, she blushed and laughed nervously. Why was everything that Sage said and did seem so charged with an underlying current of hidden meaning, often reminiscent of desire and, perhaps, even commitment? Why did she never feel so alive as she did when in his presence? She had heard of lust, though she had never experienced it, but she wondered if that was what she sometimes felt towards Sage—just a kind of physical magnetism. But she disavowed that as quickly as it came to mind. She knew that he was far more to her than just a man whom she might wish to bed. Had they not been extremely close as friends for years? She had certainly never felt these feelings towards any other man, not even Thomas. Yet the guilt she felt about these new feelings left her feeling torn in her loyalties between the brothers. Nonetheless, she graciously accepted the pie server.

"Why, I'd be honored, Mr. Danbury." With her head bent, both to cut the pie and to hide her embarrassment, Charllie felt Sage's eyes upon her once again. She was sensitively conscious of his quiet but serious scrutiny. She felt a thrill as his eyes wandered to her slender hands as she sliced and then served thick wedges of pie. Not daring to look up, she listened to him pouring the tea, smelled his spicy cologne, and felt his long fingers brushing hers as she handed him his plate. Her senses were alive as they had never been before. She felt as though she had lost her way and wandered into some mysterious new realm.

Both were famished, and they ate their pie in silence, savoring its juicy sweetness. Sharing the peach dessert in seclusion, overloading their senses with the ambrosial delight of the pie, created an inherent sexual tension between them. They avoided eye contact when possible, and a certain shyness developed as they refreshed themselves with the pie and cold drink. Though they remained silent, immersed in their picnic, it was not an uncomfortable silence but rather a companionable one. The drone of bees and the plashing of the creek were hypnotic. Charllie's lashes drooped, and her head nodded. She felt as though she had taken a drop of laudanum and had great difficulty fighting her drowsiness. Charllie vaguely heard Sage murmur something, and it sounded as if it were coming from a great distance. Then she imagined strong arms and cool lips, but knew she must be dreaming a pleasant dream. In this dream, war did not exist, and love was abundant and all-encompassing. And the man who held her gently in his arms was not Thomas. Charllie puckered her brows with a deep feeling of guilt. The pleasant dream began to gradually fade.

An irritating tickle interrupted Charllie's dream state. She ineffectually swatted at the irritant, but it persisted. Finally, she languidly opened her eyes. Looking up, she found herself gazing directly into Sage's eyes. He held a wand of grass within his fingertips, the tickling pest with which he had been teasing her. Her head was nestled in his lap, and his arms were cradling her head and shoulders like a comfortable pillow. Aghast, and still feeling the stirrings of guilt evoked by her dream, she sat up with a start. Finding herself in Sage's arms, her dream now taking on shades of true life, she dealt with the tumultuous emotions that assaulted her.

"Release me, Mr. Danbury! Just how did I get in this awkward position? Surely this is not seemly behavior for two single people without chaperones." Sitting up, Charllie quickly began to straighten her clothing and smooth her hair back into place. She felt anger and agitation toward Sage, knowing in her heart that he was not to blame. She had been the one to give in to her sugar-induced slumber; he was without guilt. She had let down her guard and acted in a most unbecoming manner. Still, she felt the anger rise and, displaced as it might be, she could not restrain it. She flashed him a withering look.

Sage was not apologetic, but he attempted to ease her emotional discomfort. "Charllie, you fell asleep. I just made you comfortable. Your head nodded and, when I was unable to rouse you from your stupor, I offered myself as your pillow. Everything was totally proper; nothing happened that could ever be labeled as improper or lacking in your total innocence. Not that my intentions are always of such a noble nature, rest assured, but *this time* I was the proper gentleman sharing my assistance and concern."

Sage grinned and extended his hand to help her to her feet. He was puzzled by Charllie's abrupt change in behavior, but he knew that he could always count on her for her emotional volatility. Still, he had hoped that this day might have provided them both with the opportunity to move forward in their relationship. He could see that his wish was most definitely impossible now.

"That is a most unbecoming statement from someone who is said to be betrothed to someone else, Mr. Danbury. I'm sure your intended would not think highly of your flirtatious ways if she were here."

Charllie regretted her barbed remark almost instantly, but the damage was done, and the spell was broken. Sage's gentle smile was immediately erased and replaced by a dark, forbidding scowl. His eyes flashed, and Charllie knew that she could not soon undo what had just been done by her over-bold comment.

"Charllie, you have tried me to my breaking point! Must you always tempt me with beauty and charm—and then chastise me for giving in to them?" His eyes became molten with hidden fire.

Sage roughly pulled her to him in an almost violent embrace. His head came down to hers, and his lips parted her lips with a forceful kiss born of anger that quickly exploded into one of pent-up passion and desire. He molded her soft body to his of hardness and strength. There was little gentleness in his caresses and yet, surprisingly, he found that Charllie's lips were answering his own in an equal measure of ferocity. He savored her peach-infused lips and held her even closer, forcing an even sweeter surrender. As his kiss deepened, currents of desire coursed through him as his attraction towards her spiraled into need. Charllie was not immune, and her body reeled with the heat of her heightened emotions. Her soft whimpers, inspired by their dueling tongues, were heady with desire and pure delight.

Sage, having expected resistance but receiving none, was emboldened to continue. His embrace deepened, and his hardness pushed against her belly. Gently, he loosed her a bit so that he could kiss her cheeks, her forehead, and the tip of her nose; he nibbled her ears; and finally returned to feasting upon her giving mouth. Charllie immediately gasped in shock when one of his fingers began tracing her nipples. A shock of electricity travelled to the warmth between her legs, and she felt herself squirming to leverage additional closeness. She cradled Sage's head between her hands and threaded his dark curls through her fingertips. She softly groaned from the passionate onslaught of Sage's kisses and felt she would positively melt as he plundered the sweet depths of her mouth with his velvet tongue that took forceful possession. She was totally swept away by a strong current of desire that was dizzying in its strength and ferocity, and this magical attraction was mesmerizing and relentless. She had never experienced such heady physical attraction, and she was loath to discontinue the joys that aroused her passion to such new heights of emotion.

Charllie was shocked at the liberties she was allowing Sage, but she was more shocked at the dizzying feelings she was experiencing, feelings she had never even begun to experience with Thomas—ever! Sage's touch, his smell, and his very closeness sent charged sensations throughout her body. She felt a total wanton! His ability to send her reeling by the slightest caress left her disturbed about the control he had over her. She knew that his attentions had begun with anger as his motivator, but she also knew that it was not anger that continued to fuel the fire that raged between them. She leaned into him, hoping that he would deepen the kisses and caresses he had begun.

Sage abruptly pushed Charllie away, and he now held her at arm's length. His eyes narrowed as his anger resumed its sway once more. Still caught in passion's grip, and realizing the necessity of bringing it to a conclusion long before his physical needs could be assuaged, he frowned—more out of sexual frustration than true anger. But Charllie could only judge what she could see, and she knew he was still holding her responsible for the hasty remark of his rumored engagement. She also felt hurt by his rejection and betrayed by her own body, which had taken on a life of its own. Yet she did not wince when his hand dug into her forearm as he angrily began to make his case.

"Was that the kiss of someone who is about to become engaged? Do you judge me of such loose character, Charllie, that I would lightly seduce an innocent maid with whom I find myself in company while being committed to another? How little you know me, my lady. Before you hurl accusations, you might want to check your sources. I do not take kindly to the gossip generated by those who know little of what they speak. And, by the way, your kisses do not seem to reflect the kisses of someone in deep mourning. If you truly believed me engaged, what possessed you to carry on in such a bold, flirtatious manner? Both of us were quick to go up in flame, Charllie, and you know it."

"What is there about our relationship that you can't accept. We're meant for each other, and yet, at every turn, you constantly paint me as the villain and refuse to see me in any light but that of a blackguard—not a potential suitor. I seem to be the only one who must take responsibility for my actions, and yet I know that your desire for me is not something that exists only in my imagination!" Sage stood there, his face ominously dark and unyielding.

Charllie flinched, and she studied his stern face in bewilderment. Was this the same man who had just recently embraced her with such warmth and passion? Her cheeks were red with embarrassment as she recalled her own part in their embrace. Unfortunately, the tenderness recently shared by them had evaporated as quickly as it had begun. She didn't know why she hid behind her past promises to Thomas because she knew without a doubt that her feelings for Sage went deeper. She gently traced his cheek with her fingertips in a subtle attempt to beg his forgiveness for the misunderstanding, but he callously pushed her hand away.

"I am tired to death of being your whipping boy, Charllie. When will you stop hiding behind Thomas and that old, lackluster love you once shared with him? I am not your enemy. You need to finally own up to the feelings that we both share. They hold the truth. Not old memories, promises that were made to be broken, and definitely not rumors about an engagement that never took place!"

She tried to explain, "I was told that you were all but formally engaged to Miss Phoebe Somerset, Sage. I had no reason to believe that the report was anything but truthful. Why I let myself be seduced by you, I have absolutely no rational explanation. Mourning someone is a very lonely pursuit, though it does not excuse me from playing the wanton. I would say that we both must share the blame for having gone beyond what is seemly. You picture us as lovers with a future, but I think that you are living a dream. I apologize if I have led you to think differently. But I can assure you that my actions will not be repeated. I kindly suggest that you refrain from any repeat performances in the future."

Charllie's embarrassment had been quickly replaced by anger, and her response was sharp and definitely out of character for her true feelings toward Sage. She knew that her stubbornness was an enemy to any future relationship they might have, yet she was entrenched in old romantic memories that continued to provide meaning for her life. When she battled Sage in her weak efforts to protect Thomas's role in her life, she did not feel vindicated by doing so. But she just couldn't risk losing her heart again with the risk that it might be, once again, broken.

Sage scowled and stood apart. He scrutinized the distant horizon, seemingly searching for something far beyond his reach. He was greatly affected by the wild turbulence he had felt as Charllie's anger sparked his hidden passion. He knew that her show of remorse was as fake as his, but he could not trust his ability to hold his passion in check where she was concerned. He knew that for both their sakes he must maintain his cold, aloof demeanor—more for her protection than for his own.

The magical spell was broken. The beautiful day was ruined. Charllie folded the blanket, emptied the jug of tea, and helped Sage rinse the dishes in the brook. He offered his arm for the walk back to the festival, but this time she declined. She was thoroughly puzzled by his anger and his rude behavior. She was also puzzled about why he would not want to acknowledge his plans to eventually formalize an engagement with Phoebe, for she could not help but believe that very often, rumor is based on fact. Perhaps Sage did not realize that Phoebe was taking his suit seriously. Maybe the couple had planned on making a formal announcement in the future. Might the engagement be more of a business arrangement than a love match between the son and daughter of the two prestigious families? Evidently, speculation at this point was totally premature. Then again, perhaps the rumor was totally unfounded! Charllie somehow took comfort in this very last possibility.

Chapter Eight

Late July dawned hot as a vat of molten bubbling soap with the humidity as thick and merciless as a cloud of gnats. Charllie awoke with a throbbing headache caused by the tension of the oppressive day, and she decided to lounge in bed for a few extra moments. She knew she should shut her windows to the approaching heat, which would surely build into a crescendo of scorching magnificence by noon, but her curtains were still stirring with the faintest cool breaths of a light morning breeze. Lying there in her dishevelment, her body betrayed her with the memories of the stolen time spent with Sage at the peach festival. The memory of his scorching kiss brought a brilliant flush to her cheeks, and her lips trembled as they relived the passion and desire they had shared in those precious breathless moments. Aghast, she sat up.

"Why am I reliving something that caused us both so much pain? His presence was odious! He portrayed himself as a lover, but he is no more than a cad! I need to stop wasting time on someone who trifles with young women's affections. After all, there is Phoebe, his future betrothed, though he is reluctant to acknowledge her yet, and who am I to him, after all, but just someone who might have become his sister-in-law. I am not interested in becoming someone's light flirtation, especially when that someone cannot light a candle to my departed fiancé. Sage talks about being in love with me; but Thomas is still very much part of me—his memory constantly intruding upon my life." She glanced at Thomas's keepsakes that lay upon her dresser, but in all honesty, she recognized them as nothing but dross.

"I wonder if a man is sometimes drawn to someone, compelled by an unreasonable attraction that urges him to pursue her because she is totally out of his reach. Have I become nothing more than a challenge? An elusive prize that begs to be won?"

Charllie knew that she was not actively looking for an eligible suitor. Finding a substitute for Thomas was most definitely not on her mind. She could never insult her beloved fiancé's precious memories, though her continued romantic commitment to a *ghostly lover* held her in an irrational bondage to him that would never allow for a new relationship.

"I must stop talking to myself! Especially second-guessing all I believe in, what I live for, how I choose to live my life. My love for Thomas is true. I am not ready to destroy it for something that was never meant to be. How can I, in good faith, turn my back on Thomas in exchange for someone else, especially his younger brother? Yet, Thomas is gone. He is dead, a precious memory that reminds me of another time and place—another life. I must be totally crazy!"

With stunning clarity, Charllie began to relive the impromptu picnic memories by the stream on the day of the peach festival. Every glance, touch, and emotion had been charged with the heat of passion. Though she had once been engaged to be married, never had she felt the heightened awareness of another's body and soul as she had felt Sage's. Not once had Thomas's presence ever created the flow of emotion that had welded Sage and Charllie together in a passion that consumed them both so totally. Her mind reeled with the implications, her body tingled with this new awareness, and her emotions ran with a joy that had never been surpassed. Charllie was shaken!

"How can I betray Thomas' memory? And with his very own brother?"

"*Thomas is dead*," an inner voice whispered. Charllie shuddered in response. The guilt she now felt was overwhelming. Certainly, she wasn't entirely to blame. It was natural that she would feel lonely at times. And perhaps Sage possessed some of the same endearing traits and qualities once belonging to Thomas. Maybe this familiarity bred a bittersweet response from emotions that had been buried during her loss.

But Charllie knew that she was only deceiving herself. There was little about Sage that reminded her of Thomas. The fires he had so easily ignited had lain dormant throughout Thomas's entire courtship, though she had to admit that Thomas himself had never been as forward with his attentions—not anytime during their entire engagement. A deep sense of guilt began to eat away at Charllie, but she refused to let it rule her. She searched for other avenues that would release her from blame and turned to Sage. He must shoulder the burden of responsibility for insinuating himself into her affections, using her weaknesses to aid him in his seduction.

"Sage always seems to find a way to get under my skin. He knows I'm vulnerable, yet he preys upon that vulnerability. No number of entreaties, threats, or bouts of anger seems to deter him from pursuing me. His conduct is loathsome because he takes advantage of his past relationship as my neighbor and friend. As Thomas's brother and intended best man for the wedding that was jettisoned by war, he should honor the loss of his brother and respect me as the sister-in-law I never had the privilege to become. It is so unfair of him to maintain these ties of familiarity that I so detest. Sage is the one who must take responsibility for the unbecoming behavior that took place between us. He needs to seriously reflect on his role as a gentleman and honor my calling as a lady in mourning, a young woman still grieving the loss of a beloved fiancé, his very own brother. He is indeed a blackguard! I need to look no further than the arrogant Mr. Sage Danbury to find the culprit for our disagreements. His rude behavior in his pursuit of my affections must end."

"Thou doth protest too much . . ."

"Hogwash! I can never protest enough when the charges are fairly leveled where they belong. If anyone is lacking in breeding, it is certainly not me. I refuse to accept Sage's reckless and unbecoming behavior. I loathe his attempt at insinuating himself into my life by using the unfair means of unsought caresses and kisses during times of my desperate loneliness. Mr. Danbury most definitely needs to begin taking responsibility for his actions!"

All at once, unsolicited, the memory of Charllie's own arms pulling Sage closer, her muffled sighs, the tremors that touched her soul, and the warmth that suffused her entire body began to resurface in Charllie's consciousness. She shook her head in disbelief. "Why do I let this man continue to mesmerize me as he does? This needs to come to an end!"

Charllie jumped out of bed and quickly donned brother Jeffrey's discarded, clean-but-worn work clothes. She braided her long tresses, pinned them on top of her head, and then crammed a wide-brimmed straw hat over them to protect her face from the ravages of the sun. She desperately needed a morning ride! Maybe she would be able to clear her head so that she could return to the day's duties refreshed and untroubled. She certainly hoped so. This association with Sage was becoming a most unwelcome burden, one she could certainly do without.

Charllie's beautiful roan mare Merrilee was soon saddled, and she stood pawing at the ground with her front leg in anticipation of her morning exercise. Her auburn coat glistened in the morning sun, and Charllie mounted her with ease and a fluid grace. She would have to go easy with her as the thermometer was quickly climbing, so she nudged her into a gentle canter and followed tree-lined lanes that led across Oak Haven and beyond. The horse kicked up little puffs of dust as they crossed the breadth of the estate. In the distance, workers could be seen hoeing corn, a flock of crows perched on a Southern yellow pine, and the lemon sun continued its heavenward climb. The horizon seemed to go on forever.

***

The gentle stirring of the air caused by the movement of the ride was delicious. Charlotte breathed deeply of fragrant grasses, tasseling corn, and sun-bleached earth. The gently rolling land ran gracefully to meet the sparkling James River in the distance, which was on its relentless journey to the sea. Charllie wished that the peace and joy she always felt on her rides could be bottled in a tonic for the times when she felt poorly. She reveled in the freedom of movement and took joy in the union between horse and rider that allowed for the speed with which she was able to traverse the Virginia countryside almost effortlessly. The peacefulness was heady, and she drank it in like an elixir.

The drone of the cicadas was incessant, and the heat was beginning to rise in waves from the dusty thoroughfares.

Merrilee's canter had begun brisk and lively but soon became more sedate and measured once her first burst of energy waned. Charllie, perched astride her mare, enjoyed that glorious feeling she always felt when out riding; she felt free, independent, and in control. Time passed in a serene blur, and it was well over half an hour into her ride before she decided to rein in her mount for a well-deserved break.

Charllie now felt perspiration trickling down the back of her neck and between her breasts, but the freedom of being astride a lively steed on a glorious day was worth any minor discomfort. She stopped by a small pool at a nearby sandy creek so that her horse could drink, and taking a handkerchief from her shirt pocket, she immersed it in the stream and bathed her face, neck, and wrists. She took off her hat, and a few wayward tendrils of her blonde tresses escaped the confines of their braid. Dressed as a man for comfort and to avoid the necessity of a chaperone, Charllie felt unencumbered by certain societal dictates. She felt more relaxed and free to be herself.

However, her brother's work clothes could not totally erase her many feminine charms. Her breasts strained against their confinement, and when she splashed her neck with the cool water, the top button came undone, showing far more cleavage than had ever been possessed by a man. Her slender waist was accentuated by rounded hips that were supported by slender legs tucked into riding boots. Her disguise may have provided a bit of confusion as to her identity had she been viewed from a distance, but anyone viewing her attributes close-up would never be fooled.

The quiet calm found in the shady nook next to the creek lulled Charllie into a false sense of solitude and security. She felt comfortable in these familiar surroundings and was lulled by the gentle lapping of the stream, an occasional whickering from her horse—tethered above her on the bank, and the subtle clacking of the branches above her head as they dueled with the slight breezes. For a moment, she consciously decided to set aside her tumultuous thoughts about Sage and just take the time to savor the morning's delights.

When Charllie bent over from the waist to rinse out her kerchief to re-administer the stream's cool water to her temples and wrists, a foreboding shiver ran down her spine. Nervous tremors ran from her neck to the top of her head, and she felt an immediate chill. She sensed that she was not alone, and this warning, based on instinct, filled her with alarm. A sense of foreboding dragged at her heart as she stood up to assess her situation. Too late, she remembered that she had removed her hat, an important accessory in masking her identity. She grabbed it up and crammed it over her braids, pulling it slightly down over her eyes. She then quickly turned to find a man with a straggly dark beard, traced with gray, wearing rumpled, filthy clothing, standing above her on the bank of the creek.

Merrilee stamped her feet in anger and nickered with nervousness as she watched the stranger begin to approach Charllie. The man cleared his throat, and a twisted smile spread across his sweat-stained face. He spat a stream of tobacco, and Charllie recoiled with distaste.

"What's a matter, little lady? I just happened to be moseying along on my way to Short Pump and decided I needed to stop for a drink. Never thought I'd find meself such a one as you along the way." The stranger began to slowly edge his way down the slope towards Charllie and, though he was smiling, it was a smile of lechery and deceit.

Charllie's eyes widened in fear and disbelief, but she gamely attempted an attitude of controlled self-assurance. She hastily rebuttoned her shirt and took a determined stance, confronting the trespasser with a firm chin as she narrowed her eyes in condemnation. She held her ground and desperately fought to remain calm. But the man came closer still.

"Right, happy to meet you. Seems like kind of a lonely place out this way for the likes of something sweet like you. I've a feeling maybe me and you could be real friendly like, little Missy."

The trespasser slowly edged his way even closer. "Might pretty piece of property. I like the peace and quiet." He eyed Charllie, and she could feel his evil intent. "The chances of me finding the likes of you way out here. This is most definitely to my liking. Looks like just you and me for as far as the eye can see. Real nice. . . Guess today's my lucky day!"

The stranger had immediately recognized Charllie for the young, unaccompanied female that she was. His quick assessment also told him that she was unprotected with no weapon in sight. He was titillated by the opportunity that a lone woman presented to him in this lonely, sheltered place—far away from the plantation and its protectors. Immediately becoming hard, he boldly surveyed his victim, assessing her for all the advantages her presence offered him. He felt confident that in bedding her here—far away from civilization—and hidden from view by brush and trees flanking the creek, that he could be just as gentle or as rough as he chose to be. Little Missy could behave herself and allow any and all of his attentions, or she could give him a fight—and that would be alright by him too. He liked to play rough! His loins tightened with sexual tension as he imagined her fear and resistance, and he began to sweat with anticipation. He salivated as he took in her soft, lightly burnished skin, her breasts heaving with her misgivings, and her blue eyes overlarge with the fear of him. He liked her fear. It sent sharp currents of lust directly to his groin. He touched himself in delight.

The scoundrel was confident that whatever attention he might force upon this woman would take place uninterrupted, and she would be powerless to even begin to deflect what he had planned for her luscious body. He knew that he towered over her by at least half a foot, and he was sure that he must outweigh her by more than 100 pounds. And if the little lady needed further convincing, why, he also had his father's deer-skinning knife strapped to his thigh—just in case. He'd hate to think of using it on someone so perfect as her, but it might just add a bit of excitement to his game.

The man crept ever closer as he ogled Charllie's feminine attributes with dark delight, and Charllie felt her flesh crawl. She sensed his agitation and excitement and knew that the danger he evoked was not imagined. His filthy body reeked of oily sweat and rancid tobacco, and his evil presence was stifling.

The odious man was emboldened further by her silence. "You must surely get lonely on a big spread like this, sweet miss," he crooned sarcastically. "Us both can certainly find something to do, I reckon—some back country lovin, real satisfyin. Ain't no need for alarm, missy, cause I can guarantee you I'm more than enough man to give a gal like you just what you need." He leered and then began to approach her as she began to tremble with fright.

Charllie was beside herself. She was desperate to flee, but he had her exits blocked, except for the creek—and running through the moving water in boots provided little chance of a successful getaway. She also knew without a doubt that it would be a terrible mistake to clearly show her fear. She needed to stall him for as long as possible, but, as she watched in horror, he continued to edge closer and closer until he stood but a few feet away.

Charllie pulled herself together and glared at him with haughty disdain. She brought herself up to her full height and placed her hands upon her hips for a show of strength rather than submissiveness. With all the courage that she could muster, she stepped forward to issue a stern command to the man who was now threatening her with bodily harm, rape, perhaps her very life.

"Sir, you are on private property! You are trespassing! My family is most hospitable, and they would take it kindly if you were to take a cooling drink and then be on your way. Get off this land! You are not wanted here!" Her tone was severe, but her lips trembled as she attempted to verbally oust him from the property. Inside, she trembled like jelly. Unfortunately, she knew that she was being less than effective in convincing him he should give up on his helpless, terrified prey—prey that offered him a glimpse of paradise with no repercussions.

The man laughed with a short bark as he pushed a greasy hank of hair off his forehead.

He continued to be emboldened by the seclusion of the area, and he knew that his physical strength was such that he could easily subdue this young woman who now stood trembling before him.

"Little Missy, you need have no fear about me. I'll just be keeping you company for a spell. Ain't nothin but love and comfort on my mind. Young woman like you needs a man like me to do her some teachin' bout the birds and the bees."

Upon reaching Charllie, he put out a leathery hand, nails encrusted with dirt and filth, and touched her cheek. Then his hand began to slowly wander down to her cleavage, which had been exposed by the loose nature of the collar of her shirt. She immediately felt dirty and defiled.

It took all of Charllie's willpower to prevent herself from flinching and then turning to run. She knew that running would be totally useless, and probably counterproductive, as the chase would do no more than excite him further. The trespasser was now between Charllie and her horse, and her options for reaching safety were getting slimmer by the moment. All she could do was hold her ground and attempt to forestall him in his plans with her continued display of scorn and disdain.

"You are no more than a lecher who is trespassing on our property. Your presence is not wanted here, and when the sheriff arrives, you will be conducted to the county jail. Make no mistake, my family does not condone criminals running freely across their land, and they will most certainly press charges. You want a drink from the stream? Take a drink from the stream— and then depart."

The man turned to her—all conciliatory, though there was no mistaking his cruel intent. "Now, lil Missy. That just don't sound terribly friendly to me. From what I see, we have this place to ourselves, and we have all the time in the world. Right this minute, I'm cravin' a might bit more than a drink from this here creek. Them britches you have on look warm and invitin', and I'm more than partial to sweet young things like you. I reckon you and me are gonna spend some time gittin to know each other before I has to mosey along. You might just as well get used to me keepin' you company for a spell."

The stranger's gnarled hand continued to trace lower, fumbling with her buttons until he finally pushed aside her blouse to peer within. Silent tears glided down Charllie's cheeks as she stood in front of the man, helpless and fearful.

A whip cracked, violently interrupting the man's physical assault of the lone woman. It brought his lewd motions to an immediate halt. The scoundrel and Charllie, both startled by this most violent and unexpected of interruptions, turned around quickly to encounter an ominous sight. Sage stood directly above them, his hat askew with his face frozen in fury. His eyes narrowed and shot green flame, his mouth was grim and unwavering, and his right hand gripped his weapon with a red-hot anger that sought to incur immediate vengeance.

The large black bullwhip whistled through the air again, but this time it went beyond just a warning, and with a ***crack!*** It immediately made contact. It ripped through the rotten fabric of the intruder's work pants like a knife through butter, and he immediately fell with a grunt. His lecherous smile was quickly wiped clean, and he now hunkered over in a submissive crouch. His pants were now shredded around his ankles, and a large strip of flayed skin began to ooze blood.

Ignoring his painful wound, the man quickly scrambled to his feet. His demeanor was now apologetic and friendly. "Meant no harm, sir. Just chatting with the little missy. Need a drink of water before setting out to town, and we just happened to bump into one another."

The trespasser gingerly walked a pace or two and then held out his hand as if to offer a friendly handshake to the man who had just administered the blistering stripe to his ankles. When his offer of friendship was ignored, and he realized that the newcomer was prepared and more than ready to continue his onslaught with the whip which had been quickly rewound, he shrugged his shoulders and stuck his hands in his pockets. The scoundrel knew that his adversary was just looking for an excuse to be provoked to further physical violence, for his temper was palpable—and now that his victim had a strong supporter in her corner, his cowardice spoke volumes. The perpetrator briefly considered bringing forth his hunting knife to counterattack, but when he glanced up at his opponent, he saw youth, virility, and righteous anger. He decided to cut his losses and retreat from his quarry.

Sage continued to glower. He had been immediately assaulted by both fear and anger when he had stumbled upon the horrifying tableau in the woods. His mind could not help but vividly imagine what he might have found had he arrived but moments later. He shuddered with emotion as he approached them. He pointed his whip at the man, noticeably trembling with anger and inner turmoil, "I don't want excuses from the likes of you. Like the lady said, you are trespassing. Get out! Leave before you tempt me to further violence upon your scurvy hide!"

Sage wanted nothing more than to be goaded to continue with his brutal punishment of the evil man. Twenty lashes would not be enough to pay the man back for his sins this day, to erase the horror that had ensued between him and Charllie. He braced himself and took a deep breath. However, Charllie did not need to witness more violence on top of what she had already experienced, and with the anger still simmering throughout his body, Sage wasn't sure that he could prevent himself from killing the bastard on the spot if he didn't quickly vacate the area. Thankfully, Charllie's ordeal had been of short duration; for it had been brought swiftly to a halt before serious ramifications could take place. He stood back to allow the man to make his exit away from the creek and away from the plantation.

The derelict began to scramble up the bank, and Sage savagely threw the man's tattered hat after him. The man quickly grabbed at it and then limped across the field to a flea-bitten nag that had been tethered in a far stand of sumac. Soon he had mounted his horse and, wasting no time, moved off in a hasty trot down the dusty lane. The distant clopping of his horse's hooves became fainter and fainter until they disappeared altogether.

The only sound that remained was the cawing of two ravens at the top of a lone pine and the gurgle of the stream. Sage was still breathing shallowly, for the shock of what he had come upon was slow to leave him.

For God's sake, she could have been raped and murdered! And no one would have even heard her screams!

He knew that what Charllie needed now was normalcy and calm, but by God, what he wanted to administer in equal measure was a severe scolding!

Chapter Nine

Sage turned to Charllie and bravely attempted casual conversation, though the anger and fear he still felt were being held back on a very short leash. “If I hadn’t recognized Merrilee, I’m not certain that I would have been so quick to interrupt this little meeting you were having. What brought you to the Danbury Dell property today, unchaperoned? Surely it wasn’t my charming presence.”

Sage knew that he was treading where no man should tread, but forced levity was all that prevented him from giving in to this ominous cloud of fear for Charllie’s safety and disgust for the man who had threatened her—both vying for the heightened emotions that threatened to engulf him.

He glanced at Charllie, clad in her brother’s clothes, and asked, “Is there a reason we are riding incognito today?” Sage, his black hair glistening in the sun, stood above Charllie next to his steed, Ebony, waiting for an answer.

Ebony nickered a greeting to Merrilee, but she ignored him with a swish of her tail. A weak smile played at the corners of Sage’s mouth. What could be misconstrued as insolence was, in fact, real concern for Charllie, who had attempted to freshen herself in the creek without the benefits of a chaperone. He took off his own wide-brimmed hat and waited for Charllie’s eyes to meet his. He knew the awkwardness of the moment was eating her alive.

Embarrassed, Charllie straightened up from her futile attempt at erasing her dishevelment. Her braid had begun to totally unravel, and strands of honey blonde hair were hanging below the straw hat, which had miraculously remained upon her head. The first button on her brother’s shirt had been ripped off by the stranger’s rough groping, and now, in Charllie's attempt to cool and compose herself with the wet handkerchief, she swiped ineffectually at the filth left by the stranger's lecherous touch. Sage gazed at the exposed cleavage and felt a tightening in his groin. His smile instantly turned into a scowl, and Charllie quickly realized from whence his reaction stemmed. She straightened her shirt to the best of her ability, refastening the buttons that remained, and then tucked her shirt back into her brother's pants. She still trembled with the pent-up horror of what might have been and attempted to deal with the recurring waves of shock that were making her feel close to hysteria.

Finally, Charllie answered. "I sometimes like the freedom of pretending to be a man. One doesn't have to deal with the confines of a skirt or a sidesaddle. It's refreshing to be independent and to wander without constant surveillance. I thought I'd be safe enough just riding through these fields. Merrilee needed a drink, and I had decided to freshen up a bit, so we stopped to rest and quench our thirsts at the nearby creek."

She looked up at Sage, who towered above her. His brows were knit with consternation, and his sensual mouth was tight as he tried to maintain control. Uncomfortable with the awkward change of mood, Charllie released a tentative smile, walked over and untied Merrilee, and then led her back up the bank and onto the trail. She let her mare crop some grass beneath the trees as she walked back over to continue the confrontation with Sage. Tears were welling at the corners of her eyes, but for her own sanity, she needed to appear as if the incident had never happened.

Sage continued to glower, "Well, don't you think that it is pretty evident to most that you aren't a man. You certainly didn't fool our *friend*. As for independence and freedom, what are they worth when you find yourself threatened? Charllie, you could have been raped or worse! I cringe when I think of what I might have found had I come by just moments later. I could have found you molested, assaulted, or even dead by the creek. Your life is precious, yet you choose to take far too many liberties with it!" Sage was not comfortable with blatantly spelling out what the consequences might have been, but he would do whatever it took to prevent something like this from ever happening again.

Charllie shuddered at what she knew might have been a horrific outcome. She had been aware of her danger from the very onset of her experience, but Sage's words severely stung her pride and thoroughly condemned her good common sense. She glowered back.

"That man was no friend of mine. And, as you can see, I'm none the worse for wear. Don't make more out of this than there is. I was just exercising Merrilee before the heat of the day became too oppressive. In fact, I hadn't realized I had wandered over onto Danbury property until you so *graciously* pointed it out. I had followed the shadiest of lanes to keep my horse cool during her exercise and must have wandered too far. Yes, I do need to be more careful, and, in the future, I will be."

Charllie knew that the way in which she responded to Sage was totally unfair and unkind. He wanted only what was best for her—her protection and well-being, but she never seemed able to treat him with the decency and kindness he truly deserved. She always felt that she had something to prove, that she couldn't let him get on her right side because just maybe she wouldn't be able to deal with the repercussions that might follow. She also knew that right now she owed him for the very safety of her life and should be thanking him from the bottom of her heart. Yet she continued to hold her ground, lifting her chin in stubbornness while attempting a weak, rather insincere smile.

"I wear my brother's clothes strictly for ease and comfort, not that I think it is really any of your business. In fact, I was having a most delightful morning until I was so rudely interrupted. Things like this so seldom happen, and I just can't go through life living in constant fear." Charllie continued to downplay the morning's experience, even though her hands were ice cold and shaking from the pent-up emotions of fright and shock.

"You know it's dangerous for an unescorted woman to go riding when it is inevitable that eventually she may meet up with some riff-raff or scoundrel. Times are still hard following the war, Charllie. Many displaced men are still on the move seeking work, looking for opportunity. Some are ruthless. Just dressing as a ragamuffin does not guarantee you safety, or kindness and respect, in such an isolated place. Your independence won't provide armor for protection or help when it is needed." Sage roughly ran his fingers through his hair in exasperation.

He continued. "God, don't you know what could have happened to you? It plays over and over in my mind! The chances you took could have been disastrous! Yes, you put yourself in jeopardy, but you also risked the love of your family and friends. You put your own life in danger, but can you even begin to imagine what those who love you would have suffered had anything happened to you?"

"Sage, you're making too much of a minor incident. True, he was a ruffian. A despicable ruffian! But I am sure that he meant me no real harm. Just a mild flirtation was all he sought. You're right. Some of it was my fault. I wasn't dressed as a lady. But as disgusting as that man was, I'm sure nothing serious would have taken place."

Charllie knew that she was deluding no one, especially herself, but she needed to falsely minimize her recent experience just to maintain some of her equilibrium, which at this moment was extremely fragile. She did not want to dissolve into a weeping, weak victim when she was made of stronger stuff. And with Sage, she always felt that she needed to exhibit strength and resolve, that she had to be the one who appeared to triumph whenever they found themselves sparring.

Sage grimaced as she made light of her predicament. Part of him strained to enfold her in an embrace that would shelter her from all harm, to blot out all the unpleasantness that had just taken place. The other part of him wanted to retrieve his whip and apply it to her pert, round derriere to solemnly punish her for being so careless with her own life. Anger, love, compassion, fear, desire—all warred within him, making his presence volatile and incendiary. He finally gave in to his emotions and grasped her none-too-gently by the upper arm and pulled her to stand beside him on the knoll overlooking the stream.

"You think that the world was made to do your bidding, Miss Charlotte, and you see me as a stumbling block—never recognizing my care and concern. Somehow, whenever we meet, you just cannot prevent yourself from using venom to flavor your conversation. A simple thank you might have sufficed, but evidently, the independent Miss Wright is always capable of taking care of herself. Well, you're not!"

Sage was heartsick over how often Charllie verbally attacked him, putting him on the defensive when all he had ever wanted was to be of one accord with her. If he could only find the perfect words that would act to bind them together in mutual respect and understanding! Love would be even better, but he bitterly rejected that possibility, totally out of hand. Dammit! He felt overwhelmingly steeped in emotions that had been concocted by both Charllie and his own brother's pasts, and his helplessness to change things for the better left him feeling constantly defeated. She fought him every step of the way, and he seemed helpless to make the kind of changes that would bring them together.

"Charllie, you're just as vulnerable as the rest of us. To this point, you've been lucky, but luck can change. Tomorrow may have a different outcome. You need to stop blaming me for what goes wrong in your life. I'm not here to attack you. I'm also not here to be your knight in shining armor. I do care about you, more than you will ever know, but I'm tired of getting the short end of the stick when it comes to your kindness and friendship. You're becoming far too predictable, Miss Charlotte, at least where I'm concerned. All sharp edges and nothing soft."

Sage turned his back on Charllie and loosed Ebony, so he too could crop grass next to Merrilee. Sage's muscles tensed and rippled as he threw the reins over the horse's head, and his long stride accentuated the tightness of his breeches as they stretched from his well-formed thighs to his dusty, worn boots. Trying to maintain her composure, Charllie quickly dashed away the tears that were lurking. She knew that Sage would never know how relieved she had been when she had seen him charging down the bank toward her perpetrator, and it was often a mystery as to why she constantly fooled herself into thinking that she shouldn't let him know her true feelings. Even now, she masked her relief and vulnerability with a façade of nonchalance and retaliated with a caustic remark.

"Predictability, Mr. Danbury, has become *your* middle name. You think that riding in here like a hero will win my good wishes, but I'm not a child. I am quite capable of taking care of myself. Your arrogance and your rudeness are just something I've come to expect." She lowered her eyelashes to suppress the threatening tears and squared her shoulders, hoping to quickly flee to her own home before all her senses finally crumbled with the reality of what might have happened without Sage's intervention. She needed to bring the morning's drama to immediate closure so that she could quickly retreat and recover.

Sage instantly pulled her to him, holding her close, but he did not touch her further. "Charllie, you needed saving. Thank God, I was here! Don't continue to pursue this false sense of independence, at least not where your life is involved and at risk."

Charllie stood in agonizing silence, her senses reeling from his nearness, his touch, his smell. She leaned into him to absorb the safety from harm that he symbolized, the compassionate buffer he now provided to an uncertain, sordid world. She breathed deeply of strong lye soap, lanolin, and his uniquely male fragrance. For a moment, she floated in a haven of serenity, and tears of relief gently and silently glided down her cheeks. The sharp memory of the harshness of the attack and the helplessness she had felt began to ebb away, and within Sage's sheltering arms, she found comfort and strength.

Charllie's body began remembering all too well the responses that Sage could elicit. Her nipples hardened, and a disturbing warmth spread within her belly's depths. She looked up quickly into jade green eyes, eyes that appeared to be examining her with both compassion and cynicism. She shuddered with the conflicting emotions of desire and anger. She knew he was preparing to kiss her, and she was incensed that he dared to be so bold, but was also stirred by impatience that he had not done so sooner. He pulled her closer, and his lips dipped to taste hers. Charllie battled with herself over all the conflicting emotions that were arising from the already steamy kiss.

"How dare you!" Charllie sputtered. But she went no further, for her lips were silenced by the sensual crush of Sage's own. The heat and power of the embrace mimicked the sultry day, and they merged with the passionate life force of their surrounding environment. The pair became lost in the exploration of each other's desire, and they quickly learned how quickly powerful emotions can quench anger and how differences may be quickly thrust aside when strong need arises, especially when that strong need has been fueled by an incident that could have torn them apart forever.

The embrace was sweet with sensual delight but fraught with the enduring passions that were complicated by inner turmoil. Sage, unfortunately, was lulled into a false sense of complacency; he was hoping against hope that his love for Charllie might now be recognized, accepted, and finally returned by the lady in question. His soul struggled to breach the gate of her heart, and the fruitlessness of his crusade up to this point had been daunting but not enough to stem his pursuit. He had nothing to lose, and his determination to win Charllie's love remained steadfast.

Charllie was beginning to realize that she should have quickly called a halt to Sage's onslaught as soon as it had begun, but she could not hold him at arm's length any more than she could stop a charging bull. Her very own body was betraying her as it leaned towards the strength he offered. Her arms, of their own volition, encircled his neck and brought him closer. Her fingers became entwined in his dark locks and then splayed against his muscular chest as she weakly attempted to push him away. Her unleashed passion warred with that of the woman who had yet to free herself from the ties of a dead fiancé, but Sage relentlessly continued to press moist kisses upon her lips, his fear and anger over her safety powerful catalysts to the desire that was bursting into flame as their two bodies sought safe harbor within this storm of emotion.

Sage's caresses were gentle but deliberate and moving. His fingertips sought her nipples beneath the soft fabric of her shirt, and the nipples hardened with tenderness and desire. Charllie heard a muffled moan and realized it had escaped from her own lips. Sage's persuasive lips sought entry for his tongue, and soon the plunder was complete. Charllie timidly met his tongue with her own and heard Sage groan with delight. She began to melt in his arms, and every part of her body struggled to surrender to the assault of desire with which Sage had met her. She wanted this day to go on forever, remaining within the safety of these arms where she was tempted with such delicious and delirious passion.

Charllie couldn't let this madness continue, for it was wreaking havoc with her very sanity. Her body was beginning to catch fire, and she knew that what she felt could be nothing more than madness. It was a madness inspired by a horrifying incident, and, though it was a delicious madness, it was madness nonetheless. It had to end! With a deft shove, Charllie sent Sage tumbling down the bank and into the creek. She trembled when she heard him hit the water with a loud splash. Fearful of repercussions, she rushed to Merrilee, where she grabbed her loose reins in a panic and quickly prepared to mount. She was frantic to take immediate flight before Sage could recover from his unanticipated bath.

But the impromptu dousing had done nothing more than set flame to the tinder of Sage's banked anger. Arising from the tepid waters of the creek, both infuriated and dripping wet, Sage was determined to quickly retaliate. In a rage, he reached Charllie before she could kick her heels into her horse's side. He roughly dragged her down off her horse and towered over her in his dripping attire. Passion was no longer etched on the rugged lines of his face, but anger most certainly was. The lips that had just recently caressed hers with sweet desire were now pinched white and grimly set with rage. His scornful eyes speared her without mercy, and his tone was no longer conciliatory.

"A bit of a coward, aren't we, dear neighbor?" Sage forced the words out through tightly clenched lips. "Somehow, I have never felt that my advances were totally one-sided. Where do the cold feet come from? Our passion was reciprocal, of that I'll stake my life. What are you afraid of? When will you stop running long enough to let love and desire into your life?" He held her arms in a vise-like grip and forced her to look up at him.

Charllie glared, her blue eyes turned to ice. "Love? Certainly, you must be mistaken. Desire, perhaps even lust, but only out of shock, perhaps a bit of thankfulness for your coming along when you did. It has been but a few years since

Thomas's death, and though you can never hope to take his place, you must realize that I am also human and may occasionally give in to temptation. But the desire I feel for you is fleeting and can never reach the depths once reached with your brother. You will never understand the love we once had. Never!"

Sage's scowl deepened, and his grasp on her arms intensified to the point where he was beginning to bruise her tender flesh. He knew that inside, he was dying. Still, he persisted. "Love!" he spat out the word as if it was tainted. "You can't even begin to understand the meaning of the word. What you had with my brother was something in a fairy tale, not something that exists between a real man and a real woman truly in love with each other. You are living in a dream world, Charlotte. You are a virgin who has never felt the true passion of what love between a husband and wife can be. You are still a maiden who has never lived in a day-to-day world where a man becomes her everything, and his world totally revolves around her. But you have most definitely become a temptress, a Jezebel who inflames a man with kisses and caresses but then turns them off like water in a spigot. You are a shrew who enjoys trampling on a heart that is yours for the taking, but who has decided to reject it with inhuman coldness. I rue the day I ever fell in love with you, Charllie. For my sake, a viper would have been preferable." Sage searched Charllie's eyes for a spark of compassion, a glimmer of warmth, but their blue depths were dark and impenetrable.

Hurt and confused, Charllie gathered her wits and composure, and then lashed out with deceptive gentleness, "Well, I can see, Mr. Danbury, that once again our views are not in step. I apologize if I have ever given you the impression that I might tender some deeper emotions for you. With Thomas in my heart, you can never be but a sorry replacement for my affections, so I prefer to forego the pleasure altogether. Now, if you will please unhand me, you are hurting me. It is time for me to go. I have duties awaiting me at home and need to return. And don't worry—I don't plan on returning to Danbury land again, alone or otherwise. Good day!"

Ashamed that he had allowed his temper to take control, Sage quickly dropped his hands to his sides in remorse and allowed Charllie to remount her horse without further interference. The feelings of hurt and anger continued to swirl within him, and if cursing his brother would have helped the situation, he would have done so; but, knowing that it would be futile, he remained silent on that account.

Before Sage released Merrilee's reins so that Charllie could freely exit the grove, he somberly made a parting gesture of appeal. "What would it take, Charllie, for your natural passions to receive me as a man who loves you, esteems you, and only wishes you the best? Do I mean so little to you that you constantly erect stumbling blocks to our relationship? Why must our friendship and concern for one another always fail to become something more? The passion that should exist between us always seems to be extinguished by the summer rain of your disregard. Charllie, why do you allow the natural warmth of your desire to be constantly conquered by the ice in your veins? I must say that I am at a total loss." Remorsefully, he released Merrilee and withdrew a step or two. "And no, my dear, this has not been a good day!"

Sage, dark and brooding, watched as Charllie forcefully wheeled Merrilee around, dug her heels into her horse, and galloped homeward. He did not see the rivulets of tears that coursed down her cheeks, blinding her on the way back to Oak Haven. Had he done so, his feelings of desolation and despair might have been slightly tempered by compassion and concern.

Chapter Ten

A week passed following the incident by the Danbury creek, a week in which Charllie did much soul searching and reminiscing. She reminisced about the time when she, Frank, and Jeffrey had gotten together with the Danbury brothers for horseback riding, swimming, and birthday celebrations. She recalled lazy afternoons of croquet, card games, and charades that took place with friendly competition and carefree gaiety. She remembered evenings of hide-and-go-seek, firefly hunts, and ghost tales. Charllie and her brothers had spent untold, delightful hours on many rambles with their neighbors, Thomas and Sage.

As she recalled the many fond memories, she remembered the Danburys as being very different in nature. Sage was the more lighthearted of the two boys, and his actions were more spontaneous and mischievous, often fueled by curiosity. Thomas had always proven to be of a far more serious nature—thoughtful, more reserved, and a bit introspective. As Thomas was the eldest, the group had frequently accepted his leadership qualities without question, and so, as children, they had often followed his lead whenever he was present. When he was not present, their adventures always seemed far more exciting, memorable, and infused with fun and laughter. Both the Danbury brothers had played instrumental roles in Charllie's formative years as a child. The roles that Thomas and Sage had played helped mold Charllie into the woman she was today, and the implications of these associations seemed to be wreaking havoc upon her current state of mind, and she feared might continue for the rest of her life.

Charllie couldn't put her finger on exactly when or why she had first become attracted to Thomas in deference to Sage. She had never consciously thought that she would ever be placed in a position where she might have to choose between the two brothers. Thomas Danbury and Frank Wright had been the older brothers in their respective families, and as heirs of their respective families and the eldest in each family, they shared many of the same responsibilities and aspirations. Thomas had always been a bit of a loner, and nothing pleased him more than being given the opportunity to plan and command change within his own household. Frank Wright, on the other hand, had always been happier working side by side with his father and directing the plantation workings of his staff as part of a team.

Charllie vaguely remembered that at the age of fourteen, she had begun to be caught up in the hero worship of Thomas. She had become intrigued by his air of command, his sharp mind, and aristocratic bearing. Thomas, as the eldest Danbury brother, was very used to taking control. When Thomas began to gift her with his kindness and deference at this very young age, his attentions bolstered Charllie's sense of awkwardness and lack of confidence, and she had begun to fall under his spell. In her eyes, he had become more of a gentleman than a boy, and he flattered her tremendously by treating her like a young lady, though she was still but a child. He soon began to take more of an interest in her pastimes, and they would often discuss favorite books, play chess and games of cards, and share duets on the Wrights' ancient pianoforte. And even though Sage was also very much a part of all their activities at this time, he often seemed to hang back a bit in the presence of

Thomas, showing respect to his older brother and seeming content to follow along in his shadow.

Jeffrey had been Charllie's favorite brother. He was only a few years her senior, and he had clearly enjoyed having a tomboy for a sister. When brother Frank was present, however, he would often become extremely exasperated with Charllie's unladylike conduct, unlike Jeffrey, who invariably egged her on to new and exciting heights of daring. She and Jeffrey had both been a bit wild and unrestrained. Thomas, the elder, had seldom wanted any involvement in their harebrained schemes; but Sage, on the other hand, could often be coaxed into joining them as well, for he too seemed to share in their love for mischief and adventure.

Once—Sage, Jeffrey, and Charllie had packed a breakfast of plums, cheese, and bread; and, having carefully crept out of their homes in the very hour preceding dawn, they had met on a knoll overlooking the river so that they could catch the first glimmer of the sun at dawn as it rose and illuminated the horizon with its brilliant, fiery first rays. They had delighted in watching the sun's climb until it rose in all its glory and displayed in its flashy rays of brilliant red and apricot, and the whole world had seemed to catch fire with its vivid glow. It had been a moment she would always remember.

Once the sky had coalesced into a brilliant blue summer sky, the three adventurers had relaxed upon the knoll and feasted on their breakfast, lightheartedly chatting about their summer plans: places they wanted to visit, things they wanted to do, and games they wanted to play. Following their lighthearted meal on the riverbank, they had then gone fishing. Jeffrey and Sage had *borrowed* the fishing rods from their fathers' stables the night before. None of them possessed any real experience with the sport, but, having watched their fathers numerous times before, they thought that it looked relatively easy.

They had been persistent in their attempt to catch enough fish for their dinners; however, their luck had not been with them. Perhaps the day was too hot, the fish too well fed, or the fishermen too inexperienced. Sage had felt a nibble or two, Charllie had eventually reeled in an old boot missing its heel, and Jeffrey had finally fallen in when he slipped on a submerged, slime-covered rock. She could still recall the hilarity of that morning. She also remembered how Sage had patiently baited all her hooks as she had been too young and squeamish to do the deed herself. The *Three Musketeers*, together they had made many precious memories.

But this adventurous side of Charllie was soon overshadowed and squelched by Thomas's powerful influence. Three years before the impending Civil War, Charllie's affections had gone irrevocably to him when he had made it clear that he was intent on pursuing her to make her his bride. As the eldest, and therefore the heir of Danbury Dell, he was seriously charged with planning for its future, he had explained at that time; and he fervently wished for Charllie to become the mother of his heirs, a hostess for his plantation, and a helpmate for his life. He felt that Charllie was the most appropriate woman for his choice, and he wanted her, and her alone, to fill these roles.

Charllie had felt touched and very honored to have been singled out in this way. Her young girl's heart quickly began to conjure up hearts, flowers, and happily-ever-afters. She had immediately begun to envision Thomas in a very different light, that of her future lover and husband. Charllie was translating all of Thomas' attention as proof that he was madly in love with her, though *love* was a word that never actually passed his lips.

Thomas began to send nosegays and charming missives to Charllie, having already won her father's permission to court her, and her teenage heart had continued to swell with the romance of it all. She could never understand how a gentleman who was so mature, dashing, and handsome could be attracted to someone so young and inexperienced, but because he had so specifically chosen her to be his wife, he made her begin to see herself as very special and fortunate. Thomas made her feel like a princess during a time when she had only just begun testing her wings as a young woman: when she still questioned her beauty and allure, when her bouts of awkwardness brought her abilities into question, and when she sought answers that she no longer felt comfortable asking her parents. Thomas had automatically become the one she looked up to, who gave her gentle guidance, and who only wanted what was best for their future as husband and wife.

Soon, the couple was spending much of their time together. Thomas had given Charllie her very first kiss, and it was a memory she still cherished. The kiss had been tender and sweet, and it had seemed to offer vague promises for the future. In less than a year, Thomas had asked her to marry him, and they had become officially engaged two years later. They had planned to marry just as soon as the war ended, which most predicted could not last more than a few months—a year or two at the most. He had enlisted right away, and it wasn't long because of personal qualifications and family connections that he had made his way up through the ranks to the designation of captain. Proud and handsome in his gray uniform, his entire demeanor exuded intelligence, confidence, and purpose.

Sage, though he too had believed in the Confederate cause, at least regarding how the politics of the Union would greatly affect the South's economy in a very negative way and would put Virginia and all its plantations in dire jeopardy, had felt compelled to stay home at the onset of the war to protect his aging parents and the family's interests. The Danbury parents were unwilling to give up both sons to the cause, and they were adamant about protecting the inheritance that they hoped to pass down to future generations of Danburys. They also felt that it was more advantageous to the cause to continue assisting with the army's requisitions for supplies so that the Confederate soldiers might be clothed and fed for the short duration of the war. Though their plantation, for numerous good reasons, had never depended on slave labor but had used indentured servants and free labor almost exclusively, their ties to the cause had never been as strong as those of many other plantation owners. Nonetheless, their loyalty was to Virginia and their neighbors who now sided with the Confederacy.

Sage, though he would always be Thomas's younger brother, was secretly guarding the nature of his own love for Charllie, a true and honest love that was not based on jealousy, a mild flirtation, or a casual admiration—but a pure, genuine emotion. It dwelt deep within him, and he was troubled by the conflicted feelings he felt about her engagement to his brother. He was tortured by the fact that once Thomas and Charllie were married, all his love and the dreams of culminating that love would quickly be torn asunder.

Sage had agreed to stay home at Danbury Dell to oversee the plantation: its people, livestock, and property. He would protect his family's interests, as well as those of the army's, but he would also be there to step in to protect the female inhabitants of Oak Haven as well, for he knew that all its menfolk would be off fighting the war. He did not want to leave Charllie, or her mother and the other members of their plantation, totally vulnerable and defenseless during these trying times. Though he was tortured every day by knowing that his own love could never be returned, he also felt responsible for ensuring the safety of the only woman in the world whom he loved without reservation.

As the seriousness of the war deepened, Sage eventually enlisted when the need arose. He was preparing to go into battle when his ill-fated visit to Thomas had taken place. Charllie was one of the few who had been privy to Sage's plan. She had helped to convince him that she and her family could weather the storm without him; it was more important for him to join so that he could provide Thomas and his army the support they desperately needed. So, though Sage had enlisted as planned, he had harbored mixed emotions about his involvement in the military. Charllie had never been privy to the confrontation that had occurred between the two brothers over her status as Thomas's future bride.

The cruel and bloody war had continued, but Thomas had not lived long enough to keep any of his promises to Charllie. Following his brother's death, Sage could not bring himself to totally turn his back on his aging parents, a grieving Charllie, and the inhabitants of both estates who were now without protection at a major turning point in the war. All parties were inconsolable over the losses of both Thomas and Jeffrey, and now that Sage was his parents' only remaining child and heir, as well as their means of safety and support, he felt he could not add to their already enormous burden by leaving them to survive on their own. He shouldered the responsibility of guarding the two estates and providing much-needed supplies for the Confederate army.

When Thomas and Charllie had become engaged prior to the war, Sage had seemed to withdraw a bit from the camaraderie once shared by the Danburys and the Wrights. He had been polite, friendly, and supportive; in fact, he had been the first to congratulate Thomas and Charllie on the news of their engagement. He had kissed Charllie gently on the cheek in a brotherly fashion and wished her nothing but happiness as a future new member of his family. Yet, as she now looked back upon that day, she knew there had been a vague sadness lingering in his eyes, and his wishes seemed to lack the joy and warmth that should have accompanied them. And then, of course, with the deaths of both Jeffrey and Thomas, and Mr. Wright's nearly fatal battle wounds that had necessitated his life in a wheelchair, the lives of both families changed forever. The carefree ties that had once existed between them had been forever tainted with sorrow.

***

Charllie poked at the dry earth around the geraniums. August's heat had turned the cemetery plots and all surrounding vegetation into a veritable dust bowl. She ladled water over a few of the bedraggled plants, but could almost see the moisture disappear as quickly as she dispensed it. The plants themselves seemed more than ready to give up their last gasp of life, and their presence did nothing more than exaggerate the atmosphere of sorrow and loss in the graveyard. Nonetheless, Charllie brushed some errant wisps of hair away from her temple and sat back to survey the hopelessness of her handiwork. She became temporarily overcome with sadness: for the pathetic flowers, for the man in the grave with whom she no longer connected, and for herself, someone feeling totally adrift in the currents of life.

Charllie stood up and stretched. Not a breeze stirred. She looked over through the glimmering haze to Danbury Dell. The stately mansion stood serene, seemingly impervious to time's trials. A couple was strolling around the pool's perimeter, and Charllie heard a gay trill of feminine laughter. Sage was easily recognizable: his commanding height, his raven locks, his self-assured manner. His companion wore a pink dress and carried a parasol, and from time to time she bent over to throw food to the ducks that were swimming over to her from all parts of the pond to partake of the feast. She straightened up and walked away from the pond, arm-in-arm with Sage, and once again, Charllie could hear a distant trill of laughter.

Phoebe Somerset! Charllie felt as if she had just swallowed lead. She watched as Sage inclined his head towards Phoebe as she attentively listened to some sweet nothings, she was sure, and then threw his head back and gaily laughed at what must have been an amusing response. Sickened by the sight of the two who casually strolled the perimeter of the pond, Charllie tried to break the voyeuristic trance she found herself in, but it was no use. Her eyes were drawn to each casual touch, the briefest of conversational exchanges, and the faintest trills of laughter. All sent daggers to her heart, yet she couldn't begin to understand the true source of her misery.

Sage, in anger, had denied that any liaison existed between Phoebe and himself. Charllie, however, knew that was very probably not the case. In truth, he had only denied that they were not about to become engaged, but she wasn't sure that he had seemed to imply that no true personal connection existed. Shamefaced, Charllie had to accept the possibility that they might at the very least be lovers, regardless of Sage's disavowals, and she recoiled at the thought. All the olive branches in the world could not make up for the true nature of their relationship, which she was now witnessing in person.

His promises, his denials, his vows of love and friendship now meant absolutely nothing to her. How he could lie in such flattering tones when he knew that these same lies could so easily be shattered by public scrutiny was more than Charllie could bear. He had been so persuasive, so seemingly sincere, and she had wanted to believe him in the worst way. Somehow, the hardest pill to swallow was Sage's duplicity, for she felt that as often as the two of them had been at loggerheads that at least their relationship was based to a large degree on honesty, too seldom found in this world. Charllie was saddened at this loss of trust that she had taken for granted as she watched the two strollers amble back to the Danbury plantation home.

When Phoebe and Sage finally withdrew from sight, Charllie breathed a huge sigh of relief. For a moment, the spell was broken, and she was able to attend to Thomas's gravesite without interruption. However, she no longer felt the motivation to continue with her duties, for they now felt so senseless. Days from now, the plants would be parched again, the weeds beginning to make a new foray, and Thomas would still be but a memory. In disgust, she wiped her dusty hands on her skirt and straightened up to look back at her own home. It was still shabby and gray with age as it nestled in the shade, but the magnificent white oak that towered above it still retained its strength and dignity. And Charllie very much needed to draw upon that strength and dignity now.

***

As Sage took the promenade around the pond with Phoebe, he could sense that he was being watched. Charllie visited the cemetery like clockwork, and he often saw her as she bent down to labor over her flowers or when she straightened up to survey her handiwork. Sometimes the sun shone behind her and, with her golden tresses and her somber dress visibly undulating in a gentle breeze, she would often remind him of an avenging angel. He tried to ignore her constant presence, but it was all but impossible. Conflicting emotions of empathy and distrust, love and anger, and joy and sorrow battled with his usual good nature, and he found himself, more and more, becoming despondent. As Charllie now stood for a moment, in respite from her labors, he felt her eyes upon him; but what emotions she harbored with that glance remained an enigma.

Phoebe was feeding the ducks, and they came from all sides of the pond to take advantage of her generosity. In their haste to reach the food, they splashed themselves and each other as their webbed feet and forceful wings disturbed the sunlight-dappled serenity of the pond's murky depths. As Sage watched them, he felt disgusted with himself, for they reminded him of how like them he had become. His very happiness seemed totally dependent on his desire to scrounge for any of the meager tidbits of warmth and desire that Charllie might cast his way; yet, frequently, she proved to be a woman who did little but provide him with scorn. He seemed to be constantly vying for her attention: waiting for her to give him any emotional crumbs of whatever compassion that she might deem appropriate. Were Charllie ever to relent and offer him any true tenderness and affection, he knew that he would immediately be the happiest of men. But he was tired of chasing an elusive dream, one that he had been chasing for far too many years. His life seemed irrevocably stalled, and he felt helpless to move on.

Sage knew that his parents were anxious for him to marry and provide them with grandchildren. They longed for a daughter-in-law and grandchildren for the legacy that they hoped to one day leave behind. He realized that both parents had finally discounted Charllie as his possible wife, knowing full well she continued to hold a torch for their dearly departed Thomas. They accepted this without question, for, in a sense, this kept their eldest son's memory more vividly alive.

Recently, they had begun to focus all their attention on Phoebe Somerset. Phoebe's father was a friend of Theodore Danbury's. They had been business associates for years as well as close friends, and the ties between the two families had gradually grown and developed. The families often met at various social functions, and they frequently visited one another in their homes. That both sets of parents had noticed the fact that one had an eligible daughter and the other an eligible son could not be overlooked. Time was of the essence, and the Danburys and the Somersets could think of nothing better than to encourage their two precious children to quickly settle down; and if it happened to be with each other, then so much the better.

Theodore had always wanted the best for his sons. Now that Thomas' death had pronounced the second son as the reigning heir of Danbury Dell, he was even more anxious to discreetly encourage a betrothal for Sage so that the future management of the estate would be safely in his competent hands, complete with a wedding to solidify the best interests of the Danburys. Phoebe seemed to play a pivotal role in this matchmaking scenario. As Somerset's only daughter, her father was also on the lookout for someone who might one day take her for his wife and provide her with a home and family. However, it was incumbent upon this person to possess education and intelligence, charm and connections, leadership experience and industry—someone suited to take over the management reins of his new warehouse in Richmond one day. It was no secret to either Sage or Phoebe that their parents hoped with all their hearts that a love match between them, conducive to the fortunes of both families, might at the very least be something for the offing in the not-too-distant future.

From time to time, John and Irene Somerset invited the Danburys to Richmond for various festivities and outings, and, of course, the Danburys often reciprocated by inviting them to their estate in the country for luncheons, picnics, and an occasional hunt. All their attempts, however, had been positively futile up to this point, especially where Sage was concerned. To him, Phoebe was a milk and toast kind of woman. Bland. She lacked the spark, zest for life, and fire that he so admired in Charllie. Phoebe was pleasant enough; she would have made a wonderful sister, and most probably a thoughtful and kind friend. He couldn't deny that she was a beautiful young woman with style and grace, but she left him cold.

Phoebe's dark hair and dark eyes evoked only mild, rather gentle, feelings of tenderness. Because she shared some of his own physical attributes, dark tresses and a high-colored complexion, he often thought that she could have been the sister he had not been fortunate enough to have. Try as he might, he could never think of her in any other way. They enjoyed each other's company, felt comfortable enough to occasionally share small personal confidences, and found each other mildly entertaining. But romance was totally out of the question. Those deeper sensibilities just did not exist between the two of them.

There were times when Sage had seriously entertained the idea of marrying Phoebe despite his true feelings towards her. He was often very lonely and felt his life was totally adrift. He knew he did not want to go through life without a family of his own, but he also did not want to waste his life by attempting to court someone who might never return his affections. But, unlike his brother Thomas, he was not willing to sacrifice either Phoebe or himself to a loveless marriage undertaken solely for convenience. Perhaps when he turned forty, and the love of his life still seemed but a distant dream, he might revisit his decision. Not now. At this point in his life, he was just not willing to make the ultimate sacrifice—one he might soon live to regret.

Sage knew that Phoebe felt much the same way about him. When the subject of marriage was brought up, Phoebe often described the man she hoped one day to marry. She would discuss his role as both a husband and father and what her expectations were for both. Her description always seemed somewhat antithetical to Sage's own personality, for the person she described seemed a bit dull and lacking in imagination. She wanted someone who was respectable, solid, serious during the day as a bastion of business, who then came to life in the evening as a dashing husband who would take on the social whirl of Richmond, escorting her to musicales, charity balls, and intimate dinners with friends. She wanted someone who directed and managed his business with the use of subordinates rather than becoming personally involved. She insisted that she needed someone who could enjoy the social whirl of Richmond during the winter months, attending endless rounds of social and cultural events.

For the most part, Sage knew that he could probably accommodate many of her wishes, but above all, he prided himself on his individuality, his determination, his desire to physically participate as well as supervise, and his lust for life and all it had to offer. He could not imagine himself sitting passively by the fire, attending to a wife and children following a day of managing a warehouse. Nor did he choose to donate so much of his time as an escort for frivolity. He did not want his life to be totally predictable and prescribed, for the world around him was not. He wanted lively, witty conversation that at times might even lead to disagreement and controversy. He needed someone who could vocalize her own beliefs and dreams, and aspirations. Sage did not view life as an orderly progression of time but as a series of exciting challenges; however, he knew in his heart that Phoebe longed for order, social standing, and routine borne of tradition. Though he enjoyed occasional trips into the city to dine with friends or attend a performance, the idea of a yearly round of wintertime social immersion was something he knew he would prefer to avoid at all costs.

Sage craved the excitement of controlling a rather unruly steed, supervising the care of crops and livestock, overseeing diligent workers, and taking calculated risks in business and in life. He could not live a life based on a boring routine. He needed to involve himself physically, emotionally, and spiritually in everything that he pursued. Phoebe could never be the woman who lived in Sage's dreams, for he needed a wife who matched him in this very same spirit. And to date, he had only ever met one such woman and, much to his dismay, she seemed to be the unattainable Charlotte Wright.

Phoebe gaily laughed at the antics of the avaricious ducks, and her laugh was infectious. Sage smiled. "Phoebe, I don't suppose I ever told you about the time my brother Thomas tried to catch Father's favorite golden carp. Somehow, he had gotten it into his head that the fish was covered in genuine gold, and he was determined to catch it for his very own trophy. He evidently thought that the fish might make him rich. He used Father's rod and a piece of raw bacon from the kitchen. The fish soon swallowed the bacon, but, with all of Thomas's flailing around with the fishing line, he ended up snagging one of our white ducks that happened to be swimming nearby instead. What a fiasco!"

"My goodness, Sage, whatever did Thomas do?"

"Well, in trying to help the hapless creature, he eventually ended up in the pond himself. He was positively furious—with both the duck and himself!"

Phoebe burst out laughing, "What a picture that must have made! I certainly hope he knew how to swim!"

"Barely, though I don't think at the time that he was very far from shore. I immediately started screaming because I feared that my brother might drown. I quickly ran to the stables for help. I remember our overseer following me back on horseback and immediately jumping down from his horse, then trudging into the pond, boots and all. He unceremoniously dragged both Thomas and the duck up out of the pond. Thomas was dripping wet, covered with mud, and coughing up pond water. The duck recovered and soon swam to the very center of the pond."

"I never knew Thomas, but I can well imagine that he must have been absolutely beside himself!"

"That wasn't the half of it. We had company expected for afternoon tea that day, and just as he was traipsing into the house, a sodden mess, their carriage rounded the bend of our drive. Two little girls, who were accompanying their parents, were gaily waving at everyone as they arrived at the front door. Not only was Thomas livid due to being seen in public in this unkempt manner, but his face was also totally red with embarrassment and still covered with mud as well."

Phoebe's peals of laughter floated across the lawn's great expanse. Sage escorted Phoebe back to the house, where he knew his mother awaited them. He was famished, and he was happily anticipating discussion on crop rotations and the political climate in Washington, D.C. with his father and Mr. Somerset.

***

Theodore and Evelyn Danbury, now in their late fifties, were aristocratic in both their appearance and demeanor. Theodore himself came from a family of old money and old titles. His family's transplantation from England to Virginia had been extraordinarily successful, and both the family and its plantation had flourished—until the Civil War had reared its ugly head, depriving the Danburys of their "heir apparent" and many of their financial assets.

Physically, Theodore was a rather grander version of the departed Thomas. Though his sandy hair had long ago turned gray, there yet remained a whisper of its sandy presence in his moustache and his sideburns. His gray eyes were more piercing and assertive than Thomas's had been, his physique was altogether more impressive, for he stood five feet eleven inches tall, and his back was still relatively straight and strong though it now carried a rather more rounded girth. However, it was still most evident that Thomas had been the one who had greatly favored his father, in both looks and demeanor.

Theodore turned to his guests and, with a smile, proclaimed, "May I toast our good friends who hail from the recovering capital of Richmond in our beloved state of Virginia? We pray that their fledgling business will continue to prosper and grow. May our ties of family and friendship strengthen as the months and years go by."

Sage knew without a doubt what his father was alluding to, though he sat quietly by without commenting. Phoebe produced a wisp of a smile and then quickly placed her napkin in her lap. She, too, did not allow the toast to provoke any reaction. Their parents were becoming more and more transparent as the days went by. They weren't getting any younger, and Sage and Phoebe understood that they were secretly praying for grandchildren in the very near future. They both hoped that their parents might possibly get their prayers answered, but they knew within their hearts that it wouldn't happen through their own matrimonial joining.

Sage glanced over at his mother to gauge her reaction to his father's toast and saw that she was totally unperturbed by it. He had to admit that he was not surprised by their collusion because he had been feeling the insidious pressure from his family in their search for a respectable wife for their remaining son for months now. And it was becoming increasingly distasteful. He was not a child, and he did not appreciate their blatant meddling in his life!

"Phoebe and I took our usual stroll around the lake earlier. We found a clutch of late duck eggs in the grasses near the cattails. It seems we may soon have ducklings joining the rowdy bunch of beggars already swimming about. That's if the foxes don't make too many hunting forays before the ducklings mature and take to the center of the pond for safety."

His mother smiled. "I do so love watching all the new young creatures. I think the baby ducks and chicks are, in my mind, the most delightful. I will be looking forward to seeing these new hatchlings."

Theodore's wife, Evelyn, Sage's mother, had once possessed the raven locks inherited by Sage. Though her eyes were a bit more hazel than Sage's green, they too sparkled with the wit and intelligence possessed by him. Now Evelyn's dark tresses were traced with silver, and they were carefully arranged in a stylish chignon at the nape of her neck. Her lace collar was crisp and flawless, and her navy-blue summer gown was graceful and demure. She chose to use her fan as a major form of communication, gesturing with it now as she invited her guests to be seated as they waited for the abundant repast that had been placed upon the sideboard—waiting to be served.

"Please make yourselves comfortable. We certainly won't stand on decorum today as we are amongst friends. Maisy has been busy all morning, and I decided that once she has served our soup and side plates that she may be excused. We have given her the afternoon off so that she may spend some time with her new grandchild. I really don't know where the time has gone! It seems only yesterday that Maisy herself had come seeking employment at Danbury Dell, and we had hired her as our new cook. She was but a child herself then, and Theodore and I green newlyweds newly arrived from England. And now, it seems that with little more than the blink of an eye, she has married and made a home, raised two lovely daughters, and has a newborn grandson herself."

Evelyn smiled as she surveyed the table to make sure that everything was in its place and that her guests were comfortable with the seating arrangements. She took a sip from her water glass and nervously repositioned her salad fork. Sage knew his mother's announcement that Maisy had recently become a grandmother was just another subtle reminder that he had fallen behind in achieving fatherhood, that pinnacle of success much wished for by his family.

I do believe my parents might be better off focusing their prayers on blessing me with a future wife, someone appropriate for the hereditary needs of this family. It is evident that my wishes are less important than theirs as they plan a betrothal for their son and Phoebe Somerset. Children may be on the forefront of their minds as they are greedy to seek heirs, but they are the least of my worries at this juncture. I must say that for me, love and romance must take center stage before I seek my bride.

Evelyn and Theodore were gracious hosts, and, even for an informal luncheon with the Somersets, they had chosen to use their best crystal and silver flatware. The candles were lit, a centerpiece of ferns and roses was nestled in the center of the table, and the wine was poured. Salad plates of garden greens, thinly sliced cold chicken, and hot, crisp rolls were passed, and the gay conversation and sporadic laughter abated until the first edge of hunger had been appeased.

Evelyn nodded towards her son. "Sage, did you show Phoebe the new foal in the stable? I was totally amazed that Francie, my favorite old mare, still had the ability to produce such a fine colt. We are all immensely proud of her, I must say." She continued to pass the pickles and jellies.

Sage nodded his head in affirmation. "I certainly did, Mother, though I do believe that the favorite subject of interest for Phoebe on our tour tended to be the three kittens that were tumbling about in the loft. I've promised her that she may take the little blonde tabby home with her today if she'd like. The little fellow is weaned by now, and he would probably relish a soft cushion by her fire. I am not sure that she has ever become a true equine fan, however. That seems to be something that exists solely in our family. Her pursuits tend to be more based on the many stores and social events to be found in Richmond."

Sage hoped to casually point out the differences between Phoebe and himself, so that when they finally made their personal preferences crystal clear to their parents, there would be no surprises. He knew that he was fighting a losing battle as his mother was stubbornly set on an immediate wedding, forcing him to seriously consider the young woman currently at hand. His mother was enterprising if nothing else.

Evelyn, however, ignored Sage's comments—as he knew she would and looked over towards Phoebe as she continued, "I certainly hope that we'll see more of you this summer, Phoebe. Your trip to Boston last year left Danbury Dell a bit wanting for female companionship." Sage was exasperated. His mother was anything but subtle, and he wished that she would call off her campaign for his future marriage plans.

Phoebe was unperturbed, however, and, since she was almost always on her best behavior, she answered politely. "I certainly hope that our families will be able to get together on a more regular basis this year, Mrs. Danbury. However, I find myself almost prostrate during the summer months and seldom participate in many formal engagements until fall. Mother often prefers a bit of travel during the summer, especially to Aunt Martha's in the Carolina mountains, while Father often stays behind in Richmond. Quite frankly, I am usually quite a homebody myself and content with sleeping in my own bed, but I have recently grown increasingly tired of this beastly heat and look forward to my time away from Virginia. Our bags are packed as we speak, and we hope to leave for Aunt Martha's in three days. Father may also be joining us later in the month if we're successful in convincing him to take some time off from his work."

Sage breathed a sigh of relief.

Theodore Danbury, who was quietly playing with his moustache, looked over at Sage, who was uncomfortably pushing a cucumber around on his plate with his fork. "So, son, maybe you could make arrangements with John and Irene to spend a week or two with them in September when they return from their trip to the mountains. I have a list of supplies and equipment that must be researched and then purchased. Of course, Richmond is the place to do it. It would give you a wonderful opportunity to combine business with pleasure. It might certainly provide a nice change of pace, for both you and Phoebe."

Mr. Danbury looked over at the Somersets: John, pink-cheeked and rather given to obesity, and Irene, a bit non-descript but exceedingly feminine and dainty. Both smiled pleasantly and nodded, and then confidently looked over at their daughter Phoebe to gauge her reaction. Phoebe just calmly smiled and sipped her wine. She had heard this foolishness just so many times before, and she was not going to give them the pleasure of providing any significant reaction. Sage, however, could feel his face tighten with chagrin. His parents, bless their conniving souls, were making his life more and more unpleasant with their endless matchmaking schemes, and he knew that one day he would have to take a firmer stand. He could only hope that they would understand. His future was his alone, and he would not tolerate their meddling.

Sage smoothed the napkin on his lap and then meticulously buttered a roll. Finally, he caught his father's eye and replied, "Father, I absolutely agree with Phoebe. The cooler autumn months are far more conducive to entertainment and social engagements. Mr. Matthews, the overseer, has always taken the requisitions and new purchases of this estate upon himself, and quite frankly, I feel he has always done a splendid job. Danbury Dell, as you know, is short of good help for both the house and the fields. We must make do with what we have, at least for now. I really do not feel that I should take time away from the estate during the harvest months, though, in fact, there may be some downtime before the holidays for me. I do need to spend a weekend or two shopping for the family and our retainers for Christmas.

His mother scowled, and Sage knew immediately she did not consider "a weekend or two" as sufficient periods of time for anyone who was seriously pursuing a matrimonial liaison.

Sage was aware that the conversation was as uncomfortable for Phoebe as it was for him. He glanced at her briefly, slightly raising his eyebrows as he did so, just to let her know he empathized with her regarding their matchmaking parents. He continued, attempting to placate both sets of parents . . . "I'm sure that Phoebe and I will be meeting for numerous special occasions as the holidays approach. Richmond is famous for its social calendar, especially as we approach the new year." Diplomacy was the best that Sage could offer his parents at this juncture.

Evelyn, bored with discussions of future social engagements that were weeks away, steered the conversation back to more mundane concerns. "Irene, have you and Phoebe had the opportunity to view any of the new fashions recently? Some seem to show a definite French influence. I'm not sure that I favor some of the new colors and designs for evening wear, but it certainly seems that the bustle is quickly going out of style." She would wait until the ladies were alone to discuss the lower necklines and raised hems of the skirts. It would not do to pursue this conversation now with the men in attendance, so they would pursue it in further detail later. First, they would settle in with their tea and dessert.

The two older men, however, both uncomfortable as well as bored with the talk of fashion, arose from the table and excused themselves. They hastened to the library where they planned to lounge in comfortable leather chairs, sip barrel-aged whisky, and talk of business and upcoming hunts. Gratefully, Sage was now left to his own devices. He too excused himself from the table, bid his guests a polite farewell, and hurriedly went upstairs to change into his work clothes so that he could resume his duties on the estate.

Sage was extremely pleased that his parents' physical declines during the war had been temporary. Today, both parents were the picture of health. They would, of course, never forget their elder son Thomas, and their deep mourning had contributed to a particularly more somber outlook than if he had returned from the war unscathed.

However, many families had lost far more than they. They were certainly aware of their many blessings.

Sage was alive and well, and he provided them much comfort as their daily lives picked up the threads of normalcy and continuity. Their estate had taken many losses both during and after the war, but the land remained fertile, and they had been able to keep and hire enough field hands to re-establish the Dell as a thriving concern. Even though Theodore and Evelyn were no longer in their prime, Sage had no doubt that some of their best years were yet to come. He knew that he was fortunate in having such loving, caring parents.

Yet Sage, running his fingers through his hair in exasperation, scowled. He wished that his parents would let him live his own life without constantly trying to interfere. They had lived their lives with little input from others, and they were continuing to do so without his instruction or unnecessary intervention. Now it was his turn to direct his own life, and they needed to respect him on this. He did not need Miss Phoebe Somerset constantly thrown his way. His relationship with Phoebe was pleasant, but totally benign; she would never be his answer to a spouse, and the continuance of the family line would never rely on her. Of that they could be assured!

Chapter Eleven

Charllie felt listless and all adrift. Her life seemed to have little purpose. Though she seemed lethargic at times, possessing little energy and direction, she felt a compelling need for forced activity so that she would not continue to dwell on the sorrows and frustrations in her life. She set aside her needlepoint. It seemed so frivolous, and it certainly did not keep her mind off her troubles. She looked around the parlor, now heavily draped to prevent the summer sun's entry. It seemed close and stifling. Portraits and framed photographs, many of departed loved ones, were arranged on the walls and on the mantle. The somber faces of those who had already passed on evoked guilt from those living; those captured within their frames looked out upon a world with dark eyes that could no longer comprehend it, and they certainly could no longer take part in it.

Charllie was too much alive to wish to spend this lovely summer's day in their company. She quickly stood, put away her sewing supplies, and planned to do battle with her somber, debilitating environment. Maybe today would provide a good time to clean and organize the attic. She had promised herself that she would deal with this task when she found a free moment, and it would certainly provide her with a much-needed purpose for this rather listless day.

Charllie swaddled her head in an old silken scarf to protect her hair from dust and cobwebs and then tied an apron around her waist. This was a task that she could have asked Aunt Bethany and Mildred for their assistance, but they both had plenty to do in the kitchen and throughout the house. Also, most of what needed to be tended to in the attic included the personal effects of the Wright family, effects which had accumulated for several generations. Decisions would need to be made by a close family member. Charllie felt it was important to bring some semblance of order and organization to this storage room herself, and she felt that she needed to do this on her own.

With a broom, a feather duster, and a trash bin, Charllie prepared for battle. She climbed the steep, rickety stairs to the attic and grimaced as every step emitted creaks and groans from the placement of her weight. The higher and higher she climbed, the more sweltering the heat and humidity became. She thought back to the days when she, her mother, and an assortment of close female relatives had resided there during the war in their little cloistered society. The nails on the wall, which were now used for dried flowers and herbs, had once been used as hooks for clothing. An old, cracked mirror remained above a three-legged washstand, which had provided the women with one of the few means for them to wash and freshen themselves in the privacy of their own home. Old trunks, once used to store their personal belongings, were still scattered around and now held keepsakes and memorabilia from many family members, past and present. It was impossible to believe that this sojourn during the war had taken place only a few years ago, for it now seemed like decades.

As Charllie moved further into the storage space, she looked around at the assemblage of travel trunks and lidded baskets, heaps of used clothing, boxes of old kitchen utensils, and piles of furniture waiting without hope for repair. The task she had set for herself seemed positively daunting. She quickly hastened to the dusty windows and threw them open to allow the circulation of fresh air. The mustiness and closeness of this oft-forgotten floor were almost overpowering, but when Charllie opened the two windows on opposite walls, a beautiful, sweet draft soon drifted throughout the cluttered space. Sunshine streamed into the dark confines and played upon the worn pine floorboards, chasing spiders into darker corners and filtering dust motes in its rays. Shade-cooled fresh breezes purified the air and allowed for the summer fragrances of new-mown hay, roses, and corn shocks to perfume the musty confines.

Hands on her hips, Charllie surveyed the assorted jumble of furniture, containers, and miscellany that seemed totally without order and purpose, and she sighed and questioned her own sanity, wondering why she might wish to punish herself in this way. It was certainly going to be a monumental undertaking. The Wrights were collectors and scavengers from way back, and it seemed nothing ever outlived its usefulness. Charllie decided that a planned attack was her only option, so she began to sort out items in the furthest left-hand corner. She would progress around the room in a clockwise rotation, going gradually from left to right as she attacked the collection of human belongings. Anything else would have seemed totally overwhelming. She knew that if she went slowly and meticulously that she would gradually reach her goal.

The large wooden steamer trunk, one of the first items that Charllie encountered, had large, cracked leather handles with metal clasps that were tarnished and worn. It opened with tortured squeaks and groans, and Charllie peered in with excitement, not really knowing what she might find but hopeful that she might have stumbled upon some forgotten valuables.

However, no treasure came to light; in fact, the truck contained nothing more than an assortment of moth-eaten woolens and shabby, faded cottons from another day and time, and absolutely nothing within appeared salvageable, not even for one of Aunt Bethany's famous homemade rag rugs. She smiled at the eccentricities of some female family member or servant who had stored these items so long ago, perhaps never realizing that these items would never survive the avaricious moths and ravages of time that sought to destroy what women had once created. Charllie dumped all the trunk's contents into the trash bin and then deftly cleaned it out so that she could use it for storing other items that were worth salvaging.

Charllie decided that she would use the trunk for family mementoes, and soon she was arranging familiar items, which she had found in various boxes or just scattered about on the attic floor, within its depths: a sampler she had made at the age of six—crooked stitches and all, toy soldiers that her father Charles had been gifted on his eighth birthday, the christening gown brother Frank had worn when he was barely a month old; and a well-worn chessboard, chess having been Jeffrey's favorite pastime—especially when he was laid up with a cold or some other childhood illness. These items were bittersweet because they linked the living with the dead in a way that evoked tender memories of what had once been and could never be again.

Other Wright and Memsey keepsakes were soon added to the trunk's collection: a paperweight from Paris, a fan from New York, a packet of letters from cousins in Mississippi, a sack of clay marbles, a butterfly collection, handmade Christmas tree ornaments fashioned by the hands of the Wright children, and innumerable diaries and journals. Some of the keepsakes Charllie recognized; many she did not. The lives of so many people had become intertwined, and their personal histories were rich with the makings of life's joys and sorrows. She gently packed these remembrances away in the large steamer trunk, knowing in her heart that they were too precious to throw away because they were the constant reminders of the richness and variety of life within her family.

Family. It was so important. Her heart ached. What was to become of her connection to this stream of humanity? Would she become a withered and solitary branch on the Wright-family tree like her Aunt Morgana who lived in Washington, D.C. with her three cats, her Great Uncle Morris, who lived like a hermit in the Blue Ridge Mountains overlooking Charlottesville, or her cousin Miss Mamie Wills, the seamstress, who lived behind shuttered windows on a lonely street close by the Norfolk waterfront? She wondered if these relatives were living their lives according to their freely chosen wishes, or had they just succumbed to bitter circumstance or the whim of fate.

Charllie shuddered. She wanted so badly to become an integral part of those in the family who had flourished with spouses and children, and grandchildren. Living a solitary life had no appeal to her whatsoever, and yet she saw that sometimes fate seemed to deal hands of unlucky cards to many unsuspecting souls. The luck of the draw. She wondered how many spinsters and bachelors were self-proclaimed and how many had just received a blighted hand from life's deck? She prayed that someday she would be one of the lucky souls who would eventually be dealt a winning hand that would include her very own family. She also questioned if she herself was making decisions that were contributing negatively to her own state of being, perhaps preventing herself from pursuing her life's dream.

Charllie closed the newly organized trunk with a bang and industriously continued the arduous task of sorting, discarding, packing, and cleaning. She occasionally sneezed from the dust she was stirring up with her feather duster, but at least fresh air was entering the sweltering upper story in intermittent gusts, purifying and sweetening its close confines. She was now able to clearly see the richly varnished floorboards of the garret; the wide floorboards of southern yellow pine dotted with square nail heads, rich with the color of age: boards that had been hewn from the wilderness of this very land upon which the current plantation had once been built. A small mouse, whose home had been disturbed by all the activity, dashed across the room. Charlotte jumped and screeched, but when she saw that the mouse had disappeared into a chink behind a rafter, she shrugged and went on with her labors.

Eventually Charllie came across a lacquered trunk of a relatively more recent date, and she hesitated to open it because she knew only too well what it contained: letters written with love from Thomas, his second-best regimental uniform (he had been buried in his best), his army pistol and saber (the regimental pistol and saber were inherited by his parents), and the jewelry box which had once contained the gold locket brooch that he had presented to her upon their betrothal. Warm, salty tears streaked down Charllie's cheeks, and for a few moments her face crumbled as she gave in to the old pangs of despair.

Life wasn't fair. Many husbands and lovers had returned from the war. "Why was my betrothed detained and held for eternity by death? Why has my life been relegated to this dark and gloomy place of limbo?" She flinched, however, when she realized that these mementoes of Thomas, carefully stored away in the trunk before her, were evoking more sad memories than the man himself.

"Thomas the man is becoming insubstantial to me, his memory no longer clear and impressionable. It's hard to remember what his voice sounded like, how he smelled, or what he liked to eat. His individual features are now hard to imagine without referring to the grainy, monotone pictures that were taken while he served in the war. Thomas is fading away into very indistinct memories, yet I still firmly hold on to the sorrow that accompanies his loss. It's sad, but these flawed memories are all I have."

Charllie knew that she was not alone in having lost someone during the war; many more women had also faced similar deprivations. The pain for many had to be far more severe and constant than her own in most cases, for it was easier for those who most likely remembered loved ones with whom long-standing relationships had existed. They had had the privilege of sharing years of conversations, embraces, mealtimes, triumphs, and losses so personal that each day had to be misery for them. Many had shared children with their loved ones, and they were now reminded on a daily basis by the gestures and countenances of these children what they had lost upon the death of their spouses.

Unfortunately, Charllie found that dealing with the loss of Thomas was much like trying to fence with a ghost. "Very few substantial memories still exist for me. Much of our relationship was based on dreams, wishes, and presumptions. My pain relies far more on what might have been, rather than on what had been. My future looks as bleak and colorless as a frigid winter's day because I am not allowing for the spring. I am treasuring mementoes and vague memories of someone who no longer exists. I do not need to be constantly reminded that my life has changed forever, for no one knows that better than I. Yet, sometimes I truly feel that I am playing the fool."

"What of my future? Shouldn't I be planning for my future? I have not died. I have not been physically maimed by this war. I am young and my heart still beats with the anticipation of what might be."

Sage and his dark good looks immediately came to mind, but Charllie quickly blocked them because she was not yet ready to fully let go of the whimsical romance that was Thomas's due, nor was she ready to capitulate to the charm and professions of love from Sage—at least not without a struggle. Her guilt for being vibrant and alive while Thomas was dead would not allow it. Her variable moods and resolutions about her very own future created nothing but confusion.

Charllie walked over to the window and was surprised to see that the sun had begun to set. It was just beginning to cast a rosy glow as it met the darkening horizon, tracing fingers of pink and amber through the tree limbs and bars of violet behind the clouds. The attic itself was becoming dark and gloomy with the absence of light, and objects were beginning to take on sinister personalities as they now loomed in sullen silence. The changed atmosphere was rather stark and intimidating, so Charllie quickly set the remainder of the room to rights as best she could, promising herself another trip in the days to come to provide a few last finishing touches.

She closed the windows and quickly dusted off their sills. She knew her mother would be wondering why she had been absent from the supper table. If she didn't make haste to fix herself a plate of cold meats and bread, she might very well have to go to bed hungry. If lucky, she might discover that Aunt Bethany had kept back a plate of leftovers and dessert for her supper, but, more than likely, she would also still be present in the kitchen to chide her about her forgetfulness. She would have to make haste with her washup and then let them know where she had been and what she had been doing.

As Charllie prepared to vacate the garret, she noticed with pleasure that at least the space was now navigable. Boxes and trunks were carefully arranged against the walls. Everything that had been deemed worth saving was now carefully packed and stored away, and that which was indeed trash would be removed and disposed of on the morrow. The mementoes of past lives now lay secure and sheltered beneath cobweb-free beams, waiting for the light of day when someone else would eventually wander up the creaking stairs, prepared to poke through the treasures of another day and time. She shut the last trunk, brushed the dust from her skirts, and stretched her arms high above her aching shoulders. Charllie knew that she herself would not be making the pilgrimage to this room again anytime soon. Too much was stored away that only served to reopen wounds still tender from hurt and loss, and too many questions as to the direction of her own future remained.

***

As the day drew down and the evening dusk settled, Sophia and Charllie moved out to the verandah with a lantern to play a game of whist. It was cooler here, and mother and daughter felt that they needed this diversion to entertain them for what remained of the evening. Charllie's father had retired to bed much earlier, for he was still nursing his old war complaints and required additional rest.

Fireflies flashed through the garden glade, and the faint fragrance of aromatic hay came in intermittent waves from the fields beyond. A campfire was ablaze at one of the sharecroppers' huts; the distant cadences of an old gospel tune could be heard, and it was being sung with much joy and emotion. Moths surrounded the lantern that they had placed on the table, and they frantically beat their powdery wings against the glass globe, occasionally perishing when they came too close to the candle within the globe. A fragile blue stream of smoke floated heavenward, and the lantern's light flickered on the rosy cheeks of both women.

The lingering heat of the day had been oppressive indoors, so mother and daughter settled in to enjoy a bit of respite on the verandah, where they found a cool breeze or two laced with evening dew. However, Sophia soon found that her daughter seemed to be lost in reverie, and, in truth, she seemed to be showing very little interest in playing her hand of cards. Charllie stirred her tea absently, oblivious to the overly repetitive clink of silver against china. Her blue eyes seemed lost in introspection, and her thoughts seemed to be far away.

"Charlotte, please pay attention! There is absolutely nothing to be gained in a contest unless one has a worthy opponent. You are not even paying attention to your cards, so when I win, I will not have the pleasure of doing it with any sense of accomplishment."

Sophia carefully arranged her cards and looked accusingly across the table at Charllie. She knew that her daughter was just not herself this evening.

"Whatever possessed you to clean the garret during the hottest day of summer, dear?" Her concern for her daughter's well-being was acute, but she was careful not to be overly obvious to Charllie. She was as headstrong as she was lovely, and she knew she would have to tread lightly if she hoped to enjoy the evening with any sense of harmony between herself and her daughter.

"I would have thought that you could have found something far more relaxing and enjoyable than poking through the bits and pieces of this family while straightening up, dusting, and organizing. In my mind, that is the most tedious way to spend an afternoon!"

"I was just a bit at odds today, I guess. I was looking for something not too strenuous that would keep me occupied and productive." Charllie looked directly at Sophia, her eyes challenging her to continue with her criticism. Then she laid her cards down in front of her.

"Mother, when you were first introduced to Father, did you fall head-over-heels in love with him? When he began courting you, did you know immediately that he was the one you would eventually wed? Did something tell you that the world could not possibly go on unless you two were promised to be joined in holy matrimony?" Charllie leaned closer, and she watched her mother carefully as she anticipated her answer.

Sophia Memsey Wright chuckled, and the chuckle quickly turned into rather more boisterous laughter. "The world was never given to really care about my personal goings on, Charlotte. My dear, your father was the most exasperating man I ever met! There were days on end when I could not abide him. I had been used to men who bowed and simpered and vied for my hand. They almost always, without exception, treated me like a fragile lily, and I simply adored their attentions. Their flirtations were the spice of my life, yet

I never paid heed to who they were as people. I was far more interested in being entertained."

"Your father, however, tended to ignore me and showed great disdain for my Southern belle coquetry. I'm sure he knew that I spent my time squandering my good looks and false posturing to antagonize my many male visitors, and that not once had I ever taken any of these *beaux* seriously. I was not a genuine, warm woman seeking to find friendship and companionship. I was a bit self-centered and thought more about myself than them, and your father showed absolutely no interest in pandering to my shallowness. Not one bit."

Sophia looked at the candle for a moment in reverie. She added an extra dollop of milk to her tea and then took a sip before she continued.

"Quite frankly, there were times when your dear father would not even give me the time of day. He positively exuded a total sense of independence and forthrightness. His personality was most often of a serious nature, for he was frequently focused on his many business objectives. Frivolous young ladies with little if any common sense were not to his liking. I think I gradually perceived him as a real challenge, and I wondered about his ability to lead a life of purpose. And you of all people, Charllie, know that a challenge is something we Memsey women have always relished." Sophia sat back in her chair, mentally casting back in time to the days of her courtship. She smiled as the tale began to spin out in her own mind. She now gladly anticipated the sharing of these memories with her grown daughter.

"The man was infuriating! I had always been able to lead men around by their noses, but not my Charles. Absolutely not! He had a mind of his own, and he soon let me know that he was not to be tamed like a fireside pussy cat. But, of course, he could not ignore me forever, and he found himself attracted to me more and more—against his better judgment. He eventually made his attraction to me known, and the passion that quickly grew between us surprised us both very much. I must say that the fireworks were very much to my liking. But it soon became evident to me that Charles had no intention of becoming tied to any woman's apron strings, especially one who appeared as frivolous as I. One day, ignoring our differences, I mistakenly taunted him for his straightlaced ways. He threw down the gauntlet then and there. He was a man comfortable in his own shoes, morally and socially competent, and interested in what was real and full of meaning. If I had an interest in him at all, I must take him as I found him or leave him be. He was never going to be a simpering, lovestruck knave that took his directions from any woman. Not even one who was the most attractive and enticing. And he meant it!"

Sophia smiled softly in remembrance. "In fact, there was a period of about three months when we did not speak. I had taken your father's dictates as an attack upon my precious new love for him. I felt he could not possibly love me if he was not willing to do my bidding. In truth, he was only defending his own beliefs and sense of self. Though I now know that he had every right in the matter, I had chosen to take offense. I was spoiled and used to getting my own way, so it took me a while to come to terms with his independent streak. So, we had parted for a time, taken a lovers' vacation away from one another. But I finally came to value some of these sterling qualities that he possessed, such as integrity, independence, and honesty—these qualities often lacking in other men. And I came to realize that not only did he wish to earn my respect for him as I found him, but he also wished to respect me, including my beliefs, opinions, and intellect!"

Another moth bumped against the lantern, and Sophia fanned the besotted creature away from the deadly flame. "Now that didn't mean that we would ever truly be of one accord! It took me quite a while to understand that true love can never flourish without both parties truly respecting and accommodating one another. Love is not just about giving and taking, but mostly it's about sharing. It took me forever, it seemed, but I soon came to realize that Charles was indeed a man who could command my attention, pique my interest, and touch my heart as no one else ever had or ever would. I realized that Charles possessed a wonderful sense of humor, was compassionate beyond belief, and did indeed have an adventurous side when pressed. I was smitten."

"Of course, when I stopped acting like a simpering fool, I finally began to earn his respect as well. When I stopped posing as an artificial flower and grew up and became a real woman, one with brains as well as a modicum of beauty, we both accepted the fact that life would be forever dull and incomplete without the other." She sat in silence for a moment and then softly muttered, "How silly young lovers can be!"

Charllie looked a bit puzzled. She shuffled the cards and then dealt them. Then she scrutinized her mother. "So, you mean you eventually capitulated to a man and gave up your own beliefs in the hopes of gaining a husband? You gave in and gave him his way, so you wouldn't be alone?"

Sophia laughed outright. "That man, my dear, is your father. A better husband and father cannot be found in this entire world. In the end, I got just what I wanted—a man who loves me for who I really am, and someone who wanted to join his life with mine and create a future. I could never abide, nor ever respect, those silly pantywaist men who gushed platitudes and feigned delight in my company. Falsity was never my Charles' suit. He is a real man, my love, not a contrived semblance of a man. He accepted me and my somewhat difficult ways, as I accepted him." She sat back and sorted the cards in her new hand.

"Charllie, love doesn't always come in soft ripples. Remember that. True and passionate love goes deep, and sometimes you must navigate rough waters. But it's an exhilarating ride—that I can assure you!"

"But, Mother, I sometimes feel that it is always up to the woman to give in to the man's demands. We are expected to give up too much to accommodate. I'm not sure I will ever be able to do that or would even want to. I'm very used to making my own decisions, speaking my mind, and living life as I see fit. Perhaps had Thomas lived, I wouldn't feel so confused. I never had a problem in taking his direction, and he never riled me up as some men do. I never questioned or minded that he set the pace in our relationship, for I knew he had the experience that I lacked. Unfortunately, most men are not like Thomas." Sage Danbury quickly came unbidden to mind.

"Perhaps Thomas was never meant to be yours, Charlotte. If strong passions were never aroused in your days of courtship, believe me, they would have never appeared later in your marriage. True love depends less on calm waters than on the blending of strong currents." Sophia scowled and then looked over the lantern at Charllie, her brow furrowed with concern. "A marriage without strong passion, my dear daughter, is no marriage at all."

"Pooh, Mother. I find friendship, courtesy, and mutual respect to be far more important than some flash-in-the-pan sentiment like passion that briefly flames and then dies out. Deep, abiding love and adoration go much further than some grand desire that is totally unsubstantial. I want a husband with whom I feel comfortable and secure—someone with whom I can converse and trust with confidences. I need a loving man willing to guide me and protect me in life while allowing for my own strengths." Charllie looked at the cards she had just been dealt with a look of disgust, and then she laid them face down.

Sophia quickly looked up. "You make the perfect husband sound like an old rug, Charllie, not a man. A good marriage can be based on all those things, but never think that you will be satisfied without the grand passion. That is one thing for which I will most definitely vouch. True love only runs deep and strong when real passion exists between a man and woman."

Charllie felt very uneasy about her mother's final statement. She remembered the way Sage made her feel when he roughly pulled her to him: his sensual lips, the hardness of his body, and his firm embrace. She knew that when they touched her heart answered his, something deep inside was ignited, and her emotions were swept away. Her very conscience rebelled as she recalled how easily he was able to make desire pulse throughout her body whenever he was near.

But he is also exasperating and controlling! Someone to love? The perfect person to entrust with my heart? Absolutely not! All my feelings and responses are born out of loneliness and despair, nothing more.

The whist game continued in its desultory way, but the tone and substance of the conversation eventually lightened between mother and daughter. Soon they were discussing a new mixed pickle recipe, which had been sent to them by cousin Halifax, and deciding whether the parlor needed a new coat of paint before winter. They smiled and nodded and continued to chat as the candle sputtered and smoked within its globe.

Chapter Twelve

Charllie was sitting in the garden under the dogwood, listlessly fanning herself. She had vacated her bedroom, completed her morning chores, and found herself longing for a breath of fresh air. The day was extremely hot and humid, and now a thick haze fell upon the landscape, obscuring all but the largest objects. The orchard swam in a surreal mist, and she could hear Merrilee nicker a greeting to the stable boy. The filly must have finally received her morning ration of hay and oats, for soon there was silence. The mail lay upon Charllie's aproned lap. She always sorted it before passing it along to her mother, who often didn't want to bother with the tedium it involved. Most mail included bills, obituary notices, and letters from friends and relatives bemoaning financial or family circumstances that were even more dire than their own.

A small letter of invitation addressed to the family piqued Charllie's interest. The stationery was quite elegant, and it gave off a very light lemony fragrance. She carefully inserted the letter opener and quickly slit the envelope open. For some reason, she felt great anticipation as she opened the engraved invitation. She read: *The Honorable Mr. and Mrs. Horace Embry, formerly of Charlottesville and more recently of Richmond, request your presence at a formal ball, on the fourth Saturday of the month of August, at seven thirty p.m., at Embry Hall in Richmond, Virginia. The ball is a celebration of Miss Penelope's sixteenth birthday. R.S.V.P.*

Charllie sat looking at the invitation for quite some time, and was oblivious to the rest of the mail lying on her lap and scattered on the lawn. A formal social event! Something neither she nor her family had partaken of since before the war, at least nothing on such a grand scale.

Charllie was intrigued, and she began to think about how her life had once been filled with so many gay events.

Penelope Embry had been just a little girl, still carrying around her favorite china doll, when Charllie had last seen her by her parents' sides. She had lost two brothers and a favorite uncle in the war, so her recent adult status was hard-earned. She was now an only child. Her young life had been overshadowed by much tragedy and misfortune, and Charllie sincerely hoped that the next chapter in her life would be written with joy and happiness. Charllie was always amazed at the resiliency of mankind, and she smiled and rejoiced that this family was continuing to find peace and joy in their lives as they strove for normalcy.

"Life must go on! Isn't that what my mother has been constantly telling me? Isn't that the message Sage promotes *ad nauseam* every time he sees me? Maybe they are right. Maybe it is time that Miss Charlotte Wright made herself seen and heard in Richmond society again. Maybe it is high time that I renew old acquaintances and discover new ones. Do I dare crawl out of my self-imposed shell of mourning and get on with living? This invitation may be just what I need to make all these exciting and intimidating changes possible!"

Charllie felt both excited and chagrined at the feelings that bubbled up inside her. She felt the stirrings of anticipation for a more joyful existence, though the guilt still existed that she was alive and could pursue a full life while Thomas could not. She also dreaded the thought of having to totally start over, by herself and for herself. There was so much that she had to overcome.

It was all a rather daunting proposition. So much time had passed since she had been thrown into the social scene unescorted. The few times when she had sat along the wall of a ballroom, chaperoned by the presence of other women who were either single or widowed, she had been but a child. She had expectantly waited patiently for a gentleman to seek out her hand for a dance, and sometimes it happened, and sometimes it did not. These had been times of great embarrassment and humiliation. She did not relish the idea of going through all of that again.

Charllie did not like to rely totally on others for so much of her happiness. Thankfully, she had never gone unattended at most of the events in the past. Her beauty, charm, and lively wit had eventually gained many dance and dinner partners. Still . . . the uncomfortableness that she knew she would undoubtedly feel upon entering society once more as a young lady, one who should already be betrothed or married, was very unnerving. She knew that it should not matter, for she truly prided herself on her independence and inner strength. Yet, in her heart, she found it difficult to overlook society's expectations and implied dictates. Whatever it took, though, Charllie was resolved to move forward on her own terms; she would never compromise herself with falseness and fear. She had to be true to herself.

Charllie could not remember the last time that an event had sparked so much interest. She had left the everyday world and taken upon herself an attitude of mourning, and little of everyone else's lives seemed appropriate or pertinent to the circumstances in hers. Yet, with this invitation to an evening that promised music, dance, and lively conversation, she felt ripples of joy and anticipation coursing through her veins. "How little I sometimes know myself and my unpredictable whims!"

Charllie thirsted after gaiety as a desert traveler for his first sip of oasis water. Her heart leapt at the thought of being thrust once more into the circle of humanity. Thomas's memory, at least for the moment, seemed to recede into the golden glow of a distant fairytale. He had become a prince in a familiar story, occasionally showing up in daydreams and wistful thoughts. Unfortunately, his absence was making his place in the family more and more indistinct, and his almost-ghostly presence was now based on memory alone. As someone who had once been an integral part of Charllie's life, his influence was gradually fading away.

"A gown. I must have a new gown!" Charllie stirred from her reverie and traced her own sad smile with her fingertips, quickly returning to the throb of life around her. "I must look my best! For too long I have lived the role of household drudge, and I never know if some other favored suitor might be on the horizon."

Charllie's fidelity to Thomas vacillated as she considered the many lonely years ahead. Perhaps she needed to at least be open to new opportunities and new acquaintanceships. She certainly knew that she was long overdue for an evening where she could be swept away by the beauty and excitement of song and dance. And then she thought with distaste about the contents of her scanty wardrobe. Nothing within her armoire would do for the upcoming engagement. She pursed her lips and gave much deliberation to solving her dilemma. But first, she must share the invitation with her family, so that they can decide what plans they might need to make to accommodate this most unexpected social occasion.

***

Once Charllie shared the invitation with her family, she immediately conferred with her mother about her dress. "Mother, whatever am I to do about a gown for the ball? You know everything I own is outdated, too small, or shabby beyond recognition."

"We're going to have to be creative and smart about it, Charlotte. You know there is currently no money in our budget for such luxuries as ball gowns. Our finances can't possibly take the strain, and even if they could, there's the problem of finding a seamstress at this late date. Do you remember finding any fabric in the garret when you cleaned the other day? Or serviceable gowns that could be refurbished?"

"I definitely didn't stumble across any stunning summer gowns just waiting for someone to wear them." Charllie didn't mean to be peevish, but she had been so excited about the ball, and she was already facing her first major hurdle—a monumental one.

"Charlotte, please don't be rude. We'll find a solution. You must be patient."

". . . and creative," Charllie added. She knew she shouldn't take her anger and frustration out on her mother, but she was tired of the family's poverty. She wished for a return to the days of plenty when she didn't have to worry about finances or how to make do. She finally stiffened her resolve, gave her mother a hug, and went up to the attic to search for the means to a gown.

Unbelievably, a return trip to the attic did bear fruit. The cedar chest, which concealed decades of men's and women's cast-off clothing and remnants of fabric, seemed to solve Charllie's dilemma. After spending much time sorting through yards of leftover fabric and bric-a-brac, she eventually found an overlooked but very usable piece of fabric, approximately seven yards of an aqua blue silk taffeta material, which had been stored since before the war. She vaguely remembered the original yardage being used for a simple gown that her mother had worn when she had hosted one of her famous tea parties. She could still remember the rather feminine rustle it had made as her mother presided over her guests with cucumber sandwiches and tea. Charllie knew that the remaining fabric would barely do for a second dress, an evening gown at that, but she was determined that she would make the yardage work— especially if the cuts were sure and conservative, and the fabric later layered over a cream-colored underskirt.

Unfortunately, Charllie did not know what she was going to do about a seamstress, but she did know that Aunt Bethany's needlework skills and fashion ingenuity were beyond compare. She could only hope that with a lot of sweet talking and a little bribery that she could enlist her beloved aunt's help in fashioning the gown.

At first, Aunt Beth stubbornly refused Charllie's pleas for assistance, mostly to temper the spoiled nature of the house's favored daughter. But eventually she gave in, as she did with most things, and it was not long before Aunt Bethany and Charllie were closeted directly after lunch for days on end to create an original gown for the birthday ball. Though Charllie detested sewing and had very little talent as a seamstress, she was competent enough to assist in cutting the fabric, basting the hems, and running errands. Gradually, the summer gown began to take shape.

"My goodness, Charllie, I swear we have spent more time on this one gown for a child's sixteenth birthday than if it had been for a wedding. I just can't see what the fuss is all about, though I must say I'm mighty pleased that you're finally leaving all your brooding behind you."

Charllie immediately stopped what she was doing, and her smile shattered. The mention of a *wedding* made her heart plummet. Did it appear that one birthday ball was going to be enough for her to heartlessly move on as if nothing had ever happened? Thomas would always be in her heart, but what if people were to misinterpret her newfound gaiety as fickleness? She gently touched the fabric and then hugged Aunt Bethany. She shook her head with a bit of displeasure and then chastised herself for giving in to her emotions.

"I can't say that I've totally left all my brooding behind me, Aunt Beth, because my precious memories are truly hard to part with. I do think that it's time to begin my journey back into a life where I can become reacquainted with old friends and family. Perhaps it's time to meet new people and foster new relationships."

"Charllie, the time is long overdue. No human alive could ever fault you with your loyalty to Thomas. But he would not have expected you to give up your life for him, especially now that he is gone. He is never coming back, and that is a fact. You should begin counting your many blessings and be happy. That is what this life is all about." Aunt Bethany gave her a warm hug and then held the newly finished gown up against her.

Charllie was amazed at the finished results of a most becoming gown. "Oh, Beth—this gown is absolute perfection! You are such a sweetheart! I can't thank you enough for taking the time to create it. I'm sure more than one young lady will be dying with envy when I wear it. I, however, will never divulge the name of my mysterious seamstress. She might just decide she wants to set herself up in a city shop."

Aunt Bethany laughed and brushed a few stray threads and cloth snippets from the gown. "It wouldn't matter a bit if you did tell her who your seamstress was. There is just not enough money in this old world to get me to do this all over again anytime soon. What I might do for love, upon occasion, is more than I will ever do for money—even if I was in need."

Both Aunt Bethany and Charllie were extremely pleased with the results, and there was reason. It was certainly true that the aqua gown was a masterpiece. Its shimmery color would contrast pleasingly with Charllie's blonde curls and peaches and cream complexion. It emphasized her delightfully rounded breasts with a tastefully plunging neckline and highlighted her slender figure with its simple lines. The floor-length skirt barely swept the floor as the many delicate flounces swayed as Charllie walked.

To be able to make a fashion statement with the scant amount of material at Aunt Bethany's disposal, the dress depended upon its simple lines and classical design. For ornamentation, Beth and Charllie had avoided showy furbelows and decided instead to provide understated flounces at the hemline and one simple white fabric rose, fastened at the waist. Charllie decided that she would also forego all jewelry. The only other ornamentation would include a single white garden rose fastened behind her ear to accent her blonde tresses, and she would carry a white rose nosegay with a matching white fan. All the costume preparations had been a balm to her wounded soul, and as she pirouetted in front of the mirror, attired in her beautiful new gown, she could not prevent her spirits from soaring.

For the first time in over six years, Charllie began to look forward to a festive occasion once more.

The Wright house itself was enlivened with this new sense of gaiety and joy due to the impending birthday gala that the family would attend. Mrs. Wright had climbed out of her own intermittent doldrums for the occasion, dusted off an elegant rose-colored gown that had already been worn to numerous soirees but was still more than serviceable, and even began to make plans to host a fete of her own at some later date. Mr. Wright, though encumbered by his wheelchair, took out his best evening jacket from the wardrobe. He had put on a bit of weight since the last time he wore it, but Aunt Bethany had repositioned a few buttons, taken out the waist a bit, brushed it free of lint, and aired it on the line. Charles looked like a new-made man.

The senior Wrights made a very handsome couple indeed. And, though Mr. and Mrs. Wright could no longer dance as a couple, they could enjoy watching from the sidelines where they would partake in the evening's lively conversation, cool mint punches, and elegant dinner. The couple was secretly overjoyed that their daughter was joining them for this birthday celebration. Hopefully, she would begin leaving her days of mourning behind her at last.

***

The night of the event was clear and seasonably warm. A full moon was just starting to rise and would illuminate the road for them upon their return. It cast shadows beyond to the dense foliage of the trees and bushes that stood indistinct and mysterious in the nearby countryside. It ascribed a rather dreamy beauty to the gold and black tinged landscape that glided by. The almost tropical night pulsed with the mysterious sounds of owls and crickets and gave off the dusky fragrances of late-blooming flowers and ripening corn. Charllie rode most of the way in silence, giving much serious thought to this new foray back into society. She listened to the pleasant chatter of her parents and rejoiced that the three of them were finally going to spend an evening together in celebration.

The recently purchased Embry residence on the outskirts of Richmond was impressive in its size and scope; however, one could easily see that many repairs had recently been made in the last two years to restore it to its present-day grandeur. The sweep of the formal drive, the glow of lanterns, and the busy cavalcade of carriages unloading guests at the front door lent themselves to a pleasant sense of high expectations. Mr. Embry was a business associate of Mr. Wright's, so Charllie herself was not quite as familiar with the family as he, but she knew that the Embrys were a family well-known in the social circles of Richmond. There would be many, young and old, attending from the wide surrounding area.

Upon entering the Embry mansion, and having been immediately greeted by the host couple themselves as well as their feted daughter, Charllie walked on through into the ballroom with her parents, surveying the lively party scene as she went. Bowls of multi-colored zinnias and dahlias, large cream-colored candles, and punch bowls (with and without potency) were positioned everywhere. A musician was playing a classical tune on a rather ancient harpsichord in a corner of the great hall. Later in the evening, he would be replaced by an ensemble of musicians who would play more lively music for the evening's dancing. Conversation and laughter floated in the air, and Charllie's body tingled with anticipation. The sights, the sounds, and the smells were invigorating. She silently prayed that the night would not go by without her being claimed for at least a dance or two by some charming young gentleman. For now, she would luxuriate in the sights and sounds of the evening as it began to unfold.

Brother Frank soon arrived with his lovely wife Emily, and Charllie and her parents greeted them and regaled them with the updates that had taken place at Oak Haven. Frank and Emily talked of their children and the plans they were making to renovate their own home. Georgia Merriwether and her husband Evan were also in attendance. Charllie hoped that she and Georgia might be able to sit near one another for supper, so they could catch up on some of the latest gossip. Abigail was absent, so it was presumed that she and her husband were still patiently awaiting the birth of their first child. Perhaps Georgia would be able to inform Charllie of Abigail's condition.

As Charllie continued to scan the crowd, her eyes eventually caught sight of raven locks sported by a rather rakish gentleman attired in a formal black jacket with a starched white shirt. Sage was absolutely stunning in his evening attire, and Charllie's heart skipped a beat. She now realized that she had been looking for him all along, and that if she had not found him, present would have been disappointed. Sage was slowly moving through the crush of guests, chatting with a few of the guests as he walked over to his host and hostess to make his greetings. Charllie saw that he had penciled his name on Penelope's dance card as she stood beside her parents. Charllie could see her blush with pleasure as she anticipated one of her first dances as an adult. Sage did look absolutely dashing, and far too handsome for his own good. She could easily understand why Penelope might be feeling a bit of pleasure and excitement as she anticipated a later dance with him.

Sage Danbury was the one person, it seemed, that Charllie was powerless in banishing from her mind. As the night progressed, it seemed that he had wasted little time, for he was soon to be spotted in the close company of a very attractive female. Charllie realized that anyone with his striking good looks would seldom need to be alone unless that was his expressed wish. As she moved closer, continuing to follow Sage's progress through the crowd, she recognized that his companion was none other than Miss Phoebe Somerset. Phoebe, who seemed to be draped enticingly over his arm, appeared to be enthralled by his presence and mesmerized by his every word. Charllie felt positively ill. She quickly turned around to avoid the nauseating sight and felt a vivid flush of heat moving up her cheeks. She shrugged aside the thought that she might possibly be jealous, yet she had to acknowledge that her earlier pleasure in seeing Sage had been blighted by now seeing him with Phoebe.

A young man, noticing Charllie's discomfort, quickly offered to bring her some punch. She smiled stiffly and then gratefully accepted. When he immediately returned to her with the punch, he politely introduced himself as Percy Atwater, owner of both a mercantile business in Williamsburg as well as a small plantation on the James. He appeared to be pleasant enough and very well-mannered.

"I hope this cup of refreshment will revive your spirits, Miss. I'm visiting relatives here in Richmond. My father is a business associate of the Embry's. I don't believe I've ever had the pleasure of meeting you before at any of these social occasions."

Charllie accepted the punch, as she continued to assess the man who had so graciously delivered her drink. “Mr. Atwater, you must be one of the Atwater brothers of Williamsburg proper whom I’ve heard frequently mentioned by my father, Charles Wright. He has also had the opportunity of doing business with your family on occasion, so I’ve been told. I’m very happy to meet you. I’m Charlotte Wright. My family lives in Goochland, west of Richmond, on our plantation, Oak Haven.”

Percy Atwater was pleased with the introductions and beamed at Charllie as he stood by her side, anticipating the evening’s festivities. “Miss Wright, please call me Percy. Mr. Atwater sounds too much like my father. I’m hoping that I won’t be presumed too bold if I request that we be on a first-name basis so early in our relationship. I’d also like to address you as Charlotte, if I may. I’m amazed that we haven’t met before. I know that I would have most definitely remembered you.”

“Percy, then. What a nice compliment, Percy. You are a true gentleman indeed. Please call me Charllie then, as it’s less formal and my favored name for family and friends. We have never met because, for many years, I guess you could say that I was out of circulation. I had been engaged to marry at the onset of the dreadful war, but since the loss of my fiancé, Captain Thomas Danbury, I chose to avoid going out socially until this evening. It has been four years since Thomas passed away.”

Percy gently took Charllie’s hand when he saw tears begin to well up in her eyes. “I was also a Confederate soldier in the war, Charllie. Let me offer you my condolences, even if given at such a late date. I did know of your Captain Danbury, though it was on a most informal basis. He was said to be a fine, upstanding officer, a soldier who successfully commanded his men and proved his worth in many a battle."

The subject matter of Thomas's death seemed to have intruded with all its poignancy and awkwardness, making Percy a bit more reticent and slightly embarrassed. Hoping to move on to happier topics, he quickly and politely invited Charllie to share the next dance with him. Charllie was delighted to accept his invitation.

As they danced, Percy thoroughly enjoyed Charllie's presence, for she was extremely attractive and engaging, and now she had confirmed without a doubt that she was single, and presumably no longer in an active period of mourning. She appeared quite open to new relationships, and he hoped that he might begin his own pursuit. Charllie, however, had immediately found Percy to be extraordinarily dull and lacking in personality. His eyes were a watery blue and lacked the fire she had come to admire; his face was light and lacking in color as it was clear he spent much of his time behind a desk in an office, and his auburn hair was fine and receding to expose a rather large, high forehead.

Still, it was not really his looks alone that made Charllie retreat from wishing to seek any further familiarity with him, for she was not that shallow. But there was no spark between them: no drama, no immediate warm gravitation of bodies and minds, and no excitement. He was a nice, young gentleman who could very possibly become a dear friend, but Charllie knew that he could never be more. Maybe, for some, his attributes would be enough to recommend him for the role of an eligible suitor for matrimony, but they were not enough for her.

Still reeling a bit from the strong emotions Charllie had felt from having seen Sage and Phoebe together, she graciously accepted a second invitation from Percy to dance. She spun gaily onto the floor with him—flashing a brilliant, though rather insincere, smile. Percy gazed down upon her and took the liberty of holding her just a little bit tighter than was quite necessary. He was not immune to her charms, and he certainly could not resist being the proud partner of such a strikingly beautiful woman. He was determined to enjoy every bit of his time with her while given the opportunity.

Charllie knew she was looking better than she had in a very long time. Sweet Aunt Bethany had triumphed with her gown, and it had just enough pleats and flounces to accentuate her youthful, curvy figure. Charllie had taken extra care with her hair and had swept it up into a loose cluster of elegant curls adorned solely by the single white rose; blonde tendrils framed her oval face and trailed past the nape of her neck. Her eyes were a bit too bright and her cheeks were rosier than normal, but in combination with full lips, delicately arched brows, and an adorable dimple, she enticed many a male onlooker. Charllie was far more affected by seeing Sage with Phoebe than she would have liked to admit, even to herself, but she maintained her composure, and only she knew that most of her gaiety was nothing more than an act.

However, the festive night was working its charm, and soon Charllie began to relax and appreciate the magic of the night for what it was worth. She was soon accepting dance invitations from eligible men of varying ages. Some of her partners were well-known acquaintances, and others were not. She found that she was beginning to thoroughly enjoy herself. The youthful blood that pumped through her veins had been starved for the life stream flowing around her, and she had to respond in kind. The music was intoxicating, and it sent new energy coursing through her body. As she whirled and glided through the overly warm hall with various partners, she found herself listening in fascination to interesting tidbits of gossip and chatting about many of her own experiences with interested partners. Charllie was not especially enamored with any of her dance partners as individuals, but she was enthralled by their various conversations, mesmerized by the strains of music that guided her dance, and entertained by the flow of dancers and servers that ebbed and flowed around her.

Mr. Atwater was slightly more persistent than many of her dance partners, and since Charllie found his attentions rather harmless, she found herself being escorted to the dance floor by him more than by any other. He was of average height, average looks, and average disposition, but his friendly nature and gentlemanly regard were promotion enough. An unruly lock of auburn hair fell across his slightly balding pate, but humor and good nature shone from his light blue eyes. And though they had yet to share few if any real intimacies, Charllie and her dance partner found that they were very comfortable spending the larger share of the evening in each other's company. It was pleasant to be able to foster a friendship when so many in attendance were complete strangers. Their seemingly exclusive togetherness at times, however, did not go unnoticed.

Chapter Thirteen

Sage boldly walked over to Charllie and Percy, meeting the two just as they were leaving the dance floor after their fourth dance. His eyes were narrowed in displeasure, but his smile was warm and completely charming. “Miss Charllie, what a pleasure it is seeing you out and about. Why don’t you introduce me to your distinguished escort?”

Sage’s greeting was dripping with affected sweetness and tinged with sarcasm. It was also charged with a bit of electric tension, but he carefully conducted himself as a gentleman who was at ease with himself and interested in those around him. His smile never left his face, but he made direct, assessing eye contact with his perceived rival.

Charllie pointedly ignored his salutations, looking past him to his companion. “Why, Miss Phoebe Somerset, don’t you look lovely this evening. It has been positively ages since we last met! Did your papa finally deliver you home safe and sound from that finishing school in Charleston? I imagine that you’re thoroughly enjoying the round of summer parties.”

Charllie knew that she was being as false as could be, but it bolstered her ego to be able to spar a bit with Sage on his own turf. Charllie couldn’t help but eye Sage’s female companion with more than a tinge of jealousy. Phoebe, who was dark and petite, was the exact opposite of Charllie, who was blonde and statuesque. Phoebe’s flowing yellow gown and delicate, expensive gold jewelry were perfect foils for her brunette tresses and dark complexion. Standing next to her, Charllie couldn’t help but feel awkward and ungainly in comparison to this diminutive goddess. Sage and Phoebe made a stunning couple, and it was very clear that they were extremely comfortable in each other's presence.

With a bit of cold scrutiny, Sage forced the issue of the identity of Charllie's escort by stepping forward to shake his hand, so she was forced to make the polite introductions required.

"Why, Sage," Charllie's voice dripped honey and affectation. "This is Mr. Percy Atwater. Percy is from the distinguished Atwater family of Williamsburg. He was a soldier who served in the war and was acquainted with your dear brother Thomas. We find that we have so very much in common. It is quite extraordinary. Percy, this is my kind neighbor, Mr. Sage Danbury."

Percy Atwater seemed a trifle embarrassed by the elaborate introduction since he had only just met Charllie that very evening, but he was game for whatever mischief in which his vivacious dance partner might be involved. He smiled pleasantly and nodded in agreement.

"We always tend to go back to brother dear in some form or other, don't we, Miss Charllie?" said Sage, unable to erase the hint of a scowl that touched only his eyes. "It is certainly less than titillating to spend so much time discussing the *dearly departed*. I haven't had the opportunity to converse with my *kind neighbor* yet this evening," he smiled, having mimicked the sarcastic salutation delivered by Charllie. "Perhaps Mr. Atwater would be open to a bit of a change of pace and might entertain changing dance partners with me, as he is a relatively new guest, especially since Phoebe is most definitely well-versed in the comings and goings on the neighboring plantations." Sage smiled mischievously at Phoebe, whose brow quickly furrowed in displeasure, though she begrudgingly agreed to the informal exchange of partners.

"I hope you are agreeable to this arrangement, Percy?" Sage continued. "I am sure that Phoebe would be delighted to dance with an esteemed visitor from Williamsburg. I hope that is agreeable with you, Phoebe?" Percy and Phoebe, knowing full well that they were both being bamboozled, maintained their composure as they politely moved towards the dance floor together.

Since the tense atmosphere surrounding Charllie and Sage had become thick with displeasure and distrust, their partners had been relieved to be given an excuse to leave the area. And, after all, it was no more than a dance.

Sage now quickly addressed Charllie, "Charlotte, my dear, I believe you owe your *kind neighbor* this next dance." His smile was closer to a smirk, and he positioned his arm around Charllie's shoulders before she could attempt an escape from the dance floor. Having known her over the course of a lifetime, he never underestimated her reactions to anything.

Charllie could not overlook Sage's artificial charade, and she grimaced at his description of her as a *kind neighbor*—he was using her earlier flippant comments against her in jest. Once again, Sage was being his exasperating self, yet her smile became tinged with just a hint of laughter. The vestiges of her recent anger, stirred up by Sage's gross manipulation, still simmered in her stormy eyes, but her sense of humor had been stirred by this most exasperating man! She had to admit to herself that she wasn't totally displeased by finding herself in Sage's company, though she wasn't at all sure that dancing with him would be in both of their best interests. However, she also knew that she did not want to make a scene, and she most certainly did not want to reward Sage by expressly letting him know that his thoughts and deeds had made a serious impact on her. Charllie also knew without a doubt that she greatly looked forward to Sage's role as her next dance partner, even though she tried to hold herself aloof and show as little emotion as possible.

Percy had agreed to Sage's suggestion with a bit of embarrassment and awkwardness, but he had been grateful to escape Sage's rather ominous presence. Percy had struck up some casual conversation with Phoebe as he led her out onto the dance floor, and they soon joined the throng of dancers. Phoebe sent Sage a withering look from halfway across the ballroom, but Sage only briefly cocked a smile and then quickly turned his attentions to his new, seemingly reluctant dance partner.

"I am thrilled to finally have the pleasure of dancing with you this evening, Miss Charlotte. Your beauty eclipses all the hopeful women in attendance, especially all who seem incredibly intent upon snaring a spouse of impeccable societal standing during this soiree. I'm convinced that they will find you to be serious competition."

Ignoring the daggers shot his way by Charllie, and not actually taking the time to wait for her acknowledgement of his back-handed compliment, Sage possessively put his arms around her and waltzed her out to mingle with those who were gravitating to the center of the ballroom floor. Charllie was furious with Sage for his rude behavior, but not enough so to make an unladylike scene. Still, she couldn't resist treading upon his feet, none-too-gently. Sage paused a moment on the dance floor, but he barely flinched at the pressure inflicted by her softly clad feet. Normally clumsy, she was not. Though she looked up at him with wide-eyed innocence and faked another innocuous stumble, he was not deceived—not even for a minute.

"Oh, Sage. I beg your pardon. I must have tripped," she apologized with a soft breathiness. She continued to flounce through the first dance steps, consciously ignoring the attentions of her escort, but he soon tired of her feigned lack of dancing expertise. He knew she had spent many hours of instruction with a highly skilled dance instructor as a very young woman, and *god help him,* he had seen her dance many times with his brother Thomas at numerous balls and celebrations. Sage's countenance took on an ominous quality, and he pulled her even closer to him, his arms tightening around her in a crushing grip.

"Any more behavior like that, Miss Wright, and I swear I will place you over my knee and deliver a spanking to you, the likes of which you will never forget. You will regret your actions and be made to realize that you royally deserve the punishment I mete out. You are acting totally childish, and the punishment would most certainly fit the crime. And, I might add, I would take immense pleasure in delivering it. I'm sure this convivial crowd that has been drawn to tonight's event would find itself highly amused by such a sight."

Sage chuckled as his threat was brought to life in his fertile imagination. He masterfully led her through a series of graceful, intricate steps, and Charllie felt compelled to follow in synchronicity under duress. She could not believe that he might possibly be serious, but she studied his face to see if she might determine his true bent.

"You, sir, are totally incorrigible; but even you wouldn't dare to go to those extremes," Charllie haughtily whispered as she tried to create greater distance between them.

"Though you are less of a gentleman than you pretend, even you would not stoop so low." She watched his eyes closely as numerous expressions flitted across his face, but she was unable to fully gauge any of them in relationship to his seriousness.

Sage immediately tightened his crushing hold on Charllie to the point where she felt positively breathless. He gently but firmly took her chin in his hand and looked deeply into her eyes. His emerald eyes smoldered with green fire. "Don't bet on it, Miss Charlotte. You have told me numerous times that I am not a gentleman, so I would be hard-pressed not to prove your own acknowledgments. You just might find that the blackguard you have painted me as has come to life. I would not press your demands unless you wish to gamble on your reputation here and now." He masterfully guided her around the hall, smiling and bowing to those he passed, belying the fact that he and his partner were not in actuality dancing in accord.

Charllie, a bit shocked and chagrined, found herself—almost against her will—relaxing enough to enjoy the dance. She didn't really believe his threats, but she wasn't stupid, and she certainly wasn't willing to risk embarrassment and public humiliation. She also couldn't ignore the feelings that had insinuated themselves throughout her body as Sage had taken possession of her as a most formidable dance master. She could feel the taut muscles beneath his dark jacket and smell his spicy cologne, hinting of lime. The entrancing music seemed to have woven a web of romance around them as she now followed his steps with grace and enthusiasm. She was astonished at how much in tune their bodies were with one another. Though they danced in silence, what their bodies communicated was a message of powerful desire and needed no supercilious language. The dance ended far too quickly and, flushed, Charllie asked Sage if they could stroll out to the balcony so that she could catch a breath of fresh air.

As Sage led her out of the ballroom, she noticed that Phoebe and Percy were busily chatting within a circle of friends, punch glasses in hand. Both, it seemed, were totally oblivious to the loss of their former dance partners. Charllie was both relieved and a bit amused. Against her will, she was also pleased that she had Sage all to herself, if only for a brief interlude. He was the most infuriating man of her acquaintance, and yet, when he was absent, she missed him. She longed for his presence and the indefinable spark that always took place when they were together. His arrogance angered her, his attraction to her was a mystery, and his good looks and personality charmed her. She knew that she spent far too much time attempting to unravel the mystery of their relationship.

On the balcony, the cool night breezes caressed her damp golden hair, and the fragrance of late summer roses was subtle but sweet. Sage kissed her hand and then continued to hold it gently in his own. The memory of their earlier confrontation on the dance floor disappeared in the swirling blue mist that had arisen on the breezes of the gentle night air. It enveloped them in a cloak providing mystery and seclusion. They looked at each other in wonderment. They had known each other their entire lives, yet tonight they were meeting almost as strangers.

For once, Charllie felt rather shy, and for a while they just stood looking out into the night, enjoying their close companionship as they listened to the sweet music that drifted to them from the ballroom. Words were rather hard to come by, for the overpowering emotions shared by them were powerful and evocative, and both were busy deciphering them with their hearts.

Eventually, when the atmosphere became a bit less charged, they began to chat about their lives at home, the friends they continued to share, the health and well-being of their families, and some of their hopes and dreams for the future. A comfortable ease settled between them, and all past recriminations and hostile thoughts seemed to dissipate. Music and laughter continued to drift to them from the ballroom, but neither felt any urgency to rejoin the throng. The only world that seemed to matter at this very moment was this new world that was bathing them in starlight.

"Sage, I'm feeling a bit parched," Charllie mentioned as she began to put her fan to good use. "I think I've worn holes in my slippers from that fancy dancing of yours, and I have certainly developed a thirst."

Sage smiled. "Charllie, you shall have nothing but champagne. I think that we should celebrate this beautiful evening, and my good fortune in being allowed to dance with the most beautiful woman at the ball." He was feeling rather light-hearted about the time he had just spent with Charllie, hopeful that perhaps they might be seriously mending romantic fences. Quite frankly, he felt like celebrating! He promised to return shortly with her refreshment, smiled a lazy, sweet smile, and was gone.

Charllie sat down on a low chair by the railing, amused by the events of the night. Sage was such an enigma; one moment she loathed the man, but the next she found him more than tolerable. In fact, she was drawn to his very presence like a moth to flame. But was it Sage who was the enigma? Or did she need to question her own feelings? She knew that she could not overlook the fluttering of her heart, the quick beat of her pulse, the bubble of laughter that swelled within her as it threatened to escape whenever she was near him. After so many months and years, she was happy— ecstatically happy. She was beginning to feel wonderfully content whenever their time together was cordial and not tense with discord. Charllie gently smiled to herself, still rather shy and unsure about these latest revelations. Was she beginning to acknowledge, even accept, Sage's plea to press his suit as her lover? A tender bud of love had slowly begun to unfurl, and its preciousness offered much hope for a joyful future for them.

Low murmurs from the porch below, along with the fragrance of cheroots, wafted up to the secluded balcony. An especially loud, boisterous voice reached Charllie's ear, "Imagine old Percy bumping into that lady Cap Thomas promised to marry. What a looker she is! Whooeee! That there blue dress is a real killer! Heard she comes from some money, lives out in Goochland somewhere. Cap used to be her neighbor. Love thy neighbor, so they say."

The man crudely snickered. There was a brief pause. "Everyone thought her and the Cap had made a match just so's they'd carry on the bloodlines of both their families. All anyone could ever hope for. A fancy looker and a rich man in Lee's army. That's how these weddings work for those with money, kind of like a business deal that has lots of perks if you're lucky."

Charllie cringed as she realized that she was most certainly the subject of their conversation, but she continued to listen—fascinated though repelled.

"A pity that old pantywaist never got to taste her wares, but then I guess her being a woman never made for a real match for good ol' Thomas anyways—seein as his tastes weren't quite on par with most red-blooded men. He would have never appreciated a fine woman like the Wright girl. She'd done okay as his own brood mare, as long as he could get her with a colt so he could get his heir. Don't think he ever saw her as much more than that. Don't know but that he might have needed some help." Rough laughter and guffaws filled the pause in conversation.

Charllie frowned, puzzled and extremely hurt at the allegations. She felt a sickness growing from within. She didn't want to hear any more but knew she must.

Another slightly lower voice continued, "Yeah, never could understand his relationship with that lieutenant of his. Disgusting, I call it. Always spending time alone in the captain's tent. Why on earth, when so many nice, rounded women are available, would you expect a man to be attracted to another man? Probably thought none of his soldiers would ever be the wiser—but most knew. Something like that's almost impossible to hide."

Charllie heard the striking of flint and smelled the newly-lit cigar. The speaker continued, "He just had that certain way about him. Kind of aloof. So neat and having certain airs about him. His men all gave him the respect due an officer, but they sometimes questioned his allegiances. Got to give him his due, though—as captain in service to the Confederacy, he did us proud. Paid for his service to the South with his life. Just seems unnatural to me that his leanings were towards other men. Each to his own, I guess."

Another murmured, "Best to respect the dead. All water under the bridge now." The uncomfortable conversation finally drifted into silence as the men, who had driven many of their patrons to the evening's ball, smoked in silence.

Shocked, Charlotte felt nauseous. She had all she could do to remain seated where she was while the destructive images were so crassly painted in her mind's eye. At first, she thought she had just been made privy to someone's vicious lies being spread about Thomas, but the more she listened, the clearer the accusations spelled out the duplicity of the man she had once loved. One of the men below finished tamping down the tobacco in his pipe, lit it, and noisily inhaled the smoke that eventually drifted up to the balcony above. He cleared his throat to speak, and Charllie leaned forward to eavesdrop on information that she felt was vital to her level of understanding.

"Guess Thomas could go both ways, but he definitely preferred the male persuasion. I suppose he needed to please the family, being a blueblood and all, and thought marriage would guarantee him respectability. Every well-to-do squire needs a prize brood mare, ya know, or that's how he sometimes put it. The man wanted his cake and eat it too. With a wife at home, no one would be the wiser about him. What a waste of prime Southern womanhood! Saw her just once with Cap—what a looker! I wouldn't have minded a turn with her myself!"

What seemed to be a few lewd comments followed, but Charllie didn't care—she'd heard more than enough! The indistinguishable undertones grated on her sorrow-heightened nerves until they were drowned out by the cries of a mournful whippoorwill. The strangers' voices finally faded away as Charllie heard their boots tromp down the stairs and proceed on out towards the stables. The last words that floated up to her were, "time for a bit of poker" and "don't forget the rum." She choked on a sob and then let her tears rain down upon her cheeks. The tobacco smoke finally dissipated, and the hoot of a distant owl sent shivers down her spine. Charllie felt overcome by cold chills that came achingly from within.

Charllie's face took on a rather pinched look and was drained of color. She was still fighting nausea, and she angrily brushed away the errant tears that continued to creep down her cheeks. Though the men had departed, presumably they had finished their conversation, but their revelations about Thomas had left Charllie totally in shock. Trembling, she somehow knew that what she had heard was true, and her very soul seemed to shrivel and die. A sob escaped her, and she quickly stood up, walked over to the railing, and stared through her tears at the full moon that swam in the distance. She felt as if she had just been doused with ice water, and her limbs had turned solid with the cold.

How a few snippets of conversation could rip apart one's life in the matter of minutes was amazing and earth-shattering to Charllie. Her precious memories of Thomas returned to her, this time with new clarity and finer definition. The farce that had been their relationship was nothing more than that. It had all been an illusion. He had withheld his affection from Charllie throughout the engagement, not because he was the total gentleman she had imagined him to be, but because she, as a woman, was not quite to his liking. He had only *endured* her glances, her touch, her presence. He had, in fact, been repulsed by his own bride-to-be.

"A brood mare," Charllie whispered in horror. She shuddered at the implication. She fought the impulse to scream, to sob wildly, and to flee. The world as she knew it, with all her once-precious memories, had just this moment come to an end in a cruel explosion of reality, and the loneliness and sorrow she now felt were overpowering and relentless.

Sage arrived with her champagne, none-too-soon, and Charllie greedily gulped it down—hoping to find the serenity and peace of mind that she had just so recently lost. Her eyes had taken on a dullness, and her face, once flushed with pleasure, was now white and pinched, almost ghostly in appearance. The glow was gone, replaced by dark shadows that traced the lids of her tear-brilliant blue eyes. Concerned, Sage took off his jacket and put it around her shoulders. He watched her full lips tremble with pent-up emotion. He cradled her hands in his—they were cold as ice.

"Charllie, are you all right? I hope you didn't take a chill. Is there anything I can get for you?"

Sage could not believe how quickly Charllie's demeanor had changed. He had left a woman glowing with the love of life and excitement, pulsing with energy and emotion, to return to a sober shadow, whose white face and cold hands showed a great reluctance to continue the festivities of the evening. He had left in a celebratory mood, looking forward to returning to the love of his life with hope and joy, only to find a stranger, a distant acquaintance who had reverted to her cold, maidenly ways.

With reluctance, Charllie voiced her request, "Mr. Danbury, what I need at this very moment, love nor money can buy. I would appreciate it very much if you would take me home immediately. It seems I am not well and cannot tolerate the press of the crowd and the cool of the night. I would thank you kindly for the sacrifice of your evening if you are able to grant this for me." All this was said very formally in an undertone, for it took all that remained of Charllie's stamina and endurance to speak at all. She was looking at her hands in her lap with downcast eyes. Her sparkle had been replaced by a deep depression.

Sage felt ice gradually pumping through his own veins. It was as if Charllie had just smashed a vase over his head with no thought to the pain that she might have caused him with either the blow or the shards. Instead of treading on his feet this time, she had gone on to trample on what was left of his heart as well. He had felt that this night might very well be a turning point for them. He had hoped that Charllie was finally relegating his brother Thomas to the past where he belonged, and that perhaps there would now be a time and place for him, someone who deeply loved and cherished her. His deepest fear was that Charllie's ongoing morbidity regarding Thomas was returning, and perhaps strengthening, in all its splendid glory as were her affections towards his dead brother. He was sickened to his very core.

Sage turned to Charllie and, though he treated her with both politeness and concern, he was also curt and cold. He replaced his jacket with her newly-sought shawl, and as soon as his horse and carriage had been brought from the stable, they departed post-haste. His dark brows came together in a scowl. The love and concern he had just recently entertained for Charlotte had been effectively obliterated. He now felt the smoldering embers of jealousy, anger, and spurned love burst into an overpowering flame. Had he known the origins of Charllie's emotions, he would never have entertained or persisted with the dark thoughts and even darker plans that grew and consumed him like a cancer.

Chapter Fourteen

When Charllie arrived home from the Embry dance, she immediately sought her bed—hoping for a bit of oblivion to release her from the power of the evening's sordid revelations. Unfortunately, she slept fitfully, tossing and turning—unable to fall into a deep, relaxing sleep. Hours passed before slumber finally overcame her troubled mind.

Unfortunately, lurid nightmares now swirled throughout her unconsciousness. At first, she saw Thomas as he had once seemed to her: sweet, devoted, and loving. As her dream progressed, however, his personality began to gradually shift, and she could sense his growing duplicity. She now noticed that his facial features were borrowed, and the true Thomas hid behind a mask that portrayed a person whose eyes reflected concern, his lips revealing tenderness. A clock chimed the midnight hour, and Thomas shed his mask like a second skin to expose a face that evoked arrogance, disdain, and slyness. He reached over to gently touch Charllie, but when his hand reached her face, he lifted her lips and checked her teeth. He nodded his head, pleased with what he saw, and started to smile. His smile was grotesque. He asked her if she was yet with colt. And then— he whinnied.

Charllie awoke with a start. She was trembling, and she found that her body had broken out in a cold sweat. Silent tears streamed down her face, and she helplessly crushed her pillow to her breasts, seeking solace— any solace.

Charllie was now wide awake and dreading more nightmares, she paced her bedroom floor—waiting for dawn to finally break. Anger, betrayal, and sorrow plagued her every step. The overheard conversation was replayed in her mind time and time again—in all its harsh detail. Charllie's emotions were plagued with a bitter grief that welled up from deep inside. She felt frozen to the core; all the love and concern she had once felt for Thomas dissipated by the cruel revelations of his true feelings about their upcoming nuptials. She recoiled at his false platitudes and selfish motives.

Charllie reflected on the days of their courtship and scoured her memory for any outward signs of Thomas's betrayal, but try as she might, she could not find any clues that would have led her to ever believe that his motives were as dark and conniving as the recently overheard conversation had implied. She had taken the time to fully question the validity of the conversation she had heard, hoping to damn it as a rumor. However, thinking back to the times that she and Thomas had been alone as a couple, she could not excuse his lack of physical and emotional warmth, warmth that should have been freely exhibited to someone with whom one is betrothed. Being a true gentleman shouldn't preclude the ability to truly express love and desire.

Charllie knew that she had been denied a genuine courtship. She had been naive and innocent, and Thomas had carefully orchestrated a most deceptive charade. All the wonderful memories she had once cherished were now forever tarnished by the cold reality that her engagement had been nothing more than a sham, her prince nothing more than a jaded dark knight, and her purpose in life twisted and distorted—she would have become nothing more than a vessel for breeding heirs. Tears of sorrow and anger coursed unbidden down her cheeks, and sobs shook her frame as she gulped for air, feeling that her very soul was in danger of suffocating.

The night, which had seemed to stretch out to eternity, had finally begun to ebb. The crickets stopped playing their discordant tempos as the dying moon now cast vague shadows under the giant sycamore. Charllie still trembled with a chill that her grandmother's quilt could not dispel. She quickly drained the glass of water from her nightstand, but it could not quench her loneliness and grief. Try as she might, she was unable to escape the heart-wrenching emotions that threatened to destroy her.

Finally, at about five in the early morning hours, when her despair hit its lowest point, Charllie ventured forth to her father's library, where she found his brandy bottle. After nursing a full glass of the pungent drink for an hour, as she tried to decipher the rosy glow that was heralding the new morning, the brandy finally traced its warmth through the frozen veins of her grieving body. She knew that the comfort it provided would not be long-lasting, but for now, it eased her pain. Her tears had been spent, and her emotions wrung dry. She finally retired to her bedroom, where she slept fitfully for the next two hours. Her slumber, though far from peaceful, did provide respite from her pain. And she was able, for a brief time, to forget the travesty of her engagement to Thomas.

When Charllie awakened, she saw that the previous night had left her face drawn and haggard, but she soon scrubbed it clean and then applied a light shimmer of rouge to her cheekbones as well as her lips to provide a bit of color. She pulled her hair back and tied it loosely with a ribbon, and then added a few drops of gardenia to her wrists. The scent of flowers was always therapeutic, and she craved any small comfort she could find.

Charllie's spirits had taken a major hit, yet she knew without a doubt that she must retain her strong backbone. She was resolved that Thomas's betrayal would not forever blight her life, no matter the personal cost. No longer would he be allowed to control her life, especially from the grave. The bonds that once held her, which she had mistakenly believed had been forged by love, had been irrevocably severed and were no more. From now on, Charllie was fiercely determined that she would control her own destiny. She would be responsible for charting her own course towards happiness, towards a future where true love might be found if she remained hopeful and open to change.

Charllie believed that life goes on, and a person's actions could either confirm or rectify any given situation. The sun still shone, the birds still sang, and the flowers still gave forth their sweetness. Whatever future sorrows she might encounter, she was determined to wring every drop of joy and gladness from her life. Thomas was now forced to relinquish his hold over her from this moment forward. He had abdicated all his power over her once and for all by his deceit, and she would not allow him the ability to blight and stunt her life for even one more minute as he had done in the past. Time would undoubtedly heal her wounded spirit, but for now, she would have to deal with the numbness and emptiness that continued to pervade her entire body.

Following her morning sponge bath, Charllie donned her favorite rose-sprigged summer dress and then put her hair up into a careless top knot that did not subdue the curly tendrils that framed her heart-shaped face. Carrying a crocheted shawl to throw around her shoulders, she stepped outside with a cup of tea that Aunt Bethany had thoughtfully left by her door. It was all that her stomach could handle.

She added a teaspoon of honey and savored its sweetness as it traced her palate with its floral notes. Charllie was determined to move on with her life. It was overdue.

The morning was so beautiful and serene, so unlike her mood. Still, it soothed her soul, and she slowly began to breathe more easily as she surveyed the countryside that still swam in the morning mist. She took a seat on the upper verandah and sipped her lukewarm tea, finishing every drop of its cloying sweetness. She heard a couple of horses whinnying in the stables, inhaled the fragrance of dew on the fields where haystacks stood as sentinels, and idly surveyed the plantation grounds. Upon hearing the light-hearted laughter of a group of workers who had just sought shade for their morning break, she smiled and was grateful that others were experiencing happiness.

***

Charllie was still at a loss as to how she could have been deceived for so long and so completely by a man to whom she had given her heart. She knew she had been naïve concerning all the intricacies of love and had gladly given Thomas total trust without absolute proof of his worthiness. But wasn't trust what love was supposed to be based on? Trust implied faith, and faith was something insubstantial, celestial, and perhaps even illogical—but it implied that true love was certainly possible.

"Did I overlook obvious faults in the true nature of our relationship because they didn't exist? Or because I didn't want them to exist? Did Thomas truly ever love me at all? If he had, how could he have done what he did to me?" Charllie knew that the answers to these, and many more, would never be fully answered. All had gone to the grave with Thomas.

A faint plume of dust gradually grew upon the horizon. The plume was now the only thing that occupied Charllie's mind, preventing her from continuing the fruitless exploration of the bitter questions that nagged her aching heart. The plume took on a life of its own. She watched mesmerized as it came closer and closer. She imagined that it was threatening to engulf her where she sat, still reeling from the shock of last night's revelations.

The mystery of the plume was soon solved, for Charllie began to recognize the horse and the rider that were the cause of it. Sage and Ebony seemed to be racing the very devil himself this morning! Yet, when they pulled up in front of the Wright verandah, both seemed relatively calm and in excellent spirits; neither one seemed a bit tired or overheated by their mad gallop across the adjoining fields. In fact, both represented that majesty of physique that could only belong to the superior male animal of its species: rippling muscles, dominance in size and stature, beauty in grace and movement, and now action in repose.

Charllie marveled at the sight and wondered what had precipitated the morning visit.

Given the cold manner with which they had parted the evening before, Sage seemed unusually cordial and composed. Drained of all emotion herself, Charllie found she did not have the strength to question his behavior or demeanor further. She greeted him with rather more warmth than her body language conveyed, and Sage could tell that her greeting was less than genuine. He weakly smiled in response, but the smile never reached his eyes. Wisely, he decided not to press her with questions pertaining to their hurried departure following last night's ball. There were many things that were probably best left unspoken.

Sage quickly dismounted and then doffed his hat. He leapt up the steps two at a time and was soon standing imposingly over Charllie. He brought her hand to his lips and gently blessed it with a cool kiss as his eyes pierced hers with both longing and distrust. She found that it was impossible to fathom the mysteries held within the icy glare of his green eyes; in fact, she was quite taken aback by their aloofness and lack of warmth. Each of them seemed a total enigma to the other. Two people who had known each other their whole lives now stood gazing at each other with questioning looks, eyebrows cocked in thought, and much distrust. Each one wondered if the other might hold the key to some unknown, unsolved mystery—perhaps the mystery as to how happiness is finally found and then experienced.

"I see you are already out and about this fine morning, Miss Charllie. And I see you are also decked out for some lucky suitor. Am I correct in assuming that Mr. Atwater may be along presently to continue what he began last evening?" Sage's possession of her hand was none too gentle, and the firmness of his jaw spoke volumes.

Charllie's vanity immediately got the upper hand, and she felt exceedingly pleased that Sage was exhibiting jealousy, even though it was entirely unwarranted. His anger regarding her ballroom friendship with Percy Atwater was almost primitive, and it acted as a healing salve to Charllie's severely bruised ego following the revelations of the evening past.

"Why, Mr. Danbury, I do believe that I see glimmers of the green-eyed monster. Is it jealousy I see lurking there? Would you find it upsetting if I were indeed waiting upon the arrival of a gentleman caller this morning? Well, Sage, to put your mind to rest—I have absolutely no clue as to the whereabouts of Mr. Atwater, though you might be more successful wondering if he might have turned his attentions to the lady you escorted for most of the evening—Miss Somerset."

The inane banter was tiring to Charllie, but she felt that anything was preferable to giving in to the feelings of depression that threatened to overwhelm her. Unfortunately, this flippant manner intensified Sage's anger, for he felt that she was mocking him and treading none-too-softly on the love he felt for her. Summoning his inner strength, he bowed in a gentlemanly fashion and then presented her with a slow, beguiling smile.

"Phoebe and I are nothing more than friends, but I must admit, Miss Charllie, that I would be positively distraught if you were to spurn me for some other suitor this morning." He smiled a bit at his exaggeration, but went on, "We didn't exactly part on the happiest of notes last evening. In fact, I never even had the privilege of accompanying you to dinner. To make up for my unwarranted lapse of duty, I was hoping you might ride with me this day to share a noonday picnic. Be forewarned that I won't accept no for an answer, at least not without putting up a valiant fight." He presented his arm enticingly and, though his manner was unusually artificial and cold, Charllie was both amused and fascinated. She remained in her chair, studying him.

"Mr. Danbury, I'm not sure that you would really welcome my company this morning. I find your mood quite questionable, and I am not sure that my presence is the tonic you seek for your doldrums. However, I too am a bit out of sorts, and a picnic away from summer's heat and humidity sounds perfectly delightful."

Charllie gracefully waved her fan, continuing to study Sage as he stood above her, hands now on his hips. He simmered within at her seeming nonchalance and artificiality, forgetting for a moment that the part he played was anything but genuine. But Sage was able to keep himself in check and finally gestured to Ebony's broad back.

"Are you too much of a lady to ride behind me upon my steed today, Charllie? Or should I fasten Ebony to your trap? I wouldn't want to inconvenience you in any way, though it might be a faster and more exciting romp upon Ebony's back. I leave the decision to you."

Sage knew he needed to be persuasive, for if he were to overstep his bounds in any way, his invitation would be soundly turned down by Charllie, who was never one to easily concede her independence. She needed to feel that the decision to go with him was, in the end, her own and only her own. Coercion, if perceived in even the minutest form, would irrevocably doom Sage's plans for the afternoon. He could not take the risk of that happening.

Charllie was intrigued. She had never ridden Ebony, and she admired his strength and power. She wanted to escape the confines of the gloom, which had sprung up all around her. A part of her, the cautious and introspective part, was reluctant to accompany Sage, for his mood was strange and rather forbidding; however, whether her perception was or was not colored by her own mood or his made her unwilling to judge so negatively and so quickly. Absolutely nothing now held her in bondage: no past tied her to tethers of a false love, and no future prevented her from leading a life of her own choosing. So Charllie flashed Sage a huge smile, one that trembled slightly, but one also reminiscent of those she had once bestowed upon him when she was a girl. She gave him her arm in reply.

Soon, because she was decked out in her summer day gown, Charllie was mounted behind Sage with her skirts hiked immodestly high enough so that she could sit astride the horse in relative comfort behind him—her arms encircling his waist and her chest pressed tightly against his back. Maybe one couldn't escape the past, but the future was always out there, beckoning those willing to risk a bit of themselves for new adventure, and perhaps a new life.

***

The ride was delightful, but it was also a bit terrifying, for Ebony was a powerful stallion. He had long strides and was very much given to speed. But the exhilaration that Charllie felt could not be surpassed. She felt she was in complete harmony with the wind, the sun, the horse, and the man. The horse and his riders covered much ground in a short amount of time, and the beautiful countryside flashed by without the appreciation of either rider as both were totally consumed by their heavy thoughts. Before long, Charllie realized that they had reached a rather isolated and distant part of the Danbury estate. She felt a prickle of unease as Sage slowed his steed to a trot and followed an overgrown road once used for commerce. They soon arrived at a dense thicket that was mostly hidden in shadow, with only intermittent sunbeams penetrating this dark congregation of shade.

Here, the trappings of civilization had been left far behind, and nature was dominant. Grapevines festooned the split-rail fences, an ancient red oak that had been split by lightning looked ready to topple over at any moment, and a dusty and well-traveled deer trail meandered into the woods.

All bespoke a wildness that predominated over an adjoining clearing. Fallow fields and copses of oak, southern pine, and sycamores radiated outward to present a perfect foil for the blazing sun, radiant blue sky, and a few clouds totally lacking in moisture. The riding trail had grown so faint and indistinct that it had become all but invisible, yet it was clear that Sage knew his destination by heart. They slowly continued with purposeful movement for a while. Suddenly, Charllie had to cling for her life once more, for Sage had nudged Ebony with his heels, and once again the horse burst into a mad gallop as the ground rushed beneath them.

As the sun continued to climb, Ebony finally took on a more sedate trot. Perspiration was beginning to show on the horse's back, beneath Sage's arms, and between Charllie's breasts. Charllie's dress began to stick and cling, and she wondered when they would arrive at this mystery destination. Truth be told, she was becoming quite faint with heat, thirst, and hunger. And even though she knew that conversation was almost impossible when riding, Sage's almost sullen silence was beginning to make her feel uneasy. He had spoken not a word since they had left the Wright estate, and his silence seemed pregnant with unspoken hostility. Charllie shook her head in disbelief. Was her own morbid mood beginning to insinuate itself upon Sage's actions? She needed to dismiss her overactive imagination and enjoy the picnic to which she had been invited.

Sage and Charllie were approaching a grove of beautiful, ancient beech trees. Ebony was finally brought to a leisurely walk, and Charllie could tell that Sage was preparing to dismount. A small stream meandered through the cool depths of the woods, and Charllie saw a picnic basket, which had been placed on a blanket beneath the shade, and a crockery jug cooling in a deep, opaque pool. Evidently, Sage had been very sure of himself when he had extended his invitation. Or very hopeful. The site for the picnic had been well planned, and the preparations for those partaking of it—meticulous. Fern fronds, sun-dappled leaves, and trailing woodbine surrounded a sprawling patch of velvety moss, which provided a picture-perfect setting for a midday meal.

Charllie exclaimed in delight, “Sage, this is absolutely perfect! Why haven’t you ever shared this spot with me before? It is so wild and yet so quiet and peaceful. I love it!” For a moment, she was answered by silence.

Sage’s brow was deeply furrowed. His somber mood no longer seemed imagined, and Charlotte felt misgivings about having accompanied him to this rather isolated location. “Our lives, Miss Charllie, have not exactly been very harmonious lately. It seems that you have been preoccupied with other things, and I have spent more time playing the fool than I care to admit.”

Charllie winced at the implied mention of Thomas, but she kept silent. Sage went on, however, in a more conciliatory tone, “Some actually say that this spot is haunted by the many souls who once lived here. Most of our workers and many of the locals who wander by stay clear of this site. Sightings of ghosts from the war, seen by both negroes and whites, seem to have scared most folks away. If you look behind you, you will see an old slave homestead, still intact after all these years.” Sage turned around and gestured to a dilapidated building that swam into focus as one’s eyes adjusted to the gloom projected by the deep shade of the surrounding beech trees. He casually brushed his hand across his forehead to replace an errant lock and attempted a casual smile.

"I've yet to see anything supernatural here myself, but many do swear by their sightings. I'm sure that those who once lived here saw much sorrow as well as joy. Maybe it's just all those memories that continue to linger. I see little but the beauty. However, I guess I have never been quite sure what you might see upon your first visit." Charllie glanced over her shoulder at the shack and shuddered.

The door of the shack had swung permanently open, and the one glass window had been shattered. Shards of glass lay strewn on the rotting porch; its roof was barely held in place by the two remaining posts that were decayed but still upright. A patch of sunlight filtered through the dense foliage, and it danced across the front of the building, mocking the more serious tone that pervaded the structure. Charllie bravely made a serious attempt at levity.

"Well, Sage, right now all I seem to be able to think about is food and drink. I am totally famished and parched. I certainly hope you haven't misled me about that fine picnic that you promised me this morning."

Chapter Fifteen

Sage smiled and led Charllie to the blanket, which had been carefully arranged on a bank of a stream, seating her in a small clearing fringed by fern and wild geraniums. He opened the picnic basket, and Charllie was amazed at the array of delicacies: biscuits and strawberry jam, cold fried chicken, bread and butter pickles, hard-boiled eggs, and garden-fresh tomatoes. He poured her a tumbler of cool, sweet tea and urged her to fill her plate with the enticing lunch.

The couple quietly nibbled at their feast, though neither one really did justice to the delicious meal. They were both feeling rather uncomfortable in each other's presence. Though Sage had chosen the seclusion of their picnic location, he had not been prepared for the awkwardness that would exist between them: two people who had been unable to reconcile their many differences. What should have been a festive occasion seemed no more than a meal for two lost souls who seemed only to be going through the motions of friendship. Both avoided eye contact, and the luncheon appeared to be nothing more than a communion of strangers.

When Charllie could eat no more, she trailed her hand in the cool water of the stream, trying to fathom its depths. There was little to break the silence in the secret copse save for an occasional whinny from Ebony or a melodious song from a sparrow seeking refuge in the mountain laurel. The brook passed by with a muted gurgle, and the glade sheltered the picnickers from the sun's noonday glare. All on the surface was peaceful and serene, though Charllie was now realizing that nothing is ever really what it seems.

Charllie, exhausted by the emotional tumult she still felt regarding her recent knowledge of Thomas's duplicity, languidly chose a stone from the water's depths and studied it more intently than necessary. She sincerely hoped it might become her lucky talisman. She smiled sadly and leveled her gaze with Sage, blue eyes questioning green. "I certainly hope that we are able to break this evil spell we have been under whenever we spend time by a stream, Sage. It seems that you and I are always at cross purposes, continually bringing out the worst in each other. I know that I shoulder much of the blame, as I have often treated you abominably. I hope you can find it in your heart to forgive me. I certainly do not want our friendship to continue to flounder. We used to be so close."

Sage turned silent and his face became rigid with restrained emotion; he fisted, then relaxed, his hands in his lap—finally furrowing his brow into a harsh frown. But he didn't answer her entreaty. As he began to gather up a few of the picnic items, he seemed almost absent and looked inaccessible and troubled. It almost appeared that a sense of guilt flickered across his face. Charllie became very uneasy and tried to break the awkward silence. Haltingly, she began an attempt to share some of her most recent revelations about Thomas, "You know, Thomas and I . . ."

Sage angrily stood up, his lips settled in a firm, severe line. He scowled at her and sharply interrupted her train of observation, "Charlotte, for God's sake, let Thomas rest in peace! Can you ever, even for a moment, let yourself move on beyond his spell?"

Sage had had quite enough of her fine sentiments towards his brother. He could tolerate no more! Then, realizing that he had disturbed Charllie with his anger, Sage gently offered her his hand and immediately took a more conciliatory tone. "I have something special to show you. I think you will appreciate it. Follow me."

He slowly pulled Charllie to her feet, and they wandered over towards the ancient hut. It seemed his intentions were to share the hut's mysterious interior with her, and though she did admit that it piqued her curiosity, she could not ignore how ominous it now appeared.

Charllie was reluctant to enter the crumbling abode that appeared unsafe and inhospitable, but she was not one to show her fears and vulnerabilities, especially after all that had occurred during the previous day. She bravely followed Sage in through the door without any sign of discomfort or distaste. The interior was dark, but the cobwebs seemed to have recently been swept from the rafters, and a large, chunky candle glowed in the furthest corner, radiating a soft warmth over some very simple furnishings.

Charllie was startled to see a large bed covered with an heirloom quilt at the back of the room and a large vase of wildflowers perched on a windowsill. A lonely window gaped open, permitting some weak light and a bit of fresh air. A nightstand with a cracked wash basin stood to the right of the solitary window. She looked up at Sage questioningly, but he answered her by insolently putting his arms around her and resting his head on the side of her bun so that his lips nestled in her hair. His mouth moved down to her neck, and he began to gently nuzzle the softness there, while inhaling her fragrance.

Immediately feeling shock, dismay, and anger, Charllie sharply slapped his face and was a bit dismayed at the loud crack it made. Sage seemed impervious to having been physically chastised for what Charllie took as an insult, though his green eyes smoldered with rage. His hold became an iron vise.

“Miss Charlotte, I had hoped we would eventually come to a mutual understanding, but I have become convinced over time that that is never going to be the case. You have spent years turning away from me and running towards something, and someone, who never truly existed. My brother Thomas never loved you, not as I did, not as I still do—with all my heart. And now it’s past time for you to stop running.”

As Sage’s actions, more and more, became those of a stranger, Charllie’s distress became palpable. In dismay, she saw him retrieve some velvet cords, cords used to tie back draperies. She no longer knew this man who now stood before her, and she began to feel extremely uneasy and fearful. She cringed when he came near her again. Before she could move away or protest, Sage gently—but forcefully—tied her hands and then led her over to the bed, where he gently pushed her down upon it and then quickly fastened the ties to the headboard. She was in shock. It had all happened within a matter of minutes, and Charllie trembled with bewilderment as she sought to understand what was happening to her with this man who had once been her closest friend, but who now seemed intent upon bedding her against her wishes and without the prefaces of love. Horrified by so many imaginings about what she might be facing, Charllie trembled and shrank within herself as she became swamped with fear and foreboding.

She began to struggle frantically, albeit much too late, for Sage had already finished tying the cords, and though she thrashed with her still-free legs, it was all to no avail. He had quickly pinioned them beneath him. She couldn’t believe this was happening to her, especially not involving someone she truly trusted. Not Sage! Not someone who had guided her, protected her, and saved her from imminent harm. Not her childhood friend, her neighbor, the man who had made her feel so many emotions. Hysteria began to build within Charllie, and she took a deep breath to form a scream.

But Sage knew her only too well, and he warned her, "I will not tolerate any noise from you, Charllie. I will not gag you if you promise not to scream—but be forewarned! If there is one peep out of you, I will. It would do you no good anyway—of that you can be assured. We are a great distance away from any neighbors, and no one will hear you. I am sure that on our ride here that you realized just how remote this location is. The only ones around, except for my horse and various wildlife, are you and me."

Sage quickly grabbed her ankles next, the last limbs to experience free movement, and soon they, too, were bound and then tied to the footboard. She was now truly his captive. Much of Sage's countenance seemed to reflect remorse, but his mannerisms were those based on determination and purpose.

"Sage, don't do this. Don't ruin a lasting friendship." Tears began to slide down Charllie's cheeks. The man she thought she had known since childhood was revealing a terrifying side. Sage now wore the mask of an indifferent stranger, and he seemed totally unapproachable and distant. Though she felt completely vulnerable and in shock, she was still too proud to beg for her release, and she would never show fear to any man—especially this one.

Charllie still believed in Sage's innate goodness and prayed that this momentary insanity would disappear as quickly as it had begun. However, she shivered when she realized the premeditation that had been necessary for this whole scenario to take place. So much planning had gone into this foray: their transportation to the deserted homestead, the enticement of a picnic, the friendly banter by the stream to placate her—all meticulous and clever. And now, because never once had she questioned Sage's motives for their liaison, she found herself tied helplessly to a bed in a hut in the middle of nowhere. More frightening still, she could not fathom Sage's true purpose for restraining her here on this bed in such a remote location.

When Charllie thought of the most lurid of possibilities, especially that of rape, she flinched. It was hard to keep her sense of terror at bay, but she had to believe that all was not as it seemed. She looked through the open door longingly, to freedom and a return to sanity. In desperation, she thought of what she might say to plead her case, to beg him to mercifully discontinue what he had already begun. But she was in total shock as to what was transpiring and with whom—a man she had always respected and trusted. Evidently, having been betrayed by one brother had not been enough; for it seemed that she was now being forced to deal with the horrendous betrayal of the other. Charllie could only shake her head in disbelief as the tears continued to freely course down both cheeks. She had been so sure that Sage had not lied about his love for her!

Sage, having finished the task of restraining Charllie, looked up and saw the tears, and for a moment she felt him waver. She hoped against hope that he would relent and release her. But then he scowled. Evidently, the fiendish force that controlled him had reasserted its dominance. He casually and tenderly brushed a stray lock of her light hair back away from her forehead and traced her trailing tears with his fingertips.

"Believe me, Charllie, I am not mad. Desperate, maybe, yes. But I have all my wits about me. And if it were not for the true love I hold for you, you would be released this minute and be totally free to become another's. But I have spent so many years loving you, deeply and truly, but have been constantly forced to walk in Thomas's shadow for what seems like an eternity. You have never given me anything but the crumbs of your affection, scorning every attempt I have ever made to seriously court you. I am so tired of waiting for your approval, Charllie. Selfishly, I have finally become determined to have something of you for myself." He sat on the bed beside her, and his look was both imploring and unbelievably vulnerable.

Charllie wanted to speak, but her mouth was dry with fear, and the emotional questions she needed to pose could find no voice. She continued to stare in disbelief at this man, once friend and neighbor, and now a total stranger, who sat menacingly near her. She knew she must have wandered into a bad dream and that if she were only patient, she might soon awaken.

This could not be happening, and she refused to accept the reality of her situation or to give up hope.

"Miss Charlotte, it seems that our time alone is finally at hand. You see, I have finally tired of waiting for someone who is intent upon chasing ghosts. I am tired of being rejected by the woman I love because she prefers to chase the specter of a man who never deserved her in the first place. I am tired of being spurned and told I am no gentleman, that I am a blackguard. And though you have told me many times in no uncertain terms that I am unfit to be your suitor, you must know that my intentions, until today, have never been anything less than honorable."

Charllie's eyes went wide with fear at the inherent threat, and she nervously continued to test the ties on her wrists and ankles with quick jerks. Her lips trembled, but not once did she avert her beseeching blue eyes from the determined green ones that now pinned her like a butterfly.

"Have no fear, sweet Charlotte. I still hold you in the highest of esteem. I have absolutely no plans for destroying your virtue. Your precious virginity will remain intact, and whoever beds you on your wedding night will find a precious, chaste bride. But be advised, I *will* brand you as mine, of that you can be sure. After today, what transpires between us will never be forgotten for as long as we live, and I will take away with me the memories of this day as my cherished keepsakes. Though you will not possess my engagement ring or gold brooch, my mementoes will be all the more memorable, for they will have been given to you in passion and love. They will come directly from my heart. In turn, I will take away memories of your awakening passions and desire, culminating in your sweet surrender to someone who loves you above all else in this world."

Charllie shuddered. She knew only that whatever memories were to be gained by her this day would not be memories of her own choosing. And that whatever high regard she had once held for this man would be forever destroyed. His message, his stance, and his very presence were ominous. She was about to speak on her own behalf, but her words were quickly silenced by Sage's hot and hungry mouth, totally primed by desire. His lips met with Charllie's, and they stole away her very breath and left her reeling. Pent-up anger and frustration were forging kisses that were both passionate and sensual, yet tinged with hostility; but they were, nonetheless, precursors of strong sexual need.

Sage quickly changed the tempo from bold onslaught to gentle, sweet kisses that first centered on Charllie's lips but then gradually began to seek succor elsewhere. He nibbled her earlobes, and gently laved her neck with delicate kisses, and traced her eyelids with his pliant tongue. Soon his velvet tongue began to plunder her mouth again, and, surprisingly, she felt an overwhelming need to meet his tongue with her own, though she managed to hold back.

Charllie tried to remain stiff and unresponsive within his embrace, to fan her flickering anger and outrage to life, but his kisses were beginning to fall like molten rain, and his mouth, desperate in its need, had sealed her own mouth with passion. His lips felt like soft, moist velvet, and she heard herself moan. She felt herself melting in his embrace, her emotions swamped with pulsing heat.

She strained at the bonds that held her to the bed, but her heaving breasts did nothing more than draw Sage's attention away from her passion-bruised lips to the mounds of her breasts that rose between them. Soon Sage was deftly and impatiently unfastening the buttons on her dress. His fingers gently touched her rosy nipples and then cupped her heaving breasts with his warm hands. He lowered his mouth to her nipples and began to gently suckle as they hardened into succulent fruit that trembled with passion. For a moment, he discontinued his attention, and then, with an almost imperceptible touch, he caressed her nipples once more, sending a sharp stab of desire throughout Charllie's body. She whimpered in fright and closed her eyes, not accustomed to the ripples of reaction that had begun to course hotly throughout her body.

Charllie's dress was damp from her perspiration and, though still in a bit of shock, confused by the new feelings that were now being unleashed, and still shaking with pent-up anger, she felt as if she had entered a dream from which she could not escape. Her heated body felt very much as if it were melting, but not from the temperature alone; and when her clothing was loosened, and skirts and petticoats were boldly loosened or removed, she felt a cooling draft—and also experienced a sense of freedom. But the fever that plagued her body did not diminish.

Sage hiked much of her clothing above her hips to reveal her long, slender and shapely legs. Undergarments were loosened and pulled to her ankles. Sage gently caressed the unencumbered Charllie, who was now exposed so that he could truly feast upon her nakedness with his eyes—focusing on her limbs, her belly, the tender flesh between her thighs. Her sweet mound trembled with the newness of this assault by desire, and Sage began to gently worship it with his full attention. He traced his index finger slowly down to the crossroads where pleasure awaited, barely touching the dampened ringlets, softly entering the moistness that spoke of newly-melting desire. And then he plied his soft tongue to her nub that was as yet reticent, but soon became hot and swollen from the sexual onslaught.

In total fear and embarrassment, Charllie attempted to jerk her body away from Sage's forced attentions and stammered, "I thought you were not going to ravage me. You promised, Sage. You said that I would remain chaste." More tears pooled within her pleading eyes, but their presence was ignored. She felt she needed to close her legs tightly together, for the area between them was beginning to feel sun-scorched and drenched with heat. She felt assaulted by currents of need that were being aroused by the flame that had earlier burst into flame by Sage's molten kisses.

Sage looked down upon Charllie, and for one brief moment, it seemed that he had turned to stone. Still, the determination that she spied within his eyes was unwavering, and she quailed at the sight. He finally answered her, "As pure as the newly fallen snow, my love. But I also said you would be branded. Some part of you will be mine before this day is through, and I intend to be very thorough about it. Mark my words."

In loosening and rearranging her garments, much of Charllie's beautiful, translucent body now lay naked and glowing before him. Sage gently traced her entire body with his fingertips, as if paying homage to it. He was enraptured by this woman whom he had been in love with for so many years, but who had constantly belittled him and kept him at a distance. Charllie had seemed to diminish his worth as a suitor and a man, yet his love ran so deep that all attempts to dismiss her had been totally futile. Her beauty and preciousness had been enticements for far too long, and he savored the exotic sight now spread out before him. Her body's soft texture and the sweet, floral fragrance that arose from her dewy skin were like balm to his wounded soul. Her body positively glowed as he bent to savor his love for her with every whisper, touch, and kiss.

As Sage continued his gentle ministrations of love, he brought forth so many cataclysmic feelings within Charllie's body. She attempted to remain rigid, still, and aloof for as long as she possibly could. She shivered slightly and stared at Sage, wide-eyed and a bit in shock. He met her eyes but disregarded her unspoken entreaties to cease his attack on her senses. Soon his fingertips began to play a seductive melody upon her that enraged her, soothed her, gentled her, and eventually totally aroused her. Her body began to feel a drowsy hum as if it had taken one too many teaspoons of laudanum. And through this languor, her body began to experience an unbidden awakening that coursed through every vein, an awakening that was leaving her breathless and frantic with heat; it inexplicably forced her to wish for more.

Charllie's mutinous body started to join Sage in collusion as it began to melt, tremble, and vibrate to his skillful lovemaking. She felt totally removed from herself. Her responses seemed beyond her control, and she sensed that she must soon surrender to her body's dictates. She felt confused by this dream state that was leading her to a place she had never been, a place where her body was straining for a resolution that would be quenched with finality. A tense heat continued to build, and her body was in thrall with an unexplained anticipation that coiled and grew between her legs.

Charllie tentatively bucked against her bonds one more time, not wanting Sage to think that she had finally surrendered to him, but he was oblivious and continued to soothe and gentle her with his touch, his lips, his tongue. She found herself sinking deeper into the bed, floating on a gentle wave that was drifting to another world. Her mental state had been subordinated by her body's complete capitulation to overwhelming desire that left her reeling with wanting more. She no longer knew who or what she was, but she knew that she was on a journey of sensual discovery. And as Sage continued to tempt every part of her body with awareness, she began to throb with an intense need, a need that was beginning to clamor for release.

Sage gently kissed her forehead, and then he began to unwrap a thick piece of folded leather apron that had been tightly wound around an item that he had stored in a small earthenware crock. When he held it up, it glistened and glowed by the light of the candle. It was a very hard and dense piece of ice. He held it to Charllie's throbbing temple, and very gradually it began to melt—cool water began to trickle down her cheek. She writhed upon the bed, in a vain attempt to free herself from the ache being aroused by the ice, but to no avail. She could not begin to imagine its purpose, and she recoiled. She whimpered in both fear and dread.

Sage began a slow, meticulous assault on her body with the ice. He went from her face to her throat to between her breasts. Her feverish body relished the cool properties of the ice as it unceasingly continued its journey. The ice thoroughly explored every rounded mound of flesh, and each indentation: her nipples puckered, her belly tensed, the curve behind her elbow relaxed, and when it finally reached her woman's core, it quivered and flexed with anticipation. The assault was gentle, hypnotic, and erotic.

As the ice melted and cooled Charllie's feverish body, Sage's molten kisses slowly followed its glacial path, and he ignited passions within her that she never knew existed. The alternate administration of ice followed by flame sent passionate desire swirling through her veins. She felt herself melting at her core, where a gentle ember was beginning to burst into flame and spread. Her writhing was still an attempt to free herself, but not from the paltry silken bonds that prevented movement of her hands and legs, but to free herself from the raging fires that had been ignited throughout her body. The ice had teased and aroused her latent sexuality, cooling and calming in its approach, but it was also creating a path for Sage's scorching kisses, kisses that held promises of ecstasy and fulfillment.

Sage nestled the ice between Charllie's breasts, and she whimpered both from the cold and from the ache growing within. He sweetly nuzzled her, and his words of love and passion flowed freely. He paid homage to her reclining body: each touch, kiss, and embrace was relentless in its pursuit to ensnare Charllie's desire, to clear a path for her own feelings of love as glacial ice is soon melted by a blazing sun.

Sage played Charllie's body like a finely-tuned instrument, and she became feverish with this new melody that was pulsing through her: the rhythm was undeniably provocative, and her body's responses could not be denied. Charllie whimpered, and Sage silenced her with a long, passionate kiss that drugged her very soul, the taste and feel of him so very powerful and sweet. Charllie found herself responding to his deepening kisses, and the two lovers began to sense a shift as their passion began to meld. This change in the passion of the moment brought a low, earthy groan from Sage himself. He disengaged himself and moved back to the ice, which had settled between her breasts. Once more, the ice traveled over the hills and hummocks of flesh while his molten kisses trailed close behind until he could tell that Charllie's passion had grown to such an extent that he needed to temper its rise with slower, more deliberate moves.

Sage traced her belly with his fingertips and settled the ice in the hollow surrounding its very center. While Carllie flinched at the ice-cold waves that emanated, she felt Sage's warm fingertips gradually tracing her body lower and lower. She began to mouth the word “no,” but Sage quickly silenced her protest with an ever-deepening kiss. This sweet distraction heightened Charllie’s awareness, and soon Sage’s fingers had begun a plunder that was both merciless and gently persistent. Charllie began to feel a desperation that centered on want. Her breathy moans sent shockwaves of desire coursing through Sage, and his own body was caught in a maelstrom of passion that begged him to quickly complete what he had begun. But Sage was determined to pleasure only Charllie.

Charllie felt the utter betrayal of her body as it beckoned the desire evoked by Sage’s every caress. Sage had continued his assault and, like the ice, Charllie could feel her body beginning to melt and become fluid with an edgy response that was both new, yet as age-old as time. She had been plunged into a restlessness that began to elevate to a feeling of desperation, and her fear of this new assault on her senses forced her to struggle against this new, fledgling desire.

The more Charllie thrashed to escape Sage’s assault with his fingertips, the more Sage was determined to seek it out, and now Charllie was crazed by his touch and began to urge him to continue. Waves of pleasure and frustration emanated throughout her. In distress, Charllie heard herself whimpering, “Please, stop.” But she knew that she did not want any of this wild madness to stop. Not yet! Her body was on fire, and she knew that if she wanted the fire to be quenched, the last thing that she needed was for Sage to stop whatever it was that he was doing.

Sage continued the intimate caresses, but much more slowly. The building throb, which went to the very deepest core of Charllie’s existence, remained, but she no longer felt like she was scaling a peak from which she must fall at any moment. Sage looked at Charllie's beautiful, aroused body. Her cheeks were flushed with passion, and she had never looked lovelier. Her eyes tried to hold his. They pleaded for an end to this madness, which was taking place between them, but Charllie realized that her true desire was for him to continue because this precious fire needed to be extinguished, or she knew that she would perish. Sage alone was the only one who could provide her with that mysterious relief for which her body craved.

For a moment, Sage regretted the way in which he was taking Charllie's innocence, but he knew he must complete what he had so ruthlessly begun. He was committed, and though he knew he risked the possibility of Charllie forever hating him, he also knew that there was nothing he wouldn't do for this one small glimpse into Paradise. She would be his, if only for an afternoon, if only in the foreshadowing of what love can be between a man and a woman, a true passion shared only once in a lifetime. Sage also wished to gift Charllie with something that could only be given once, something so precious that unless the person giving it chose to give it with love, its value would be greatly diminished. Sage wanted to teach Charllie how to scale Heaven's gates, and this one memory alone might very well have to last him a lifetime.

Once again, Sage tasted Charllie's lips, and if Charllie could have freed her hands, she knew without a doubt that they would have held him closer. The fever that was pounding through her veins was unquenchable without his love, and it was a fever she desperately hoped that he would cure. The fires continued to lick at her very core, and they were both frightening as well as enervating. She felt as if she stood on the threshold of something magnificent and was fearful as well as impatient. Would he never continue!

Sage took what remained of the piece of ice and held it to Charllie's lips. It soon melted, leaving only traces of dewdrops upon her full, love-swollen lips. He removed the drops with the warm caress of his own lips and then gently touched her cheek.

"Miss Charllie. Though we shared a lovely picnic, we never did get to our dessert."

Sage withdrew a jar from a sack, and the substance within, when held to the candlelight, glowed gold—honey. He tilted the jar to see the changes in the honey's viscosity, and then he smiled in anticipation. The thick, golden liquid shone with a subtle light as it absorbed the candle's rays. He began to remove the lid as he prepared once more to go to battle with Charllie, carrying the banner of desire.

Charllie reclined on the bed, and an enervating lethargy pervaded her limbs as she puzzled over what Sage might possibly have planned for the honey. Her state of arousal was uncomfortable and gnawed at her with the teeth of desire, though cessation had tamped it down to a more endurable level. The cabin was getting darker with the deepening shadows of late afternoon, and there was a stillness and surreal quality to the drama that was slowly continuing to unfold. The velvet bonds had become totally superfluous, for the bondage now experienced by Charllie had little to do with earthly ties. She now knew that freedom was highly overrated and that it could never provide her with what she truly desired. She looked at the golden liquid, enthralled and, without knowing why, felt her body begin to tremble.

Sage slowly removed the lid, and then he trickled a drop of honey upon her temple, and then continued to trace a thick and viscous path of sweetness down her slender neck, across her breasts, onto her belly, and finally to the pass between her thighs. Charllie moaned deep within her throat, and this guttural response quickly brought Sage's mouth to the honey's first sweet location. At the onset, his warm and moist kisses seemed to do nothing more than remove the stickiness from her temple; however, Charllie quickly began to feel the repercussions deep within. The heat of his ministering kisses was creating sensations within her that were languid, sweet, and strong. Charllie closed her eyes, and as Sage licked, lapped, and laved the sweetness from her body, she began to feel an incredible pulsing heat that answered the gentle, lapping movement of his tongue. She felt herself being swept away on a current of sensuality, and she couldn't stop it—she didn't want to stop it!

As Sage slowly kissed the honey away from the many sensitive locations found on Charllie, his fingers traced arousing paths of scorching heat down her feverish body. She was totally pliant, and as her body continued to throb from the constant assault of her senses, her reactions became slightly more frenzied. Sage knew that her passion was frantically seeking relief. He slowly gentled her with the warm and passionate kisses that removed the honey from her navel and then her gently rounded belly. Here, delicious passions of their own were also stirred, but they did not evoke the frenzied passion that had ignited at her nipples and raced to between her legs. Yet, though Sage was not physically touching these sensitive areas, Charllie could still feel them throb and swell with need. She tossed and turned, becoming anxious that her heightened senses might never return to normal, that the exquisite heat that was tormenting her would never be doused by a momentous, cooling finale.

Charllie felt that she was gradually going insane with this mysterious need that she had no power to define or control. As Sage gently licked the honey from her warm and responsive body, she felt every nuance of his desperate love. Her body craved his fevered touch with a sharp hunger; it was set on fire with the ministrations of his tongue, but it was nowhere near being sated. Her body wanted something more, it desired something more, and it screamed out with need for something more.

Charllie tried to anticipate his next foray against her passion-slicked body, but she could not. The touch of his fingertips, each lap of his moist velvet tongue, and the warmth of his breath sent tremors of sweet desire throughout her entire body. She craved his ministrations even while she was slowly being consumed by the ravenous flames of love and desire, flames she prayed he would soon be able to douse.

As Sage very slowly and sensuously moved down the length of her body, Charllie pleaded with him, “Please stop, Sage. I don’t know what you are doing to me, but I am so overwhelmed. I wish for it to end!”

But Charllie’s moans and gasps of pleasure gave lie to the fact that she wished it to end so soon. Her soft and fervent pleas to end her pain, to make the blessed agony cease, continued. She moaned Sage’s name with blatant entreaties that, when spoken aloud, shocked her. But her whole body was in the throes of some mysterious, magnificent passion, and she no longer recognized this woman who was so distraught with need. She felt that she would die if this feverish agony did not end in some final resolution.

"It won't be long now, Sweetheart," Sage gently answered her. He slowly eased himself down her body until his mouth was now whispering against her mound.

Charllie gasped in horror, and she tried in desperation to withdraw herself from his seeking mouth. Then Sage's warm tongue plunged between her pouting lower lips, and it quickly sought the moist nub, which was already swollen with desire. Charllie knew that she was totally lost, and she felt herself beginning to melt. Sage's tongue began to rhythmically stroke her, and like tinder to flame, Charllie began to feel herself beginning to slowly ignite once more. She shirked away her cloak of modesty and repulsion, replacing it with an overwhelming addiction to the desire that coursed through her veins. She would not beg him to stop, for all her senses cried out for more.

Charllie felt her passion expand and swell and increase at every lap of his plundering tongue. Not knowing what to expect, and fearful of these new and overwhelming sensations, she moaned and bucked—feeling like she was riding the bare back of some magnificent stallion. The wild and spirited ride was worth any danger or repercussions that might follow from the foolhardy venture, and it must continue. It was a splendidly erotic matter of life and death. If the ride continued, and no destination came in sight, she knew without a doubt that she would die.

Charllie recoiled as a sharp surge of electric desire struck her, spurring her passion to new heights. Sage had provoked temptation with his honey gathering, and charged currents wildly pulsed as Charllie experienced both exquisite pain and pleasure. She now envisioned herself as an orange-red bloom of honeysuckle availing itself to a persistent hummingbird, intent upon emptying it of all its sweetness. She opened herself to it, and the warm and increasingly greedy bird continued to lap the honey as it sent tremors of lightning within; she felt her very core turn molten, with heat and sweetness painfully intermingling.

Extreme desire held Charllie in its throes, racing her to heights where nothing but this agonizing, sweet torture had ever existed. Nothing mattered but the honey within her body and the tongue that plundered it with flames of fire. The waves of desire built and built until she thought she could absolutely endure no more, and still she felt the desire continue to build. And then, she heard herself boldly cry out in delight and wonderment as this heightened pleasure exploded in sweetly violent waves of cresting delight that consumed her in flames. Fires that had just recently been the cause of her torment abruptly subsided, mercifully dousing her desire with repletion. The warmth from her passion gradually dissolved and slowly ebbed away, leaving her with the gentle waves of warmth that receded in sweet ripples of repose. She had been consumed, and now she was drained. Charllie had briefly spied Heaven, and she would never be the same!

Charllie lay there, numbed by the fleeing desire and the newness of the passion that Sage had aroused. She felt embarrassed that he had been able to evoke such wanton behavior from her, feeling ashamed of the unladylike manner that had been provoked. She had done little if anything to protect her own honor the whole time. She felt a criminal, a willing accomplice. What he must think of her, she could but guess. In quickly scanning the time spent with Sage in her mind, she was aghast to realize that the entire episode had evoked nothing but her own pleasure and an exciting awakening. She had been at first a most unwilling victim, but a victim too soon transformed into a more than willing participant.

The entire experience had been a true epiphany, an epiphany of both love and desire. She felt that she had been reborn as a woman who had come to grips with the desire with which she had been born. So many mysteries had all at once been answered, but so many remained. She should be experiencing feelings of anger, revulsion, and loss. But she wasn't. She felt euphoric, joyful, and replete. She felt like a woman who had come into her own. She felt like a woman in love!

Charllie looked up to gauge Sage's response to all that had recently transpired between them, but he was no longer nearby. She finally saw him in a corner of darkness, seemingly gathering his wits; and she secretly willed him to speak to her—to acknowledge her presence. She huskily whispered his name: once, twice, three times. But it was as if he were totally deaf to her, and his own silence was complete. His normally handsome face had become engulfed by a massive thundercloud of emotion: his brows were solemnly knit together, and his once warm, sensuous mouth was severe and compressed.

Sage had sought to find some semblance of finality to a most untenable situation, to allow free rein to a desire which had been tamped down for years, to show Charllie what true passion can be like between a man and a woman. He had hoped to free her from his brother's ties, ties that had been both false and inadequate. Instead, he had found only a true hell of his own making. It was a hell in which he had sullied the innocence of the one woman who absolutely meant the world to him. She was the one person who was in total control of any happiness that he could ever hope to realize.

He had wanted so much to forge ties of love with Charllie. Instead, he had done everything in his power to ensure there would forever be an insurmountable chasm between them.

Slow, torturous moments passed, moments in which Sage stood aloof and silent, but eventually he rejoined Charllie. He savagely cut the cords that bound her, cursing softly as he flung them to the far corners of the hut. Then he tenderly brought some semblance of order to her clothing as he buttoned, straightened, and smoothed her underclothes and her gown—treating her much as one dressing a small child might. His fingertips brushed her errant curls back into place, and they lingered for a brief, tender moment on her lips. He slowly backed away and stood erect, scrutinizing the results, but Charllie could see that there was much regret in his every move and action. At last, when he finally deemed Charllie respectable for her return trip back into society, he helped her up from the bed as he continued to smooth the wrinkles from her gown.

Straightening, Charllie looked up at him imploringly, willing him to speak, to explain, to give emotionally of himself. Only prolonged silence was elicited. Sage walked over and extinguished the candle, and retrieved his rucksack. Wordlessly, the couple departed from the shack and, in the guise of a gentleman, Sage gently took her arm. Impulsively, Charllie attempted to shrug him away, but then, with a deep inner sadness, she acquiesced and accompanied him to Ebony, where he graciously provided her with a seat behind him once more.

The intimacy, which they had so recently shared, now tormented them both like a black, suffocating cloud, and it continued to plague them on what seemed to be the longest, loneliest journey back to their estates. Charllie thought about

Sage's promise to retain her virginity, and she realized he had meticulously kept that vow. Physically, no one could ever question her purity. For all intents and purposes, she was a virgin and would remain so until her wedding night. But she was most definitely no longer innocent, nor was she untouched by any man. Sage's prediction had come true. From now on, and forever more, a part of her would always be his.

Charllie could not understand why she was not feeling particularly happy or comforted by her remaining virginity, but she knew that in her heart of hearts their recent lovemaking had forged ties that encompassed far more than the actual mating ritual that normally took place on a wedding night. Their afternoon in the hut had involved an intimacy that spoke a language of pure love and desire that could never again be fully replicated by either of them with anyone else. It had been a sharing that had transcended time and place, and it had brought them together in a once-in-a-lifetime meeting of two bruised hearts. She knew that Sage had been right when he said that she would always remember this day, regardless of where she was or whom she was with. She would never ever be able to forget this day or this man. This truth brought her unspeakable pain, as well as boundless joy. Though her body was intact and remained pure, that was not the case with her soul— it no longer belonged to her alone. And so much of her rejoiced in that. Yet so much between them was left unresolved.

Chapter Sixteen

Two weeks had passed since the episode in the hut, and Charllie had immersed herself in numerous plantation duties. The entire episode with Sage had been disturbing, eye-opening, earth-shattering, and memorable. She could not think about it without feeling sexual stirrings, tender memories, and a bit of guilt and shame. She felt, however, that it had been an epiphany of magnificent proportions—that her body and soul had blossomed into a woman that day. Charllie had finally begun to come into her own as a woman, and she had been forced to see the world as a vibrant, forward-moving environment in which she must take part if she wished to capture and enjoy the true beauty of it. Not one day went by that she did not think back to the bittersweet rendezvous with Sage, a day in which she had been totally overwhelmed by desire and emotion.

Charllie had hoped that Sage would call upon her at home to discuss what his motives had been that day, and to allay her fears that this new beginning was nothing more than a precursor to the demise of their relationship. She secretly prayed that he did genuinely love her, and never once did she completely attribute his seduction to malice or vengeance—knowing full well that his feelings were far more complicated than that. She had realized for a long time how he felt about her, but her stubbornness in maintaining an ongoing allegiance to Thomas, a Thomas who had never truly existed, had been totally misguided. Charllie had finally begun to recognize her genuine stirrings of love for Sage within herself, stirrings that had begun long before the incident at the hut. Everything had culminated in her recognition that she had, in fact, chosen the wrong brother as the object of her affections.

She had been wronged by Thomas but had been too blinded by romance at the time to recognize the error of her ways. And then, years after Thomas's death, she had been positively hurtful to Sage, mistreating and maligning him, even when he had continued to profess his love and affection for her. Her world had been out of kilter for so long that she was now most anxious to right it so that she could embrace life and all the sweet fruits it might possibly bear. Unfortunately, she had no idea what needed to be done to correct their blighted romantic history. Sage seemed to have disappeared, indicating that he was now reluctant to meet with her so that a reconciliation could take place.

Charllie, totally at a loss as to what she could do about her quandary, knew she needed to keep busy, or she would go insane. Summer was on the wane, and autumn was just around the corner. She set about drying herbs, making preserves, plying her needle to winter bedding, and planting an autumn garden. The plantation buzzed with activity: wood was cut and stacked, Mrs. Wright busily knitted stockings, Aunt Bethany packed away the summer clothing, and the last fruits of autumn were canned, dried, or pickled. The house took on a more somber look as the winter drapes were hung, evening fires were lit, and wooden bowls of plums, pears, and early apples were placed on the buffet. Charllie was involved in it all.

Charllie welcomed the additional activity, but she always found the time to explore her newly discovered feelings for Sage. She allowed herself the precious time necessary to finally reject the tender feelings she had once held for Thomas. The prolonged grief that had once guided her sheltered life had come to a most abrupt end, and she began to get on with her life—a life in which she hoped Sage Danbury would one day play a major role.

Over the summer and into the fall months, Charllie dried many bunches of herbs, flowers, and grasses. They had been hung in the attic and were now dry, yet they still retained much color and a strong whisper of their fragrance. She spread out the dried flowers and grasses on the dining room table and began to fashion arrangements for the many vases she had set out. They would add cheer to the dining room, parlor, and bedrooms during the dreary days of autumn and winter. Charllie noticed a sadness and poignancy that surrounded her bouquets, for they reminded her of lost love. With a sigh, she thought of what she and Sage might have shared together had she not been so blinded by Thomas's duplicity and had Sage not been totally consumed by anger and jealousy over Charllie's continued ties to his deceased brother.

As Charllie placed her arrangements throughout the house, she wistfully thought of a future spring when very real flowers, not these dried shadows of bloom, would once again adorn the gardens and dooryard. She wondered what the new year would bring and if she would ever realize her dreams of marriage and family. The low sun slanted its final rays onto the dining room buffet, and the dried yarrow shone celestial gold for a moment before the evening shadows convened. Charllie began to set the table with plates and silverware; her thoughts were as somber as the late day had become.

***

The very next morning, Charllie made a memorable trip to the Danbury cemetery, where she made her formal good-byes to Thomas. As she walked around his stone, her mind chose to skirt around the fact that their engagement had been based on duplicity. Chastising him at this late date would only be counterproductive. Instead, she chose to forgive him for attempting to forge a life for himself without taking her needs into consideration. She knew that his death on the battlefield had actually freed her to live an honest life, which would hopefully be based on love and common desires shared with his very own brother, whose heart was far truer and accessible than his had been. It was fine to grieve over Thomas, for he had lost life's battle without being given the time to live it. In many ways, he was to be pitied, for he had been deemed worthy of roles that would never suit him. Both he and his future wife would have been made miserable by society's dictates.

Charllie had already boxed Thomas' brooch and engagement ring and buried them at the very bottom of the old leather trunk sequestered in the attic. They were nestled in the original red box, in which Thomas had presented them, under piles of vintage clothing, memorabilia, and numerous journals. Perhaps in the years to come, some ancestor would discover these *buried treasures* and delight in them as keepsakes from the past. For now, they no longer existed for Charllie; they were devoid of any meaning and had become nothing more than baubles that could only remind her of insincerity and deceit.

Charllie bent over the red clay soil in the graveyard, pulled a stray weed or two, and then finally straightened up to survey the burial plot. Thomas was interred with many generations of his family, but he no longer held a place in Charllie's heart. He had totally abdicated his power. This tender spot in Charllie's heart had recently gone to someone far more deserving. As she turned to walk away, she knew that she had finally found closure for this chapter in her life. She felt reborn, free, and anxious to begin anew.

She looked across at Danbury Dell, hoping to catch a glimpse of Sage, perhaps riding Ebony, walking with his mother down a shaded garden path, or conversing with his plantation manager. But the place looked deserted. The dogwoods were just beginning to show a tinge of maroon, and the white ducks swam disconsolately around the pond's perimeter. For a moment, Charllie felt panic. Had their love been destroyed before it had even had a chance to bloom? She had never seriously considered Sage's interest in her as a life partner, foolishly distancing herself from the very person who eagerly stood by—eager to provide her with all of life's precious treasures: love, children, and home. How sad that she had been instrumental in not only blighting her own life, but also blighting his. She wondered if she would ever be able to forgive herself.

So much of what Charllie had once believed in as being true had been destroyed. Thank goodness for that because Thomas's love and loyalty had been nothing more than a sham.

Thankfully, they had not had the opportunity to go through with the marriage, for she would have taken her place as a devoted wife and probably mother; but her husband's heart would have always been elsewhere. She shuddered. The cold pond mirrored the gray clouds whose sterile shadows floated below, casting silver ripples that lapped at the stone-cold shore. A blue heron dipped for fish, but finding none, took wing and flew to a nearby copse.

Charllie glanced at the gardening implements in her hands, and she marveled at the countless hours she had spent at the gravesite to commemorate a *hero* who had never truly existed, and she thought with revulsion how he had planned for their future together. She also shuddered when she re-examined how she had mistreated the younger brother.

Sage, whom Charllie had come to totally overlook, had remained true to her all these years, with little hope that she would ever return his love. And his love was based not on his heart and constancy alone but included a searing passion that was barely restrained by convention and sensibility. For one dark moment in time, an overriding anger had been allowed to set precedence over his actions. Having been spurned for years by his one true love, his passion for her had been unleashed, causing him to be wild and reckless in his initiation of love with Charllie. But, even in losing all restraint, he protected her virginity—taking only memories for himself while imparting a precious awakening for her. The deep and abiding love that he continued to feel for her could not be ignored.

Sage's passion had burst the righteous bounds of civilization, but in its stead, an almost pagan belief in the power of desire had goaded him to awaken her passion. In doing so, he had gifted her with pleasure born of love, the most precious treasure that can ever be given to a woman by a man who loves her. Sage had established his own creed, worshipping Charllie by giving her ecstasy beyond all her dreams while denying physical pleasure for himself. He had been truthful when he said that part of her would always be his. The memories of her sexual awakening would stay with both for a lifetime.

Charllie knew that her surrender that day in the hut had been total and complete, and it was a forever surrender. The velvet ties that had bound her to the bed had only been symbolic because the true ties that now bound Charllie to Sage were those of the heart. The passion that had taken place had erased the falsehoods of the past and allowed for another love—one which was constant and true. There would never be another man who could arouse Charllie's love, passion, and desire as Sage could; for the love she felt for him was deep and everlasting. There could be no other. Not now. Not ever.

***

The days flew by, and Charllie was caught up in the mad rush of life, even though her own personal life seemed to float listlessly within an eddy. Some of her friends' lives, however, were full to overflowing with joy, and they wished to share them with friends and family. Charllie was invited to an anniversary party, an engagement party, and later in the month, the christening of Abigail Cory's daughter, Grace. She looked forward to experiencing a full social calendar, for it took her mind off Sage's absence.

Abigail Cory was ecstatic with the arrival of her newborn daughter, and well she should be. The child was adorable, and she had quickly wrapped both her mother and father around her tiny finger. Abigail and her husband Seth had gone from a couple to a family in a matter of minutes, and yet neither one seemed to be able to remember what life had been like before the presence of little Grace. They were truly infatuated, and it wasn't hard to understand why.

Baby Grace was precious: her baby cheeks plump and pink, her light brown curls soft and fine, and her chortles and coos delightful. Charllie felt rather envious of her childhood friend, for she couldn't help but wonder if she herself would ever be similarly blessed. Since falling in love with Sage, she had begun to ache to become his wife and bear his children, and she now envisioned a child with ebony locks, emerald green eyes, and a devil-may-care grin. She held Abigail's daughter in her arms, and the child became her child, and Sage's. She wondered at the rapid change in her own nature: the strong up-swelling of maternal instinct and the incessant waves of maddening desire that she felt in relationship to the man who had nurtured so many physical longings.

Charllie agonized over how blind she had been for such a long period of time, overlooking and mistreating the one true love who had always been her champion and close friend. She thought with sadness of Thomas's betrayal and willingness to deceive, even knowing that their very marriage would have pronounced Charllie a victim of his lies. But it was now only with joy, tinged with more than a bit of wistfulness, that she thought of Sage.

***

On the third Saturday in October, Charllie hosted a surprise tea party for Hattie Mae's sixty-second birthday. The family had arranged for Hattie to take the pony trap into town early in the morning to purchase some thread, paraffin, and pickling salt. Not a soul had even mentioned that it was her birthday. While she was gone, they had worked their magic. Hattie had arrived home to an uproarious welcome from friends and family, and she exclaimed at the tables laden with refreshments and gifts.

The tables were spread out beneath the bronzed oak trees in the backyard and were covered with multi-colored tablecloths. Cold platters of sliced ham, rolls and freshly churned butter, mixed pickles, an enormous spice cake, and gallons of cold apple cider and hot mint tea were set out with the gifts and the many bouquets of late hydrangea that Charllie had artfully arranged. Hattie Mae's cousin had brought his trusty old fiddle, and its golden strings permeated the early afternoon air. A few small children practiced some comical dance steps on the back stoop, some of the older children went off to play a pickup game of croquet, and the buzz of happy conversation amongst neighbors, relatives, and plantation workers drifted across the lawn.

Charllie felt pleased that the day was progressing so well. She soon found Hattie surrounded by family and friends. "Congratulations, Hattie Mae. I hope you were able to find everything in town." Charllie smiled.

"Child, you sent me on a wild goose chase, and that's all there is to it! Had I known you all were planning such fine festivities, I would have done more to fix myself up than to just remove my apron! I never expected such a fine show in tribute to these old bones. My, doesn't everything look so nice, and smell so good!"

Charllie knew that Hattie would always treasure this day. Seeing that many others wanted to wish her well, she gave her one final hug. "Hattie, you deserve every little bit of happiness that this old world can give you. Enjoy your birthday celebration! You know you deserve it."

"Bless you, child! You have truly done me proud. This is a day I will remember for as long as I have breath. I know you have lots to do, Charllie. I will make it a point to catch up with you later."

Charllie began to scan the assembled guests because she was looking for one special person. She finally saw the Danburys, Theodore and Evelyn. They were taking tea with her mother over near the mulberry tree, but as she walked over to greet them, she quickly discovered that their son was not with them. Charllie felt her spirits plummet.

"Mr. and Mrs. Danbury, so good to see. It has been too long since we last met. I hope you've both been well. Sage has been making himself scarce at Oak Haven, and I thought he might be joining us today." Charllie had taken Evelyn Danbury's hands within her own and gently squeezed them. She had always held nothing but love and respect for Sage's parents.

"We had hoped so, too, Charlotte. Unfortunately, he has been so immersed in the doings of our plantation these days that we hardly see him ourselves. That boy seems so intent upon making up lost time for all that went begging for attention during the war. He works from dawn to dusk every day of the week but Sunday. He could certainly use a day of leisure, but neither my husband nor I had any luck in swaying his decision not to attend Bethany's birthday celebration."

"Please tell him that I was asking for him, will you?" Charllie didn't want to sound too interested, for she knew that the elder Danburys were not privy to the drama that was playing out between Sage and her, but she did want Sage to know firsthand that he was in her thoughts. *Goodness, how she missed him!*

"We certainly will, dear. I'm sure that Sage will have second thoughts about missing such a lovely party. We're so pleased that you thought to invite all of us, and we will certainly tell him you sent your regards."

Charllie smiled, a bit wistfully. "Mother, please take good care of our neighbors. Make sure they have a comfortable seat where they can relax and enjoy the day. Would anyone like another cup of tea or a slice of cake?"

Sophia answered for both the Danburys and herself, "I think we'll wait until after we've made our rounds with introductions and greetings, Charllie. But thank you so much for offering. You may wish to remind our guests that Hattie Mae will be opening her gifts soon. I know the young children always enjoy watching in suspense, curious to discover what lies beneath all the wrappings."

Charllie nodded her head to acknowledge her mother's instructions and then moved on to mingle with the crowd. She felt downhearted, sadly only going through the motions now. She had so hoped that her handwritten invitation would have enticed the entire family to attend the birthday celebration. Charllie had so looked forward to finally seeing Sage again. She walked over to the refreshment table and began to assist with serving cider and tea while reminding her guests that Hattie would be opening her gifts very soon.

Sage had become such an integral part of Charllie's life that, even though they continued their lives apart, his presence on earth filled her with love, light, and hope. She knew that she was acting totally moonstruck and that it was not logical, nor probably even quite sane, to spend so much time thinking about him. But like the fly that is fatally trapped in the spider's gossamer web, Charllie's body and soul were lovingly caught in breathless anticipation, waiting for the acknowledgment of Sage's affections.

Charllie watched Hattie Mae open her birthday presents, and she feigned interest and delight, but her thoughts were far away with the man of *ice and honey*. Hattie held up a beautifully crafted teapot, and Charllie remembered sipping tea by the edge of the stream with Sage. A new candlestick brought memories of the candle that had glimmered by the bed while she was in the throes of a relentless passion on that one forbidden afternoon. And a handmade comforter reminded her of the quilt, which had cushioned them in the dark depths of the slave hut. Other gifts were opened, but Charllie was already lost in reverie. The memories were bittersweet and stirred many conflicting emotions. However, all were overshadowed by her love for Sage and how she had missed him over the past two months.

Charllie attempted gaiety while assisting Hattie in disposing of the gift wrappings. "Looks like Christmas has already come and gone with this haul you made today, Hattie Mae. Are you sure you're going to find a place for all of this in your house?"

"I'm not sure, honey, but I'm surely going to try. I feel positively rich—like a queen! Have you ever seen so much fine stuff? And have you ever seen such a crowd for a plantation cook's birthday? This is certainly a day I won't soon forget. You must be pleased as punch, Charllie. You and your mother have certainly done me proud today."

"Oh, Hattie Mae, you're dearly loved by many, here and all about these parts. You've been bringing more casseroles to funerals and soups for illness than I can count. Probably birthed almost as many babies as Doc Brown. And there's never been anyone than can make medicine from the herb patch as good as you. Doing good deeds and going the extra mile for neighbors have made you a very important lady. You have a right to expect good things now and again, especially when you're such a sweetheart."

"Child, you're sweet-talking me now. When you was a little girl, I always knew when you had been up to some mischief cause your tongue would just about drip honey. I would always know when you were using flattery for some purpose. But I thank you anyways! By the way, I haven't seen your young man here today."

Sage was most definitely avoiding her, of that, Charllie was convinced. "According to the Danburys, Hattie, Sage has been up to his elbows with work on the Danbury plantation. Seems he is trying to catch up on all those projects that were left begging during the war. He wasn't able to get away today, but he sent his best wishes along. By the way, who told you he was my man?"

"Just a little bird, Charllie honey. That boy does nothing but work these days. I used to see him visiting here often, but lately he has become as scarce as hen's teeth. Any fly in the ointment between you two, Charlotte? Something just doesn't seem right."

"Not as far as I know, Hattie, but I'll keep you informed. Just don't hold your breath about Sage being my man. Right now, I would settle for a good friend." Charllie maintained a façade of levity, hugged Hattie Mae one more time, and then left her to wander the yard alone.

***

Charllie attended a few small parties and gatherings in the neighborhood over the next few weeks, but Sage's presence was never forthcoming at any of these either. Prior to each event, she had taken special care with her dress and hair, hoping that he would be in attendance and that he would seek her out, courting her as he had not deemed appropriate in the past. She considered sending him a letter, but decided against it. Sage was not keeping busy at Danbury Dell out of necessity; he was keeping busy out of misplaced guilt. She'd lay money on it.

Charllie's cheeks still flamed in embarrassment when she remembered how she had reacted to Sage's touch in the slave hut. She would not confirm her unladylike conduct with a bold and presumptuous personal note, especially one that was unsolicited. Whatever he might think of her, she would not compound her misconduct with additional unbecoming behavior. They would meet again—soon, she hoped. Only this time, Mr. Sage Danbury would not be the pursuer. Charllie was not willing to leave her future happiness up to fate or a reluctant suitor.

Chapter Seventeen

In early November, Charllie had the honor of receiving a gentleman caller, Mr. Percy Atwater, who stopped by to thank her for having introduced him to the incomparable Miss Phoebe Somerset.

Once Percy had been ushered into the parlor, he wasted no time in addressing Charllie with his wonderful news. "Miss Charlotte, you need to know how grateful Phoebe and I are after you introduced us at the birthday ball. Phoebe and I have most recently become engaged, and we are already planning a spring wedding."

"Why, Percy, that is such wonderful news! You must realize, however, that I was far from being your personal matchmaker. Sage Danbury was far more instrumental in your introductions than I. But none of that really matters. I am as pleased as punch that the two of you have become engaged. Isn't this a bit precipitous?"

Percy looked down at his hands, and then his eyes finally drew level with Charllie's. "Sometimes it just happens that way, Charllie. One moment we were total strangers, and the next—the best of friends. And, before we knew it, we had deep feelings for one another. It's hard to explain, but we soon realized that we do not want to live apart. Both of us have been lonely for far too long. And when we met, we just clicked. You know what I mean?"

"Yes, Percy. Somehow, I think I do know what you mean."

Percy continued, "The war lasted such a long time, and so many people were forced to put their lives on hold. It seems Phoebe and I had both done the same. We're older now, and we both know what we want. We've both been anxious to find a marriage partner, to establish a home, and to start a family. When we found each other, we soon realized that we could make each other's dreams come true. Neither one of us wants to waste precious time with a lengthy engagement, and, though we plan to have a very nice wedding, we aren't set on one that is overly elaborate, costly, and time-consuming. And, believe it or not, Charllie—both of us are really and truly in love. I guess you'd say that we are anxious to be husband and wife." Percy blushed and spent a bit of time nervously reshaping the brim of his hat

"Percy, I'm positively thrilled for both of you! You make a wonderful couple, and I couldn't be happier." Percy would never know just how happy Charllie really was in seeing the one woman in Sage's life who could consistently spark her jealously being promised to another in marriage. She had never received such wonderful news!

Shyly, Percy responded to Charllie's well wishes, "Phoebe and I would be honored if you would set aside the date for our upcoming engagement party. Phoebe is having the formal invitations printed, but we know that it is rather last-minute notice. We wanted to give everyone time to make their plans. I've already stopped by Danbury Dell on my way here to inform Sage of our betrothal and the engagement party, and I did extend my thanks to him as well for doing his part in introducing us. He didn't immediately commit himself, but I'm very hopeful that he might be able to arrange his schedule to be there as well."

At the mention of Sage, Charllie resisted the impulse to question Mr. Atwater further. *How did he look? Did he ask about me? Was he well? Why has he failed to call upon me?* She squelched all latent stirrings that the mention of his name brought forth and, though it was painful, she went ahead and offered Percy refreshments and casual conversation for half an hour prior to his leave-taking.

Percy finally stood up to go and, as he prepared to don his hat, he thanked Charllie for her hospitality, "I really must take my leave, Charllie. I promised Mother that I would complete my rounds this day. I have enjoyed my visit so much and look forward to seeing you at our party. Take care, and send my best wishes to your parents and brother and his family. By the way, they are all invited as well. Have a good day now!"

Charllie breathed a sigh of relief as she walked him to the door. It was difficult experiencing someone else's joy while watching from the sidelines, wishing that your own life could find such happy parallels. Was there even a possibility that someday she, too, might hope to plan her own nuptials with the love of her life?

***

Charllie knew she should be recalling their last day together in the hut with shock, revulsion, and hostility. But she could not be a hypocrite. With the revelation of Thomas's betrayal, she had finally looked at Sage with a fresh, new perspective. She understood how her treatment of him over the past two years, and even before that, must have eroded his confidence, his sense of self, and his plans for a future. She could imagine how his love for her had turned to anger when she constantly rejected him and reviled him. Charllie knew in her heart that Sage had most probably been aware of Thomas's betrayal as well, but he had protected Thomas's good name nonetheless with the selfless love of a brother. Not once had he ever tried to come between them. He had most probably been forced to come to grips with the cost of that selfless love and his inability to successfully press his suit with Charllie, the woman he himself had hopelessly desired to marry one day.

Charllie couldn't help but feel a bit selfish, callous, and mean for her past conduct, but she realized that she, too, had been a victim, an innocent one at that. She felt both pride and anger that Sage had most probably kept the knowledge of Thomas's dual life from her, but she knew that what he had done had been the honorable thing to do, even though it had prevented them from following the true leanings of their hearts.

"If Sage does indeed love me, why has he given up the fight so easily? Why hasn't he continued to press his suit? Why hasn't he persisted in trying to woo me to make me his wife? And now, why is he distancing himself from me when all I want is to be with him? I will never understand why he completely gave up on our chance to find true love."

Finally, it dawned on Charlotte through the subtle strains of a woman's intuition. Sage was overwrought and feeling self-recrimination for having despoiled her innocence that day in the slave hut. He felt that when he had taken her hostage and ravished her that he had irrevocably destroyed all his rights and privileges to respectfully choose her for his own. He was feeling guilty for losing self-control, for planning a rendezvous where he planned seduction—lavishing her with so many of the pent-up emotions that he had been forced to bury beneath his role as a gentleman. Forcing his affections upon her, someone whom he dearly loved but who did not seem to return his love, had been his only opportunity to show her what passion might be between lovers while also giving him at least a taste of his own heart's desire.

Charllie scoffed as she followed her thoughts through to the end. "The poor, misguided man cannot see that he has, without a doubt, won his heart's desire because he has never been made privy to my knowledge of Thomas's deceit. He does not know that I have finally realized that all my affections are now tied to him, not Thomas. He must think that I now view him as an absolute criminal, a blackguard of the worst kind. I am sure that he sees himself as one who sullies the purity of virgins, having corrupted my innocence with his lovemaking. In truth, I now view our memorable day together as an epiphany, a bright new beginning free from Thomas's hold."

The only bondage that had been harmful and destructive to Charllie had been the self-imposed ties that she had willingly accepted in grieving unnecessarily for Thomas. She was now a woman who could reason, feel desire, and make decisions for her own future—a future in which she hoped that Sage Danbury would become predominant. Charllie could only hope that Sage did indeed continue to love her as strongly as he once had.

Charllie knew that Sage was wrong in placing so much of the blame upon himself for what had happened between them. They had both been Thomas's pawns. Without their knowledge and against their wills, they had played his sordid little game. And he had almost ruined both of their lives. Now, however, Thomas was dead, and his lies had been exposed. He was forgiven, remembered, but no longer directing the future of either plantation.

"It is time for Sage to stop feeling guilty for any misbegotten deeds of the past and to look to the future. In fact, it is long overdue. I know that I love Sage . . . with all my heart. I have always loved him. The velvet cords with which he bound me that day would never have been strong enough to totally subdue me had I truly wanted to escape. I was mesmerized, curious, and reluctantly willing. I know that now without a doubt. Sage probably presumes that I am now nursing my anger, totally outraged over the "ordeal" that he put me through while, in fact, I was most grateful for the wondrous epiphany of the miracle of love that I had been allowed to experience."

"I am truthfully very disappointed that Sage has not immediately renewed his pursuit. Men! Do they not understand that women sometimes take the prerogative to change their minds? And now that he is totally avoiding me, perhaps I will never get the opportunity to let him know about my change of heart. Therein lies my dilemma!"

If Sage had given up the pursuit and retreated to hide in his shell, it was up to Charllie to remedy the situation. After all, she was partly to blame for the huge misunderstanding. She had not had the time nor the opportunity to share important intimacies with Sage during the picnic prior to the seduction, when she could have so easily resolved the misunderstanding of changing loyalties that lay between them. She had not taken the time to inform him earlier that afternoon because she had not wanted to spoil the rather congenial mood that the couple had first experienced. Sage had discouraged her as well because he had assumed that, once again, she was about to proclaim Thomas's many virtues. And this, of course, had allowed his anger to ignite one more time. A lost opportunity had jettisoned love and understanding.

"Will it never end? Now this immense gulf exists between us. How will we ever begin to bridge it?"

Charllie had been almost relieved that she had never discussed Thomas's deceit with Sage, for she had lived in the hope that they could start a new life together without sullying another's name. Yet maybe truth and honesty are always the bedrock from which enduring love must spring. Perhaps it was time for them to lay all their cards on the table. Perhaps desperate measures needed to be answered by even more desperate means.

"Could the upcoming party for Percy and Phoebe be the catalyst for an important showdown? I really don't know. But I do hope that sooner or later I will have the opportunity to let Sage know my true feelings, and that what he finally does with them will be totally up to him. I can only pray that his feelings of love for me are as strong as mine are for him, and that they have not been diminished by time and circumstance."

***

Shortly after Percy Atwater's visit, the formal invitation Charllie had been waiting for arrived at the Wrights. It requested the presence of the family at an engagement party being held by the Somersets for Miss Phoebe Somerset and Mr. Percy Atwater. The party would be hosted by Phoebe's parents in the Somerset mansion. Charllie smiled, for she certainly had absolutely no animosity toward Phoebe now. At one time, she had seen Phoebe as a formidable rival for Sage's affections, but that was when she had still harbored confused loyalties between the two brothers.

She wondered, "Just how long have I deluded myself into believing all that claptrap about *only one true love*, or has my own one true love always been Sage? Have I been too besotted and confused to recognize it? Maybe Phoebe and

Percy's party will give me the opportunity I need to rekindle my relationship with Sage. I can but hope."

Charllie spent the next day exploring the huge wardrobe in the attic, looking for something that she could wear to the engagement party. The weather had turned far too cool for her new silk gown, and besides, Sage had already seen her in that gown. In the very back of the wardrobe, she found what she had been looking for, a becoming sapphire blue velvet gown. She held the gown in front of herself, remembering that she had worn it years ago when she had been a bridal attendant in her brother Frank's late autumn wedding.

The gown had kept well, and though the velvet was slightly crushed in a few inconspicuous places, it could undoubtedly be revived by a damp cloth and a good airing. Charllie had been slightly heavier the last time that she had worn it, so, hopefully, Aunt Bethany could be persuaded to take in a few nips and tucks at the seams. It was hoped that with a fresh new ribbon around the bodice and perhaps a lowering of the neckline that the velvet gown could be refashioned and brought back to its original charm. The style was simple, yet very feminine. When she tried it on, both Aunt Beth and her mother had exclaimed just how becoming it looked on Charllie. She knew that she could count on both women to give her further creative ideas for adding fresh, decorative touches to her dated gown.

Charllie wanted to look her very best if Sage should be there. The gown itself would really be of little importance, for what she really hoped for was that he still held tender feelings towards her and that he would finally come forward again to begin the process of claiming her as his own. She smiled with rapture as she imagined his strong arms guiding her in the intricate steps of a dance.

***

The engagement party for Phoebe Somerset and Percy Atwater was scheduled to take place on the first Saturday in December. The day had been gray and blustery. Rain clouds had threatened but not delivered. The meadows and copses had been drenched by the rain of two days past, and the trees hung their heads with clinging leaves that refused to succumb to the bitter approach of winter by dropping to the ground. A pale lemon sun peered through the horizon in the scant few hours left until nightfall. The dreary outdoors, however, had very little to do with the atmosphere within the Wright home. Lamps, candles, and fires chased away the gloom, and all was hustle and bustle within.

Mr. and Mrs. Wright were already dressed and ready to depart, but they kept their own counsel. Aunt Bethany, attired in her Sunday-go-to-meeting best dress, placed a pot of tea and matching teacups before them in the parlor where they continued to reminisce about past balls and engagement parties. They knew that Charllie had not completed her toilette, and God forbid any parent who tried to hurry that process along. While they were pleasantly chatting, they smiled at the noisy activity that could be heard filtering down the staircase. Charllie was most certainly *in a mood* this evening, and one only had to guess the reason why. Charles lifted his wife's hand to his lips for a gentle kiss and then winked.

"I wonder if Charllie's *mood* has anything to do with a certain childhood friend?" Mr. Wright wondered aloud. "It seems that Mr. Sage Danbury has been making himself noticeably scarce over the past few weeks. An ominous sign, my dear. An ominous sign."

Sophia's round cheeks dimpled, and her eyes shone with youthful glee. "Oh, I certainly do hope so, Mr. Wright. Those two have been meant for each other ever since they were little, running about the estates chasing the ducks, fishing the creeks, and capturing butterflies. It's a pity that it has taken them so long to recognize it. They were always so compatible, yet both are so outrageously independent and stubborn. Those two have never been able to see the forest for the trees. But there's one thing that puzzles me, Charles. Just who do you think is doing the chasing? Of that I am positively unclear."

Charles Wright chuckled. "Well, Sophia, in my mind it really makes very little difference as to who is doing the chasing, for the final outcome is really all that matters. However, at this point, my money's on Charllie, and God spare the man who tries to get in her way when she's determined. For him, I have nothing but pity. Mark my words, Sage will one day find himself with a wife who holds sway over his every move. You can count on his days of bachelorhood, if my predictions run true, as soon being nothing more than a fleeting memory."

"Pshaw, Charles. Somehow, I fail to ever see Sage as a henpecked husband, even with our Charllie. He is one headstrong young gentleman, and, if anyone can tame the wildness out of our daughter, it is he. Somehow, I feel they are totally deserving of one another. Their life together will certainly be a most interesting balancing act, and one that could never, by any stretch of the imagination, be considered dull. Their marriage, at least, might be a wonderful catalyst for rebuilding the two plantations. But I suppose I mustn't get ahead of myself on this." Sophia chuckled as she continued to gauge the presumed romantic conquest and the future ramifications that would link both families to happiness and prosperity.

Charles smiled to himself and thought about how headstrong his own Sophia had been, and still was, yet he wisely kept these thoughts to himself. "It sounds like peace finally reigns above. Perhaps I should request that Beth fetch our wraps for us. Though this tea is delightful, I would certainly enjoy a little stronger libation this evening. The weather has turned cold and damp, and much too suddenly."

Indeed, peace finally did reign above. Charllie stood in front of her looking glass to survey the final results, and, though she was not totally satisfied, she shrugged and felt that the effort expended had made her at least presentable. Truthfully, Charllie looked stunning. Though some of her golden tresses had been caught up in a chignon, the rest had been allowed to flow to her shoulders, where they cascaded in waves and ringlets. The twilight-blue gown was a superb foil for her fair skin, and it accented her brilliant blue eyes. Charllie was wearing a sparkling crystal earring and necklace ensemble that captured the firelight and diffused color and light like a prism. Their crystalline fire, which glowed against the backdrop of the velvet gown, introduced the sun to a midnight landscape where dark and light intermingled dramatically.

Charllie's true beauty, however, seemed to emanate from some undefinable source. This evening, as she posed in front of her mirror, a womanliness in her presence was revealed—exhibited in her full red lips, her sparkling blue eyes, and her barely concealed breasts. Having experienced passion, she would never look the same, feel the same, or be the same. She had taken the first steps across the threshold of womanhood, and she would never again be able to subscribe to the naïve concepts of love once held by her when but a child who dreamed of romance. She had become a real woman in love with a real man.

Charllie had been fortunate enough to find true love and passion, though being able to capture them for her own remained a problem with no solution. Her eyes went soft and her nostrils flared slightly as she recalled what it had felt like to be in the raptures of full-blown desire. Her heart quickened as she recalled strong arms, bruising lips, and a velvet tongue. She felt herself beginning to tingle at the vivid memories of the sensual onslaught that had been the awakening of a lifetime.

Unfortunately, these vivid memories had been thwarted by the circumstances of the situation and subsequent misunderstandings. If Sage was unable or unwilling to rectify the situation, then perhaps she would have to do something about it herself. She caught herself peering into her own eyes and laughed impishly, "And now, Mr. Sage Danbury, may I have this dance?"

To ask a man to partner one at a dance was totally forward and unladylike, but Charllie knew that Sage's defenses were up and, though his walls might seem impenetrable now, perhaps she alone might be able to find a solution that could tear them down. She knew that it would be rather awkward and risky to the extreme, but she was more than willing to sacrifice much to bring about some resolution to this hurtful stalemate. Both she and Sage had so much to lose unless they could begin to find common ground.

The soft velvet folds of Charllie's dress caressed her body with a seductive softness. The velvet was a reminder of the cords Sage had once used to subdue her, but these new, invisible cords of love that Charllie now felt surrounded her very heart and soul. As she crossed the room to find her wrap, the dress whispered and played around her thighs and emanated warmth throughout her body as she dreamed of his kisses of fire, and the drugged passion that had pulsed through her veins by the administered ice and honey. One day, Sage and she must come to an understanding of the heart and soul if they were to pave their way to any kind of happiness. Charllie could only pray that perhaps tonight might be that all-important beginning.

Chapter Eighteen

During the long, cold ride to the engagement party, Charllie chatted amiably with her parents, never once giving them any insight into her secret longings. Had she known they were already privy to the workings of young love, especially regarding their daughter and a Mr. Sage Danbury, she would have been quite surprised, perhaps mildly outraged. All along, she had been congratulating herself on her ability to keep her own life private from the world, overlooking the fact that family often possesses perception and intuition that far outweigh even the talents of a skilled fortuneteller.

Charllie was extremely nervous, and her constant chatter was an outlet for these emotions. She knew what her goals were, but that didn't mean that Sage would agree with them. She knew he had a mind of his own, and perhaps he had totally tired of this game of cat and mouse, deciding it was a game not worth playing. He might have experienced too much hurt to his pride and been shunned by Charllie just one too many times. Perhaps his love had finally chilled and died, or he had found someone else who could reciprocate the love and tenderness he had once felt for her. Charllie shuddered at this final thought and then squared her shoulders, lifted her chin, and mentally prepared for battle. She refused to believe that it was over between them. A bright new future had to be possible.

Entering the hallway at the Somerset residence evoked many memories of the last ball that Charllie had attended. She wondered, somewhat in a panic, if Sage would even attend. He had been able to make himself scarce at any number of social functions recently, functions which she herself had attended. There was no guarantee that he would now deviate from that pattern. And, sadly, Charllie knew that social obligations were almost the only avenue she could count on in the hopes of meeting with him on neutral territory unless he himself chose to approach her at her own home. However, the festive atmosphere quickly dispelled her gloom, and as she handed her wrap to an attendant, she began to get caught up in the evening's gaiety.

The engagement party had just begun, and the rooms were aglow with firelight and candlelight. The aromas of roasting apples and aromatic spices filled the air. Dried flower arrangements with gold accents and bowls of fruit accented the large buffet, which was groaning under the weight of hors d'oeuvres, pastries, and hot and cold punches. Gay chatter and laughter accompanied the merry melody played by a trio of musicians. A few hardy souls had already taken to the dance floor, and it was not yet quite eight o'clock.

Phoebe and Percy approached Charllie, Phoebe a bit more reticent than Percy, as Charllie had always seemed a rather formidable young lady to her. Nonetheless, her welcome was cordial.

"Thank you so much for attending, Charllie. You look absolutely breathtaking this evening." Percy stood proudly at Phoebe's side with his arm linked with hers.

"Thank you for inviting me, Phoebe. You are the one to be congratulated on your attire. What a beautiful gown! You are the belle of the ball this evening, as well you should be. Your satin gown is so unusual and so becoming. In fact, you both make an extremely handsome pair. My congratulations to you both! I am really so happy to be here."

Phoebe and Percy, upon first acquaintance, had seemed like an unlikely couple to Charllie, but, upon getting to know them better, one quickly realized how well they complemented one another. They constantly sought ways in which they could chastely touch one another. When one spoke, the other listened attentively. And both constantly smiled as if they shared a marvelous secret. Charllie felt uplifted just by being in their presence. It was clear that they were of one accord and were quite content in finally having found their lifelong partner.

When the couple moved on to greet other guests, Charllie felt momentarily at a loss. Without an escort of her own and not knowing many of the guests assembled, she wandered over to the fireplace to find an inconspicuous seat. As she gracefully maneuvered through the milling crowd to claim a secluded corner chair, she came face to face with Sage, who was conversing with a young lady who was artfully pursing her red lips and fluttering her dark lashes. Her dark red tresses, Charllie would later swear that they couldn't possibly be nature's gift alone, were a perfect foil for her emerald green gown. An enamel hair comb, which accented her hairstyle, bobbed erratically with her head as she chattered away, emphatically making a point to her charming attendant. Charllie squelched a giggle and proceeded to take a seat just steps beyond their rather intimate location.

Sage had not even acknowledged her presence, and she was not about to intrude on his new friendship, at least she assumed—and hoped—it was a new friendship. Charllie stared into the depths of the fire, and she became slightly aggravated when she heard Sage's voice mingled with the shrill laughter of the redhead. The musical ensemble was now tuning up for the traditional engagement dance, the first dance, which would honor the happy couple. Charllie watched in dismay as the redhead placed her hand on Sage's arm, and he gallantly acquiesced— leading her out onto the dance floor.

Tears threatened to dislodge themselves from Charllie's sparkling eyes, but she bravely smiled and accepted an invitation to dance with a young widower, a rather attractive cousin of Phoebe's who was visiting from Philadelphia. The cousin was rather debonair with his chestnut brown wavy hair that included the merest touch of silver threading through his sideburns. His eyes were a deep and rather solemn gray, he had a fascinating cleft in his chin, and he possessed the most engaging smile. However, Charllie was beyond appreciating all these attributes, for she only had eyes for Sage, who was at this moment being totally monopolized by the vivacious redhead.

Mr. William Somerset, Charllie's dance partner, had quickly introduced himself as he guided her around the dance room floor with graceful moves and much finesse. William was an excellent conversationalist who also possessed intelligence and charm. Yet Charllie found little joy in the dance they shared. It was evident that many young women must see him as a real *catch,* and he most likely caused many hearts to flutter, but he left Charllie cold. She might as well have been dancing with the hat rack that stood in the hallway. Her heart was spoken for, and any new partner who might choose to pay court was only wasting his time.

William, trying his best to be cordial and engaging, opened their conversation. "I am privileged for the opportunity of an introduction, Miss Charlotte Wright from

Oak Haven, and I am honored that you accepted my invitation to dance. Your dear mother has informed me that you hail from Goochland. I have never had the opportunity to visit Goochland. However, from what I have seen of this part of Virginia, it is truly magnificent country. And, I must say that I have been favored by fortune to find such a beautiful dance partner."

William found Charlotte to be very desirable, and, truthfully, he felt he would be a very lucky man indeed if he could but sweep her off her feet. "I have been a lawyer in Philadelphia for a good number of years and have prided myself on my success in the profession; however, I would have gladly traded it all away for a home filled with love and joy."

Charllie looked more closely at him, noticing that his gray eyes had become slightly overcast with sorrow. He went on, "I own a house on the outskirts of the city. My wife and I decorated it to our taste over the years with items from our trips abroad. It's a beautiful home, but, sadly, I really don't enjoy it as I once did. Helen passed away five years ago from yellow fever, and, unfortunately, we did not have the time necessary to establish a family. The family manse is now empty, and I can't tell you how quickly a home can become just a house when it's no longer filled with love."

"Mr. Somerset, I'm so sorry. These must be very trying times for you." Charllie attempted to be interested in his plight, but her thoughts were not on William. In fact, nothing about his story, bittersweet as it was, seemed to touch Charllie. He was a stranger who deserved politeness and sympathy, but no more. She remained cordial but removed.

"You're right, Charlotte, those were trying times. I am now intent on finding happiness once again, if it is at all possible, for I hope to one day make my beautiful house a home again."

William soon realized that his partner was showing little interest in him or his conversation. As he watched her scan the crowd for a special someone, he had to accept the fact that his pursuit of Charllie had been doomed from the start. Their conversation, which had begun lively enough as it was laced with interesting tidbits of the people they knew in common and the places they had been, soon became rather stilted and artificial due to Charllie's inattention. He had shared some of his life's sorrows with her, but her empathy had been rather lacking. In fact, she was spending altogether far too much time keeping track of another gentleman's progress around the dance floor instead of paying attention to her own dance partner. He continued to politely whirl Charllie around as the music played, but his ardor had been thoroughly squelched by the lack of reciprocity.

Charllie was totally oblivious to the many mixed emotions that went through her current dance partner's mind. Her eyes constantly sought out Sage, and she was greatly distressed to see that his hand had intimately spanned his dance partner's waist. She flinched when she saw him bend his head so that he could share some intimate conversation with her. She felt that Sage held *Miss Red* much too closely and that her attentions were bordering on the obscene. Her dress showed far too much cleavage, she pressed herself up against Sage in a most unseemly way, and her coquetry was overdone and too casually coy. Charllie was in constant self-imposed torment during the entirety of the dance, and when Mr. Somerset escorted her back to her seat at the conclusion of their dance, so that he could continue his pursuit of more amenable dance partners, she felt nothing but relief.

Charllie, caught another glimpse of Sage and *Miss Red* together, and she felt her cheeks flush with hurt and anger. She acknowledged that she was jealous, perhaps needlessly so. "I know that Sage and I do not share an understanding. He is a free agent and may attend to any woman of his choice. He certainly does not need my approval for his selection of dance partners, for any of his actions, or for any of his choices in life. Perhaps I should get on with my own life, and perhaps I need to discount the possibility of Sage ever being part of that life." Charllie edged closer to the fireplace, and she basked in its warmth as strangers babbled around her.

With relief, Charllie noticed that *Miss Red* had finally left Sage to saunter over to some other beau whom she had not seen in a long time. Sage took a seat for a moment, became restless, and then wandered over to a more private alcove. Charllie ached to be with him. She wanted to talk to him, touch him, and be near him. However, she knew that as things currently stood between them, he would not ask her to dance, and he certainly wouldn't seek her out. His guard was up, and he was not about to approach her and acknowledge their friendship. If she truly wanted to salvage this evening, the impetus would be left entirely up to her. She drew in a deep breath, smoothed her skirts, and then casually strolled over to Sage as the ensemble began a sweeping waltz.

Sage scowled as Charllie approached, but he stood his ground and did not try to evade her. As she drew near, he inclined his head and graciously bowed, but little if any traces of a smile lit up his rather somber features. Charllie, nervously smiling and attempting nonchalance, placed her hand, no longer sporting an engagement ring, on his forearm. Sage involuntarily flinched as if he had been scalded, and his eyes narrowed as she began to speak.

"Mr. Danbury, I know you have been avoiding me this evening, and that's your right entirely. However, I feel it is most unkind. I currently find myself adrift amongst a sea of strangers without a single dance partner. I was hoping you might take pity on me and graciously consent to lead me out onto the dance floor yourself."

Sage found himself in an uncomfortable dilemma. He had hoped to avoid a confrontation with Charllie. He had acted abominably on her behalf, and he could not forgive himself for the travesties that he had orchestrated on one late summer afternoon. Though he could never forgive himself, he had hoped that in time she would be able to forgive him, at least partially, enough so that they could resume some sort of friendship.

"I'm sorry, Charlotte. I would never have overlooked you intentionally. I must admit that I did have the notion that I might be the very last person you would like to acknowledge. We have a very star-crossed history, as you know, and I must admit that I shoulder most of the blame."

Sage continued to ache for Charllie with a deep and abiding love, and he could not ignore the fire that swept through him when her small hand touched his arm. He might have reacted by briefly flinching, as if the most minor of touches from her was abhorrent, but this reaction was in direct opposition to how he truly felt. Her touch was a jolt to the entire wellspring of his very being, a warm current that pulsed with a life of its own. Without her touch, he felt bereft.

Sage ached to hold her closer than any man had ever held her before and to allow his body to worship her body with all the fires of desire that were inspired by this casual touch. To still the emotions raging within him, he presented Charllie with a rather bland, passive mask.

"Charlotte, please excuse my lax manners this evening. I would be honored if you would consent to be my partner in the next dance." Sage stood up and offered his arm to Charllie. Though he had agreed to do her bidding, he did not express any warmth or enthusiasm as he awkwardly escorted her to the dance floor and then took her in his arms.

"Sage, though it is so kind of you to agree to dance with me, I must admit that I had hoped for slightly more enthusiasm on your part."

Sage ignored her comment and gently swept her into the rhythm of the waltz. Charllie was downhearted by the lack of emotion that he displayed, but she was moved by his closeness, and her spine tingled with his touch. The dance began as a methodical exercise of two strangers attempting to follow the music in a concerted effort. Their smiles were artificial, their touch unemotional, their dance steps impersonal. Charllie held back sobs that threatened to wrack her body. She was dancing with the man whom she loved above life itself, and they were dancing like total strangers.

Charllie moved closer, attempting to close the distance between them. She knew that her forwardness was a gamble, and that if Sage no longer felt the same way about her that her gamble would fail hopelessly. Charllie could only pray that Sage would relent, wish to resume their relationship with a modest show of intimacy, and at least meet her halfway in her attempt at reconciliation. Her very soul went out to him as it looked for its home, but it was not to be.

Unfortunately, as Charllie closed the distance between them, she could sense that she was making Sage extremely uncomfortable. He immediately stiffened and made a greater effort to hold her at arm's length. Charllie interpreted this move as indifference or a complete unwillingness on Sage's part to acknowledge any ties of intimacy. Evidently, Sage had no wish to resume their relationship where it had left off. A part of Charllie shriveled and died.

She would never know with what restraint Sage had placed upon himself to remain the cold gentleman while wildfires of passion ruled within, threatening to consume him. She would never know how much he wanted to crush her to him, to kiss her until she was breathless and panting. His hands were cold, but they belied the passion that flamed beneath the oh-so-cold exterior. His restraint was the only thing he possessed that could save him from the overwhelming rush of feelings that threatened to engulf him as Charllie attempted to embrace him. Holding her at arm's length was necessary for his self-preservation and to ensure decorum in this moment of passionate longing for the one in his arms who was so close to him, and yet so far.

Acknowledging Sage's rejection as he distanced himself from her, Charllie immediately stepped backward a pace, feeling thoroughly humiliated and insulted. Her face became suffused with high color as she battled with the emotions of shame and rejection. A wave of emotion, similar in nature to the grief one feels upon losing someone dear, threatened to crash over her; so she immediately disengaged herself from Sage's arms and sedately backed out into the hallway—away from the crush of dancers. Once free of the public eye, she lifted her skirts and dashed to the furthest reaches of the house, where she finally sought solace in a vacated sitting room where one lonely candle kept vigil by fighting away the shadows.

She threw herself upon a horsehair divan where she quickly gave in to wracking sobs that were soft and low, though they reached down to the very innermost depths of her heart. The man she loved no longer reciprocated those tender feelings. Having only just found him, she had now truly lost him. The time they had spent in the hut had not been an affirmation of love; it had been an annihilation of it. The desire they had shared had not been the means to a new beginning but the finale to the hopes of what might have been between them. She was no longer an important part of Sage's life, nor would she ever be.

Charllie reeled with the emotions that swirled through her. She thought with much regret of all her meetings with Sage when she had reviled him, kept him at a great distance, and urged him to look elsewhere for companionship. She had been young and thoughtless in her dealings with him, but, at the time, she had still been chasing a ghost. Why hadn't she realized the depth of love that Sage held for her then? Why hadn't she even tried to understand her own attraction and feelings toward him? She felt as if she had once held the whole world in her hands only to carelessly allow it to fall and smash to smithereens—all the precious memories they shared destroyed forever by her own stupidity.

The lilting music that gently swept through the corridor from a distance seemed to mock her. Charllie could picture the couples dancing together, their arms around each other, their bodies swaying to the music. Their imagined laughter and intimate whispers invaded her gloomy thoughts, and she felt nothing but despair.

"Am I forever doomed to loneliness?" "Will I ever be able to rectify the many mistakes I have made?" "Has Sage been forever lost to me?"

A dark, towering shadow momentarily blotted out the candle's light, and Charllie quickly dabbed her eyes in embarrassment. She had hoped no one would choose to inhabit this rather secluded room, for she had wished to lick her wounds in private, so no one would witness her feeling sorry for herself. The candle flickered, and she looked up to find Sage looking down upon her. His thoughts and purpose for being there were unfathomable. His face was dark, his mouth drawn in a fine line, and his eyes scrutinized her in a most uncomfortable way. "Miss Charllie?" He stepped out of the shadows and slowly approached her, standing just a few feet from the divan.

"Why, Sage. What are you doing here? I was just overcome by the crowd and the excitement. I decided to find a quiet place to rest for a moment. I will be fine shortly. Would you be so kind as to bring me a cup of warm punch? I do believe I have become chilled."

As Charllie uttered these words, she was catapulted back in time to another moment and place where her senses had been totally overwhelmed by the revelations that she had unwittingly overheard regarding her betrothal to Thomas. The tenseness of that situation, caused in large part by having just been apprised of the duplicity of Sage's brother, had forced her to realize the complications of relationships based on romance rather than on love, and it had left her reeling with emotion. Another ball, another celebration, another misunderstanding. The painful memories soon had Charllie cringing on the sofa, avoiding any eye contact with Sage, but his eyes remained narrowed in scrutiny.

"Do the crowds and excitement often bring on tears, Charllie? Or is it something I said or did? If I am to blame in any way, I humbly offer my apologies. You know that I would never willingly do anything intentionally to hurt you."

Sage immediately realized what he had just said. He had made his own internal references to their encounter in the slave hut, reacting rather violently to these memories. "Damn! I have no right to talk to you of apologies and sensibilities after what I did to you, Charllie! I am a blackguard—just as you always said I was! I have no right to question you about your feelings, not with my callous past overshadowing my every action. I will bring you your punch, Miss Charllie, for that's the very least I can do." And with that, Sage bowed and quickly left the room.

So, his guilt was eating him alive! It was just what Charllie had originally suspected. A wave of relief and tenderness went through her. Perhaps he did still love her. At least he still showed that he was concerned for her well-being. There was much between them that was tangled and confused, and she needed to think long and hard as to how she could possibly find a way to get them to a point of reconciliation. Both were to blame, of that she was sure. But she knew that if he continued to paint himself as the villain, there was little hope that their love could ever begin anew from where it had left off.

It seemed that gentle attempts at friendship to re-establish camaraderie were not going to be enough. Not at this moment. If a dance could not rekindle the romance, the tactics needed to become far more determined, perhaps even blatant. She would just have to salvage whatever feelings of friendship they still had for one another. A major offensive would have to wait for another day.

Sage returned with her hot punch, and after handing her a napkin and setting the drink on a nearby table, he sat at a distance. His look was one of concern, but it was also one of caution. Charllie gratefully sipped the steaming drink and smiled tremulously. Sage's heart seemed to be caught in his throat. He was overcome with emotions that he had sought to dispel with icy disregard, yet he was now reeling with the warmth of Charllie's closeness. The desire to wrap his arms around her surged within him, and a reckless passion encouraged him to whisk her away and make her his own.

These thoughts, however, were unreadable to Charllie; and she felt at a loss as to how to react to the cold, silent man who sat across from her. His concern for her seemed to be based on etiquette alone, the polite offerings of a stranger. A small tear glided down Charllie's cheek and glowed like a diadem in the candlelight. Sage watched it, entranced, and his heart melted. He quickly stood, moved to Charllie's side, and gathered her to him. He rested his head atop her soft curls and inhaled her sweetness.

Charllie looked up at Sage with her large and questioning blue eyes, and his lips crashed down upon hers with the heat and hunger of one who has been starving for many days. His strong arms enfolded her with a protective fierceness born of desperation. His warm tongue sought its home within her sweet mouth, and he heard her gasp in what he misconstrued as dismay. He immediately disengaged himself from her and stepped away. He broke their connection of desire as with a cleaver, for he wrongly believed that her response was one of fear and disgust. He was not yet ready to reconcile his past behavior on her behalf, for he was unwilling to believe that he had been forgiven. That he was now the object of her regard—he could not fathom.

Charllie felt her frustration swell. She had not had adequate time to respond to his embrace with her own rising passion. Sage would never know that she had been more than ready to acknowledge each of his kisses with her own. Perhaps he would never have broken their bond so readily if he had known. But in misinterpreting her gasp as one of reprimand and repulsion, Sage restored his mask of cold politeness. There had been no time for conversation between them to heal their broken relationship with understanding, and it now seemed that it would not happen.

"Pardon me, Miss Charlotte. I had no right to make bold with my unwanted advances, so I hope you will forgive me. I suppose I could blame my unpardonable behavior on my weakness for ladies' tears, but I owe you an apology for my inability to maintain a sense of decorum. My manners often seem lacking when you are near, and I find myself constantly overstepping my bounds. If there is nothing more I can do for you this evening, I will take my leave. I hope your recovery is brief and that you will be able to rejoin the festivities shortly. Once again, my apologies." Sage bowed briefly and then quickly exited the room, leaving the candle to sputter in his wake. He soon called for his overcoat and melted into the night.

It seemed that lately Sage spent an awful lot of time bowing and exiting. A blight had fallen upon a relationship that had once promised the potential of bearing sweet fruit. His departure had come about so suddenly that Charllie had not even had the opportunity to react. She wanted to clasp his hands in hers, protest his departure, and assure him that she had tender feelings for him. Yet no opportunity had been given, and the barriers he constantly erected now seemed overwhelming. Charllie felt totally dejected and wished for nothing more than the privacy of her own room in her own home, where she could hide away in abject misery. But she was not a quitter!

Charllie repaired her tear-stained face in front of an ancient, cloudy mirror, re-arranged a few errant curls, and forced a smile. Though she felt totally dispirited, and her limbs felt made of lead, she rejoined the assemblage and danced with a handful of random dance partners. However, this time her eyes no longer sought out the green eyes of Mr. Sage Danbury. His time had not yet come.

Chapter Nineteen

Time seemed to go by at a snail's pace for Charllie. She did not hear from Sage, nor did she dare communicate with him, and, thankfully, memories of the devastating engagement ball soon faded. The Christmas holiday was just around the corner, and preparations had already begun in earnest. This was both healing as well as torturous for Charllie. Thankfully, she was able to keep herself occupied with all the preparations and activities of the holiday so that she was not constantly tormented by her failure to reconcile with Sage. However, the loneliness and dejection she felt whenever there was a lull in her daily activities were devastating. She found herself going from smiles to tears in a matter of minutes. Her existence became a roller coaster of happiness and sadness, and she found the ride far from exhilarating. Emotionally, she felt drained.

The Wright family always hosted numerous festive socials and family gatherings during the holidays, and this year they seemed to be pulling out all stops as they celebrated continued good health, prosperity, and a return to normalcy following the war. And, of course, Charllie was expected to participate in all of them. Mr. and Mrs. Wright watched with concern from the sidelines as Charllie went through the motions of her life without any sense of true joy or excitement. She smiled as often as she ever had, she made pleasant witticisms, she sang and even played the pianoforte on occasion, but you could tell that her heart just wasn't in it. Her outgoing personality had been changed to one of somber introspection and withdrawal.

Even Charllie's appearance told a story of sad change. Though she had long ago foregone the trappings of mourning, prior to the war, she had always been given to splashes of color with artfully arranged ribbons, an occasional flower, carefully selected jewelry—all to complement a simple, but attractive, gown of a particularly vibrant color. But lately she had chosen to wear more serviceable attire, usually of a rather colorless and featureless variety, becoming in its own way but not stylish, and with few if any accessories. If visitors were expected, she would dress in a comfortable, but rather staid, dark maroon velvet gown for those few festive occasions. Her mother, Sophia, would often grumble at this lack of spirit on Charllie's part, but Charllie would continue with stubborn resolve. All her clothes that bespoke a world of fun and joy had been banished to the back of her closet, where they patiently waited for a more auspicious day and time.

Charllie was also less apt to ride Merrilee as frequently as she had in the past. Winter had set in, and the spitting snow and brisk winds had sent most to their crackling hearths—this included *Miss Charlotte*. In years gone by, she had chosen to brave the inclement weather, and nothing would have deterred her from enjoying an adventurous romp on her favorite horse. She had always loved to bundle up and ride off to visit shut-in neighbors, trade in the quaint shops, or assist in overseeing the care of the fowls and livestock that remained on the estate.

During past Christmas holidays, she had delighted in tramping through the woods to search for the best Yule log, the perfect sprigs of holly, a cluster of mistletoe, or the most magnificent Christmas tree. This year, she politely begged Mr. George to do what she had once delighted in doing herself. She listlessly penned a few Christmas letters, crafted a few pomanders from oranges and cloves for the crystal bowl in the parlor, and cut out a few paper angels for the tree, but she did these activities for therapy rather than enjoyment. The sense of joy was totally missing in Charllie's life.

Charllie made a scant few holiday deliveries to her neighbors with the sedate pony trap. Most of the holiday gifts that she brought to her friends and relatives were handmade, simple yet elegant gifts that she had labored over to honor these longstanding relationships. Needlework, scarves, and mittens had all been carefully wrapped in tissue paper and delivered with homemade Christmas cookies, jellies, and preserves. Though she sometimes missed her daily visits to the horses and chickens, she knew that they were in the capable hands of the staff who now cared for them in addition to the pigs, the sheep, and the pigeons. She did continue to visit Merrilee once a week, bringing the mare a carrot or an apple, but, in her self-imposed lethargy, it was seldom more than that. Charllie rarely left the comfort of the hearth with its crackling fire, for she had lost her spirit.

There was a listlessness about Charllie as she wrote in her journal, read lengthy, rather somber Gothic novels, and patiently worked on her cross-stitch. She had lost weight because she often substituted tea and toast for supper, frequently begging off from joining her parents for the evening meal, always fabricating a headache or some other ailment. Mrs. Wright had become alarmed, and she eventually called in the family physician, who pronounced Charllie perfectly healthy but in need of a prescribed winter tonic—a liquid medication that was made of various unknown additives with wild cherry wine being the predominant ingredient. In truth, her ailment needed nothing more than time, and perhaps circumstance, to provide a cure. Charllie knew what that cure needed to be, but she was powerless to provide its prescription. Unfortunately, Charllie had not seen Sage since the fateful engagement party. It seemed he was avoiding everyone.

A festive event that might have brought the two of them together. Christmas came and went, and Charllie was disappointed to the point of tears when no thoughtful gift, Christmas card, or casual salutation arrived from him. She had hoped that he would, at the very least, wish her well for the new year, but she realized that was not meant to be. She had devoted countless hours to knitting him a bright red lamb's wool scarf to protect his neck and throat from winter's blistering cold, and she had sent it along with an anonymous note wishing him well. Though he would never know it was a gift of love from her, at least she would know that her token of love might bring some pleasure and comfort to his life. When the scarf was sent along to his home, she thought about the cherished connection that had once existed between them, and then she dissolved into tears.

Charllie would never know that Sage, upon opening the gift of her scarf, had actually prayed that it had been sent by her, but, because it was anonymous, and he was still remorseful about their summer interlude, he was forced to believe otherwise. However, from the moment Sage received the scarf, he never left the house without winding it snugly around his neck. Whether or not Charllie had given him the scarf, its presence seemed to bring her closer and was a comfort to him. She constantly pervaded his mind as he remembered her warm smile, flirtatious blue eyes, and golden hair. The many fond memories of their times together constantly flowed through his mind, and he cherished them. He often visualized the summer sunbeams that had filtered to the forest floor by the edge of the slowly meandering brook that wound past the slave hut in a distant glade and thought about that day which would forever remain bittersweet.

***

Sage's holiday was altogether mirthless. His parents had decided to spend the holidays with relatives in Philadelphia, and quite frankly, he was happy to see them go. He begged off by reminding them that someone needed to remain at home to supervise, to provide the retainers with a festive holiday hosted by a Danbury family member, and to be at hand in case of any emergency. His own world had become lifeless and colorless, and the last thing he needed was for well-meaning friends and relatives to constantly prod him with holiday cheer that came off as artificial and insincere.

Sage had organized a Christmas party for the plantation staff and the few sharecroppers. A tree had been cut and decorated, a ham and turkey slowly roasted, and presents purchased and wrapped for the children. All had been invited to partake of a feast on Christmas Eve. He dutifully acted the host, making sure that the Danbury Dell mansion was welcoming and festive—at least in appearance. The mansion exhibited a believable facade of celebration: a decorated tree with gaily wrapped gifts beneath it, steaming bowls of wassail, trays heavily laden with a variety of succulent foods, Christmas carols sung in the parlor, and even a sprig of mistletoe hanging above the doorway in the entry. But little cheer had existed for Sage this Christmas, and all the decorations and fine food seemed like nothing more than window dressing.

As the welcoming host, Sage had felt his face freezing into place with a rather forced smile for the entire evening, for he had felt no true warmth or gaiety. He shook hands, distributed gifts, raised a toast to all assembled, and finally bid them adieu. He was totally relieved when the whole event was over, and he was finally left alone to his own devices. He looked around at the devastation: the leftovers, the strewn gift-wrappings, and the smoldering Yule log, and he felt cold and empty. The Christmas spirit had totally passed him by. The one gift for which he truly ached was not to be found under his Christmas tree, and he had no one to blame but himself.

The next day was Christmas. Sage sat before a roaring fire, spending most of the afternoon whittling away at a cold roasted chicken, nursing a bottle of whiskey, and watching fiery red embers race up the chimney. Charllie would never know how often his heart and mind had turned to her. "Charllie, I was such a fool."

Chapter Twenty

Shortly after the holidays, a letter of good tidings reached the Wright home. Brother Frank had decided to take his wife to Raleigh, North Carolina, on a trip that would incorporate both business and pleasure. Frank would attend to some necessary business while Emily visited some first cousins there. In the evenings and on the days with an open schedule, the couple would partake of the city's delights. Both looked forward to a bit of sightseeing, some fine dining, and perhaps a theatre or musical performance. They were to leave at the beginning of February and wished to entrust their children, Gerald and Sarah, to their grandparents and Aunt Charllie for the duration.

Charllie was delighted, for she desperately needed a diversion to break the monotony of the short winter days, and she loved her nephew and niece dearly. She spent the next few days preparing for their visit. The guest bedroom in which they were staying adjoined Charllie's, and it had a large feather bed complete with a trundle bed beneath it. It was furnished with gaily colored quilts, a rose washbasin and pitcher for Sarah and a hunting theme washbasin and pitcher for Gerald, children's books for nighttime reading, and cozy scatter rugs throughout.

Charllie took great pains to decorate the reading table with a large bouquet of dried flowers and bowls of apples, pinecones, and nuts. Antique glassware lined the mantelpiece. She brought down an old chest from the garret and filled it with the discarded toys from the older Wright children's youth. The fireplace was prepared with kindling, aromatic pinecones, and smaller boughs for its first lighting, and larger logs were stacked neatly nearby to be added when the fire needed replenishment. Spicy orange pomanders remaining from the holidays were placed in a bowl on the children's nightstand, and fresh cinnamon sticks and cloves were added to augment their spicy fragrance. All was in readiness for the arrival of the grandchildren.

A few days later, the children arrived, escorted by parents who were anxious to leave right away on their own journey while the weather held. Sarah and Gerald had seldom been away from home except on very rare overnight visits, and they felt a bit of trepidation at first, knowing they would be staying with their aunt and grandparents for over two weeks. But when they were shown to their bedroom where a fire was gaily crackling on the hearth, and they saw how close in proximity they were to Aunt Charllie's room, they soon felt safe and secure within their new surroundings. It would be a joyous time for the Wrights, especially Charles and Sophia, who would once again be treated to the shouts, giggles, songs, and laughter of children's voices. No one was happier than Charllie, who desperately needed to be immersed in their excitement, happiness, and love.

"Aunt Charllie, what do you think we should do today?"

"Let's see, Sarah. Yesterday we visited the stable and fed Merrilee, but today is far too cold and blustery for going outside. I could tell you some stories by the fire. We could make some hot cocoa with whipped cream. Or I could teach you charades. What do you think?"

Gerald responded first, "I could do with some hot cocoa, Aunt Charllie, especially if it comes with some of Grandma's cinnamon jumbles."

"I want everything!" Sarah chimed in. "I want stories, cocoa and cinnamon jumbles, and charades!"

Charllie smiled and hugged both children. "I think we can arrange that. As long as you promise not to ruin your supper with all the treats!"

"We won't! We won't!"

During their stay, Charllie taught Sarah some basic stitches, and soon the child was working on her very first sampler. Gerald, who was already a bit restless from being cooped up inside so much, was soon riding behind Charllie on Merrilee as they toured the estate and brought foodstuffs to some of the shut-in elderly. Merrilee nickered happily as Gerald offered her an apple on his outstretched hand, but he withdrew it in disgust when he brought it back covered with the horse's saliva.

"Aunt Charllie, that is totally disgusting!" Gerald frantically tried to wipe the saliva from his hands to his trousers. He was anxious to return to the house to wash his hands.

Charllie burst out laughing. "Gerald, you are such a city boy!"

Charllie's niece and nephew were such good medicine for her. She often caught herself watching the children wistfully. They were everything that one could hope for: a boy and a girl both favoring their parents in a multitude of ways. They were beautiful, intelligent, mischievous, loving, and well-mannered. Gerald had light, tawny hair with bright blue eyes and long dark lashes. He was ruggedly built and had already mastered riding his own pony with great expertise. Sarah was a diminutive brunette who had her Dad's own gray-blue eyes. Sarah tended to be a bit of a bookworm and was never happier than when she was curled up by the fire with either a book or a favorite doll. Though brother and sister, their squabbles were few, and they seemed to get along amazingly well together.

The children were delightful companions because they were so friendly, outgoing, and loving. Though they possessed excellent manners, they weren't above some mischievous behavior from time to time, and their presence kept Oak Haven very lively. Charllie sometimes fretted that perhaps these children would be as close as she would ever get to being a mother. Maybe the role she played as their aunt would forever be her only role. She knew of many spinsters, husbandless and childless, who spent untold selfless hours baking, sewing, and tending nieces and nephews. Perhaps she was fated to become one of them.

When Charllie thought in this vein, though she knew that she was privileged to be an aunt, she was also overcome by sadness because it was her dearest wish to become a wife and mother. She would think about the man who had once looked at her with green eyes that flashed with passion—a man with tousled black curls, a sensual smile, and a firm jaw. She ached when she recalled their first shared kiss, the dances, the embraces, and the summer of *ice and honey.* But most of all, she missed the man himself and being part of his life: their banter, their laughter, their camaraderie. When she had once grieved for Thomas, she had thought at the time that she knew what true loss was. Now she knew that it had been but a poor impersonator. Without Sage, she recognized true loss—it was total desolation.

Winter's short days and long nights were compensated in part by the children's visit, but not entirely. On the occasional silent, somber night when the moon cast blue shadows and traced melancholy silhouettes outside her bedroom window, Charllie sometimes wrapped herself in a warm robe and paced the cold floor of her room. She found herself entering the world of the frost tracings on her window, a magical world of icy plumes and crystal whirls. The winter nights seemed eons away from the passionate heat of summer, and her very heart seemed to take its cue from her surroundings and beat more slowly, suspended in the grief caused by the loss of her one true love.

The cold would eventually drive Charllie back to the comfort of her warm bed, where she would torture herself with the memories of what Sage and she had once shared. The futility of her reminiscing was all too clear, yet on many nights she was drawn once again to the provocative memories of their tempestuous relationship. She could not easily douse the tiny flicker of hope within that they might be reunited in the future, that the fragile bud of their prematurely blighted love might eventually begin to bloom once again. The hope was small, almost insignificant, but she cherished it.

During the waking hours, Charllie entertained her niece and nephew. They were not, however, oblivious to her sometimes somber mood.

"Aunt Charllie, don't spend all day moping. My mama says that if you frown too much, your wrinkles will begin to set in, and before you know it, you'll look old, even older than you already are!"

Charllie couldn't help but laugh at her precocious niece. "I certainly wouldn't want to do that now, would I? I might find myself on the shelf without a husband forever and forever."

Gerald piped up, "That'll never happen, Aunt Charllie. You're too beautiful for that. Someone will come along and ask you to marry him. It's bound to happen. You just wait and see." He patted her on the knee to give her some comfort.

Charllie was heartened by the optimism of her nephew and gave him a big hug.

Sarah came around the table so that she could hug her aunt, too. "Gerald and I want to do something exciting today, Aunt Charllie. What can we do?"

"Well, maybe we could make some homemade ice cream. I think the hens laid a few eggs this morning, and Aunt Beth still has a few vanilla beans left over from Christmas. Of course, I would need someone strong who could keep the paddle churning until it turns the custard into ice cream, and I'm not sure anyone here is big enough or strong enough to do that."

"I sure am, Aunt Charllie," said Gerald as he flexed his arms, so she could see his muscles.

"Me too, Aunt Charllie, I'm strong like Gerald. Can I beat the eggs? Can we put strawberry preserves on our ice cream?"

"I think we can manage all that. Let's find Aunt Bethany and ask her if we can borrow some of her aprons. Maybe we'll have the ice cream made in time for dessert tonight."

Charllie knew that her brother would most probably accuse her of spoiling his children, and he would probably be right. But she learned that by making them happy, she was able to find a bit of happiness for herself as well. The time they shared together in the various activities provided nourishment to one who was starving for human affection. During the day, Charllie acknowledged the sun and all it had to offer: its joys, its delights, its hope for the future. During the night, she anticipated the rising of the moon with dread, for it brought the aching loneliness of empty hours, poignant memories, and disturbing dreams. Charllie found herself in a wretched state of limbo, vacillating between the two worlds of joy and pain.

***

One day, Charllie took Gerald and Sarah for a walk in a meadow just over the ridge from Oak Haven. The children chatted nonstop about the imminent return of their parents. Charllie realized this pleasant respite, which had been so wonderful for her own well-being, was swiftly coming to an end. She knew that the children's leaving would most definitely create a void in her life. Their stay had provided her with purpose, entertainment, companionship, and laughter.

As they approached a nearby pond, which was still covered by ice and snow, Gerald let out a shout. He picked up his feet and began to race towards the pond. As Charllie scanned the pond, she saw a terrible struggle taking place. A black creature was thrashing wildly and helplessly in a patch of open water that was surrounded by chunks of shattered ice and bobbing islands of frozen snow. Soon, they all heard the desperate, rather meager barking by what could now be identified as a dog—a dog frantically floundering in the frigid waters. The dog was desperately trying to reach the shore and safety, but all its efforts were unsuccessful. All who watched in horror from a distance were aware that if he wasn't saved soon, he would perish.

The pond around the open patch of water, most of which was still covered by ice and snow, appeared to be deceptively solid to the child who was speeding to the dog's rescue. It was clear that he was going to attempt a rescue of the drowning dog by crossing the ice with no thought to his own safety.

Charllie now heard the sharp, frantic barking of the dog more clearly, and then in terror she realized that Gerald was determined to save its life at any cost. The dog continued to frantically tread water in a futile attempt to reach the shore. Gerald finally reached the bank of the pond, grabbed a tree limb that lay in the frozen grass, and awkwardly walked out upon the ice, attempting to reach the dog in trouble.

Charllie began to call out to her nephew in terror, ordering him to stop in his efforts to save the animal. "Gerald, get off that pond! Now! It won't hold you!" She, too, began to race towards the pond with Sarah close behind her. She knew the inherent dangers of the situation and was frantic to prevent anything tragic from happening to the child.

Gerald either ignored his aunt's commands or couldn't hear them. He leaned forward, gingerly tried to give assistance to the dog with a stick he had found on his way to the pond. Teetering on the fragile ice, he called to the dog to grab the stick, but it was useless. The limb was not long enough, the dog was not given to taking demands, and Gerald could not reach him without walking further out onto the ice. He slowly inched his way forward, but he was far too heavy for the fragile ice. With a sickening crash, the child broke through the ice, plunging into the frigid water just inches from the unlucky dog. Unbeknownst to both dog and child, the beginnings of an early spring thaw had already begun melting much of the ice from beneath the pond's surface, and the crusty white surface was dangerously thin and nothing more than a facade. No rescue could successfully take place from the pond's surface. And now—two souls needed rescuing.

In horror, Sarah watched her brother break through the ice and saw both the dog and the boy helplessly flailing in the icy water. She began to loudly scream and wail. Her cries were shrill and heart-rending. Charllie tried to comfort her, knowing that she alone was now responsible for making a rescue, and she would have to do something immediately if her nephew were to be saved. Though Charllie could swim adequately, she knew she was encumbered by her heavy winter clothing, but, unfortunately, she did not have the time necessary to fully disrobe. Every moment lost puts her nephew further in peril. She was not going to stand by and watch Gerald drown if she had anything to do with it! She began to quickly stride toward the pond, intent upon doing whatever she had to do to rescue the child.

As she reached the edge of the pond and prepared to plunge in herself, she heard a man's deep yell and the loud pounding of a horse's hooves. "Charllie, get back! Mind the girl!" She then felt herself being forcefully thrust aside as a horse and its rider rapidly galloped past her, charging into the pond's depths to attempt the daring rescue of both dog and child.

Charllie gratefully recognized Ebony and Sage, and she awkwardly stood up from where she had been unceremoniously pushed onto the muddy bank. She watched as Ebony balked upon first entering the frigid water, and then his muscular body broke through some of the chunky layers of ice that encircled the pond. With Sage's guidance of the reins, the stallion used its powerful legs to navigate forward to the middle of the pond, the churning swim eventually bringing Sage close enough so that he could attempt a rescue of both the boy and the dog. He swiftly grabbed Gerald beneath his arms, quickly lifted him up and out of the water, and then unceremoniously plunked him behind him—ordering the boy to hang on tight.

By this time, however, the dog had gone under and disappeared beneath the surface with barely a ripple, and Sage feared that he had been too late to rescue it. But with a valiant struggle and a frenzy of churning water and ice, the dog resurfaced one more time, and Sage quickly made a desperate, final grab. He was able to hold on to the dog by its thick coat and hoist it in front of him, where it lay panting in exhaustion.

The journey back to the safety of the solid bank was a tremendous struggle for both Ebony and his rider, but their passengers were now safe upon the horse's back. The horse was becoming numb by the frigid water, the thrashing of his limbs was slowing, and the burden of a man, a boy, and a dog, all soaking wet, greatly weighed him down. However, the valiant horse determinedly used its powerful legs to reach the shore, fighting the freezing cold water and chunks of ice, constantly struggling to find solid ground for its hooves.

Sage stubbornly continued to balance his precious cargo with great difficulty upon the back of his horse. He had relied on Ebony's great strength and determination the whole time to bring them to safety, and he continued to provide gentle nudges with his knees and tugs on the reins to communicate guidance and encouragement to his horse during the ordeal. Eventually, all made it to the shore, dripping wet and frozen—but alive and safe. Ebony whinnied in triumph as he plodded up the slippery bank, exhausted, drenched, and covered in mud. But he still retained his precious burdens. Finally, he reached Charllie's side.

While Charllie had remained at the site watching the unfolding of events in the pond with terror, thankfully, she had also had the presence of mind to send Sarah back to Oak Haven for help. The child had obeyed immediately, racing across the fields with her adrenaline pumping. Just as Sage was gently lowering Gerald and the dog safely to the ground from the back of Ebony, and then dismounting himself, Aunt Bethany, Mr. George, and Sarah came riding across the pasture in the pony trap filled with warm woolen blankets and a large container of steaming hot chocolate. Sage had gently handed Gerald and the dog to Charllie, who quickly brought them to Aunt Beth for blankets and refreshment. Mr. George immediately threw a warm blanket across Ebony's back and then began to lead him across the pasture towards the stable where the horse would be rubbed down and curried, fed warm oats and hay, watered, and bedded down in soft straw in a stall for the night.

Sage and Gerald, along with the friendly stray dog, were quickly wrapped like cocoons in the remaining heavy woolen blankets, and then the entire group boarded the pony cart, where they sipped their hot chocolate and prepared for the ride back to Oak Haven. Charllie and Sarah, both still shivering from concern and shock, were also each swaddled in a blanket, and they, too, gratefully cupped their hands around mugs of hot cocoa, greedily indulging in its warmth.

As the shock of the event began to wear off, Charllie gradually recovered from the horror of what had so recently transpired. It would take a while for the result of the dramatic rescue to sink in, for the positive outcome of this day had by no means been certain.

When they arrived home, they were welcomed by the Wrights, who had seen to making accommodations at the house for the return of those who had taken part in their unfortunate dunking in the pond. They had been fearful and concerned, not knowing the outcome, but had prepared for the best nonetheless. Tubs of warm water with clean linens and clothing awaited everyone, including Sarah and Charllie, the frantic bystanders. Aunt Bethany, always a gentle soul with animals and children, enticed the dog that appeared to be a young female into the kitchen, where she was bathed, dried, and fed. Then she was installed in a soft bed of hay that had been covered with burlap and set in front of the cook stove.

When everyone had bathed, dressed, and finally reassembled downstairs, Sophia Wright directed them to move on into the parlor. "Sage, Charllie, children—come along," Mrs. Wright urged. "The fire on the hearth is blazing. Come in and take a seat around the table. Aunty Beth has laid out soup, baked bread, and applesauce cake. Hurry before your dinner goes cold." As Sage and Sophia's family members filed by her, Sophia grabbed each one for a quick hug, so thankful that all had returned to their home safe and sound.

The evening was just beginning to draw down upon them, but the candles had already been lit and their flickering flames on the table and mantle cast gentle light upon those who were seated and about to partake of the hearty meal. Mr. Wright had pulled his wheelchair up to the head of the table, and he poured Sage a bracing measure of bourbon. He also poured one for himself and a smaller measure for Charllie. Aunt Bethany served Gerald and Emily mugs of hot cocoa, and Mrs. Wright presided over the family teapot for further refreshment.

"I'd like to make a toast to our neighbor and friend, Sage Danbury, for being our hero of the hour," announced Mr. Wright with a wide grin. "He was in the right place at the right time and had the strength and fortitude to see the rescue through. The Wright family will never forget his daring feat of courage. We will forever be grateful and indebted to him for his help in our time of need."

Sage, though enjoying the warmth of the bourbon that spread throughout his limbs, was still chilled by the icy water of the pond. This additional warmth provided by the grateful family that surrounded him was greatly welcomed and touched his heart. He, too, was pleased with the day's outcome and replied, "I was certainly fortunate to be where I needed to be, and grateful that luck and good fortune were with us in the rescue. It's indeed a blessing that I was able to bring both the boy and dog back home— safe and sound. I must also commend one bright, young lady who had the presence of mind to scream for help, and I must say—she has most certainly been blessed with a fantastic pair of lungs!" He looked across the table and acknowledged Sarah with a broad smile of thanks.

"Her screams carried clear across your pasture to the Danbury stables, loud and clear as a bell. I had just ridden in from checking the fence lines, and I can tell you her cry for help certainly allowed me to spring into action as quickly as I did. Thank goodness fate was with us today. I must say, however, that most of the thanks and congratulations must go to Ebony, my magnificent stallion. Our rescue mission would never have succeeded without him."

"Hear, hear!" Mr. Wright responded, pounding the table with his mug of bourbon.

Mrs. Wright pointed an accusing finger at Gerald, who appeared to be acting rather sheepish throughout the proceedings. "I, my dear friends, would now like to chastise my darling grandson for acting in such a dangerous, foolhardy manner. Don't you ever dare to attempt another stunt like that again, my young man, or you will have to face your grandmother's wrath, which can be considerable! You should know ice is never strong this time of year, especially under snow with spring just around the corner. And to top it off, you can barely swim! You're just lucky that I have a stout heart and the patience of a saint! You will forever be indebted to Mr. Danbury and his fine horse Ebony. Never dare to forget it!"

"But, Grandmother, I couldn't let the poor dog drown in the pond. I had to save it," Gerald responded, though his response was rather timid and lacking in conviction, especially knowing the outcome of the recent fiasco.

Mrs. Wright scowled. "And look who ended up needing to be saved. Both of you! If Sage hadn't come along when he did, you both would have drowned. Knowing Charllie, she would have undoubtedly been the next one in the pond to try to save your sorry skin, and then we might have had three floundering in that pond!"

Charles Wright chuckled. He winked at Charllie because he knew with a certainty that his wife had been right in assuming what the outcome might have been if Sage had not arrived when he did. Then he threw his arm around his wife's shoulders and gave her a gentle squeeze. "Now, now, wife. All are safe and sound, and we'll all look back upon this day as some great adventure. Our grandchildren, daughter, and dear neighbor are all warm and dry and none the worse for wear, and on top of that, we have ourselves a fine dog. We're enjoying a wonderful dinner, thanks to Hattie Mae's fine cooking, and all are going to sleep soundly in their beds tonight. We can thank the Lord for the blessings of this day. Let's raise a toast to happy endings!"

The glasses and mugs clinked, and following a familiar toast of good cheer and happy smiles, the chatter of family and friends continued. Though Sage too had a pleasant smile on his face and was most convivial with the family, not once did his eyes seek out Charllie's, nor did he direct any conversation her way. Charllie sat demurely at the table, drinking in the sight and sound of this man whom she loved without question. However, she didn't trust herself to speak to him directly, so she contented herself with feasting on his presence with her eyes.

The plates and cutlery had finally been removed, the fire had died down to glowing embers, and Gerald and Emily prepared to tiredly climb the stairs to their room. Now that the excitement of the rescue had begun to ebb away, and the warm beverages and hearty food had lulled them into drowsy comfort, the adults were also beginning to contemplate seeking their own beds.

Charllie glimpsed Sage's way and finally dared to address him, "Sage, I'd like to thank you for being there today for us. Sarah and Gerald mean everything to this family, and I don't know what I would have done without you. You not only saved Gerald, but you went the extra mile and risked your own life to save the dog as well." There was so much more she would have liked to say to him, but she knew that she couldn't at this time and in this place.

"I appreciate that, Charllie. I did what anyone would have done for those in need, and as I said earlier, so much was dependent on so many other factors as well: Sarah's cry for help, Ebony standing ready to go, some old-fashioned good luck, and the Lord's blessing."

Charllie then poured herself a cup of tea and quietly nursed it while her eyes remained a bit downcast. She felt her heart plummet from Sage's avoidance of anything personal. The ensuing silence was awkward, but the clock soon broke it by chiming the time. Sage scraped back his chair, stood up, and appeared ready to prepare for departure.

Mr. Wright pushed his wheelchair back from the table to detain Sage for a moment. "Let your horse stay the night in our stable, Sage. Mr. George has him settled in a comfortable stall, and I'm sure the poor horse is deserving of an uninterrupted night of rest. I will have George bring round the carriage, and he can drive you back. A lap rug lies ready on the seat for your comfort on the ride home." Charles wheeled himself away from the table as he prepared to escort Sage to the door.

"Don't bother George at this time of night, Charles. It's a mild night, and the sky is rather clear. Lots of stars for lighting my way. I'll walk across lots and be home in no time. I appreciate the fine care he gave my horse after the rescue, and I know that Ebony is enjoying your fine accommodations. I am looking forward to a bit of fresh air before I retire, and it will give me a chance to stretch my legs after such a fine meal. I enjoyed the fine dinner and even better company. Please tell Hattie Mae to send her applesauce cake recipe along to our cook. It's certainly a winner. Gerald, I'll look forward to seeing that fine dog you rescued, once she's clean and dry. Take care, and no more swimming until the summer! Good night, all."

Sage smiled and then ran his fingers through his damp hair. He quickly said good-bye to all, though he did not personally address Charllie, and his eyes totally avoided hers. It was clear that for now she was but one of the family, and his departure, lacking in any personal acknowledgment or friendly banter, was blatant.

All afternoon, with all that everyone had been through, Sage had never once attempted to single her out in any way except to push her aside at the pond so that she herself would not venture into it as he made way for his rescue of Gerald and the dog with Ebony. Charllie did not think that she could feel any colder than she did right now, even though she herself had not been exposed to the depths of the pond. She poured herself another generous shot of bourbon and then stiffly climbed the stairs to her room, where she knew she would face another sleepless night.

***

The two weeks went by much too quickly, and soon Gerald and Sarah were reunited with their mother and father, who graciously thanked Charllie and their parents for the loving care that they had provided for their children while they were away. Over tea, the children's parents filled them in on the many friends and relatives they had visited in Raleigh, the restaurants they had frequented, and the performances they had attended. They passed out souvenirs to everyone, and then they luxuriated in the warmth of the evening fire while sipping mulled cider.

When Frank and Emily were introduced to the family's adopted dog, they were told the story of the new dog's dramatic rescue. This had included, of course, the narrative about their own son's reckless and daring rescue attempt, which had ended with his own dunking in the icy pond and followed by his own rescue. They were horrified at first, especially as they could vividly imagine what the horrific outcome might have been. But since they were soon apprised of the daring rescue by Sage and Ebony, and told of their daughter's role in bringing about the rescue, they were soon comforted. Since both parents had also been raised on rural plantations where risky occurrences naturally took place from time to time with adventuresome children, they accepted the event as part of the ongoing family lore.

The hapless dog, the instigator of the mad adventure, was now clean and well-groomed. She sported a shiny black coat with silky curls and two floppy ears. Her pedigree might have included a mix of Labrador retriever and cocker spaniel, though no one would ever know for sure, but she was certainly a comely miss. She was clearly a mutt, but her liquid brown eyes spoke of love and devotion. It had been clear from the very beginning that she had been just one of the many abandoned animals trying to fend for herself without an owner. She had become house-trained in no time, and her quiet and gentle presence provided much happiness to the family. Though loved by all, she had become Charles Wright's constant companion and best friend. Her name, proclaimed by Charles, was now Gertrude.

Sarah and Gerald flung their arms around Gertrude for a final hug and promised her that they would see her soon. They were effusive with their hugs, kisses, and waves to all the loved ones from whom they were departing, including their grandparents, Aunt Charllie, Aunt Bethany, Mildred, Hattie Mae, and Mr. George; and soon they were bundled and seated in the carriage along with their belongings for their trip home. It was very clear that their parents were once again their everything. They were ready to return home to continue life as a family.

Chapter Twenty-One

The seemingly interminable winter was finally in its death throes. The lengthening days promised an early spring as the returning brilliance of the sun sent warmth and light into even the most obscure corners. Signs of spring, gradual at first, were beginning to take precedence and were soon found everywhere. Green shoots followed by new buds pushed up through the leaf mold, seeking this new brilliance of the sun, and soon a parade of blooms made a cheery processional: crocus, daffodil, mountain laurel, pear, cherry, and magnolia. New life was to be seen everywhere: bawling calves, awkward foals, fluffy hatchlings, and cuddly kittens. The rolling lawns undulated with the miracle of new green, freshly plowed fields became seas of activity as workers planted new seeds and seedlings, and the James River roiled with chocolate waves from melting snow from the Blue Ridge Mountains.

Charllie's spirit, so long dormant it seemed, began to swell up within her, and she sought to discover all the rapid changes taking place on the Wright estate from the back of Merrilee. Often, as she rode off to visit cultivated fields, pastures, or hidden glens, she was totally unaware of the green eyes that often watched her go on her way, haunted green eyes that fell upon her with a hunger and wistfulness that sought healing balm for a broken soul. Sage's days were now filled with the many responsibilities of Danbury Dell, but his heart was empty.

Charllie had certainly not forgotten Sage. He was, after all, her everything. But she had a very practical streak that made her realize that until she could meet him face to face and deal with him on an equal basis, she was forced to get on with her life in the best way possible. Even though large chunks seemed missing from her life, making her feel empty and incomplete without him, there was delight in life and happiness in hard work, and Charllie set about to savor both. She would not let herself believe that their day would never come, for her love for Sage was far too precious.

Charllie's life took on a somewhat comfortable pattern: riding in the early morning, caring for the livestock, tending the kitchen gardens, baking breads and pastries before the heat of the day, writing in her journal, dining with family, and visiting friends and retainers. Sometimes her busy life would be enough to provide her with deep, sweet sleep at the end of the day. Often it would not. On those occasions when she paced her room restlessly, awoke from disturbing dreams, or read until dawn by candlelight, she knew there was only one cause and one cure for her insomnia—Sage Danbury.

***

Sage, too, was feeling the effects of living an entire winter away from the presence of Charllie. As the manager of the Danbury estate, he was caught up in all the necessary work that went on in maintaining it for the family's welfare. Sometimes he wondered if the estate's success had any correlation to his future happiness, for he knew that if a Miss Charlotte Wright were to be forever removed from his unknown future, that he would be thoroughly impoverished, and that wealth and success could never make up for that deficit.

Sage knew that he had no one to blame but himself for her absence, and his guilt for having compromised her innocence remained. Still, he felt her loss deeply. Three times he had ridden to the family cemetery and had impatiently watched and waited for Charllie's approach while Ebony noisily cropped grass, but she never came. He had hoped that this location might now be neutral and could provide them the much-needed privacy to begin anew. But Charllie no longer haunted the site, and his brother Thomas's neglected grave was proof positive. Sage's brow furrowed in consternation as he wondered about the reason for her absence. Either Charllie no longer felt compelled to visit Thomas's grave, which could be interpreted in a positive way—her period of mourning had finally come to an end, or she no longer chose to maintain emotional ties to either Danbury son—this thought plunged him into deep despair.

Sage began to ride the perimeters of the Wright plantation, hoping for a glimpse of Charllie, and when he saw her ride by, his heart beat faster, his palms became moist, and he felt so many bittersweet emotions swelling within him that he could but stare and watch until she eventually withdrew from his sight. He never approached her because he had convinced himself that she did not seek a renewal of their relationship—that she was probably better off without him. Still, he monitored her comings and goings.

He never allowed her knowledge of his trespass, always seeking concealment within a small copse of trees or in the shelter of an outbuilding. He did not want her to think that he was given to skulking about, and he certainly did not want her to feel uncomfortable as he observed her from a distance, for it was purely innocent and harmless, at least as far as she was concerned. His avoidance of Charllie made him feel like the very worst coward; unfortunately, he was not at the point where he could forgive himself for his past travesties. But as for Sage's own emotions, he was constantly plunged into self-imposed agony whenever he saw her, for Charllie had become a spirit that haunted his every move, his every thought, his every breath.

Sage took on many backbreaking challenges on the Danbury estate. He physically assisted the workers with the strenuous labor of erecting new split-rail fences; plowed additional acreage, which had lain fallow for years; shored up and rebuilt barns and outbuildings; and cut, split, and stacked wood from huge, storm-damaged trees. When time allowed, he madly galloped across the entire estate to inspect the grounds, the livestock, and the crops. All the physical energy expended was never sufficient to purge Charllie from his every thought, and so Sage lived day to day in constant torment.

Unbeknownst to each other, Sage and Charllie were living parallel lives of deprivation: each starving for the love and recognition of the other. They were using excessive activity and involvement as a salve for their open wounds—a salve that did not have the power to heal any more than phony medicine peddled at a medicine show. Both stubborn and proud, they seemed to bide their time, waiting for fate to take them by the hand and lead them to their destinies.

***

An engraved invitation with hearts and flowers arrived at both Oak Haven and Danbury Dell on the very same day. It was the promised invitation that announced the upcoming nuptials of Miss Phoebe Somerset and Mr. Percy Atwater. Sage and Charllie were both delighted and chagrined about the upcoming event: delighted in the good fortune and happiness of two acquaintances and chagrined that their own lives were still held in subjection by a very tangled web of love. Sage and Charllie's separation had erected emotional barriers over which neither seemed able to scale. They remained lonely in their self-imposed solitude. Perhaps the upcoming wedding would provide some access, a crack in the wall through which perhaps a glimmer of love's light might peek. Both lovers, separate and apart, felt a promise of hope and a foreboding of despair at the upcoming social event, which would inevitably bring them together. Would their own futures be determined so soon, so irrevocably?

***

On Saturday, May 23rd, the day of the Somerset-Atwater wedding, the morning began with a warm, sweet rain that dissipated shortly before noon. Diadems of moisture danced and glistened on the rolling green lawns to be shortly lapped up by the greedy tongue of a late spring sun. The many celebrants who were preparing for their departures from their homes to travel to the church thrust aside their raincoats and took parasols to protect themselves from the sun and not the rain.

It was a glorious day! The whole world seemed to have conspired to assist in the upcoming wedding. The many conveyances that were traveling country roads would eventually converge at the one destination, the country church. The carriages and wagons were filled with men dressed in their summer-weight suits, women in their light and airy pastel gowns, and children in their Sunday best. Beside them on their seats nestled packages wrapped and beribboned for showy display, cloaks for the evening return, hidden flasks for passing amongst the menfolk, and a blanket or two for sleeping children. This special outing would provide much entertainment, both for the day and in the telling for years to come.

The elder Wrights rolled smartly along in their open carriage. Charles, though paralyzed, was feeling the new stirrings of returning health. He felt well enough to take the reins and direct the horses, though his wheelchair and Mr. George were established in the back of the carriage as necessary backup for his disabilities. Sophia rode proudly by his side, chattering gaily about past weddings, the wedding at hand, and even about a possible future wedding. Had Charllie been present, she would have been shocked and embarrassed, but she was not.

Charllie was following her parents in her brother Frank's carriage. Frank and Emily occupied the front seat with Frank at the reins, and Charlotte was sandwiched between her nephew and niece in the back. Though her summer gown was gaily colored and very becoming, one of the first new items she had been able to purchase in years, she, in fact, had taken little real care or interest in her appearance. As a matter of fact, she felt rather funereal about the whole depressing day ahead. She wasn't sure that she could selflessly give the newlyweds the unreserved well-wishes they so deserved. Her spirits were at an all-time low, for her estrangement from Sage had gone on for far too long, and it was beginning to wreak havoc on her. She pretended joy and excitement, but instead she felt only dread for the day's activities.

Charllie knew she should be ecstatic over the good fortune of her friends, but she also knew that the day would but emphasize her own loss. It would showcase a dream that she had long held for Sage and herself: a grand commitment of exquisite proportions—marriage. She also knew that Sage would be present, and she didn't know how he would react to seeing her after such a long period of time.

Charllie thought with longing back to when Sage and she had both been comfortable and open with each other, when they had shared an easy relationship that included close friendship. But that had been before her engagement to Thomas, before Sage's avowal of love, before the passion shared in the hut, and before Charllie had learned to recognize her own true feelings toward Sage. It seemed that Charllie had taken far too long to recognize the true love and passion that existed between Sage and herself, love that was not falsely sugar-coated with romance but included friendship, respect, and devotion.

With great nervousness as well as misgivings, Charllie realized that the vehicle in which she was riding was swiftly approaching its destination. People who had recently arrived before them were already stepping down from their carriages and milling around in front of the church. Charllie scoured the churchyard for Sage, and when she found him missing, she breathed a sigh of relief. She was not yet prepared to deal with their first encounter after so many months. The gay chatter and lilting laughter were oppressive to her nerves, proving to be totally counter to her true emotions at the time. Though the sun was gaily shining for this wonderful event, its warmth barely touched Charllie's chilly demeanor.

For moral fortitude, Charllie linked her arms with Sarah and Gerald, and with a nephew and niece on either side, acting as an emotional buffer against the world, she prepared to enter the church. She smiled at friends and family as she made her way through the crowd, but she avoided stopping to chat. She envied those who were truly blessed with happiness on this special day and only prayed that, upon entering the church, she would be able to find her seat without having to deal with a confrontation with Sage.

The church door was decorated with grapevine wreaths sporting starched lilac bows and white flower blossoms.

Melodic church bells sent out peals of joy and gladness. The guests were seated by ushers on the hard, wooden pews while the quiet buzz of conversation filled the church as the families and guests waited for the ceremony to begin. Charllie did not look to either her right or left but focused on the altar instead, which was tastefully decorated with plumes of lilac branches and glowing candles. She finally entered her family's pew and settled her skirts around her. Her nerves were highly strung, and she self-consciously smiled and nodded at something inane that was conveyed to her by her sister-in-law. She noticed the impressive stained-glass windows, attempting to take delight in their jewel-like colors that were reflected upon the pulpit by the late morning sun.

Finally, the organ began a lilting, inspirational prelude, and it was soon followed by the traditional wedding march. The entire congregation quickly rose to its feet and waited in anticipation for the wedding party to enter. Diminutive flower girls gently tossed fragrant petals in the aisle and giggled when the ring bearer ran to his mother for comfort when stage fright got the best of him. Soon, however, Phoebe proceeded down the aisle in her gown and veil of silk and satin, and when she arrived at the altar in her flowing gown of white, Percy came forward to stand proudly at her side. The bride and groom looked radiant; both looking forward to stepping over that mysterious threshold which would welcome them as husband and wife.

The ceremony was breathtaking, moving, and inspirational; however, little of the event was attended to by Charllie. She was too wrapped up in her own emotions. Her imagination had given wing to the wistful fantasy of seeing herself as one of the leading players in this romantic event, a culmination of so many hopes and dreams. Perhaps she and

Sage could have taken part in exchanging lifetime vows had their own romance not been derailed by bitter circumstances and misunderstandings. However, her imaginings were as insubstantial as the wind, and she realized she might never come to experience the depth of the passion that she had hoped to share with him.

She heard the participants' exchange of heartfelt vows as in a dream, and some strange force compelled her to look to the row of seats directly to her right. She immediately caught sight of Sage, and her heart stopped. He, too, was looking her way, and the looks they both shared became locked with vulnerability and openness. Their very souls were briefly plundered as his green eyes, fathomless and dark with emotion, met her blue eyes that were softened by pain and swimming with tears. They quickly, with embarrassment and a lingering sense of longing, looked away. The ceremony culminated in the couple's first kiss while the congregation cheered and clapped.

Sage and Charllie had to endure further traditional activities, such as going through the reception line, pelting the newlyweds with rice, and greeting and conversing with the friends and family in attendance. Soon came the jockeying for seats in various carriages as the guests prepared for their journey to the reception, which was being held at a nearby inn. Charllie felt like she had walked into a bad dream, for her somber thoughts all focused on Sage's aloofness.

Once at the reception, everyone was soon seated at tables bright with lavish bouquets, colorful napkins, and shiny silverware. The bride listened in rapture to a comical story being told by her new husband, and the air was punctuated by laughter, gay conversation, and the clink of crystal. The ceremonial toast to the bride and groom was met with the approval of all those assembled, and soon the champagne was flowing freely. A tide of gaiety had swept all away on its heady current, except for Charllie and Sage.

Charllie had finally lost all the hope that she had once harbored for a reunion of lovers with a positive outcome at the wedding of their friends. She wondered if perhaps Sage's love was not as strong as she had once thought it to be. She drank a bit more champagne than was perhaps prudent, but it did not quench the growing anguish within. She looked down at the ring-less fingers of both hands and realized that, though no token of commitment was evident, her affections had already been promised to Sage—she had committed her heart to him many months ago. She wondered how her own life would play out, now that it was quite evident that she might have lost Sage once and for all.

Sage, too, was rather glum as he sat at his parents' table. He was sure that any chance he had ever possessed for sharing his life with Charllie had been forever blighted by his past callous actions. He felt like the pauper who gazes in upon a rich man's feast but is forced to continue experiencing the pangs of starvation. He knew that his misery was of his own making, but that knowledge did not ease the pain, nor will it to go away. When the ensemble began to tune its instruments for the first dance, Sage abruptly threw down his napkin and hastily prepared to leave the reception.

Charllie, looking on from a distance, saw the quick flush of anger that suffused Sage's face as he stood and hastily left the room. She was puzzled by his abrupt departure and watched as he offered his hasty farewells to the newlyweds, offering little more than a few words to them along with a brief nod. She also nursed her own hurt, for not once had Sage even attempted to extend even the most innocent gestures of friendship towards her. This day, which she had in all honestly dreaded for weeks, had also been a day in which she had secretly cherished some hope of mending her relationship with Sage. But that was clearly not to be. The disappointment that the occasion would not bring about a much-wished-for reunion was hard to bear. But attempting to hold back the threatening tears—harder still.

Unfortunately, Charllie depended on her family for transportation, so she was forced to remain until the day's festivities finally concluded. When her brother made a point to find her, with her wrap in his hand to prepare for their journey home, she felt like soundly kissing him. She was so thankful that this painful day had finally come to an end, and she could return to Oak Haven, where she could lick her wounds in private.

Chapter Twenty-Two

As spring became summer, and the warm, gentle breezes were replaced by heat and humidity, Charllie began to feel an ominous presence, like that of an approaching summer storm. She knew that something had to happen to irrevocably determine whether Sage would, or would not, become an important part of her life. She had many misgivings because she knew that she was faced with the very real possibility that there really was no future for the two of them. She also knew that if she hoped to see the issue resolved that she would have to take the lead in these matters, for Sage was proud, if inordinately so. He continued to make himself a whipping boy over last summer's romantic liaison. And Charllie knew that while he felt responsible for having *forced* his passion upon her, which—in actuality—had been a wondrous and joyous gift, he would politely keep his distance.

The intense labor on both estates had subsided. Until tender seedlings became riddled with weeds vying for space, until spring crops matured and were ready for harvest, the pressing needs of labor and care had subsided for a spell. The inhabitants could go about their daily chores, knowing that the afternoons could be spent languorously lazing about until the more urgent demands of farm life resumed in a week or two. Adults sat sipping cool drinks on the verandahs, napping on porch divans, and reading light material in the cool parlors with the draperies drawn. Children often napped as well, and dreamed of the fish they had caught in the early morning or the fireflies they would capture at dusk.

Charllie had a presentiment that the idleness brought about by the time and weather had most likely chased Sage into grave introspection. Intuition told her that he was beginning to haunt the grounds of last summer's rendezvous site as he sought solace in solitude. No one would dare to interrupt his self-loathing or recriminations there. He could wallow in his guilt without ever being disturbed. But Charllie had had quite enough of this self-induced punishment where Mr. Sage Danbury was concerned, and, furthermore, she had a plan— a very bold and forward plan.

***

Friday dawned bright, hot, and humid. The kitchen fire had been allowed to die out, for all the cooking for the day had been completed long before noon. Mr. and Mrs. Wright had left the plantation to visit friends, a day's travel from Oak Haven and would not be returning until the following Monday. The plantation's retainers would care for the livestock and maintain their daily responsibilities, but whatever time was free was theirs to spend with family and friends.

Charllie was awash with mixed emotions. She was nervous and excited, yet also filled with great misgivings about what she had planned. Today was the day when she would lay down all her cards, and Sage would be forced to decide whether she was worth the gamble. She could only pray that it would pay off, for if it didn't— she would be forever plunged into a world of loneliness and regret.

Charllie took great pains with her appearance. She washed in a basin of cool well water, splashed on a light, rose fragrance; and then carefully donned her favorite rose-sprigged frock.

Her hair was swept up into a cluster of damp curls, and she wore nothing for jewelry but an inexpensive heart necklace that Sage had once given to her on her twelfth birthday so many years ago. She checked the picnic basket that Aunt Bethany had packed earlier that day: ham biscuits, slab pickles, and dried-apple tarts. She had told her aunt that she was visiting a childhood friend, and, indeed, Sage was just that. Charllie knew that she herself probably would not be able to eat a bite of the picnic as her nerves were already taking their toll, but these props were necessary to help carry out her scheme. She filled a pottery jug with sweet mint tea and then hurried to the stable where Merrilee was saddled and waiting.

Charllie's hands shook as she attached the picnic items to her saddle horn. She wrinkled her nose a bit when she thought about having to ride sidesaddle to accommodate her attire, and then she realized that no one was around to notice her. Her comfort far outweighed decorum, especially on this day, so she hiked her skirts well above her knees and sat astride her mare. She looked toward the distant Danbury meadows and copses, squinting her eyes as she attempted to discern any movement, looking for that one lonely horse and rider that would eventually determine her future fate. But all the landscape before her appeared empty, and nothing stirred. She nudged Merrilee forward and then began her journey to set her bold plan in motion.

The pace was leisurely, for Charllie had to balance the picnic items, and she had no desire to push Merrilee faster than was wise in the heat of the day. She also did not want to greet Sage, drenched with perspiration and wilted like a week-old nosegay. She tried to focus on the beauty of the day, smiling at an adolescent colt rolling on its back in the pasture, and looking with wonder at the fleecy clouds outlined by the azure blue sky. But, in truth, her mind was on the distant copse of trees, the slave hut, and Sage—all destinations of her very heart and soul. The journey she had begun was beginning to seem both interminable and far too brief, all at once. Her heart was beating wildly, and her eyes grew large as she contemplated what she had planned. She cringed as she considered the boldness and possible ramifications of the rash gamble that she had decided to make.

Eventually, Charllie realized that she had traversed the entire Wright plantation, and the wild acreage located solely on Danbury Dell property, land which she had visited with Sage a year ago, and now her destination appeared to be on the horizon. Merrilee was forced into a sedate walk, and as they began to enter the wooded grove, Charllie looked warily around. At first, she felt great disappointment, for the woods seemed devoid of anything or anyone—neither horse nor rider could be seen. But as her eyes became accustomed to the gloom of the shady dell, she saw a ghost of a man sitting near the creek, his back leaning against an aged sycamore. He had not heard her approach, and his very attitude spoke volumes of sadness and despair. Charllie silently slid off Merrilee's back and tethered her. She cautiously approached the man, lost in thought.

"I knew that if I were ever to be invited on a picnic again, that I would just have to do the inviting myself," Charllie boldly proclaimed. She retrieved the picnic basket, jug, and blanket. Sage's head snapped around as she announced her arrival, and his eyes now narrowed warily as he watched her approach.

Charllie was shocked by his appearance: noticing the loss of weight, a week's growth of beard, and the longish raven hair that now grew considerably past the nape of his neck. But his very presence was precious beyond belief. Ignoring

Sage's lack of a welcome, she continued, "A beautiful June day like this just can't be improved upon for a picnic. The heat has certainly become oppressive, but it can only be expected at this time of year. I feel like a withered posy myself. At least this shady knoll offers a lovely pool where I might refresh myself if I were to be so forward."

Charllie deposited the picnic basket in the shade of a mulberry tree and then set the jug of sweet tea in the stream. She then spread the blanket on a patch of grass above the creek. She bent down, slowly unlaced her shoes, and finally took them off. Then she painstakingly removed her stockings so that she was soon standing barefoot. But Charllie had no plans to stop with her shoes and stockings. She continued to slowly and methodically undress by deftly unbuttoning her frock and letting it fall gracefully in a pile at her feet. Then she quickly stepped out of her cotton knickers. Since she had foregone all additional frilly undergarments, she soon stood in front of Sage totally naked. She looked like a woodland nymph who had lost her way and found a new home in a Virginian dell. Charllie's alabaster skin shone translucent in the shady glen where sunbeams and shadows flirted with one another, and she made no attempt to hide her rose-tipped breasts, the swell of her belly, or the thrust of her buttocks. Looking neither to the right nor to the left, she slowly entered the cool stream and began to lower herself into its crystalline depths.

As Charllie nervously immersed herself in the stream, she felt the cool, limpid waters caress her legs in a gentle lapping motion. She had all she could do to continue her act of nonchalance, for she could feel Sage's scorching stare as it traced her body's every movement. She began to gently hum a tune and continued to gently splash the refreshing water over her fevered limbs. Time seemed to stand still, and the world became a world of opposition: hot and cold, light and darkness, joy and pain, love and hate. She was caught in a warp that held nothing but ambiguity. In her search for final answers, she prayed that she would not be left wanting.

As Charllie continued to bathe in the stream, Sage could do little more than stare. He felt as if he had become an unwitting voyeur in a dream, a dream that had immediately captured his imagination and ardor. He became instantly aroused as he responded to the beauty and grace of the woman who now taunted him with her naked presence. His whole body caught fire, passion stirred within him until he felt painful desire, and he trembled with months of pent-up need. Yet he did not act upon his full-blown desire, and he did little more than watch guiltily as the object of all his affections flirted dangerously before him.

Sage could not for the life of him fathom the purpose of Charllie's visit or her most indiscreet actions. *Is she so innocent that she feels such a display will be perceived as nothing more than a childish romp? Is she trying desperately to re-establish our relationship on par with that of a doting brother and sister? Yet surely, she would never even consider disrobing in front of her own brother, much less in front of someone with whom she shares no blood ties.*

Sage felt guilty of the pleasure he felt as he took in all the nuances of the feminine flesh that was displayed before him. The beauty and grace that belonged to the most precious woman in his world were now his alone for this moment in time, and, though he tried to look away to protect her modesty, he was unable to keep his eyes diverted away from her for long. He was totally mesmerized. He was a thirsty desert traveler who had finally found a precious watering hole in an oasis, and he drank in her loveliness and presence in long and deep draughts.

Charllie provocatively frolicked in the stream for what seemed like an eternity, but she finally stood up and stretched her arms above her head as water cascaded down around her shapely shoulders. Her nipples were tight and hard from the cool water, and her beautifully rounded belly was dappled by the sunlight and shade of the dell. She made no attempt to modestly cover any of her womanly attributes, and her natural beauty shone for Sage alone. Sage felt overwhelmed by the enticement of Charllie's femininity before him, and he now understood what it meant to be breathless with desire.

Charllie casually strolled up out of the creek and, when she reached Sage's side, she dribbled a tiny rivulet of water down his face. At that instant, she knew they were both remembering the ice. The trickle slowly crept down his cheekbones, and tiny droplets lay glistening near his sensuous lips. Charllie gently caressed them with her fingertips, and then she traced his lips with the lightest of touches with her tongue—feeling Sage shiver from the onslaught of desired that smoldered within him.

Sage dared not move a muscle, fearing that this insubstantial dream might quickly evaporate to leave him stranded in a world of heartache. He continued to remain seated as he cautiously watched Charllie stand above him in all the glory of her nakedness. His eyes traveled above to the wonders that were now fully exposed to him: her rose-infused and alabaster skin, the gentle curve of her cheeks, the pout of her lips, her perky breasts with the raspberry-hard nipples, the feminine swells of her belly, and the silken triangle at her apex where her blonde whorls caused his very groin to pulse and ache. Sage shuddered as if the embers of a banked fire were struggling to burst forth in flame.

"Sage, isn't the water just so cool and refreshing? You should have joined me. I feel so refreshed." Charllie bent down and began to unbutton Sage's shirt. At first, he thought to discourage her from her explorations, but soon the smoldering passion in her eyes made him as docile as a child—he knew that Charllie was beyond his control at this point, and he was beyond wishing her to be so. Sage luxuriated in the feel of her fingertips as they caressed his newly exposed chest. He closed his eyes in wonder as licks of flame, caused by her gentle hands tracing his body with an ardor that threatened to ignite him. He marveled at just how incendiary her presence alone could be.

Sage finally made a weak attempt to halt Charllie. Maybe it would be best, far more proper, and more befitting of their circumstance if he were to prevent her from going further with this provocative charade. He didn't want either of them to come to regret anything that might transpire this day, for he knew firsthand how guilt and regret could eat a person alive.

"Charllie, you have absolutely no idea what you're doing. This isn't a game. If you are determined to continue, I cannot promise how long I'll be able to resist you and remain a gentleman." His voice trembled with naked want, and he remained mesmerized by her very presence, her every touch.

He trembled, aching to gather Charllie to him, to hold her naked body close to his, to trace her loveliness with his hands and lips; but he withheld himself. He felt her fingertips continuing their assault as they scorched their way to the waistband of his trousers. He sharply inhaled a painful breath, and his eyes followed her fingertips' movements in fascination.

Charllie was beginning to revel in the power she knew she now had over Sage. The very air was fairly vibrating with the sexual tension of it, and she herself was not immune. She smiled a sweetly seductive smile, continuing to allow her fingertips free play with Sage's waistband. Sage inhaled sharply, and he appeared to be experiencing much agony from her touch.

"I'm not sure that I was looking for a gentleman this afternoon, Mr. Danbury. However, I am sure that I was looking for a man, the kind of man with the ability to arouse passion—something that sometimes seems to exist in this lovely dell. You, of all people, know that I'm a firm believer in fair play, and I think that your conduct last time we met here was totally abominable. Why, you had the audacity to undress me as if I were nothing more than your play doll, and you conducted all kinds of wicked games with my innocent body. Yet now you act as if I am trifling with your affections. Nothing could be further from the truth. There is nothing trifling about what I plan to do to you and with you. But this time, I do believe it is my turn to play a game of my own making, a game I plan on winning. I am now determined, Mr. Sage Danbury, to see you in all of your male glory, and I am also determined that we will at last finish what you once had the boldness to begin."

"Charllie, don't throw caution to the wind. Passion is not a game, not between us. It is something that you have to seriously consider because the stakes are far too high."

But Charllie decided to answer him without using words; she gently invaded his breeches with gentle fingers that soothed his swollen manhood with trembling caresses that promised untold delights. Sage groaned, closed his eyes for a moment, and then made a half-hearted attempt to stand.

Sage knew that he was beginning to lose control, but he felt that he had no right to become the one to make any decisions in further compromising Charllie's chastity. In his powerlessness, he allowed Charllie to continue with her plan. Charllie gently pushed him back to a reclining position and then concentrated on unbuttoning his trousers, ignoring his faint attempts at protest. Her gentle, tender explorations resumed, bringing him exquisite waves of passionate rapture that sought release. Sage knew immediately that he was lost. Charllie's innocence was now overruled by her love and desire for him, and she was determined to lay siege to his every thought and deed. She knew that he had once loved her, and it was clear that he desired her now. She had nothing to lose and would continue to act upon his every weakness.

Sage could no more resist her than he could prevent himself from taking another breath of air. Sage's arms enfolded Charllie, and he crushed her to him none-too-gently. Soon all his clothing joined hers on the bank of the stream, and the passion that had been banked since the previous summer burst into glorious, searing flame. There, on the moss touched by sunlight and shadow, he was finally able to become more aggressive in the expression of his love; his kisses were hard and demanding, falling like molten rain; and his tongue plundered her with velvet waves of flame. Charllie reciprocated by matching in equal amounts every kiss, every caress, and every ardent whisper of desire and delight. She welcomed the heat that came from Sage's exploration of her body with his fingertips of flame.

Charllie, though still a novice in lovemaking, was completely emboldened by her deep feelings for Sage and the passion he was arousing deep within her. Soon her hands were timidly beginning to trace the contours of his body. Sage groaned, and then stifled that groan by gorging himself on her lips and feathering her nipples until they hardened with erotic need. His warm lips soon found her nipples, and he began to suckle her with an urgency and sense of purpose. Charllie found herself writhing in both agony and delight. She couldn't get enough of this man. She delighted in the feel of him, the smell of him, the taste of him. His groans of delight set new fires ablaze within her, and she continued her exploration of his maleness as their lips sought each other and their fingertips continued to familiarize themselves with each other's erotic zones.

Sage finally broke free from a lingering kiss, and Charllie trembled as his lips began their exploration of her body. The sensations that he stirred with his lips were electric, and the heat radiating throughout her body became overpowering and impossible to quench. She lay back upon the moss, encouraging Sage to continue with his explorations. Charllie whimpered as the precursors of ecstasy set her entire body aflame. Sage pulled back to temper this desire, leaving her destitute and hungry for completion. His voracious appetite for Charllie's love must be gentled by restraint, and he could not allow his hunger for her to spoil this, their moment.

Yet Charllie immediately pulled Sage back down to her, and she greedily met his mouth with her own passion-swollen lips. Sage took shallow breaths of delight as he experienced Charllie's aggressiveness with wonder and disbelief. She surprised him with her passion, and he delighted in the fragrance of her sun-kissed body—it was so soft, warm, and giving. Though he would have liked their passionate foreplay to go on and on, the fires she was stoking within him were begging for release, and he needed to make love with her right now—in every sense of the word. Yet still he held back . . .

"Charllie, don't! You don't understand. I can't take you like this."

His entreaty was almost a sob. But Charllie didn't stop, and soon her warm, passionate kisses and trembling touches were falling like rain upon him; and he was reciprocating with fingers that trembled as they explored more of her. He shuddered with the anticipation of the delights that he knew awaited him, and he heard Charllie's sharp intake of breath followed by subsequent moans as he realized that she was aching with much the same need as his. Charllie was now tracing his manhood with her tentative, warm tongue, and Sage was writhing in agony.

Charllie found that her whole body was on fire, and her voice shook with desire as she made her entreaty. "Sage, make me yours. I have always been yours. It's what I want—what we both need."

Charllie knew that this was the ultimate gamble, and what Sage chose to do in the next few moments would decide their destinies forever. Charllie gently began to pull Sage closer, and with a low growl, he capitulated and crushed her to him. Bruising, passionate kisses followed shortly, and with all his restraint gone, he was soon seeking entrance to the delights of her body, his manhood carefully pushing through the resistance it met. And though Charllie gasped for a brief moment when her passion was interrupted by sharp pain, her entreaties for him to continue did not cease; and Sage, gently though forcefully, joined them together as one for the very first time. Charllie delighted in this new togetherness, and a happiness beyond all description began to steal her soul. Then, as her pain lessened and the passion between them began to blossom once more, the two lovers continued to seek the stars.

Sage's pulsing rhythm was neither gentle nor fierce, but it was constant, calling upon her body to answer in kind. Charllie's body was beginning to hum with need in reaction to their coupling, and she soon joined in the sexual dance with Sage. Her body was now totally under his spell, and their intent was to totally complete this exquisite dance of desire. Having experienced both pain and pleasure at Sage's entry, Charllie had been mesmerized by the exquisitely sharp longing she had felt in their passionate joining. Sage's persistent thrusts within the confines of her thighs were drawing them closer and closer to the promise of completion.

Both were climbing, climbing a peak that promised ecstasy and a quenching of this fire that was rampaging throughout their bodies. Sage's tempo increased even further, and he sought peace for both by pushing deeper and faster. Charllie immediately shattered, her scream was quickly muffled by Sage's kiss, and she shuddered in the aftermath of her joyful release.

Sage's release came soon after Charllie's, and it was explosive; for his abstinence, his love for Charllie, and the many fires of desire which had been so passionately stoked had created a powder keg. Having breached Charllie's virginity in his attempt to seek heaven, he had lit the fuse and then prepared for the following explosion. His release had been almost violent, and his moans were primitive and deep. He lay nestled on top of Charllie, his head cushioned in her hair—replete, satisfied, and very reluctant to move. He did not want to awaken from this long, sought-after dream.

Charllie gently sighed as she felt further tears slide down her cheeks. She felt a deep sense of completion and rightness. She felt truly tied to this man whom she loved above all others. They belonged together in a way in which they could never belong to another in this lifetime.

Sage captured her face between his hands and then kissed her sweetly and gently. Passion was once again entering the fray, and it was clear that Sage and Charllie were not through with their lovemaking. His fingertips continued stroking her, now focusing on her nub where an intense pleasure was once again taunting her for release. Soon she began to feel hot desire pounding relentlessly through her veins. And though her passion had once-upon-a-time been released in this way, it was clear that Sage was bent on prolonging her torture.

The brief pain Charllie had felt at their first connection had quickly receded as a wave leaves the shore, and soon all she could feel was an overwhelming need again. Sage's manhood had also recovered its heat, and he, too, sought far more from Charllie than before. He slowly positioned himself above her, and with slow and liquid moves, he impaled his hardness within her slick, hot mound. Sage slowly moved upon her, and soon Charllie's moans spoke of torture born of desire. She could no longer hold back from thrusting her own hips up against his; she needed him, and she was losing patience with the slow tempo. Soon, a faster rhythm began, a rhythm that was quickly spiraling with intense heat and light throughout them. Their bodies became taut with desire as they sought release from this agony that now held them imprisoned by rapture.

The tempestuous ride they took was unlike any either had ever taken. Their passion crested in a frenetic storm of lightning bolts and crashing thunder, and they were spirited toward the heavens where they cried out in unison—both awash in the light of a plummeting comet. Replete, they lingered many long moments before disengaging. For both, a dream had come true, and neither wanted to break the magical spell.

Chapter Twenty-Three

Sage kissed Charllie gently on her lips and then planted kisses around her face and in her hair. "Charllie, Charllie, Charllie . . . What have I done? I never meant for us to go this far. Passion is one thing, but I have taken your virginity without the benefit of marriage. Whether you like it or not, Miss Charlotte Wright, we are now most definitely engaged to be married, and our marriage will take place within the month. You might be carrying my child this very moment, and, though that would be a blessing from above, you deserve all the sanctity of marriage in a timely manner. I've loved you, sometimes it seems like forever. Charllie, I just couldn't resist you." Though Sage protested the very intimacy that they had so recently shared, his arms continued to possessively encircle her.

"And why should you, Sage? I meant to have you, for you are all I have ever wanted. However, you don't have to marry me, not for a child's sake. I am not a brood mare, as your brother once insinuated. I know of Thomas's duplicity—all of it. I overheard all the sordid details when I was in the wrong place at the wrong time. But our love was always meant to be, and the responsibility is not yours alone. It's my love for you that spurred me on, and my hope that you might love me as well. If there are to be any regrets, they will be shared. If I am with a child, that child is our child, one made from our love and our passion. You told me once that you would have precious memories with which to remember me. Well, I, too, want memories, memories that will link me to you with love."

Now that they had finally made love, and Charllie had made her own confessions, she was beginning to have misgivings. Though Sage's passionate response to her had been everything she had ever dreamed it would be, and he had indicated that marriage must be their next step, he had not told her directly that he still wanted her, loved her, cherished her—and she needed that confession. She hoped Sage would confirm his feelings of love for her now, professing that they were just as strong and deep today as they had always been. Just feeling a sense of responsibility for her would never be enough.

Sage hugged her to him ferociously. "You knew about Thomas? That he had mixed allegiances but still planned to seek an heir with you? I could never tell you, not when I held you so dear. I couldn't besmirch a brother, and at the same time destroy the tender feelings of someone I loved above all else. These last few months, I used to wait for you at Thomas's grave, but evidently, you had stopped visiting it. I couldn't allow myself to dare hope that you might have gotten over him. Charllie, you have always been my one and only love, though I had finally stopped hoping that one day you might be mine and I yours. I love you with all my heart and soul. It seems that I always have and always will."

Charllie disentangled herself from Sage and sat up. She wanted to look deeply into his beautiful green eyes so that he would finally know the truth. "Sage, I think I have always been in love with you as well. I may have been infatuated with Thomas for a time, it's true, but only because I was still a young girl and he made me feel like a desired woman. Thomas was good with words and made me feel special. He fed my hungry ego. But there was never any real passion there. I wondered about that sometimes, but I was young and naïve. And, of course, later, when I overheard a conversation that indicated Thomas preferred other diversions, I came to realize that I could never have been anything more to him than a brood mare and constant companion. I knew then that I had been totally blind, not only about Thomas, but most especially about you. I never really loved Thomas, for my feelings were based on nothing more than a fairy tale, but I have always loved you. I know that now."

Sage gently took both of Charllie's hands and held them to his breast. His loving silence allowed her to continue, "And that day at the hut? I was in bondage only because I chose to be in bondage. Do you think flimsy ties would have held me if I had been set on freeing myself from you? How could I deny my own desire for you and not accept the gift you so freely chose to give me that day? You gave me a beautiful gift, a lovely awakening—both of heart and soul. You selflessly gave of yourself to pleasure me. And you made me believe that you truly loved me—above all else. Your lovemaking might have been planned in anger and frustration, but it was carried out in love. Sage, you've been punishing yourself for something which we both desired. You wanted to be mine, and I wanted to be yours. I love you!"

Sage was overcome by Charllie's confession, and it took some time for him to drink it all in and to understand all its implications. He held her close and rained kisses down upon her. Never had he cherished their love more than at this very moment.

"I certainly do not want a brood mare, Miss Charlotte. But if I could find a wife to love me half as much as I love her, who would accept me as her doting husband, and who would welcome me and any children we might conceive with love and warmth and joy—I would be the happiest man alive."

"Well, Mr. Danbury. If that is indeed a genuine marriage proposal, I most certainly accept. As to welcoming you and any children with love and warmth and joy, I guess you'll just have to let me prove myself. Though I'm warning you, Sage, it just might take years and years."

Sage scooped Charllie up into his arms and deftly carried her to the slave hut. Charllie looked up at him and laughed, "What, no candles?" Sage silenced her with a kiss and proceeded across the threshold.

The building was musty, dark, and damp, but it seemed alight with the glow of their love. When Sage went to lay Charllie down upon the bed, a vagrant sunbeam caused the locket on Charllie's chest to glow. Sage gently picked it up from where it lay nestled between her breasts, and when he recognized it as his very first gift to her those many years ago, he swiftly brought it to his lips and kissed it. His eyes misted over with deep emotion, and then they began to glow with renewed warmth and passion.

Charllie lay on the bed, her body still warm from their earlier lovemaking, yet she held her arms out to Sage in enticement once again. This flowering love was leaving them both insatiable. Sage gathered Charllie to him, and he buried his head between her breasts and gently began to explore her newly-awakened body with his many fervent kisses. He was rewarded with a breathless moan from Charllie, and he silenced her with urgent kisses that fired her imagination and drove her passion to new extremes.

Charllie may have been a novice where lovemaking was concerned, but she was already on fire with the wild passion that pulsed throughout her body. Each of Sage's kisses was equally matched by her own, and her seductive touch was delightfully aggressive and immediately inflamed wild responses from him. The hut became charged with the steamy atmosphere of passion that imprisoned both lovers in velvet chains of desire.

Sage and Charllie spent the next hour in each other's arms, where rapture created a special world where time is but a vague concept, and the language lovers speak is undecipherable to all but themselves. And then, in the afterglow of love, they spoke of sad days past and happy days to come. They reveled in the delight of the very present. They could not get enough of each other, for their many months of emotional starvation had become a precursor for their feast of love.

***

When Sage and Charllie finally emerged from the hut, they walked over to the creek arm in arm. They couldn't help but compare the events of this idyllic day to those of a summer day of less than a year ago. What had begun a year ago, tainted with both hurt and longing, had been carried out now in deep and fervent love, and had been followed immediately by an eternal pledge. Once again, Charllie entwined her arms around Sage and pulled him to her for a sweet and lingering kiss. The love she had found with this special man could never be quenched, for the flame was bright and true.

The last glow of sunset tinged the glen with a warm amber glow, and the heat and humidity of the day lingered and made the two languorous. At the water's edge, Charllie, now comfortable with her own nakedness, cautiously dipped a toe in the stream and then proceeded to enter its gently swirling depths. This time, Sage found himself more than willing to join her in the tepid water of the creek. Their naked bodies glowed in the rosy light that filtered through the sycamore's branches, and they quickly came together, their skin silk upon silk, in the ripples that eddied to the shore. The sensuous waters lapped at their love-sated bodies, and the warmth they now felt was almost celestial, for it was the warmth of tender love and togetherness. Their bodies caressed each other with flesh against flesh, and neither could discern where one left off and the other began, for they had truly become one in both body and spirit.

When they arose from the pool, Charllie and Sage's marble bodies seemed sculpted by the hand of time and placed in this timeless glen to remind nineteenth-century man that love can conquer all and that the passion that surrounds it is indeed ageless. They evoked the blessing of the world for all those who have finally found their soulmates, even though their life paths may once have been crooked and long.

As twilight drew down upon them, Sage and Charllie found themselves ravenous; they sat upon Charllie's shawl and finally did justice to Hattie Mae's picnic. Each bite was magical. They took turns feeding themselves and each other. They gloried in the sensual experience of eating, drinking, and conversing as lovers. They toasted each other with the elixir of sweet tea, and the finest champagne could not compare.

As Charllie and Sage lay upon the bank, secure in each other's arms, they were content to watch the new moon rise while listening to the soughing of the night breezes, the plaintive song of the whippoorwill, and the gentle murmur of the creek. Ebony's whinny finally broke the spell, and the couple knew it was time to leave. After carefully assisting each other with dressing, combing damp hair, and finger-pressing wrinkles, Sage assisted Charllie behind his saddle on Ebony's wide back. He then tied Merrilee's reins to his saddle horn so that she could amble along behind them. Once Sage mounted his horse, Charllie pressed up against Sage's back and lay her head snugly against him while her arms encircled him and held him close. As Ebony took off in a gentle trot, Charllie knew that Sage would bring her safely back home this night and then on to the beginnings of a new life. Her smile was gentle and warm, and she snuggled even closer.

Epilogue

As Charllie approached the clearing, she smelled the sharp and pungent aroma of fresh pine shavings. The sound of a hammer punctuated the otherwise still autumn air, and then a handsaw joined its brethren in the noisy activity. Charllie couldn't believe her eyes. The once forlorn slave hut, which had been the site of so much heartache and so much joy, was being totally transformed.

The sagging porch had been replaced by a wider, more ornate verandah. The rest of the house had been shored up, rotten sills and siding replaced, and insulating pine straw installed beneath the house. New windows sparkled all around the freshly painted white building, and they gazed out upon the enlarged clearing. Black shutters had been installed on either side of each window, and a freshly stained door sported a new iron knocker, beckoning guests to enter. Charllie walked across the porch, and she smiled as her footsteps rang out across the solid planks of fir. She remembered her last visit and how she had feared that at any moment she might fall through the rotting boards before she got the chance to go inside.

She gently pushed the door open, and it swung inward on well-oiled hinges. The interior was totally unrecognizable. The main room had become a dining room and kitchen: new wide oak floorboards had been sanded and varnished, the walls had been patched and painted, and the new windows were adorned with white, starched curtains. A large cookstove as well as a brick oven took up an entire wall, a dry sink was positioned in front of a window that looked out upon the backyard, and an oak table with six matching chairs stood upon a red braided rug. Kitchen cupboards flanked the dry sink, and a large bookcase was positioned between two easy chairs in the room's furthest corner.

A large addition had been added to the back of the hut, an addition which included a modest but functional summer kitchen; a parlor—complete with fireplace and hand-carved mantle, a comfortable rocking chair, and a gold settee; and a master bedroom with a cherry bedstead, a matching bureau and armoire, and a washstand. Multi-colored braided rugs covered the varnished hardwood floors, and crisp curtains fluttered at every window. Charllie strolled through the refurbished house, looking in amazement at all the miraculous changes. She walked through the back door and stood poised on the kitchen stoop, where she surveyed the work area, where the sounds of industry were currently taking place.

Sage stood poised in front of two sawhorses in the backyard, hammer in hand, and stripped to the waist. Charllie couldn't help but smile at the magnificence of his tanned upper torso and muscled arms, and then her eyes lowered to his tapered waist and well-defined thighs. Though their wedding had taken place a few months ago, she still felt warmth spread throughout her body as she drank in his masculine physique. Their life was now filled with love and passion, and she was addicted to him—body and soul.

Charllie thought back to the first Saturday in September when she had become Sage's wife. They had decided to marry as soon as possible without a lot of fuss and fanfare. They had married in a small chapel with fewer than fifty of their closest family and friends present. Charllie had worn a very simple white cotton gown and had carried a bouquet of daisies and purple asters.

Sage had worn his summer-weight gray suit with a purple aster in his buttonhole. Their wedding vows had been pure and heartfelt, and they had but mirrored the pledges of love that Sage and Charllie had already exchanged in private weeks earlier. The couple had been toasted with champagne, the wedding cake had been sliced and devoured, and the traditional wedding dance performed. But to Sage and Charllie, both spellbound by the other's love, the only truth of the day was found in the light that shone in the depths of their lover's eyes.

Married. Sometimes, Charllie could still not believe that she had realized her most precious dream. This was something she had wished for as a child, but she had never quite known if, how, or when her dream might come true. Now she could not imagine herself without this man beside her. It was as if all memories of Thomas had been erased, for the Thomas she thought she had known had never truly existed. But Sage certainly did, and his reality was what made her sun rise each morning and her moon to ascend each evening. He was her everything. She now found it hard to remember a time when she had eaten alone, walked alone, or slept alone. Her life had become filled to overflowing, just as a barren creek bed swells with water following a late summer thunderstorm, so too had Charllie's life been filled with a miraculous abundance of love.

Sage and Charllie were currently living with the Danburys at Danbury Dell, but soon they would be taking up residence in this newly refurbished honeymoon cottage. The delight of living together in this secluded and beautiful dell promised to bless all their expectations. They would be able to walk the wooded trails, wade in the shallow stream, and ride their steeds between their new home and the two plantations. They would be immersed in the beauty of nature as they awoke to birdsong, listened to the creaking branches above their heads, and shared the evening meal as they witnessed the western sunset. They would be able to live as a couple and learn about each other without the distractions of others. Charllie sighed happily.

The hut would be a temporary home, for plans were already being made for a wing at Danbury Dell to be refurbished and modernized to the couple's liking, complete with a remodeled nursery suite to be established on the second floor. Charllie placed her hand upon her belly and smiled, for she knew that deep inside a small seed had been planted and now grew. She was pregnant with Sage's child, and the thought of this miracle brought tears to her eyes. In less than a year's time, she and Sage would live at Danbury Dell as its future inheritors, and she hoped that she and Sage would fill it with the warmth and laughter of the many daughters and sons that they hoped to bring into the world. For now, they looked forward to luxuriating in the intimacy provided at the honeymoon cottage.

The cottage would eventually become Hattie Mae's retirement home. A small settlement of homes would spring up around it for the free planters, nieces and nephews interested in homesteading, and perhaps a healer and a teacher. New houses would also spring up in the glade, for there would be plenty of work on both plantations to provide work and a future for all. Hattie was already planning to share her home with a widowed niece. She had begun making plans for a kitchen garden, an herb bed, and a chicken house. She was also looking forward to the prospect of having her own home where she could sit in the rocking chair on the porch while she shelled beans, knitted, or gossiped with friends.

Charllie knew that the Wright family would never be able to force Hattie Mae into total retirement, for she would undoubtedly be present at every birthing, would most likely continue baking her favorite breads, cookies, and pies for both households, and would—as a matter of course—supervise the plantings of all new gardens. Any new cook would have the impossible task of replacing her, but change was in the air: here in the glen, on the two plantations, and in Richmond and beyond.

But Hattie Mae's labors would soon be relegated to her own wishes and desires, not those of others. She would be free to spend her days with as much or as little activity as she chose. Charllie smiled. Somehow, she could not envision Hattie spending her last days rocking on the new verandah. More likely, she'd be found with her hands and apron covered with flour or red garden soil.

Sage looked up and caught sight of Charllie. His smile was slow and easy, and it lit up his whole face, especially his beautiful green eyes. He put down his hammer and quickly swallowed up the distance between them with quick and powerful strides. Their embrace was gentle but passionate, and Sage rather gingerly touched her belly, which had just begun showing an emphasized roundness. Charllie grinned widely. "Why, Mr. Danbury, I do believe you are taking a few too many liberties. Perhaps I need to provide you with a few lessons on how a true gentleman should treat a lady—that is, if you have more than ample time for me."

Sage threw back his glistening raven-haired head and laughed. And then he swept Charllie into his arms, gleefully preparing to learn just how a gentleman should treat his lady.

The End

www.ingramcontent.com/pod-product-compliance
Lightning Source LLC
Chambersburg PA
CBHW070640310726
48982CB00001B/345

* 9 7 8 1 9 7 0 3 7 9 2 9 7 *